Take Me If You Can

"A sexy, riveting read!"
—*New York Times* bestselling author Christina Dodd

"Flirty, fun, and fabulously original."
—*USA Today* bestselling author Julie Kenner

"Sexy, witty, fast-paced, and full of delicious plot twists."
—*USA Today* bestselling author Cherry Adair

"Sexy, charming, witty, and irresistible."
—national bestselling author Roxanne St. Claire

"If you're looking for a fun, entertaining read that will keep you on the edge of your seat, then look no further than *Take Me If You Can.* It will make you laugh, make you cry, and keep you glued to the very end."
—Romance Reviews Today

"A swift, smart, and sassy suspense with lots of romantic tension . . . reminiscent of smart, sexy movies like *The Thomas Crown Affair.* . . . A delight."
—Fresh Fiction

continued . . .

Fit to Be Tied

"Sexy-hot delicious and laugh-out-loud delightful! Karen Kendall is my new favorite author!"

—*New York Times* bestselling author Nicole Jordan

"Kendall's lively tale about breaking up, making up, and shaking it up is funny and poignant. Fans of Lori Wilde, Susan Donovan, and Connie Lane will appreciate Kendall's humorous take on tying the knot." —*Booklist*

"Kendall again presents a story that mixes humor with a more serious plot. The journey of the two main characters toward an awareness of what really matters, and secondary characters who make their own discoveries, give this light-hearted romance substance." —*Romantic Times*

"This funny, sexy romance will keep you reading."

—Fresh Fiction

"Be prepared to laugh, cry, and feel some emotions for the characters and their plights . . . an unforgettable read."

—Romance Reviews Today

The Bridesmaid Chronicles

First Date

"Lighthearted comedy . . . the snappy talk keeps the plot in constant motion. . . . Something fun . . . to read on the beach."
                                        —*Publishers Weekly*

"A sharp, sexy, and fun read with engaging characters who steal into your heart right away. Karen Kendall's newest romance contains all the ingredients required to make it a supersassy romp, and practically thrums with vibrant, snappy dialogue. Utterly delightful and very highly recommended!"
                                        —The Best Reviews

"*First Date* is a magnificent, captivating read that will keep you totally entertained from the first page until the last."
                                        —The Romance Reader's Connection

First Dance

"Hilarious and downright sexy! Karen Kendall will delight you!"   —*New York Times* bestselling author Carly Phillips

"Kendall's sparkling third installment in [the] Bridesmaid Chronicles series offers both zany romance and serious probing of her protagonists' emotional depths. This witty, well-crafted entry bodes well for the final volume."
                                        —*Publishers Weekly*

Take Me Two Times

Karen Kendall

A SIGNET ECLIPSE BOOK

SIGNET ECLIPSE
Published by New American Library, a division of
Penguin Group (USA) Inc., 375 Hudson Street,
New York, New York 10014, USA
Penguin Group (Canada), 90 Eglinton Avenue East, Suite 700, Toronto,
Ontario M4P 2Y3, Canada (a division of Pearson Penguin Canada Inc.)
Penguin Books Ltd., 80 Strand, London WC2R 0RL, England
Penguin Ireland, 25 St. Stephen's Green, Dublin 2,
Ireland (a division of Penguin Books Ltd.)
Penguin Group (Australia), 250 Camberwell Road, Camberwell, Victoria 3124,
Australia (a division of Pearson Australia Group Pty. Ltd.)
Penguin Books India Pvt. Ltd., 11 Community Centre, Panchsheel Park,
New Delhi - 110 017, India
Penguin Group (NZ), 67 Apollo Drive, Rosedale, North Shore 0632,
New Zealand (a division of Pearson New Zealand Ltd.)
Penguin Books (South Africa) (Pty.) Ltd., 24 Sturdee Avenue,
Rosebank, Johannesburg 2196, South Africa

Penguin Books Ltd., Registered Offices:
80 Strand, London WC2R 0RL, England

First published by Signet Eclipse, an imprint of New American Library,
a division of Penguin Group (USA) Inc.

First Printing, April 2009
10 9 8 7 6 5 4 3 2 1

For Don, as always

Acknowledgments

Thanks are due to so many people who helped with this book!

To my editor, Kara Cesare; my agent, Kim Whalen; and authors Lisa Manuel, Linda Conrad, and Marianna Jameson for reading drafts and providing thorough and insightful feedback—the good, the bad, and the ugly.

To Claudio Cambon, for vetting my terrible Italian. To Dennis Pozzessere for being a sounding board on my Carnevale research. To Judie B. Raiford for sharing her expertise on how a solid gold Venetian mask could be forged—and who could do it. To Mona Risk, for her insight on how to poison such a mask.

To my husband, relatives, and friends, for putting up with me during the writing process and understanding that authors are strange and complex beings.

And, of course, many times over to everyone at Penguin: Anthony Ramondo, for brilliant covers on this series. Angela Januzzi for great PR. Kara Welsh and Claire Zion for sticking with me throughout the vagaries of the publishing market.

You guys are all my heroes more than any fictional characters. Thanks again.

chapter 1

Gwen Davies had a license to steal. Though she'd once been paid to re-cover furniture, she now got paid to recover missing art. For all intents and purposes, Gwen was a high-class repo man—just one who wore Dolce & Gabbana instead of a bad toupee. She stole for justice, on commission, and because it made her feel alive.

But a thief—even one with a permit—often encountered people who objected to her activities, so she had to stay in top shape. That explained why she was in this brutal joke of a gym on Brickell instead of at a coffeehouse with a venti mocha and a nice, fattening Danish . . . or on Miami Beach, watching the sun come up.

Gwen was also there to kill off a relentless, recurring dream . . . starring a man she never wanted to see again—naked or not. Quinn Lawson wasn't welcome between her sheets, but he turned up there almost every night she turned them down. He'd never been a man who waited for an invitation; he'd engraved his own right underneath her skirt.

On her fourth set of crunches, the tiny hairs on the back of Gwen's neck rose, despite the fact that they were drowning in sweat at the end of a murderous workout. She couldn't hear a sound over her own labored breathing and the groan of her muscles, but she acted on pure instinct.

Gwen hurled her body to the right with all the stamina she had left. She spun on her tailbone, raised her feet, and kicked out, taking her would-be assailant down with a solid hit to the knees.

Armando Romeu, aka "Cato," crashed to the ARTemis gym floor and lay blinking for a moment before he grinned up at her, his spiky bleached hair making him look like a hungover Miami sun. A very muscular, Cuban sun. "Not bad, princess."

Gwen grimaced at him, refilled her lungs with the cold gym air, and flopped onto her back. She caught a whiff of stale sweat and eau de rubber from the mats under the fitness machines, as well as the more pungent odor of paint from the room's freshly touched-up trim.

She sucked in another lungful of air and ignored the ripe odor emanating from Cato, despite the valiant efforts of his deodorant. He must have gone for a run in the Miami heat.

She stared up at the scratches and smudges on the bottom of a punching bag above her. Beyond it stood all the other exhaustion-inducing equipment: the weight circuit, the elliptical, the treadmill, and the rowing machine.

The sight of it all was enough to scare any self-respecting slug right back to the Godiva shop in the mall. Gwen briefly fantasized about her former days as a not-so-busy interior designer. A leisurely latte, a book of fabric swatches, a manicure followed by a long lunch . . .

And you were bored to tears. Remember?

Then there were the clients you wanted to tar, feather, and ride out of town on their own custom curtain rods. Not to mention the battles with workrooms . . .

"Yep, not bad at all," Cato said, sitting up in one fluid motion. His torso was a perfect isosceles triangle of buff, South Beach male.

"Not bad? You mean it was great." Gwen shoved her feet under the toes of his trainers and finished her set of crunches. "Not only did I anticipate, but I brought you to the floor."

"Don't get a big head, missy. I caught you napping last week," he reminded her.

"It was an off time of the month."

"Oh, *that* old excuse . . ."

Gwen sat up and leveled her gaze on him. "Listen, Cato—"

"Yes, Inspector Clouseau?"

"If you'd ever had PMS or cramps you'd understand. You got me *one* time out of the last, what, thirty attempts? Give me a break."

"It only takes once. And a dead art recovery agent is not an effective art recovery agent."

"Yes, Cato. Thank you, Cato. May I have another scare, please, Cato?"

"You bet, *mamita.*" He winked at her and got up. "That's my job: to keep all of you worthless agents in shape and on your toes."

"And here I thought my Jimmy Choos took care of that."

"They do, they do. But me and Jimmy? We're like this," Cato said, holding up two fingers close together. Then he laughed. "And we *both* make your ass look good."

Gwen shook her head at him and wiped her face and neck with a towel. "Go do a sneak attack on someone else."

He rubbed his hands together with glee. "Gladly. I can't believe I get paid to have this much fun."

An hour later, Gwen walked into the Miami offices of ARTemis, Inc., art recovery specialists. Outside, the breeze off the water seemed unseasonably humid, and the royal palms yawned languidly under the insistent sun. Like most of the city, they weren't eager to wake before ten a.m.

Gwen had traded her gym shorts for a silk Pucci dress

with an empire waist, no panty hose, and a pair of cream sling-back sandals. She'd dried and gelled her short hair; the soft orange streaks picked up the tangerine hues in her dress. She looked pretty good for a repo man.

"Hiya, doll face," said Sheila. Sheila Kofsky was the ARTemis office manager and looked like a trendy white raisin with a cloud of improbably blond hair. She presided over the reception area and the wardrobe room, her inch-long acrylic nails striking fear into any would-be interloper's heart.

Sheila always cut a somewhat astonishing figure. Today's reading glasses were electric blue with little hot-pink flamingos painted at the top outside corners of the rims. She wore matching hot-pink lipstick and nail polish, tight black pedal pushers, a tight black cleavage-revealing top, and a hot-pink faux-linen jacket. But the pièces de résistance were the electric-blue calf-hair mules that she had to have dyed herself.

Gwen still hadn't figured out why anyone had hired Sheila. She swore like a sailor, had no couth, and didn't fit in to the elegant atmosphere of the office. But she never missed a day of work and was a true genius with the recovery agents' wardrobes and, when necessary, disguises.

"Hi, Sheila. How are you today?"

"Never mind that. There's another package for you from Sid Thresher." Sheila reached under her desk and handed Gwen a box from Van Cleef & Arpels.

"You opened it?"

"Of course I opened it, doll. It's part of my job." Sheila grinned.

"It is *not* part of your job to unwrap it and steam open the personal card," Gwen said, wondering why she bothered. Sheila was incorrigible.

"Saves you the trouble. Sid's begging you to taste just a

little of his Subversion and he wants you to wear these with the satin bustier and thong he sent last week."

Subversion was Sid's world-famous British rock band. Gwen had been targeted for seduction by an older, uglier, less stable Mick Jagger. She sighed and opened the box.

Inside was a pair of diamond chandelier earrings so long that they'd bang her shoulder blades if she were to put them on. They glittered in the fluorescent lighting.

Agent Eric McDougal sauntered through the front door, took a look, and raised his ginger eyebrows. "Gwendolyn," he drawled. "Whatever did you do to earn those?"

Gwen ignored him, shut the box with a snap, and turned to Sheila. "Please return these immediately. Send Sid a computer-generated note saying thanks, but I can't possibly accept."

"Such a nice girl," McDougal said sardonically. "So well brought up."

Sheila closed the mouth she'd left hanging open. "You're kidding me, right?"

"No." Gwen dropped the box on her desk.

"Listen," Sheila said. "Why waste the postage? Just let me keep 'em."

"Send them back. I don't want to encourage him. Sid is crazy and he makes my skin crawl."

"Doll, I could do a lot of lying back and thinking of England for these beauties, and maybe the matching necklace, too. . . ."

"Now, there's a visual," said McDougal. He turned to Gwen. "Coming to the assignments meeting?"

Gwen nodded and followed him down the hall to the conference room. She sat down at the long maple table as if she belonged there with all the other art recovery agents.

She sipped at her morning fruit smoothie and reminded herself that she *did* belong there. Today she'd get her first solo assignment. She was a newly minted coin just being put into circulation—and it was up to her to prove her worth.

Gwen scanned the faces of the other agents on the team.

Dante di Leo, who looked as if he owned the place but didn't, leaned casually against the end of the table, reviewing his notes for the meeting. Since he was out of the field for now as he struggled with a broken leg, he ran the presentations and handed out assignments. Gwen much preferred Dante to McDougal. Dante looked out for her, tried to help her.

McDougal, despite the fact that he looked like a hot cross between Prince Harry and a young Paul Newman, could go kiss a speeding MTA bus. His wiry auburn hair looked as if it hadn't been combed in a week—probably the last time he'd stopped partying and slept. On the table, he tapped out the rhythm to an unknown song with his thumbs, his laser blue eyes far away.

Avy Hunt typed furiously into her BlackBerry. Dressed in slim, dark leather pants and a snug T-shirt, her light brown hair piled messily on top of her head, she did own the place—or at least half of it.

Little blond Chloe Atwell seemed hip and studious with her rectangular, trendy black eyewear and smooth asymmetrical haircut. As usual, she had a Starbucks cup in her hand.

Valeria Costas wore a smug feline expression, her black hair gleaming blue under the fluorescent lighting. She looked well massaged and oiled, as if she'd just stepped out of an exclusive spa. As she dug into her Vuitton satchel, the diamonds on her fingers glittering, Gwen couldn't help but hope that Cato would go after her next.

They all waited for Dante to start the meeting. Avy glanced at her watch and then at him.

Dante met her gaze calmly and took his time, maneuvering on his crutches to the laptop computer that would run his PowerPoint presentation. "Lights, please."

Gwen got up to hit them, but Sheila chose that moment to pop in. "Communiqué from Kelso." Over her bizarre reading glasses she gave a look that was a little self-important.

"And what does our fearless and invisible leader have to say?" Avy asked. Nobody had ever seen Kelso, though he owned fifty-one percent of the company. He operated off the grid and out of the ether—rather like Liam, Avy's former-thief fiancé.

Sheila employed a hot-pink nail to shove the reading glasses higher on her nose. "Word on the street, Ave, is that the Greek ambassador you got arrested is out for revenge. Kelso doesn't know how or when, but he says to keep your eyes open. Possible Mob connections."

Avy nodded. "Is that it?"

Sheila stared at her. "Yeah, sweet cheeks. The Mob could be after you, that's all. No biggie."

Avy's face remained serene. "Okay. The phone's ringing. Will you shut the door on your way out, please?"

"I serve at your pleasure," Sheila growled.

"And you give me so much of that, Kofsky." Avy said it with a grin.

Sheila snorted and stomped out.

"Ambassador?" Gwen asked.

Avy nodded. "Three years ago, way before we brought you in to train, I did a recovery through Lloyd's of London that ended with the arrest of Constantin Tzekas, the U.S. ambassador from Greece. He was prosecuted for the theft of a Masaccio painting and deported in disgrace."

"And now he's out to get you?"

Avy shrugged, seeming unconcerned. "Apparently so."

Gwen shivered. Avy was her former college roommate at Sweet Briar. She was close to fearless, but Gwen was not. She didn't like the idea of anyone being after her best friend. Particularly not anyone with Mob connections.

Dante looked concerned as well. He gestured with his head toward the lights, though, and Gwen turned them off. The first slide flashed up on the screen. "Toulouse-Lautrec," Dante said, "circa 1892. Worth just shy of eight hundred thousand." A damning portrait of a night on the town in turn-of-the-century Paris, the painting exhibited the ghoulish, overly painted faces of tawdry women in a nightclub and the men who leered at them. The hues were weird and bluish, the contour lines exaggerated—half-witty, half-menacing.

"This was stolen from the home of an elderly couple in Paris. There was no sign of a break-in, and one of the possible suspects is their bachelor nephew. They want this kept quiet—no police. Chloe, you'll take this one. The insurer is Giroux Freres."

Chloe nodded, looking pleased, and Dante slid a file down the long table toward her.

"McDougal, you're going to Scotland." Dante flashed the next slide. "An entire suit of armor, sixteenth century, has walked out of the great hall at Edinloch Castle. It belonged to the current Duke of Edinloch's ancestor, who fought in the Battle of Arkinholm while wearing it, so he wants it back. It's not insured."

Dante's lips twitched. "As he put it, 'Ach! Why the fook would I insure a bloody bit o' tin?' So he's paying us a flat ten-percent fee for the recovery, plus expenses."

"Just tell me the ancestor's bones aren't still rattling around in there," said McDougal, yawning. "What's the Tin Man worth?"

"Conservative estimates put it at four hundred thousand."

Dante sent another file folder spinning toward McDougal, who didn't look as pleased as Chloe.

Poor guy, he'd collect a mere forty thousand for his troubles. Gwen would be lucky if they gave her a piece with a five- or ten-thousand-dollar commission.

The sight of the next slide produced a couple of audible gasps within the room.

A Venetian mask stared sightlessly out at them. It was not made out of painted paper, but of pure gold, with stylized peacock feathers picked out around the eyes in diamonds, sapphires, and emeralds. A fringe of faceted diamonds, sapphires, and emeralds poured like a priceless waterfall from the bottom of it and would completely obscure the face of the wearer.

"You are gazing at five-point-four million dollars," Dante said. "This mask is a Columbina Oriente dating to 1508. It was created for a cousin of the Borgia family who resided in Venice. He was being cuckolded by his wife, who had a much younger lover.

"While the wife enjoyed her fresh meat—please pardon the expression—the husband plotted revenge. He had the inside of the mask painted with a lethal poison, just in time for the Venetian Carnevale, a celebration before Lent.

"Not coincidentally," Dante added in a dry tone, "the term *carnevale* means literally 'to remove meat.'"

A ripple of laughter went through the room.

"*Eccolo*," he continued, "the wife's lover, delighted to receive such a lovely gift from his inamorata, donned it immediately and paraded about—only to die writhing in agony hours later. And voilà," Dante said with a flash of white teeth and a flourish. "The husband's rival meat was . . . removed."

As Avy's BlackBerry vibrated on the conference table, Valeria said avidly, "I want this recovery."

Dante didn't even cast his hooded eyes toward her as he shook his dark head. "The mask, as the plum assignment, goes to Avy."

Avy wasn't even listening, her gaze intent on the screen of her BlackBerry. She began to type a response with her thumbs.

Valeria blew out an audible breath of resentment and tossed her hair over her shoulder. "Of course. I should have known."

"This mask was, until recently, part of the corporate art collection at Jaworski Labs, right here on Brickell. It was stolen from there two nights ago—"

"Wait," Gwen interrupted. "Why would a pharmaceutical company have an art collection? Isn't that odd?"

"Not at all," Dante said. "Banks, insurance companies, technology giants—many of them seek to diversify their assets through acquiring art. And in the case of Ed Jaworski, the founder of the lab, his wife was an artist. So the old man began stockpiling art in the seventies, before the insanity of the eighties market. Smart move. That art collection is one of the only reasons the company has been able to ride out some of its storms."

"Like the recall of their cholesterol drug and the resulting class action suit," McDougal said.

Chloe frowned. "Wasn't there some kind of scandal with Jaworski about a year ago, something about a painting?"

Avy finally punched send on her BlackBerry and looked up. "Yeah, you could say that. The CEO of Jaworski was taking great care of a Renoir original acquired with company funds—he hung it over the couch in the living room of his Fisher Island home. He claimed, of course, that he only had it at his place for safekeeping."

"Nice," Gwen murmured.

Avy stood up and shoved her BlackBerry into her battered Dior saddlebag. "They found other irregularities, too. Old Jaworski is still on the board, and he made sure the man got canned. He brought in some whiz kid to run things. The guy's only thirty-five."

She looked around the table and drummed her fingers on top of the file folder Dante had slid down to her. "I'm sorry, but I have to catch a plane. I'll be in Europe for a couple of weeks, but I'll stay in touch."

Her eyes came to rest on Gwen's face. She nodded once decisively, and then turned to Dante. "Give the mask assignment to Gwen. She can handle it."

Dante's jaw went slack as he stared at her. "Gwen is a rookie!"

"Green as a goddamned salad!" said McDougal.

Around her, Gwen could feel the resentment pulsing in the room as the other agents simmered. She couldn't really fault them. "Ave, I don't think—"

"Gwen will do the recovery on the mask," Avy repeated. "This isn't up for debate."

Valeria stared coldly at Gwen. Her eyes were baleful and promised trouble. She turned her gaze back on Avy. It didn't get any friendlier.

"You're the boss," Dante said at last.

Avy headed for the door. "Glad you remember that." Her departure didn't ease the tension in the room and nobody would look at Gwen.

She felt exhilarated. Guilty. Terrified. Alive. And possibly unworthy. Her first assignment had a commission of more than half a million dollars? Crazy.

Dante switched to the next slide. "Valeria, you're going to Brazil. . . ."

Gwen opened the file folder Avy had pushed at her and stared down in silence at the mask. The thing was breathtakingly beautiful, the epitome of mystery and glamour. It spoke of sultry Venetian nights, elegant debauchery, freely flowing wine . . . and evil.

The mask was instantly recognizable. Once the alert

went out and it got listed on the international Art Loss Register, the mask would be impossible for anyone to sell on the open market. It would be almost as challenging to unload the piece on the black market. So who had stolen it—and why?

chapter 2

Quinn Lawson, president and CEO of Jaworski Labs, ordinarily thrived on having his feet held to the fire. The open flame got his juices flowing and warmed up his many and varied arguments for change in the business environment. And if his toes got a little charred in the process, well, that was the price of progress.

But today took him right back to when he was age ten, the spit drying up in his mouth as he prepared for a paddling in the principal's office at Fullerton Junior High in Nowata, Oklahoma. He had that same funny feeling that things weren't right—that the man behind the desk had an agenda for taking Quinn's pants down.

Of course, this Palm Beach Mediterranean-style mansion with its private beach and full staff was a far cry from the Fullerton Junior High administrative offices, with their shiny, puke green linoleum floors, faux-wood-grain desks, and cheap framed educational posters.

Nobody at Fullerton had ever offered him bourbon in a Baccarat decanter on a silver tray, either. Go figure.

But old Ed Jaworski, like Principal Goodwin, took an implacable inventory of Quinn, as if he'd like to strip him of his full head of dark blond hair (Ed was down to about three wispy gray strands), his muscular build, and his hard-earned, full-scholarship-funded double degrees from Stanford: BA and MBA.

Ed was nine days older than God. He didn't like the way Quinn did things, his lack of respect for tradition. But he hadn't been able to argue with his results—until now. And even now, the results had nothing to do with numbers, which always turned to music in Quinn's hands.

"You'll get the Borgia mask back, or you're fired," Ed said. "I will personally see to it."

And he could, as the still-powerful founder of the company. It didn't matter that he'd be cutting off his nose to spite his face; that the old son of a bitch would have to undergo an exhaustive executive search for another CEO.

A man like Jaworski didn't care about the consequences of flexing his muscle—he just wanted to show that even withered and gray, with the prime of his life behind him, he could do it. Ed wanted to show that he could still get it up, so to speak.

"I can promise you that the mask isn't hanging over my couch," Quinn said in an attempt to lighten the atmosphere.

That failed miserably.

"Gross negligence!" Ed thundered. "The security of Jaworski Labs has been compromised under your watch."

"If you recall, I recommended an overhaul of the entire security system soon after I accepted the position." Quinn gazed at him for a beat too long before adding, "Sir."

"If you can't keep the art collection safe, then how is the board supposed to have confidence that you can keep the research and development of this company's products safe?" Ed overrode him, choosing to conveniently forget the meeting in which he'd pooh-poohed Quinn's concerns.

In other words, Principal Ed was telling him to bend over. It didn't matter that the meeting was documented. Ed could screw his career here six ways to Sunday.

Quinn gripped the arms of his chair and fought to keep

his temper under control, because if he lost it, Jaworski could add gross insubordination to his list of reasons to get rid of the whiz-kid CEO that he'd had to have at any price and now couldn't abide. With anyone else, Quinn would bark right back. With this old man, it was more effective to keep his cool.

It briefly crossed his mind that Jaworski himself could have had the mask stolen to set Quinn up. But that seemed a bit extreme, even for him.

"I'll get the mask recovered." Quinn said it quietly but firmly. "I have ARTemis on it already. Avy Hunt is handling this personally."

Jaworski nodded grudgingly. "She has a good reputation."

"In the meantime, sir, the theft can only back up my original argument that our security needs updating. The system is"—*as old as you are*—"antiquated. It's my understanding that it's the same one that's been in place since you retired."

Old Ed's eyes snapped as Quinn deftly pointed out who was truly responsible for allowing the breach. "You've got a lot of nerve."

"Yes, sir." He kept his voice neutral. "That comes in handy when running a company."

Jaworski glared at him.

"So I assume that I'll have your full support now in authorizing funds for a total overhaul of headquarters security." Quinn smiled. *Now who's got whom bent over, you old bastard?*

Ed made a strangled noise. "Get the hell out of my house," the old man growled. "And don't come back until my five million dollars' worth of art has, too."

Quinn stood up and calmly exited. He'd learned a few things over the years since he'd been in Principal

Goodwin's office. He'd learned not to bend over for anyone, no matter what their authority.

Because once your pants are down, it's hard to defend yourself—in school, in love, in life.

Goodwin had violated every moral, ethical, and social code he supposedly stood for that day. But who would have believed a dirty, troubled, bastard kid whose grandfather was the town drunk?

Quinn had taken care of himself. He'd stabbed the principal with his own letter opener, but nobody had bothered to ask why—and Quinn certainly hadn't volunteered the shameful information. They said he was just a violent punk and expelled him.

He'd then had a choice: a publicly funded military school or running away. But he'd known even at age thirteen that running wouldn't solve any of his problems; it would just intensify them.

Ironically, military school had been the making of Quinn. When he'd graduated, he'd put on his dress uniform and paid a visit to his old friend Principal Goodwin. Watched him shake like a leaf. But that was in the past.

Today was all that mattered, and Quinn refused to let Jaworski get to him. Quinn had hired the best there was in the art recovery business, and if ARTemis couldn't find the mask, then he'd damn well go after it himself. Sure . . . in all his spare time.

He left Jaworski's expensive Palm Beach air-conditioning and drove his Mercedes the hour and a half to the lab's corporate headquarters in the Martinez-Rochas Tower on Brickell Avenue.

The buildings in downtown Miami, like the people, all seemed to wear designer sunglasses that kept them anonymous. The Martinez-Rochas Tower, like all the others, was tall, white, and full of tinted glass to keep the sun out and cool air in. It was facelessly modern, without any particular architectural significance. The interior attracted more attention, because of the art.

As he walked in, Quinn's eyes swept the rotunda that housed the lab's corporate art collection, which included a range of pieces as diverse as original sheet music by Puccini to studies of dancers by Degas to works of minor German expressionists.

He braced himself to see the mask's empty niche. Despite his calm demeanor in front of the old man, the empty niche drove him crazy. It was as if someone had thrown a brick through his own living room window, and he had to step over the mess every day without sweeping it up.

He gritted his teeth and fervently hoped that ARTemis was going to rectify the situation, and fast, so that he could turn his attention back to the business at hand. He was an expert at supply chain development and management, market positioning, competitive positioning, pricing, and financial analysis. He could design a business infrastructure and innovate cost-management strategies.

What he could not do was understand the insane art market or comprehend why anyone in their right mind would pay fifty-four? fifty-six? *million* dollars for a single painting by van Gogh, van Went, or van *Gone with the Wind*. A few daubs of paint by a lunatic.

Quinn also didn't understand why anyone would pay five million bucks for a silly Venetian mask, no matter what its provenance, which was a fancy word for where it had originated and who'd owned it in the five centuries since then.

Besides Jaworski's art consultant, the enterprising Angeline Le Fevre—who was driven by fat commissions—only one person had ever tried to explain art to him. He thought of her as little as possible.

He shook his head as he approached El Chivo, his nickname for the bronze sculpture that stood in the center of the rotunda. Maybe some artistic type would accuse him of lacking a soul, but the thing looked to him like a kid had smushed together a bunch of mud and stuck two horns at the top.

And yet Angeline Le Fevre insisted that it was a goat. She said it was by Picasso, worth millions. And she swore it was made out of bronze, not mud.

Quinn guessed he was just an uncultured schmuck, but apparently others in the building were, too. Because some joker occasionally stuck a burger or a taco in the goat's misshapen mouth, and that tickled his funny bone.

"*Buenos dias*, Manny," Quinn said to the round security guard in front of the elevators. "*El Chivo* looks hungry."

"*Buenos, señor.* Nah, he's not hungry. I found half a McDonald's milk shake in front of him earlier, so I figure he's still digesting a Happy Meal."

Quinn laughed. "A milk shake, huh? That's a new one." He got into the elevator when it opened, but his smile vanished as his gaze moved again to the empty niche.

Gwen stared intently at the video screen as she watched the Jaworski surveillance tapes for the seventh or eighth time, focusing in on the two shadowy figures in wool caps. The caps were pulled down low and the collars of the men tugged high, effectively concealing most of their features.

"There," she said, pointing. "Stop the tape. D'you see that?"

"What?" asked Dante. As usual, he wore a black designer T-shirt and formfitting jeans with beautifully crafted Italian loafers. Sheila called him GQ.

"That glint. Just a tiny silver glint near the edge of this guy's cap."

Dante peered more closely at the screen, then lifted a shoulder. "And what significance does it have?"

"I don't know. Looks like the guy wears an earring."

"Aha!" Dante teased her. "Now you're onto something. Only three-quarters of the Miami population wears an earring, *bella.*"

Gwen made a face at him and peered more intently at the tiny silver gleam in the grainy picture. "How's your leg?"

"Misery is going through a south Florida summer in a cast," Dante said, grimacing.

"It's not summer," Gwen reminded him with a laugh. "It's early February."

He raised an eyebrow and gestured out the floor-to-ceiling plate-glass window. Biscayne Bay sparkled below under a relentless sun. "I must dispute that statement."

He was right—eighty-six degrees with 83 percent humidity was summer, no matter what the calendar claimed. This winter felt like August.

"*Caliente,*" he said.

"So are you ever going to fill us in on exactly how you broke your leg?"

His eyes glinted under their sleepy lids. "Ask Avy. Ask her about the Berlin job—and how I tried to watch out for her."

"Well, that explains it. Avy doesn't like to be looked after. She probably broke your kneecap just for that."

Dante laughed, but the sound was a bit humorless. He grabbed his crutches and headed for her office door. "May I get you something to drink? A Pellegrino? Espresso?"

Dante drank espresso even though everyone else in Miami was hooked on café cubano. His voice reminded her of a café cubano, though—rich and smooth and sweet, full of character. It had hypnotized more than one woman in Miami. Apparently there'd been a few of those in his two years with the agency, but they were only arm candy, nothing serious. The rumor was that he had an ex-wife in

Milan and was still in love with her. Gwen found that romantic, if sad.

"Dante, why don't you sit down and I'll get the espresso? Oh, right. You don't trust me to make it decently."

He winked at her and swung himself to the door. With his head he gestured to the tape, still frozen on the close-up of the man's ear. "I don't think that will get you anywhere. Make a list instead of anyone who stood to gain from the disappearance of the mask."

"I've done that, and it's a very short list," said Gwen. "The Jaworski corporation owns it. They'll get the payout from Chubb if we don't recover the mask. But nobody else benefits."

"So maybe it's a cash-flow issue," Dante suggested.

Gwen nodded. "Possible."

"I'll leave you to it."

"Thanks," Gwen muttered, staring again at the shadowy figure's ear. Dante was right—she should have the Nerd Corps dig into the backgrounds of the executives at Jaworski. But it stood to reason that a crooked executive wouldn't do his own dirty work. This had been a smash-and-grab operation: The two dark figures on the surveillance footage had come in through a loading dock and had gone right to the rotunda that housed the corporate art collection. Then they'd immediately headed for the glassed-in niche that held the mask. They'd destroyed the glass simply by annihilating it with a fire extinguisher pulled from a wall on the way.

Nothing creative about the whole operation. The men moved as if they were following instructions to the letter, and they never deviated from them. They'd acted on orders. They'd been directed to take one piece and one piece only. Why?

She didn't have to make a list. There were two possible

motives for this crime. One was money. The other was lust for the mask itself. Art lovers could become obsessed with the idea of possessing a piece. Obsessed to the point of stealing it to hoard and admire it in secrecy.

Gwen hit the eject button on the tape. If she found these men, she'd save herself a lot of guesswork and grunt work. A threat of cops, maybe a bribe—and she'd not only track down the mask itself but find out whom these guys were working for.

Gwen pocketed the tape. Then she called Miguel in the Nerd Corps to see about possibilities for magnification.

Miguel looked like a choirboy in his polo shirt, with his neatly combed black hair. His skin was olive brown, his eyes a startling pale blue, his mouth a sweet Cupid's bow. To all appearances, butter wouldn't melt in his mouth. Nobody would ever guess that he was a wizard and spent his days doing highly illegal hacking and research for ARTemis.

Within twenty minutes Gwen knew the glint on that shadowy figure was indeed an earring, a small silver shark.

Miguel caught his lower lip between his teeth and tapped the screen. "I know that guy. Vargas? Vasquez? Wait, lemme see. . . ." A few clicks of his fingers on the keyboard and he brought up a database with photos and rap sheets. Gwen had a feeling that it was highly irregular for him to have access to it, but she said nothing as he scrolled through it.

"*Velasquez* brothers," he said. "They're pretty well-known as muscle for hire. Esteban and Carlos, the one with the earring. They live in east Hialeah. Small-time crooks, petty break-ins and some smuggling, some dealing."

"Why would they be involved in something like this?"

Miguel sat back in his chair and shrugged. "Easy money. You want me to set up surveillance?"

Gwen nodded. She'd gather as much information as she could before talking to them.

"Consider it done."

In the end, electronic surveillance wasn't necessary. Gwen herself had no trouble tailing the Velasquez brothers the next day from their house in dicey east Hialeah to a warehouse along the Miami River, where they stowed some boxes and then drove away, the brake lights of their old Chevy Impala winking conspiratorially at her.

Gwen waited for five minutes to make sure they didn't come back for anything. Then she got out of her little Toyota Prius, gingerly made her way through the thicket of bushes concealing the car, and picked a trail across the gravel drive leading to the warehouse.

The structure was a bizarre amalgam of brick, cinder block, wood, and corrugated aluminum, and it looked as if it would crumple in a hurricane. She just hoped the roof wouldn't fall in on her.

The door was sealed with a heavy industrial padlock, one that would have discouraged most people. Gwen just lifted an eyebrow and dug into her bag. She bypassed her nail file, her mints, and her wallet for a sweet little set of lock picks in a handy microfiber pouch.

She never left home without it.

chapter 3

Inside the warehouse stood several huge pallets of boxed Cuban cigars and liquor. Gwen easily climbed one. The roof wasn't an issue, but the security presented a problem: Gwen didn't expect to be greeted by a sixteen-foot-long reticulated python.

Maybe she should have—after all, she was in a dark, suffocating, ramshackle warehouse along the Miami River, where dead bodies and "square grouper"—packages of cocaine—washed up on a regular basis.

After years of her mother's cocktail parties and dinners for thirty, Gwen could charm admirals and generals with a simple dimple. But this reptile? To say that she was at a social loss was putting it mildly. For openers, she screamed—and it wasn't one of those ladylike chirps, either. It was raw with fear, loud enough to blast off her carefully applied lipstick and leave an appalled kiss print shimmering in the humid Miami air. Edvard Munch's *Scream* had nothing on hers.

The python struck as Gwen hurtled backward off the tall pallet of boxed Cuban cigars she'd unwisely climbed. As she hit the filthy concrete floor and rolled, she thanked God for Cato's training.

Gwen got as far as she could get from the crates and the

cold-eyed, now motionless reptile, then pulled the SIG Sauer P-230 that was standard issue for all female agents at ARTemis.

The cold weight of it in her hand reassured her as she wrestled for control over her breathing and her heart rate. The python, still lording it over the Cubans, did a funny little rhythm-and-blues thing with its head and peered into the middle distance.

Gwen had always scoffed at the urban myth that those in illegal imports/exports sometimes used snakes to discourage anyone from disturbing their products. Only in Hollywood . . . But it was just her luck that the Velasquez brothers had been watching too much bad television.

She drew up to her full five feet four inches and squinted at the python while she steadied her shaking, sweaty hands.

The creature's ugly, flat, lipless head swiveled in her direction and she shivered. As she forced herself closer and aimed her flashlight at it, she could see the snake's eyes: black and beady. She took aim right between them.

Nobody in this dangerous area between Seventeenth and Twenty-seventh avenues would blink at the noise. The shot exploded in the uninsulated, aluminum-roofed warehouse and almost deafened her, but it was well worth killing the snake. The resulting mess wasn't pretty. No time to think about that, though. She needed to get what she'd come here for.

At the top of the mountain of Cubans, which towered behind an equally tall mountain of crates of a Peruvian liquor called *pisco*, was an ornate carved mahogany box, the same one she'd seen in her file. Inside that box should be the stolen Venetian mask.

Easy. Too easy? If anything, Gwen would have expected to track it down in Europe, among priceless bottles of wine or an aristocrat's cache of jewels. The Miami River was a bit of a stretch—but it was certainly convenient. Yet maybe the brothers simply hadn't had the chance yet to ship the mask out of the country.

She clambered back up the pallet of cigars and gingerly used her foot to push the body of the python off the edge. It fell to the cement floor with a couple of heavy, meaty thuds. She swallowed her bile at the sight and turned her eye to the prize, glad that she was a good shot. She should be, after all the ARTemis target practice.

The wooden box was heavy under her left arm as she navigated her way down the big pallet with her right one. She set the box down on the ground and squatted in front of it as she lifted the lid. The golden mask with its empty eyes glinted up at her. It brought back memories of a silver mask she'd once worn, memories she ruthlessly threw back down the dark well of her past.

The slides and photos hadn't done the Venetian mask justice. Studded with swirls of inset jewels in peacock designs and hues, it almost took her breath away. She traced the cold contours of it with her index finger, stopping at the places where an ornately chased, Florentine leather strap fastened to the edges. It buckled at the back of the wearer's head.

As she gazed at it, unease coiled at Gwen's neck and then slithered down her spine. An image flashed at her: of convulsed, agonized hands trying to pry the mask off, fingers scrabbling hopelessly to unbuckle the strap. A writhing, shuddering body in its death throes. Black betrayal.

She almost dropped the box. Instead, she quickly shut it, tucked it under her arm, and hitched the handle of her big handbag over her shoulder. She turned toward the aluminum door, which hung a bit drunkenly on its hinges now that the heavy padlock was off, the only thing that had held it on straight.

Gwen stabbed open the door with her manicured index finger and stepped out into the humid, fetid Miami air, which moistened her skin like the surly breath of an alligator.

She still couldn't quite believe that her $5 million assignment had been this easy. Something about this recovery didn't feel quite right—but then, it was the first one she'd ever done on her own and she didn't know exactly what "right" *should* feel like.

Gwen wanted to savor the moment, bask in the thrill. But as she walked to the Prius, the mask inside the box seemed to pulse ominously. She couldn't wait to get rid of it.

Quinn glanced at his watch, impatient for two o'clock to arrive along with Avy Hunt and the Borgia mask. He was impressed that she'd made the recovery in such a short time. Now he could get old Ed Jaworski placated and off his back, while Quinn himself returned to doing what he did best: running the company.

Any more security breaches and the lab's investors would scatter like cockroaches before he could get funding for the R & D on a drug with huge potential—it could break the cycle of alcohol addiction. Things were too late for his grandfather, but not for others.

Quinn's mouth twisted as he signed a stack of letters. They'd found old Jack Lawson on his sagging front porch with a bottle of Popov still in his gnarled, clawlike hand. He'd died as he'd lived, in shame and squalor.

It was the shame that drove Quinn still. Never again would he be the object of pity and ridicule, a kid that some old pervert felt that he could take advantage of because nobody would notice—or care.

If he could get Alaban produced and distributed, he'd leave a mark on the world, and not just a skid mark. He could quit remembering the days when he'd had to apologize for his very existence.

As Quinn signed yet another piece of correspondence, his phone rang. "Sir," said his assistant, "your two o'clock appointment is here."

"Thanks, Chris. Send her in."

Quinn picked up the dark suit jacket he'd tossed on the couch and pulled it on. He sat down in the brown leather chair behind his desk and tried not to be bothered by the oppressive dark paneling and taupe upholstery of his predecessor. He made a mental note to have Chris remove the mounted bear's head that loomed over the credenza and had been the former CEO's unsubtle gimmick for intimidating people.

The rest of it could wait—Quinn was here to get Jaworski's bottom line healthy, not prance around with some interior decorator or spend whole days playing golf, as his predecessor had.

Quinn was curious to meet Avy Hunt. What kind of woman spent her days running down stolen art? How did a person get into that kind of profession?

His office door opened and he got courteously to his feet. Then he saw who waltzed in and he almost fell back into the chair.

It was her. No doubt about it. Those were the same sweet doe eyes that belied her intelligence. The nose that was narrow at the bridge and widened into an upside-down heart at the tip. The contours of her face, also heart shaped. And the mouth he'd loved until she'd given him the big kiss-off fifteen years ago.

He didn't know whether to laugh or throw something. "Unless you've changed your name, Gwen, you're not Avy Hunt."

Her face had drained of color and she took a step back, then another. Her mouth formed his name but no sound

came out. She shook her head as if to clear it of his image,
but he sure as hell wasn't going anywhere. His journey for
the past fifteen years had led right to this desk. It had been
spurred by her, people like her. Quinn had seen to it that
he'd never feel inferior again.

The silence stretched on.

It made him angry: He'd worked for years to get her
voice out of his head, and he suddenly wanted to hear it
again. Why? And still she said not a single word. Damn her.

*Talk to me. Open that sultry, dirty-angel mouth. Or do
you need a pen, so you can write me another note?*

Long-repressed, long-forgotten emotion bubbled to the
surface in him, simmering like lava under a thin, scarred
crust. He wanted to take her by the shoulders and shake her
until she spoke to him, even if only to swear. But he didn't
move from behind his desk.

"Your hair is different," he said at last, stupidly, eyeing
her short cut with the subtle orange streaks. They were
supposed to be rebellious, he figured, but they were oddly
elegant. Reminded him of Grand Marnier in a firelit glass.

She nodded. The expression on her face hadn't changed
since she'd entered, but even after fifteen years, he still
knew her well enough to note the small signs of shock
she'd exhibited: the quick, subtle double blink, the surge of
color in her white cheeks, the small hand tightening on that
ridiculously large pocketbook. Her left knee, exposed by
the hem of her skirt, quivered.

So she hadn't engineered this meeting on purpose . . . or
had she?

He wished he didn't know what she looked like naked.
How she had a birthmark that looked a lot like a chocolate-
chip cookie on the inside of her right thigh.

Hey, Cookie Monster . . .

The memories were so silly. So juvenile. So bittersweet.
And so out of place.

He pushed them away and made a last-ditch attempt to get down to business while Gwen stared up at that stupid, goddamned bear's head with an expression of polite disgust. He wanted to yell that he hadn't shot it and hadn't stuck it up there, but doing so would reveal that she'd eviscerated the famous Quinn "cool," and damned if he was about to do that.

"Gwen," he said evenly, "what are you doing here? It's great to see you after all these years, but I have an appointment right now. My assistant must have thought you were Ms. Hunt."

"Avy's busy on another job. They sent me instead. Since the results are the same"—she pulled a familiar mahogany box out of the huge handbag—"we didn't clarify that I'd be the point person instead." Gwen set the box on his desk and took a step backward.

"C'mon, Gwen. You knew damn well that I was the CEO."

"No." She met his gaze without flinching, and there it was: the triple blink that meant she was annoyed. "I knew that the CEO of Jaworski Labs was our client. That's all. So at the risk of being rude—"

He laughed. "The Gwen Davies I remember never took any risks. She found herself a man at the first sign of trouble."

"—at the risk of being rude," she repeated, "don't flatter yourself."

"She was never rude, either. She wasn't brought up that way."

Gwen's soft, full mouth flattened into a thin line. "Things change, Mr. Lawson."

Mr. Lawson? He nodded. "And they also stay the same."

She inclined her head. With a small smile, she stepped forward again and flipped open the hinged mahogany box. "I believe this is what you were looking for?"

The gold mask stared up at Quinn, its eyes as empty as Gwen was trying to make hers.

He nodded. "You work for ARTemis." He said it dubiously, almost mocking the concept. Gwen was some kind of art world Jane Bond? With her total lack of a sense of direction and nonexistent street smarts?

"Yes." Her gaze might be steady, but he could read the defiance there, no problem.

"Honey, you used to get lost in a mall."

She nodded. "And you used to be a grease monkey," she said, eyeing his Rolex, his Hermès tie, his three-hundred-dollar shoes. "I guess you've come a long way, baby. Any further questions?"

Nicely done. Even he had to admit she'd scored with that one. "Where did you find the mask?" Quinn asked, suspending his disbelief for the moment.

"In a warehouse on the Miami River."

Jesus H. Christ. He pressed his fingertips together, hard, under cover of his desk. "Please tell me you didn't go there alone."

"Mr. Lawson, how I do my job is none of your concern. ARTemis doesn't make a policy of sharing details."

He supposed he deserved that.

"And the thieves?"

"The thieves aren't my concern, either. We're recovery agents, not police officers."

"But you must have some knowledge of these crooks, or you wouldn't have found the warehouse. . . ."

"I can't help you. I'm sorry."

"Isn't that a little immoral, Gwen?"

There was that small smile again. A little bit sad this time. "Amoral, Mr. Lawson. And again, it's part of the job."

He wanted to shout at her not to call him friggin' "Mr. Lawson" in that cool, snotty way. But he wouldn't give her the satisfaction. "Part of the job you like?"

She shrugged. "Do you like every aspect of yours?"

Score again. "The Gwen Davies that I knew had very clear ideas of right and wrong. She was neither immoral nor amoral."

As the words spilled from his mouth he had a quick, unwelcome flashback to a narrow, dark alley in Rio and the living color of an intoxicating Carnevale.

Oceans of alcohol, raucous laughter, and intemperate music that stole taboos and hurled them to the four winds. Wild, fantasy-spurred costumes. Gwen's silver mask glinting in some form of celestial communication, flashing signals of pleasure and madness to the moon . . . her lovely mouth open to drink everything in . . . him utterly lost to reason between her bare thighs . . . the stone wall scraping his knuckles as his palms supported her naked bottom.

He'd made her come against that wall without even knowing her name.

Amoral? Immoral? Right? Wrong? Did it matter? They'd simply been two kids woven into the sexual tapestry of an exotic, foreign celebration. Drunk on freedom, anonymity, and desire.

He shoved the memories aside, but not soon enough. God damn it, he was hard. So hard it hurt. How fucking ironic that she, of all people, had returned this other mask.

Gwen stepped forward again and leaned over the desk that now trapped him instead of lending him executive power. She was close enough that he could smell her perfume, which was an edgy, citrusy blend, not the sweet floral he remembered. It, like her hair, was different. And she wore smoky, mysterious eye makeup with a lot of mascara, so that her eyes appeared huge.

He liked the fresh-scrubbed nineteen-year-old version of her better, the one who'd had a tiny zit near her nose the last time he'd seen her . . . even though this thirty-four-year-old polished woman was undeniably gorgeous.

"The Gwen Davies that you knew, Mr. Lawson?" she said softly. "She no longer exists."

And as Quinn absorbed that statement and argued with it mentally, she turned on her heel and walked out of his life just as suddenly as she'd walked back into it.

chapter 4

Gwen held her head high and aimed a smile at the young man who occupied the desk outside Quinn's big executive office. "Thank you," she said.

"Have a nice day," he told her.

A nice day? She almost laughed, except she was shaking under the bravado, and if she let the hysteria escape, she'd probably sound like a helium-inflated squirrel on a bender.

Of all the gin joints . . . No, wait, that would have been *his* line. What was hers? *Play with me again, Sam?*

She'd never thought she'd see Quinn Lawson again, after the night she'd packed her bag while he studied late at the Stanford library for the GRE. She still remembered the Yellow Cab that took her away.

Dents testified that the vehicle had been in more than one accident, and the interior smelled of pot and salami. The stuffing poked out of a jagged hole in the vinyl bench seat, and it had seemed a metaphor for her emotions. She'd stared at the crumbly foam all the way to the airport.

The driver, a grizzled man in a soiled Oakland A's baseball cap, asked casually if she was going on vacation.

Not exactly . . .

Even now she still remembered the words she'd written

to Quinn before she folded her good-bye note and left it on
the kitchen counter of their rented apartment.

> *Dear Quinn,*
>   *You've done the best you could in a bad situation
> and I love you for it. But given all that's happened,
> it's time that we end this now. I'm leaving because I
> know that you never will; that your sweet stubborn
> streak and your endearing sense of what's right will
> hold you on a course that's wrong—for both of us.*
>   *I wish you nothing but happiness as you build a
> better life, Quinn: the life you deserve. I'll always
> think of you fondly.*
> *Yours,*
> *Gwen*

Cold? Cowardly to leave a note instead of saying good-
bye in person? Perhaps. But she'd ruined enough of his life
already, and for his sake as well as her own, she needed to
make a clean break.

If she'd tried to leave in person, he'd have taken her in
his arms, locked her against him, made it impossible for
her to go. She had never been able to fight his sexual mag-
netism.

They'd have ended up in bed. Or up against a wall,
which was how they'd gotten into trouble in the first place.

Quinn Lawson, CEO, Jaworski Labs. How ironic that
he'd ended up running a pharmaceuticals company, given
the chemistry between them.

She put her hands to her flaming face as the recurring
dream came back to haunt her. Dear God, she'd had it
again this morning before she awoke. . . . Had she conjured Quinn somehow? Pulled him psychically back into
her life? Or had he done it to her?

She'd always thought it odd that he hadn't come after

her to have a final confrontation. The fact that he hadn't didn't fit his personality. He could be relentless in pursuit of what he wanted—and he'd have wanted closure. The chance to rail at her, the chance to control the final act of their story. Quinn would've wanted to scrawl *The End* himself before closing the book.

Some might call him a control freak, but she knew that it stemmed only from his utter lack of power as a kid. As an adult, he *had* to manage things—and judging by his current position, he'd done well at managing them.

Quinn Lawson, CEO. Fine-art collector, judging by the mask. Big-game hunter, judging by the horrible dead-animal trophy. Player of golf, judging by the picture of him with Tiger Woods behind his desk—a game he'd once insulted as one enjoyed by men in pastel sweaters, with little balls.

Who was this guy? Not the man she remembered.

There'd been no fishing rods in sight, no muscle cars, no sign of the ropers and beat-up jeans he used to wear. Just a big, dark-blond guy in a suit, studded with status symbols, in the blandest, beigest office she'd ever seen, with a snarling bear's head proclaiming his virility to anyone who entered.

She didn't like this Quinn. He'd once had a personality and a soul. Now he'd sold both, it seemed, to the corporate devil.

Her hands shook as she unlocked the door of the Prius. Her stomach turned over with the engine, and the alternator seemed to fuel her frayed nerves as well as the car. She wanted to get home and pull a bottle of crisp white wine out of the refrigerator . . . and stop thinking about Quinn Lawson.

Cookie Monster. Her idiotic name for him came back to torment her. How dumb could an eighteen-year-old girl get?

She'd erased all of it, damn it! Rubbed out that chapter of her life. It wasn't supposed to come alive now in full Technicolor and Dolby stereo, presented as a major motion picture.

Gwen closed her eyes but still saw his inflexible cleft chin, his wide mouth and jaw, the slightly Roman nose, the intelligence in the long-lashed eyes that were the exact color of tawny port.

C'mere, Daddy's Girl . . .

Back then, he hadn't meant it as an insult. Back then he'd just been teasing her about her overprotected life and her trust income, her parents who adored their only child to the point of suffocation.

She'd gone to Brazil to study Latin American art and to taste a little freedom. She'd had exactly a month of it before she let Quinn step between her thighs that night. She'd woken up with him and he'd never left.

A horn blew into her consciousness, and Gwen realized that she'd run a stop sign without even registering her actions.

Pull yourself together before you kill someone!

She heard a clicking noise and couldn't figure out where it was coming from until she looked at her own hands. They still shook, and the ring on her right hand rattled against the hard, molded steering wheel.

She wanted to call Avy . . . but Avy, who knew everything else about Gwen's life, didn't know about Quinn. And Avy was off on some secretive mission of her own. Gwen had a feeling that it involved her new fiancé, "former" thief Sir Liam James, but she couldn't confirm it, and if Avy had wanted her to know, she'd have told her. Avy had been odd and moody lately, and not eager for Gwen to meet Liam. Why? It confirmed all of Gwen's suspicions about him.

She called Avy as she pulled into her driveway, just to

hear her voice and break the news on her recovery, but Ave didn't answer.

Gwen lived in one of the last little 1930s houses still standing in her neighborhood. The developers had bought most of them and torn them down to build condominiums instead, and who could blame them for wanting to get ten purchase prices instead of one from the same lot?

But she had steadfastly refused to sell her little two-bedroom house, even for the exorbitant sums they'd eventually offered her. She didn't need the money, and she didn't want to live in a condo or a high-rise, even if it was becoming the Miami way of life. She didn't need a spa, a gym, a restaurant, or a retail space below her, and if she wanted a view of the ocean, she went to the beach.

Gwen didn't bother garaging the Prius. She pulled a stack of envelopes and catalogs out of the mailbox chosen by the previous owner, which was also yellow and had pink flamingos and blue dolphins glued to it. Then she climbed the four concrete steps to the tiny porch, picked up a half-full pitcher, and stopped to water the hanging ferns and the peace lily before she unlocked the front door.

She threw the mail on a chair and went immediately to the 1950s fridge she'd salvaged and paid an electrician hundreds of dollars to rewire and update. She had a retro stove, too, and no microwave or dishwasher.

She pulled a bottle of cold chardonnay from the refrigerator, closed the door, and stared at the appliance in sudden unpleasant recognition. Why had she never noticed—or admitted—that it looked exactly like the one from the apartment in Brazil? When she'd gone retro with the kitchen she hadn't examined her reasons closely.

Gwen fumbled in a drawer for the corkscrew and proceeded to break off the cork in the bottle. She threw away the top half and reinserted the screw. The cork finally came free.

She took a glass and the bottle into the bathtub. Insisting to herself that she was celebrating her first recovery, she drank most of it before falling into a fitful, uneasy sleep . . . and woke the next day after having the dream yet again.

Quinn was being briefed on some clinical trials of Alaban when Chris knocked on his office door.

"Yes?" he called.

Chris was tall, gangly, and well dressed. Unfortunately his short, black ponytail made him look a little like Olive Oyl. He came in, said a quick "excuse me" to the two junior executives who sat in front of Quinn's desk, and said into his ear, "Jaworski sent a car for you."

"What? I'm in the middle of a meeting."

Chris said, "He wants you at the Breakers for an emergency board meeting in ninety minutes."

Quinn's eyebrows shot up. "Excuse me for a moment," he said to the junior executives. He went outside with Chris and closed the door. "Jaworski can kiss my ass. I'd have to get into the car this second to make that."

"Just relaying the message, sir. Don't shoot." Chris tried to grin but his expression betrayed his worry. Emergency board meetings were not at all normal.

Quinn nodded. "Call him back and tell him I'll get in the company hearse when I've wrapped up this meeting, and not before." He paused. "Sorry you're stuck in the middle of this pissing match."

Grimly Quinn went back into his office. The junior executives went on with their report, clearly enthusiastic about Alaban's continuing excellent trial results. He listened to them with half an ear. An emergency board meeting called on two hours' notice was ominous, to say the least. Trouble loomed on the horizon, and his total ignorance of it didn't bode well for him.

Jaworski should be in a decent mood—he had his damned Venetian mask back, and the quarterly earnings reports looked good. What was going on?

A full two hours later, the company limo pulled up to the spectacular Breakers Hotel in Palm Beach and Quinn got out, running a million scenarios through his mind.

Jaworski could be entertaining a buyout offer. A member of the board might have had a health crisis. Someone might have resigned . . . or a major PR issue had developed. Had a class action lawsuit been filed?

Quinn walked in knowing that Jaworski wouldn't be pleased that he was a half hour "late," but he was damned if he'd be the man's puppet. Even in an emergency it was normal to give directors a day or two to juggle their schedules.

The Breakers sat on 140 acres of prime beachfront property. Built by Standard Oil magnate Henry Flagler, the luxury hotel had been founded in 1896 as the Palm Beach Inn. Over the years it was expanded and then redesigned from the ground up by the Beaux Arts—trained architects Schulze and Weaver.

Inspiration for the Breakers came from various palaces and gardens of the Italian Renaissance. Quinn thought wryly that Gwen would have felt much more at home here than he did. She'd have been able to talk intelligently about the architecture and decor. Him? Mainly what he noticed was that the corridors of the main lobby were wide enough to drive a Hummer through, and the chandeliers looked like they'd be a hell of a lot of fun to swing from. Other than that he enjoyed the miles of pristine ocean view.

Jaworski had brought Quinn here a couple of times—to embarrass him on the golf course. Ed was a scratch golfer and liked to rub it in.

Quinn strolled into the massive Italianate building, then

found the meeting room with no problem and knocked on the door before pushing it open.

He was greeted by a funereal mass of pin-striped suits. The directors sat around a long table like a gaggle of unusually polite vultures staking out a carcass. Jaworski glared at him through a pair of steel-rimmed reading glasses. Then he looked at his watch. "Nice of you to show."

"The meeting was called on very short notice. I couldn't get away immediately," Quinn said, pulling out the last available chair. He helped himself to some coffee.

"Mr. Lawson, the board has assembled here today in light of some disturbing developments having to do with the Borgia mask."

Quinn took a sip of coffee. "Is there a problem? The mask has been recovered."

"No, Mr. Lawson, it has not."

Quinn knit his brows.

"The item returned to you by ARTemis is not, in fact, the Borgia mask. It's a cleverly made copy."

The table, vultures and all, seemed to spin as Quinn absorbed this information and processed it in disbelief. He set down the coffee cup.

"It was you who hired ARTemis to recover the mask, Mr. Lawson. Is that correct?"

"Yes—on the recommendation of Angeline Le Fevre, our company art consultant."

"And it was you who authorized a five-hundred-thousand-dollar commission check to be cut and made payable to ARTemis, Inc."

The faces of the vultures melded together as Quinn absorbed the implications of this statement. "Are you questioning my integrity?" he demanded.

"You authorized the check without testing the authenticity of the mask."

"I'm not an art expert. It didn't cross my mind that . . ."

But Quinn couldn't deny it. This was worse than anything he'd imagined.

"And it must have been you who requested, in fact, that Ms. Gwendolyn Davies make the recovery, not Avy Hunt."

Quinn's gut clenched. "This is *outrageous*. I had no knowledge that Ms. Davies even worked for ARTemis."

"I find that extremely difficult to believe, Mr. Lawson, especially in light of the fact that you were once *married* to Ms. Davies."

Jaworski dropped the information like a bomb, and it had the desired effect: The rest of the board exploded in a blur of pinstripes and power ties, accusation and acrimony.

Quinn stood up and braced his hands on the table. "I don't believe this," he thundered over them all.

"Is my information erroneous, Mr. Lawson?"

His throat felt full of sand. Quinn shook his head and tried to calm down. "It's not erroneous, Ed, but you're leaping to conclusions that are erroneous. Gwen Davies and I were married for about five minutes when we were very young. I haven't seen her in *fifteen years*. I haven't spoken or e-mailed with her in fifteen years. I certainly didn't cook up some half-baked forgery plot with her to defraud Jaworski Labs, which is clearly where you're going with this!"

"So you're telling this board that all of these connections are bizarre coincidences?"

"That's exactly what I'm telling you."

Jaworski scoffed. "Lawson, how can you expect us to believe that?"

Quinn pinched the bridge of his nose between his thumb and forefinger, as if this would stop the top of his head from blowing off. "How can you believe I'd have anything to do with stealing from this company?!"

"So you're the unwitting buffoon, then, of your ex-wife? Is that what you're saying?"

That possibility was almost worse than being called a criminal. Could Gwen have targeted the mask, stolen it, had it copied, and then "found" the copy for a fat commission? Quinn couldn't bend his mind around it. What motive would she have had? Disgracing him? But why, after all of these years? It didn't make any sense. And she'd claimed that she didn't even know he worked for Jaworski.

Gwen was many things: too pretty, too careless, too rich, too flighty. She was also an emotional coward, in his book. But he'd never known her to be a liar. And though she was now a thief of sorts, she played for the good guys. None of this added up.

"That's your story, then. Your ex made a fool out of you." Jaworski's voice dripped with scorn, and it acted as lighter fluid on Quinn's flaring temper.

"No!" he said. "I'd stake my reputation that she had nothing to do with this, either."

"Your reputation is in shreds," Ed said sharply.

"Then I'd stake my life!" Quinn shouted. Why he felt so strongly, he didn't know. Why in the *hell* was he defending a woman who'd betrayed him? Who'd broken her vows, walked out on everything they had? A woman who'd destroyed his budding faith that he could have a happy ending in life, in spite of his miserable beginnings?

"Lawson, I don't much care at this point what you stake. I don't think any of us do."

Quinn stood up and buttoned his jacket. Then he raked his gaze over the vultures. "Fuck you," he said evenly.

The room fell to a dead silence, which suited him just fine. He stared directly at Jaworski.

"You can question my business decisions. You can question my numbers. You can question any of my strategic forecasts and recommendations. But I will not allow you to question my integrity! I won't stand here and be called a crook."

One of the other directors spread his hands wide. "Calm down, Lawson. Nobody's calling you a crook."

"Yeah, you are. Deny it," Quinn said to Jaworski.

The old man's face creased with even more wrinkles, more suspicion, more ill will. Bereft of hair, his head looked a lot like a sphincter sitting atop a custom-made suit.

I'm done. Unbelievable, but after less than a year in this job, I am done. Quinn's stomach pitchpoled like a catamaran in a Miami hurricane.

So be it.

There wasn't a damn thing he could do. They couldn't go backward from this, and they damn sure couldn't move forward.

"As of this moment," Quinn announced, "I'm resigning as president and CEO of Jaworski Labs. It's clear to me that I no longer have the confidence or support of the board of directors, and it will be impossible for me to function effectively as a leader in this hostile environment.

"For the record, I think that you've been hasty, sloppy, and misguided in your investigation of this matter, and if any word of these accusations comes out in the media I will sue each director, the board as an entity, and the company for damages. That's not a threat; it's a promise. Are we clear, gentlemen?"

Nobody moved. Nobody spoke.

"Are we fucking clear?"

Finally Jaworski said, "None of us wants a breath of this released to the press. This company doesn't need any more bad PR, especially not bad PR having to do with our security or possible executive corruption and embezzlement. The whole business with Shankton last year cost us dearly, and our stock has only just begun to recover in the wake of the scandal.

"In light of all that, I'd like to move that we do not go

to the police with this matter. I move that we accept Mr.
Lawson's resignation and give him exactly two weeks to
recover the real Borgia mask. If in two weeks' time we are
still not in possession of our property, then we will recon-
vene and consider pressing formal charges against both
Mr. Lawson and ARTemis, Inc."

The motion was seconded and voted upon. Within minutes, Quinn found himself back outside the Breakers,
blinking in the sun. An old expression of his grandpa
Jack's came to him: *A rooster one day, a feather duster the
next.*

He wondered exactly how his world had just disinte-
grated. All he knew was that it had to do with his lovely
and mysterious ex-wife.

He walked like an automaton toward the company limo,
the long black Lincoln Continental that he'd always called
a hearse. It had certainly brought him in style to his own
corporate funeral today. The driver, a blond kid named
Peter, opened the door for him, and Quinn got in. He stared
straight ahead as Peter got behind the wheel.

"Back to the office, sir?"

Quinn shook his head. "No," he said grimly. "Take me
straight to ARTemis, Inc."

He might have just instinctively defended Gwen, but
she had a lot of explaining to do. He thought about tactics
on the ninety-minute drive and decided to be very aggressive. His best offense was to put her on the defensive. He
was more likely to catch her off guard and get the truth that
way.

chapter 5

Gwen was working at home, compiling her report on the Borgia mask, when the phone rang. "Hello?"

Sheila's voice crackled over the line. "Gwen? Honey, you need to get over to this office right away."

"Why? Is there a problem?"

"Uh-huh. You could say that."

"What is it, Sheila? You're scaring me."

"Just get your little buns over here, doll face, and make it snappy."

Gwen slipped on the spike-heeled sandals she'd discarded by the front door and ran outside to the Prius. She gunned it straight into rush hour, downtown-Miami style. As her hands sweated on the wheel and she mentally cursed every brain-dead moron who slowed her down, cut her off, or gleefully endangered her life, she wondered what could be wrong at the office.

Had Sid Thresher ordered an avalanche of red roses? Had an arrest warrant been issued for the couple of parking tickets she'd forgotten to pay? Had Quinn Lawson complained that she'd been rude? She couldn't imagine him being that petty.

She finally inched down Brickell to the parking garage ARTemis employees used and pulled in so fast that her tires squealed like a teenager's. She all but ran to the elevators and emerged still breathless.

She took three deep lungfuls of air before rounding the last corner and approaching the modern glass doors of ARTemis, Inc.

A very unwelcome electric current shot through her when she saw Quinn, still looking so different from the shirtless guy in the well-worn Levi's she remembered. Impossible to reconcile this businessman with the tough, edgy, incognito lover who'd taken her hard against a wall in Brazil. God forgive her, she could still feel him inside her, those rough stones against her spine. Gwen slapped away the images.

Quinn was wearing a dark suit similar to the one he'd had on a couple of days ago. It was his expression that had changed. Instead of looking nonplussed, he looked . . . grim. Even angry. And at her.

"Mr. Lawson?" she said. "How nice to see you again. How can I help you?"

"You can help me," he said in clipped tones, "by cutting the bullshit."

"Excuse me?"

"You heard what I said, Gwen."

It was her turn to grow angry. "Yes, I heard what you said. But I don't understand what you mean."

"Don't play games with me, Daddy's Girl."

"I'm not playing any games, Mr. Lawson. And don't call me that."

Sheila's eyes were avid and wide as dinner plates behind her electric-blue reading glasses.

Gwen squared her shoulders. "Would you like to step into my office so that we can discuss this privately, Mr. Lawson?"

"No, I wouldn't. Where's the mask, Gwen?"

"What are you talking about? The last time I saw it, it was on your desk."

"The real mask. Where the hell is it?"

"I gave you the real mask!"

"Did you think Ed Jaworski wouldn't have it examined and tested? Did you really think he was that stupid?"

Her stomach dropped to her knees and she stared at him blankly. "You're telling me . . ." Sweat broke out on her palms, under her arms, and at her hairline. She couldn't seem to take in enough air. "You're telling me that the mask I brought to you is not the original? It's a *duplicate*?"

He shot her a withering stare. "Were you trying to make me look bad to my board of directors? Were you setting me up?"

Sheila's eyes almost popped out.

"Quinn, listen to me. I don't know what's going on, but I delivered what I thought was the original mask to you, in good faith—I promise you. You have to believe me."

A pulse jumped at his jaw. He stood there shaking his big, dirty blond head. "No, Gwen, I don't. You made me another promise fifteen years ago, and it turned out to be worthless. So I don't have a whole lot of faith in this one."

She opened and shut her mouth, but the words wouldn't come. This situation was too awful to comprehend. She'd made her first big recovery for ARTemis, but instead of appearing cool and competent, she appeared to be a fraud.

She'd known in her gut that something was fishy. And what was Avy's first mantra? *Listen to your gut. It never lies.*

Right now, her guts were twisted up and starting to heave. Sweat from the back of her neck gathered and poured in a stream down her spine, soaking her blouse.

"For the last time, *where is the mask*?" Quinn roared.

Gwen met his stormy, implacable eyes and shook her head. At last she found her voice. "I don't know."

"I'm going to get to the bottom of this, and if you had anything to do with it, I will shut down your sleazy operation here so fast that your little pseudo-hip head will spin."

Sleazy? Pseudo-hip?

"Who are you callin' sleazy?" Sheila shot Quinn the hairy eyeball. He ignored her.

"ARTemis has a stellar reputation," Gwen said evenly. "Just what are you accusing me of? Say it, Quinn!"

"You slipped me a bogus mask so that you can sell the original and make a boatload of cash."

"Is that right?" she said. She eyed him stonily. "You've got it all figured out. I need the money so badly that I made the duplicate in my kitchen sink with papier-mâché and a can of gold glitter."

He stopped ranting long enough to raise his eyebrows at the sarcasm in her voice. They both knew that with her trust, she didn't need money. They both knew the duplicate was a very sophisticated piece, impossible to tell from the real one with the naked eye.

"You have the connections to find someone, Gwen. Years of interior design work and commissioning custom artwork for your clients . . . or did you hire one of your mother's jewelers to pull this off?"

"You're being ridiculous," Gwen said. "What possible motive would I have for doing that? Give me just one."

He shook his head. "I don't know."

She held his gaze and raised her chin a notch, elevated one eyebrow, and mutely challenged all his assumptions. And to her surprise, Quinn dropped his gaze and looked away. Well, wasn't that interesting.

Then he stared back at her long and hard. He stood flat on both feet, head thrust forward, hands by his side, fingers curling into fists. He looked like a boxer, and the reception area was his ring. For a moment Gwen wished she were back in the warehouse, face-to-face with the python rather than with Quinn Lawson, whose dark gaze clearly communicated that he thought less of her than he did of a cockroach.

The perspiration at her spine dribbled lower.

She focused on his face, trying not to inhale the scent of him, a mix of clean deodorant soap, laundry starch, fine light wool, and hot, agitated male. Funny how he didn't smell so civilized when he was angry. The faint cologne she'd detected in his office the other day had evaporated.

His dark pupils continued to drill into her. He blinked once and then he was at it again, perforating her character, the very essence of her being. And then . . . she saw it. The softening in his irises as a smidgen of doubt crept in.

He pinched the bridge of his nose and cursed softly. "You're not lying."

Her knees went weak with relief. "No, I'm not."

"I wish you were," he said, and sat down heavily in one of the visitor's chairs.

Gwen sat down opposite him. "I need to see the mask. Do you have it with you?"

"Oh, no, darlin'. Understand that when they fire a man, they don't generally let him take company assets with him—even fake ones."

"Fired," she repeated stupidly. "They *fired* you over this?" No wonder he'd come in swinging. She'd caused him to lose his job. If possible, she felt even sicker.

Had she been put on this earth just to repeatedly wreck Quinn's life?

He sighed. "Actually, I quit before they could. But the results are the same, and yes, our little disagreement was over the fake Borgia mask. You see, the board hired someone to do some digging, and they turned up the little-known fact that you and I used to be married, sweet pea."

Sheila, who'd just picked up the phone, dropped the receiver with a clatter onto her desk. "Married!"

Gwen closed her eyes and prayed that any moment now, the floor would open and swallow her.

"Your daddy's lawyers must have left some threads dangling, honey, even after all their efforts to seal the records and whitewash his little debutante."

"Debutante!" Sheila was having a field day. She now had enough gossip to dine out on for a month.

Gwen did her best to ignore her. "Look, Quinn, in order to figure out what's happened here, I need to see the mask that I delivered to you."

"Too bad," Quinn told her. "Because neither one of us can get our hands on it now. I'm quite sure that my access codes to the building have been terminated."

Sheila clattered away on her ergonomic keyboard, her acrylic nails jamming into the plastic keys in a little technological symphony. She peered avidly at the screen, the tip of her tongue barely visible at the right side of her tangerine mouth. What was she up to? Was she already getting in touch with Kelso?

Gwen came to a reluctant conclusion: She was in over her head here. Much as she dreaded the shame and mortification of confessing her incompetence to any of the agents, it was time to call in reinforcements.

"Quinn, let's go to my office, where we can talk privately about how to proceed."

"Oh, fine," said Sheila. "Just leave me in suspense, why don't you."

Quinn glanced from her to Gwen with a slightly bemused expression. It was one she'd seen countless times on the faces of other clients.

"With pleasure," Gwen told her sweetly. "By the way, have you mailed that package back to London yet?"

"Working on it," Sheila muttered. "Well, doll face, what a kick in the pants, huh? To quote that seventies song, 'Reunited and it feels so good . . .'"

Gwen felt heat flash to her face for the umpteenth time that day. "Has anyone ever threatened to fire you for gross insubordination?"

"All the time," Sheila said cheerfully. "All the time."

Gwen led Quinn down the corridor to her office, which was small but cozy. She'd furnished it with a sunny yellow armchair and ottoman, an oil painting of a woman reading, and a vase of tropical silk flowers. On the floor she'd tossed a brightly colored throw rug.

She sat in a leather rolling chair at her corner computer desk, leaving the armchair for Quinn. "All right," she said. "I think it's time to call in a more experienced agent. My boss, Avy, is overseas, but she'll have good advice. How is Jaworski Labs going to proceed?"

"The desire is to keep this situation out of the media. The company cannot afford the bad exposure. I have two weeks to solve this mystery and track down the genuine mask. After that, Ed Jaworski and the board of directors will contact both their lawyers and the police. They'll sue ARTemis for breach of contract and quite possibly fraud. I'll warn you right now: They have deep pockets."

Gwen swallowed hard. "If they win a judgment against us, ARTemis could be bankrupted."

He didn't deny it. He just clasped his hands together between his open knees. He stared at her in silence.

"Quinn . . . we'll get to the bottom of this. I know how you must feel—"

"Do you, Gwen? Do you really? For the past few years, during my 'meteoric' rise in management, I've been able to look into the mirror without shame. I've been able to leave all of old Jack's drunken escapades, all of my mother's humiliations, all of my hometown's scorn in the past. I've been the bastard kid who made good—and I've been proud of it. Too proud, maybe. But as of two hours ago, the shame is knockin' on my door again. Rumors are swirling—did Quinn Lawson conspire with his ex-wife to defraud Jaworski Labs? Is he a low-down, rotten thief?"

His hands shook almost imperceptibly, and that small tell, the only one, broke Gwen's heart.

"I am not about to open that door," Quinn said in a low but deadly voice. "I will not be shamed, not ever again. Whoever's behind the theft of this mask has made a big mistake, because I will hunt him down like a dog. He can rip off a hundred art objects, he can cost me my job, but he will not steal my reputation and get away with it. I've worked way too hard to make it."

For the first time, Gwen saw again the tousled, rumpled, rough-around-the-edges guy who'd commanded an intense three months of her life. The unstoppable man who'd taken more than his share of her sexually, emotionally, spiritually. Taken her fast and almost ferociously, because nobody had ever *given* him a thing.

Her skin broke out in goose bumps, and a frisson of pure sexual awareness skated down her spine.

She was the girl who'd been raised to say *please* and wait politely for everything. She couldn't help but be attracted to a man who didn't ask anyone for permission. She'd been given far too much, and she'd never encountered anyone like Quinn.

And yet, when he'd taken her, put her in a niche like the only precious object in his life, she'd felt trapped, unable to come out from behind the protective glass.

Taken . . . Was it the right word? He'd given, really. Given his all, too much and too fast, with all the expectations that entailed. But she hadn't wanted to be the center of his universe—she'd spent too long being the center of her parents' world.

Gwen hadn't headed for the wilds of Brazil to be imprisoned again. And yet, as she stared at Quinn's long, lean fingers with their short, square nails, she remembered them stroking her skin, slipping under her clothing, bringing her erotic joy.

Warm. His hands had always been warm. Never cold, never clammy—just warm, steady, unerringly skilled. Patient—surprisingly patient, considering their first meeting and how it had ended with him under her skirt, her legs wrapped around his hips in the moonlight. Did he remember that night when he looked at her now? Or did he remember only how she'd disappeared?

"So," Quinn broke into her thoughts. "You're going to call your boss?"

"Yes. We're going to recover the mask. And we're going to recover your reputation—not to mention my own."

chapter 6

Before she dialed, Gwen took a deep breath and then tried to exhale her sheer mortification, her guilt at having let Avy down. Avy had recruited her, hired her, staked her own reputation on her, trusted her more than Gwen trusted herself. She didn't patronize her or treat her like a pinhead.

Don't you see? Your strength lies in the fact that nobody would ever think you're dangerous. People are careful around me. They're not on their guard with you.

Yeah, great. A whole lot of good that had done her on this recovery so far.

Gwen hit the autodial for Avy on her phone. It rang and rang, finally clicking into voice mail. "Avy Hunt. Leave a message."

"Hi, Ave, it's me." *Fudge.* How to encapsulate this situation in a sound bite? "Just touching base. Hope you're having fun." She ended the call.

Quinn stared at her. "Just touching base?" he repeated, his tone scathing.

"Look, I can't leave that kind of message. I'll wait till I can talk to her personally." Her mind raced. "We'll call Dante instead." He was out of the office, but she'd call his cell.

"Dante," Quinn said dubiously. "Like Daunte Culpepper?"

In spite of the circumstances, Gwen laughed. "I doubt it. He's probably named for the Italian writer."

"Yeah, whatever."

Gwen dialed his number, relieved when he answered. "Dante, it's Gwen. I have a big problem."

"What kind of a problem?" His rich voice exuded calm and logic.

"I'm going to put you on speaker, since Quinn Lawson, the CEO of Jaworski Labs, is here with me." Gwen swallowed her ego and filled him in on everything. Almost everything.

"*Madonna*," he said, after a long pause.

Gwen resisted the urge to tell Quinn that it was just an Italian expression, not anything to do with the singer.

Dante said, "Okay, so let's try to narrow this down: Who knew the value of the mask?"

"Mr. Lawson," said Gwen. "His whole board of directors."

"All the shareholders," added Quinn, "since mention was made of the piece in the company's annual report."

"The previous owner," Gwen continued. "And Jaworski's art consultant and curator."

"Is that all?" Dante asked dryly.

"Hundreds of people."

"Then we need to find a way to narrow it down. Get the Nerd Corps on it. I would look at the previous owner and the art consultant first. They have direct ties to the mask. Then I'd look at the board."

"Okay. And I'll run checks on all the other executives at Jaworski, delve a little into their finances."

"Good. I'd go after the Velasquez brothers, too, and see if you can get them to talk."

"Uh-huh. How do I do that? Just walk up to them in their favorite bar and strike up a conversation?"

"I doubt they'll talk for tequila," Dante said. "But they

56   Karen Kendall

might respond well to a threat or a bribe. Tell them how you identified them. Hint that the police might be very interested in that information. But be very, very careful. Don't meet them alone, even armed."

"You can rest assured that my ex-wife is not going near any thugs," Quinn broke in. "I won't allow it."

Silence came from Dante's end of the connection.

Gwen cringed and closed her eyes.

"Your *what*?"

"Quinn's just kidding," Gwen said hastily.

"No, Quinn is not," he said.

Gwen narrowed her eyes on him. "And he has absolutely no control over whom I meet—or what I do regarding this case."

"The hell I don't! It's my case, too."

"You were married, Gwen?" Dante asked. "When?"

"Um. Well, it happened in college, over the semester I went to Brazil. Quinn and I met there. We got married in California shortly afterward. Palo Alto, near the Stanford campus."

"I knocked her up," Quinn said helpfully.

Gwen felt the blood drain from her face.

Dante said nothing.

"Dante," she said, hating the urgency in her voice. "Please, you have to promise me that you won't say anything about any of this to Avy. I need to be the one to break it to her, all right?"

He sighed. "It's not me you need to worry about. It's Sheila."

"Right. I'll take care of that immediately. Thanks." She hung up, whipped her head around to Quinn, and said ominously, "Stay here. I'll be back in a sec. Then we're going to chat."

Gwen walked to the reception area and stood over Sheila's desk until she looked up. "Yeah?"

"Sheila. You just overheard some personal information of mine. I'm here to ask you to keep it confidential. *Please.* And don't mention this whole fiasco to Avy until I can tell her myself, okay?"

"Hmmm." Sheila lifted a heavily penciled eyebrow. "It's really good gossip, though. Juicy."

"Yes, I know. That's exactly why I don't want it getting out!"

Sheila tapped a pencil against her teeth, coating part of it with lipstick. "What's it worth to ya?"

"What do you mean, what's it worth? Are you trying to *extort* money from me?"

"That seems like an awfully harsh word. And it's just that, well, I got this credit card to pay off."

Unbelievable. Gwen fought against stooping to her level, but was so mad she lost. "Listen, Sheila. Would that be the secret card that Marty doesn't know about? The one with thousands of dollars on it that would give him a heart attack if he were to find out?"

Sheila bit down on the pencil, and the eraser popped out and onto her tongue. She hacked like an old cat to spit it out. When she could speak again, she said, "Get out of here. My lips are zipped, long as yours are."

Gwen blew her a kiss.

Sheila shot her the finger.

Gwen stomped back into her office, folded her arms, and glared at Quinn, which somewhat amused him. She tilted her head like a dainty, pint-sized bull about to charge. If she'd had horns, she would have tossed them. "How *could* you? How could you do that to me?"

"Do what? Tell the damned truth?"

"To my colleague!"

"As long as we're on this topic, let's ask another question, Gwen. How could you have done *me* like that, fifteen years ago?"

She swallowed, blinking rapidly. "You know why."

"No, I don't. How could you disappear without a word?"

"I left you a note," she said, a funny catch in her voice.

"Yeah, you sure fuckin' did. That was such a great note, too. Explained a whole lot of nothing. That letter touched me so deeply—I fed it down the garbage disposal." He'd then kicked the under-the-sink cabinet so hard that the door had splintered, but she didn't need to know that.

"This is all ancient history, Quinn. There's no reason to rehash our relationship, and you still had no right to air my dirty laundry at work."

Quinn got out of the yellow armchair and paced to the window. "Well, tough, darlin'. I ain't gonna apologize."

He could see her reflection superimposed over the cityscape, dominating hundreds of cocaine white buildings, all lined up in a wide, bleached, shake-your-moneymaker Miami leer. Gwen looked too pure for this city.

She still disarmed him, this mouthwatering, stacked, slightly punk Audrey Hepburn. His gaze hovered at the vee of her blouse, on the smooth, enticing skin there. He remembered the feel of it against his lips. He remembered the scent of her, and her heat. The edge of his anger dulled, then sharpened again into something disturbingly like desire.

He couldn't help his next question. "Is that all I am to you, Daddy's Girl? Dirty laundry?" Then he got mad all over again—this time at himself—for asking it.

Gwen hunched her shoulders and pressed the toe of her shoe against the wall as if trying to push it back, escape the confines of the room and his presence. She didn't answer.

He continued to watch her reflection as she picked up the phone again and stabbed out the numbers for someone's extension. But her gaze drifted from the phone. Was it Quinn's imagination, or was she checking out his rear view?

"*Dígame*," he heard a voice say.

"Hi, Miguel," she said. "Can I come down and see you?"

"We," corrected Quinn, turning to face her. "Can *we* come down."

"Thanks," Gwen said, and hung up. "Quinn, I can't take you with me. There are things about this company—like our methods of gathering information—that we keep private. The Nerd Corps is off-limits to you."

Quinn opened his mouth to argue, but she cut him off. "Look, I understand that you're a control freak and you're used to running the show over there at Jaworski Labs. But let me make something clear to you: This is not your turf. Okay? This is *my* territory and *my* case and I will handle things my way."

"Yeah? Seems to me your way hasn't worked too well," he retorted. "And it's my ass on the line here."

"Your ass is not on the line. Mine is," Gwen said coolly. "Your ass has already been fired."

His jaw worked. "That was a real cheap shot."

"Quinn, I'm sorry. It *was* cheap. But I'm good at my job—despite this temporary setback—and you're not going to tell me how to do it. You're also not going to get in my way."

"I'm the goddamned client!"

She leveled her gaze on him and he broke eye contact.

"Fine," he said. "I'm not the client anymore, but I have a vested interest in locating this mask, same as you. So let's put the past behind us and pool our resources."

Gwen shook her head. "One quarterback, Quinn," she said, bending forward to pull her huge handbag out of her desk drawer. "Only one."

Something twinkled at her navel as her blouse peeked open—and then it was gone as she straightened.

Gwendolyn Celeste Davies had pierced her belly button since they'd last met. He stared, incredulous and ridiculously turned on.

"Fine, one quarterback," he repeated unwillingly. He really had no choice if he wanted access to her information—or her. "I'll defer to your judgment. But don't shut me out."

"I can't take you to the Nerd Corps. So why don't you focus on pulling together information on the Jaworski executives. You know them, after all." She drummed her fingernails on her desk for a moment and then asked, a little too casually, "Quinn, where do you think the mask I recovered might be? The fake?"

"Forget it," he said. "They'll have it locked up."

"Yes, but where?"

"Why do you want to know?"

"I'm just curious, that's all." She put a hand up to her hair and fluffed the little orangey spikes.

"There's a heavy-duty safe in my old office," he said. "If the mask's not with Ed Jaworski, it'd probably be there."

"Heavy duty, huh? Too bad."

"You wouldn't even think of breaking into a high-tech lab, right? You're not insane."

She laughed. "Quinn, don't be ridiculous. If I got caught I'd go to jail." Gwen slipped off one of her shoes and massaged the ball of her foot.

He couldn't look away from the peach nail polish on her toes and the delicate gold band encircling her second one.

"So," she said, slipping her shoe back on. "We'll meet back here tomorrow morning to compare notes."

He looked at her suspiciously. "And where will you be this afternoon?"

"Out." She shot him a tight little smile.

"What do you mean, out?" He crossed the room and stood next to her desk.

"Out working on something. I don't know yet, okay? Back off."

Quinn almost swallowed his tongue as Gwen calmly removed a handgun from her la-di-da designer pocketbook and checked the clip.

"Gwen, what the hell is that?" The very idea of his little boutique princess packing heat was ridiculous.

"My SIG. I'm leaving right after I speak with Miguel."

"You can't just . . . just . . . walk around with a gun!"

She lifted her eyebrows. "Actually, I can."

"Do you have a permit?" he asked incredulously.

"Of course I have a permit."

"When did you learn to *shoot*, for chrissakes?"

"I took a class," she said casually, as if it were basket weaving or macramé.

"A class. Great." He dragged his hands down his face. He suspected that his reaction amused her, and that pissed him off even more. "Well, the world is a safer place now, I'm sure."

"Don't patronize me, Quinn." But she said it without rancor, and as she uncrossed and recrossed her legs, his breath hitched in his throat as he got a flash of tiger print.

Tiger print? What had happened to the white cotton panties he remembered? The white bras?

His ex-wife was walking around in racy lingerie with a *gun*, for God's sake. What was next, a grenade in her cleavage?

Who did she think she was? Having an art history degree from Sweet Briar didn't qualify her to be some secret agent. Or to carry a gun.

What if she left the safety off on that SIG and accidentally blew off her fingers one day while she applied her lipstick? What idiot had issued her a gun permit?

And why did the tiger-print panties and the SIG turn him on? He was a sick, sick man. Not to mention a stupid one.

"Quinn. Relax. You'll find that taking orders from a woman isn't nearly as bad as you think. You'll survive."

"I'm not taking orders from my ex-wife," he growled.

"Okay, we'll call them suggestions, then." She smiled. "How's that?"

How dared she stand there and bat her eyelashes at him? Smug, sexy little nightmare of a woman.

"In the meantime, get me some information on those executives and I'll meet you back here tomorrow at nine. We're going to find the mask, Quinn. Don't worry."

He knew they'd find the mask. He was in no doubt. But he was torn about working with her. If he didn't cooperate, he'd lose precious time and insight. If he did, they were inevitably going to have power struggles—not to mention that he might start to worry about her and the risks she was taking.

Quinn repudiated that idea immediately. Because if you worried about someone, you cared. And he was long, long past caring about anything to do with Gwen Davies.

chapter 7

Revenge was a dish best served cold. The man's temper ran hot. He kept it under control with difficulty. He had waited so long and plotted so intricately. How had this plan gotten derailed?

He should have just killed her quickly and cleanly, as he had others when the need arose. But no, his uncle didn't like to harm women and had insisted on humiliation, public disgrace. An elaborate scheme that involved too many people . . . people who could talk. People who must now be silenced proactively, before they were pressured or bribed.

The old man was soft. He no longer had the stones for business, but he still called the shots.

So much careful planning and money up in smoke because of the whims of a crazy bitch. A bitch who'd been predictable as hell up until now. A bitch whose arrogance knew no bounds.

So she thought she was on her toes, did she? Considered herself untouchable? Well, she had another think coming. It was time to move on to plan B, a more permanent solution— after he'd tied up the loose ends on plan A.

The man drove deeper into Miami, despising the lousy car he sat in, but needing it to blend in with the environment. Sweat trickled from his scalp down his neck and from there to his spine. No AC in this stinking climate . . . though he should be used to it by now. And perspiration was the least of his concerns.

He headed east, the houses getting smaller and more derelict as he went, until they were nothing but little shit-boxes inhabited by the rodents of the city. Crack whores. Drug dealers. Kids who'd grow up to be the same. Mangy, starving dogs. Clotheslines. Cars on blocks in the front yards, if you could call them such.

He missed his home, his family—though family was the reason he'd come. He despised this city and everyone in it, and he'd been here too long trying to put this plan into action. Even in the high-end areas—Coral Gables, Key Biscayne, Brickell—he saw nothing redeeming. Conspicuous consumption, whorish women, no work ethic, easy highs.

As he stopped at a red light, he pulled his Glock from under the seat and checked the clip. The sight of it discouraged a pierced, tattooed guy in a ripped T-shirt from coming any closer.

The man adjusted his baseball cap and didn't look at the kid. He wanted nobody to remember him, not even a punk looking for trouble.

The light turned green, green for go. And he progressed down the street, turned the corner, and came to his destination. He made sure he had the custom silencer he'd paid dearly for. And then the man got out of the car, shut the door, and faded into the shadows as the sun went down.

For someone, it wouldn't come up again.

chapter 8

Gwen could breathe and think better on her own, without Quinn sucking all the oxygen from the room and distracting her. Knocking her off balance . . . though she'd done a pretty good job of fighting back. His expression upon sight of her SIG? A true Kodak moment.

Do you have a permit for that?

Yeah, baby. I can also knock you on your big, sexy butt in two seconds flat and crack that heavy-duty safe after breaking and entering the lab you think is so off-limits. But we'll get to that later.

For now, she concentrated on looking sweet and addicted to fashion and generally unthreatening. She'd tried to call Avy again an hour ago, but there was no answer. Weird.

But as Gwen approached Le Fevre Art Consultants to speak with Angeline, Avy called back.

"Gwennie, it's Ave. Wait— Liam, take a left up there. And don't hit that cow."

"You're with Liam? I knew it. Where are you?"

"Loire Valley, France. Château country— Left, Liam, *left*! Your *other* left. You freaking wrong-side-driving, British— No! *No kissing.* Drive."

Under any other circumstances, Gwen would have laughed. "When do I get to meet Liam?"

"Oh, you know," Avy said vaguely. "Soon."

"Has he really retired?" Liam had had a long and productive career in grand larceny. Maybe he could be a consultant in this situation. . . .

"Of course he has, or I wouldn't be with him." Kissing noises came from the phone, without protest this time. Gwen held the phone away from her ear. At least Avy was happy.

She opened her mouth to tell her about the horrendous situation back in Miami, but opted to indulge her curiosity first. "So, what is it exactly that you two are doing in France?"

"Huh?"

"What are you doing in—"

"Vacationing," Avy said. "We'll go to Italy next. We'll be in Venice for the opening of Carnevale."

"Right. You didn't give up a five-hundred-thousand dollar commission to go on vacation," Gwen said.

"What's that?" Avy's voice suddenly sounded faraway. Hissing noises came over the line. "You're breaking up. . . ."

"You are *terrible* at faking static," Gwen told her, but the line was already dead. So much for coming clean with her boss.

Gwen stowed her phone and tried to open the door in front of her, but it was locked. The name, Le Fevre Art Consultants, was trumpeted across it in big gold letters, and underneath was an ornate, rococo gold picture frame with a dollar sign in the middle of it. Subtle.

From the other side of the door she heard a man swear and a woman hiss at him to be quiet. It dawned on Gwen that she'd arrived at an inopportune time, even though it was two forty-five in the afternoon on a workday.

She'd turned around to leave when the door opened to reveal a small woman in a short green skirt and a gold silk blouse. Her hair looked freshly combed, though her rust lipstick had smudged at the left corner of her mouth. She was pretty in a hard sort of way, but owed a lot of it to good cosmetics and careful grooming.

"Yes?"

"Ms. Le Fevre? I'm Gwen Davies from ARTemis, Inc. I was hoping you'd have a moment to talk about the Jaworski collection's Borgia mask."

The woman hesitated and then shrugged. "Come in." She stepped aside and Gwen entered the office, only to stop short at the sight of a familiar figure. McDougal had his back to her and was busily buttoning his cotton shirt.

"You've got to be kidding me," said Gwen. She guessed it wasn't all that surprising. The Miami art world was small, and he had a habit of making conquests at art openings and galas. To him, women were canapés—and most of them couldn't resist those Newman-blue eyes. But in the middle of the business day?

McDougal the man-whore turned around, finished his last button, and ran a hand through his unruly ginger hair. He winked and held out his arms. "Gwendolyn! What a pleasure."

Angeline Le Fevre's desk was clean—too clean, since a stack of papers and files had clearly been swept right off of it and onto the floor. McDougal's shirt was untucked, and the unmistakable essence of sex permeated the air.

Gwen wished that the vanilla candle on a side table, the faint odor of mildew from the air-conditioning vent, and the smell of old cigarette smoke had covered it, but she wasn't that lucky. Raunchy hormones buzzed through the atmosphere like flies.

"What brings you here, sweetheart?" McDougal asked,

dropping his arms, since it was by now evident that she wasn't going to step into them.

"My job," she said evenly. "And you?"

He didn't even flinch. He just grinned shamelessly. "A different kind of job." He waggled his eyebrows.

Angeline bit her bee-stung lower lip.

"Maybe I should come back some other time." Gwen turned to leave.

"Not at all," said McDougal. "We're finished here, aren't we, babe? Was everything . . . to your liking?"

"Very well-done," Angeline said.

"Glad to hear that. I'll send you an invoice."

Gwen presumed he was kidding, though she didn't know why she was giving him the benefit of the doubt.

McD blew them both a kiss and didn't let the door hit him on the way out. An awkward silence ensued, and then Angeline said, "Please sit down. How can I help you?"

Gwen eyed the chair suspiciously, but it looked clean and free of McDougal cooties. She sat down on it.

Angeline eyed her curiously, waiting for her to speak.

"Ms. Le Fevre, I'm here to ask you a few questions about the stolen Borgia mask that Quinn Lawson acquired through you for Jaworski Labs."

Angeline's expression went from curious to puzzled. "I was told that it had been recovered."

"Yes. A mask was recovered, but not the original. What we repossessed was a very good copy."

"*Mon Dieu.* A fake?"

Was it Gwen's imagination, or was Angeline's expression of polite surprise not all that surprised?

"But how can that be? It is not easy to duplicate such a thing."

"No, it isn't. I was hoping you could help me discover who might have done it and when."

Angeline fumbled in her desk drawer for a pack of cigarettes, which she was not allowed to smoke in a high-rise. She lit up anyway, without asking Gwen if it would bother her. It did, but she gave no hint. This wasn't her office, after all.

"The mask was purchased at auction, correct?"

"Yes. From Christie's." Angeline lit her cigarette with a gold lighter and inhaled deeply.

"Was it tested there before the auction?"

"Of course. A house like Christie's would never risk its reputation. The mask was examined by experts."

"And how long was it in your possession before you delivered it to Jaworski Labs?"

Angeline exhaled, and deliberately in her direction. "It never was. I bid for Jaworski at the auction, but Christie's delivered the mask through their fine-art carrier."

"Do you know who that is?"

Another drag on the cigarette, a shake of the head. "You'd have to check with them."

"So the switch could have been made by the shipping company."

Angeline nodded through a cloud of exhaled smoke. "It is possible. I would certainly start there." She tapped the end of her cigarette into a crystal ashtray.

"Or it could have been made after the break-in."

Angeline's heavily made-up gray eyes met Gwen's. She shrugged and nodded. Crossed and recrossed her legs. Inspected her Robert Clergerie pumps for scratches. "What does this really have to do with me, Ms. Davies? I wish I could help you, but I cannot. What's happened is very unfortunate, but . . ."

Gwen aimed her sweetest, butter-wouldn't-melt-in-her-mouth smile at the woman. "I'd surely call the disappearance and duplication of a five-point-four-million-dollar art object, one that you brokered the deal on, more than unfortunate."

Angeline sucked on the end of the cigarette until it glowed fiercely. Gwen wondered if she'd sucked on McDougal that hard, and then banished the revolting thought.

"Are you accusing me of something, Ms. Davies?"

Gwen widened her eyes. "Oh, no. Of course not."

"Because I'd be extremely careful if I were you. My reputation is at the core of my business, and if you slander me, I can assure you that you'll pay for it in court."

"Angeline—may I call you Angeline? As I told you, I'm only gathering information. Because, as you can imagine, it's not good for *our* reputation at ARTemis to have recovered a fake. I'm sure you understand why I'm trying to cover all the bases."

Angeline blew some more smoke at her, and Gwen resisted the urge to empty the ashtray into her bright green lap. "*Oui*, of course. So begin with the fine-art carrier, eh? After the break-in, nobody could make a duplicate so fast. You found the fake when?"

"Two days ago."

"Far too little time to reproduce a piece of that intricacy and quality."

"Unless the forger has been working on the piece for a long time."

Angeline's hand stilled in the middle of ashing her cigarette. Then she resumed. "How? He'd have to work from the original, which was in the possession of the auction house."

"Where was the mask before it went to Christie's?"

"It belonged to an old man. He was sick, terminal, and needed the proceeds from the sale to pay his medical bills."

Thanks to the Nerd Corps, Gwen had done her homework before coming. "Right. So you had access for months while he was dying."

Angeline laughed. "That's a ridiculous theory."

"Is it? Why?"

"I told you, Ms. Davies, that Christie's runs tests. Now I think you'd better go."

Gwen stood up. "Thank you for your time. I'll leave my card in case you think of anything else that might help." She dropped it on Angeline's desk and turned to walk to the door.

As she opened it, she heard the woman rip the card in half, and then presumably again into quarters. Lovely manners Miss Le Fevre had. And she'd had a lot of lovely opportunity, too.

Gwen pondered this. Gosh, she might have to water Angeline's plants for her one day when she was out. Feed her cat. Take in her newspaper.

Then she brightened. There was no need for her to break in to Angeline's home . . . because McDougal could walk in legally the next time he wanted some raunchy sex.

She texted him, because she didn't want to hear his voice.

McMan-whore. Oops, looked like she'd gotten ruder since her Sweet Briar days . . . not that Eric would care.

Check out your girlfriend's closets for me. I'm positive she had something to do with the missing mask. Let me know if it's in her panty drawer. Yes, I'll split the commission.

Gwen plotted out her next course of action as she sat in Sheila's domain, the wardrobe room, her face being covered in what felt like spackle.

Three walls of the room were fitted with California Closets and stuffed with clothes of every size and description: male and female, highbrow to lowbrow, rocker style to rocking-chair-appropriate.

Two mostly naked department store mannequins stood in the center of the room, staring vacantly into the middle distance. The male one sported a pair of boxers printed with half-peeled bananas. The female wore hot-pink panties with a black cat face on the crotch.

Gwen's bare toes curled into the plush polypropylene zebra-print rug on the floor. The dust on the fake potted trees had made her sneeze three times, incurring Sheila's wrath as she worked her magic on Gwen's face.

Her butt hurt from sitting for so long on the awful reproduction rococo vanity stool. Sheila peered at her intently as she continued to layer on the age makeup, her tongue caught between her teeth.

Behind her turquoise reading glasses (studded with small tropical plastic fish) Sheila's face had the texture of crumpled aluminum foil, but it was fascinating, full of character and experience. Her skin was a map of her life.

"Quit staring," Sheila said, reaching for a big, fluffy powder brush. "One day, Little Debbie, you'll have a face like a leather bag, too."

Gwen sneezed again as an avalanche of mineral powder poured down her nose. "I didn't—"

"And if I'm still kickin', I'll laugh my ass off. You think I wasn't something to look at when I was your age? I had men begging to lick my boots."

Gwen tried not to imagine Sheila's accountant husband, Marty, sucking on her stiletto heel.

"Today Marty may look like a dumpling in Sansabelts, but he used to have the sexiest little tushie."

Gwen blanched.

"Yeah, he used to get his TLC for free when he was hot. Now he has to save up points."

"Points?" Not that Gwen was sure she wanted to know . . .

"Yeah, points—like you do with rewarding kids' behavior. Or that weight-loss program. Marty unloads the dishwasher, he gets a point. He peels off his dirty socks and leaves them under the coffee table, he loses a point. He washes my car, he gets a point. He farts under the covers, he loses two points. See how it works? We start it every Sunday morning. If he racks up enough points by Saturday, he gets some after dinner."

Speechless, Gwen just nodded.

"It's a great system," Sheila maintained.

"I-I'm sure it is," said Gwen.

"All right, doll face. We're done with your mug."

Gwen spun in the chair and gazed into the mirror over the dressing table. She resembled her grandmother. Actually, she looked worse—as if Gran had been smoking crack under a bridge for the last ten years. "Did you have to go quite this far?"

Sheila cackled and marched toward her with a small, salt-and-pepper-colored dog under her arm. "Couldn't resist, doll. I've been itching to do this—you're too darn pretty."

Sheila shook the dog, which revealed itself to be a mangy, flea-bitten wig.

Gwen eyed it suspiciously. "Where did you get that?"

"Mwah-ha-ha-ha. You don't want to know."

"Has it been washed? Does it have lice?"

Sheila's eyes sparkled with cheerful malice as she stuck her hand in a jar of goop and slicked back Gwen's real hair with it. Then she brandished the dog again.

Gwen ducked. "Get away from me! Did you skin that off some poor animal?"

"Would you relax? I got it from a defunct dinner theater. And yes, it's been dry-cleaned, so c'mere. You asked for my help." Sheila stretched what looked like a stocking over Gwen's scalp and tugged the wig into place over it.

"Damn, girl, do you look hot. Your ex sees you like this, he'll marry you all over again for sure."

"You're so not funny."

"You want that man," Sheila said around a bobby pin.

"I do *not* want him."

"He wants you, too."

"He does not." So why did the thought of Quinn wanting her get the back of her neck tingling? Why did she feel heat under all the muck on her face?

Sheila snorted. "He wants you so bad, he'd even do you in a chicken suit. And while we're on the subject—"

"We are not on the subject!"

"—how could you divorce a man with those buns? That chest? Those arms . . ." Sheila moaned. "No point system necessary."

"Stop salivating," Gwen said in a severe tone. "And stop being nosy."

"Can't help it. Okay, let's get you fitted with some body padding—ooh, how fun to make you fat! And then find a uniform. Really ugly shoes, too. I've never seen you in ugly shoes! This will be a pleasure. . . ."

chapter 9

Why scale a twenty-story building when you could dress like a Guatemalan grandma, grab a mop and bucket, and shuffle right in? That evening, Gwen followed on the heels of the regular janitorial staff as they arrived at the Martinez-Rochas Tower around nine p.m.

She spoke Spanish into a clunky old cell phone and wearily flashed a fake ID at the guard. He barely gave her a second glance, and Gwen got onto the elevator with the rest of them. She had a cover story if they asked her any questions, but nobody did.

She got off the elevator with three of the workers on the seventh floor and dodged into the nearest ladies' room. She waited there until she was sure they'd dispersed and then headed for the stairwell with a duster and a few extra garbage sacks in her left hand. Jaworski Labs occupied the ninth floor of the building.

Gwen entered the stairwell, climbed two floors, and timed a convincing sneeze so that her face would be hidden from the surveillance camera near the door. She pulled a pocket hankie out of her ugly dress and buried her face in it until she was inside the corridor that led to the offices. These measures were probably unnecessary, given her makeup job, but she couldn't be too careful.

The Nerd Corps had provided her with a scanned duplicate of an employee key card—Gwen knew by now not to question their methods and just to be grateful for the results.

She slid the key card into the slot on Jaworski's door, expelling a silent breath of relief when a little green light blinked. A simple turn of the handle and she waltzed right into the corporate reception area, all of their security be damned.

Her gaze went straight to the alarm keypad in the corner. She had thirty seconds to enter the correct code . . . except apparently that wasn't necessary. The alarm wasn't set.

The little hairs at Gwen's nape stood to attention. Why wasn't it set? It wasn't a question of someone having forgotten to do it. No, there was somebody here.

She shrank back against the wall near the reception desk and listened. Hum of the watercooler. Electronic groan as the air-conditioning cycled off, the room having reached the correct temperature. A phone rang a few offices away. Other than that, silence.

Gwen was about to move into the hallway when she heard the murmur of voices. Two men? Two men and a woman. A smothered yawn, a slap on the back, a "Yup. See you tomorrow."

The female voice said, "Triple-check the results—he's going to grill you."

Snort from one of the men. "He can grill *this*."

Finally she saw them as they turned from a back corridor and made their way toward her and the main exit.

Gwen dropped to the ground and crept under the receptionist's desk, pulling the rolling chair in after her. The group didn't bother with the lights, thank God. A pair of woven, tasseled loafers, a pair of sensible navy pumps, and some wingtips walked by as she held her breath. Then the door opened, the group exited, and the door closed again.

Gwen continued to crouch under the desk, her heart hurling itself against her rib cage, until she talked herself out of the panic. She looked like a maid, someone who belonged here after hours. Someone whom the employees wouldn't think to question. Someone who was almost invisible to them. It was sad but true: Most white-collar professionals wouldn't spare a glance for a heavy woman in her late sixties in a janitorial uniform.

When her breathing had returned to normal, Gwen eased the chair back, crawled out from under the desk, and got to her feet. Wielding the duster and a trash bag, she forced herself around the corner and along the corridor she knew led to Quinn Lawson's old office.

A faint mildew smell hung in the air, despite a chaser of Lysol. Once water got into industrial carpet in Miami, it had its way with the fiber and nothing could stop it.

She looked for light under every door she passed, breathing more easily as she discerned nothing but darkness. She stopped at Quinn's door. No sign of light. No sign of any movement inside. But what if? What if the duplicate mask was still with Jaworski?

Her breathing had kicked up a notch just at her thinking about it. She counted to ten and got it under control as she used another key card to open this door. If the mask wasn't here, then it wasn't here. She could track down Jaworski and get into his house, too. The Nerd Corps wasn't just made up of brilliant geeks . . . they were essentially criminal consultants. Gwen skittered away from that thought.

The end justifies the means. Avy had repeated it patiently, over and over. *These aren't sweet, decent kindergarten teachers we're dealing with, Gwen! They're* crooks.

But Gwen didn't feel right being here . . . and she had to

get over that. She was here. And she needed to get a look at that duplicate mask.

She entered Quinn's office and shut the door behind her. The moonlight streamed through his open wood blinds and caught the teeth of the bear's head, which looked as if it might leap off the wall at any moment and grab her by the throat.

Gwen shivered in disgust and turned her back on it, walking over to the big, ugly mystery-wood credenza by the window. Outside, the royal palms that oversaw the parking lot swayed disapprovingly at her, shaking their fronds over her lost ethics.

A loud electronic tick had her whirling, but she couldn't identify the source. She stood frozen for a moment and then made the mistake of looking up at the bear's head again. Its eyes followed her every move.

Wildly, she wondered if there were some kind of nanny-cam in its mouth, and then dismissed the idea as ridiculous. What was wrong with her? She needed to pull it together and focus on why she was here.

Where was this heavy-duty safe? Behind a painting? Built into a piece of furniture?

She began with the artwork, which interestingly enough was boring and nondescript. Quinn's choices? Somehow she didn't think so.

There were some pompous herons in tall grass gazing out from one painting with an ornate frame. She lifted it from the wall, but there was nothing behind the piece.

The next picture portrayed two sailfish popping up out of the water simultaneously, like a couple of pieces of marine toast. No safe behind them, either.

She checked inside the massive credenza, since she was standing right next to it. No dice. Inside were stacks of Jaworski Labs letterhead, mailing envelopes, and annual reports. There were boxes of Jaworski Labs pens and an old-fashioned Rolodex, a series of golf videos, and a book on golf that looked more effective than a sleeping pill for knocking someone out within five minutes.

Gwen shook her head. Where was the Quinn she'd known? Who was this guy?

She was reassured by the bottom shelf of the credenza, which held a few old issues of *Car and Driver*, an all-in-one tool that did everything from open beer bottles to tighten wing nuts—and a lighter. Evidently Quinn had not stopped by yet to pick up his personal belongings.

Gwen nudged the door of the credenza closed with her foot, jumping at the sound it made. Stupid of her.

She turned to the desk, creeped out when the grizzly's eyes followed her over there, too. *God!* What was it with men and dead animals? Horns, fangs, claws?

Just in case, and half for curiosity's sake, she pulled open the top drawer of Quinn's desk and examined the exciting possibilities arrayed inside. A tube of Rolaids, a set of keys, pens and pencils galore, a calculator. A letter opener, a box of pushpins, a pair of scissors . . . no mask.

The second drawer yielded business cards, CDs filed in alphabetical order in labeled jewel cases, and a couple of notepads. In the third drawer was a portable printer that could be used with a laptop for travel.

She was beginning to get frustrated. Where was this safe? She'd headed for the file drawers when she heard footsteps in the hallway. Panic punched her in the stomach and she switched off her flashlight. She reminded herself again that she was dressed appropriately to be here.

Yeah, but most janitorial staff turned on a couple of lights and left the door open. In her discomfort, she hadn't done that. She was creeping around like exactly what Quinn had initially thought she was: a thief in the night.

So Gwen crouched and gave in to her instincts—she crawled under Quinn's desk, where she banged her knee on

something rectangular with sharp corners. Could it be . . . ?
She felt around the edges of it with her hands, and determined that it was the right size and made of ornately carved wood. This was the box that had held the mask.

Gwen made herself wait a full two minutes—she counted off 120 seconds in her head—before switching on the flashlight and fumbling for the catch on the box. She opened it with growing excitement—only to be disappointed. The box was empty.

Then she heard the electronic snick. A card swiped through the lock on the office door, which flew open.

Gwen's head came up instinctively and cracked the underside of the desk, hard. She switched off the flashlight, even knowing that it was too late. The game was up.

Quinn's voice said, "Come out from under there with your hands up." He sounded hard, angry . . . dangerous. He didn't know it was her. Did he have a gun?

Sick with fear, Gwen told her limbs to move, but they refused.

Quinn knocked his executive chair to one side with a single, well-aimed kick. Ropers. He was wearing ropers and faded jeans. "Get the hell out of there!"

Someone had filled her mouth with cotton. No moisture. No ability to draw in air. Gag reflex.

"With your hands up!" he ordered.

Did he have a gun? Why hadn't he called security? Were men on their way up already? Wait . . . he couldn't do that. He was here just as illegally as she was. It was small comfort, but it was some.

She tried to speak but couldn't form words. So she crawled out, hands in front of her, palms toward him. Maybe he wouldn't recognize her.

"Stand up."

She did so in one fluid motion before realizing her mistake. A bulky woman in her late sixties would have difficulty doing that. She'd have had to brace herself, probably huff and puff.

"Turn around."

Gwen swallowed and pivoted. First she noticed the .22 aimed at her chest. Then she focused on Quinn's eyes, which were hard and cold and just as uncompromising as the business end of that gun. They narrowed, then widened. His jaw jutted toward her. "Take off the wig," he said.

Gwen broke into Spanish, pleading and gesturing. "Don't shoot! I didn't do anything. Please God, don't shoot."

"Take off the wig," he repeated. "It's slipped, so you can save the denials."

Fudge! She must have knocked it out of position when she'd cracked her head under the desk. "*No hablo inglés,*" she claimed.

"No *hablo* any further patience," Quinn growled, striding toward her. He grasped the gray wig and pulled it clean off, tossing it to the floor. "Who are you? Who hired you?"

Gwen felt naked and exposed as she stood in front of him, even with the realization that her makeup job and the body padding still protected her.

Then he grasped her roughly by the padded arm and the jig truly was up. His expression changed from angry to puzzled and angry; he opened his fingers and then gripped her again. The latex body padding looked real, but it just didn't feel real. And it wasn't warm to the touch, like human flesh. He inhaled, then peered at her incredulously, his gaze traveling from her puffed-out cheeks to her support hose and cheap black lace-up shoes—then back up to her face again. He opened and closed his mouth as if trying to get his temper under control.

"I can smell your shampoo, Gwen," he said through gritted teeth. Then, to her shock, he ripped the maid's uniform open, sending buttons flying. He yanked off the body

padding, and she stood there, mouth open, wearing nothing
but a flesh-colored camisole and tights.

He cast her a look of pure disgust. "Well, honey, you've
just been busier'n a one-legged cat tryin' to bury shit on a
marble floor."

As Gwen blinked at that, he gouged a line down her
heavily made-up forehead with the nail of his index finger.
The revulsion on his face intensified. He whipped out a
pocket handkerchief, cleaned the underside of his nail, and
then wiped the cloth down one side of her face.

He dangled the makeup-caked handkerchief by one corner before tossing it at her. "Nice," he said. Then he
pointed. "There's a washroom in there. Clean that off and
pull yourself together. Afterward, you and I are going to
have a chat, my little double-crossing quarterback."

"I didn't double-cross anyone," Gwen said. But she
stepped out of the ruined uniform, kicked off the ugly
shoes, and walked with utterly false calm to the washroom,
shutting the door behind her.

Her whole body vibrated with tension as she leaned her
hands on the sink and took several gulps of air. She finally
looked up to meet her own eyes in the mirror and winced.
Her hair was matted down from the wig, half the age
makeup was smeared off, and he'd left a long squiggle
mark on her forehead. Her face looked like a toddler's idea
of abstract expressionism, painted in a palette of liver-olive
and chalky beige.

She reached into her mouth and removed the dental cotton that had distorted the shape of her cheeks. She dropped
that into the wastebasket and turned on the faucets full-
blast, splashing water onto her face and groping for the
soap dispenser.

Two minutes later she was scrubbed clean. She had no
makeup with her, not even a lipstick to arm herself for the
"chat" she was about to have with Quinn. And she'd have

to have it in a pair of support hose and a camisole. Lovely. Every woman wanted to look this way in front of her ex.

She ran her fingers through her hair and got it to stand up in a feeble semblance of its normal appearance. She washed her hands and dried them again, a completely unnecessary stall for more time. She glanced with little hope at the nonopening corporate window. *Riiiight.* What would she do—charge through it wielding the toilet plunger and fall to her death?

That seemed preferable to going back out there and facing Quinn like this; it really did.

"Have you fallen in, Gwen? Or are you just trying to drown yourself in the toilet so you won't have to come out?"

Hateful jerk. She pulled open the door and stalked out, glaring at him. Offense was the best defense. "Quinn, what are you doing here? How do you have access to the building? You've been fired. Your presence here and the noise you've made could land us in jail!"

Quinn's über-manly jaw slackened. "Are you actually standing there in your grandma underwear blamin' *me* for this situation? You have some nerve!"

Gwen nodded. "That comes in handy when you repossess stolen art for a living."

"What in the hell are you doing here, Gwen?"

"I came to look at the mask, to see if I can get any clues as to who made it and how and where. I was going to call you, but the makeup job took a while, and I ran out of time."

"You weren't going to call me," he said flatly.

She broke eye contact and sighed. "All right. I wasn't going to call you. I knew I could do this more easily on my own."

"You're taking completely unacceptable risks."

"Really. And what about you? You're here, too."

"That's different."

She smirked at him, which seemed to enrage him.

"Ever been in jail, Gwen? It wouldn't be your idea of a good time, trust me."

"Why, have you?"

"Yeah. I tried to break up a fight one time, and got arrested for my trouble."

She hadn't known that. But there was probably a lot about Quinn now that she didn't know.

"It's not only dangerous for you to break in here, but it's dangerous for a woman to be out alone at night in Miami. You don't even have your SIG with you, do you?"

"I didn't think I could get it through security. But I have other ways of protecting myself. How did *you* get in with a gun?"

"I know my way around the system," he said.

"How did you get in, period?"

"Like I said, I know the system."

"By the way, it sucks."

"Tell me about it," Quinn muttered.

"All we had to do was scan your assistant's key card. Our team did it from three feet away and he never noticed."

Quinn looked a bit shamefaced and shifted his weight from one foot to the other. "Same," he muttered.

Gwen laughed. "So, do you want to lecture me on my morals tonight?"

His face darkened. He stepped forward, closing the gap between them, and took her by the shoulders. His hands burned her bare skin, sending that familiar liquid heat through her system. *Oh, God.* Not this. Not now.

But her lungs had compressed; she had trouble drawing air in. Her pulse spiked. Her knees went weak.

"You lied to me about this. Don't friggin' lie to me. Not ever again."

"I didn't lie. I simply omitted to tell you I was coming here."

"Same thing! We're supposed to be working as a team."

"We don't make a good team. I tried to tell you that."

"We make a great team—until you decide that it's only made up of one person. You did it fifteen years ago, Gwen. You did it again tonight. And you know what? It's *bullshit*."

"Oh? Well, you came here alone, too. Now get your hands off me, Quinn," she said, her tone low and deadly.

His nostrils flared. White dents in his nose appeared directly above them. A muscle bunched in his jaw. His face loomed over hers, and his hands stayed right where they were.

Old attraction pitched a pheromone-laden fastball, but mutual hostility hit it right out of the park.

"*Hands*, Quinn!"

That muscle in his jaw jumped again, but he lifted his palms from her shoulders. However, he didn't step back one inch.

Neither did she. Gwen stood there in the damned support hose and glared right back at him, chin up like a battering ram.

chapter 10

Quinn stood looking down at the top of Gwen's disheveled head, opening and closing his hands in sheer frustration. The soft orange streaks lay like little question marks among the strands of her natural color.

They asked, *What are you going to do? Kill her? Or kiss her?*

She stood in front of him in a lacy wisp of lingerie and a pair of the ugliest stockings he'd ever seen—yet with no visible panty line underneath them.

Quinn had gotten a thorough and disturbing view of her sweet backside as she'd stalked into the washroom. The stockings were hideous, but they left little to the imagination. Gwen looked just as good as she had when she was nineteen. Maybe better, since she was now more muscular.

Because of his height, she had to tip her head back to meet his eyes, and her full, nude mouth played havoc with his anger. Would she taste the same?

The strappy, lacy thing that covered her upper body had been designed by the devil, who was clearly a female. *Covered* didn't really do justice to what was going on here. *Covered* was an entirely inadequate verb.

No, the lacy thing clung, and it thrust up her curves, and

it created deep, shadowy cleavage that might make a lesser man gnaw on his knuckles and shed tears into his beer.

Quinn was better than that. He had self-discipline. And he was madder than hell at this woman, so nothing she could offer would tempt him. . . .

"Quinn?" she asked uncertainly. "Quinn! What are you—"

He blocked her questions with his mouth. She tasted the same. Better. Like ripe bing cherries, firm on the outside, soft inside, dark and sweet. She was pliant under him; she made an unintelligible, shocked noise and it gave him a woody.

His hands moved to her face, then down her neck to those gorgeous shoulders, sliding the length of her sleek, defined arms. He reached her slim hips, circled around them to Gwen's so-sexy ass. He copped a good handful, but the stupid spandex stockings made things difficult.

Gwen kissed him back fervently, and as he dipped his fingers under the elastic waistband of the infernal, diabolical hose, he concluded that they were both lunatics. Stark, raving— *Oh, sweet Jesus, that ass.* So smooth, so warm, so beautiful. His eyes just about rolled back in his head as he pressed his body into hers and remembered what it felt like to be inside her.

Slowly, unwillingly, he became aware that Gwen was tugging on his wrist, that she'd pulled her mouth away from his and was shoving at his chest with her free hand. "Back off, Quinn. This is the worst idea ever to come along in the history of bad ideas."

If she were smart, she'd let him keep going. If she were smart, she'd use his unholy attraction for her to manipulate him into doing her bidding. But she wasn't that kind of girl. She was too . . . honest?

Quinn almost laughed at that. Then he decided he didn't

care. He came within a hair of burying his face in her cleavage. He almost said *please.* He thought about begging.

"*Hey!*" Gwen said, out of breath.

He stared at her hopelessly, groping around in the recesses of his mind for his righteous anger, his rage that she'd broken in here alone, without telling him. He scrubbed a hand over his face and muttered an apology, a justification, an excuse—something, he didn't know what.

Gwen said, "You taste the same." Her color was high and she wouldn't meet his eyes. After a long moment she said, "We need to focus on the mask."

Feeling poleaxed, he nodded his head. *Mask? What mask? Oh, that mask.*

"I can't find the safe. Do you know where it is?"

He inhaled, then exhaled. "Of course I know where it is."

"Well, show me."

He looked at her for a long moment, his Gwen. Messy hair, entreating eyes, swollen mouth, beard burn. Because he almost choked on whatever it was that he felt, he fell back on being flip. "Make it worth my while," he said, with a waggle of his eyebrows and a leer.

Gwen's face changed, the sweetness and the entreaty dissolving. She eyed him scathingly. "I don't *think* so." She picked up the uniform he'd so rudely stripped off of her and stepped into it. Her hands shook as she pulled the edges together to cover herself.

"I didn't mean it like that, Gwen. I was kidding. It was . . . a fantasy. All right?"

"Do you tie me up in this fantasy, Quinn?" she asked, in those soft, perfectly modulated tones of hers.

Uh . . . that doesn't sound so bad.

"Get your revenge for the past, maybe spank me a little?"

He almost choked on his own spit.

"Well, dream on." Gwen released the plackets of her dress and put her hands on her hips. The dress gaped open and he tried not to stare at her breasts, at the clearly outlined nipples.

"Quinn, could you have left me one button? Just one? How am I supposed to get home like this?"

He stared absently at the scattered gray plastic buttons on his beige carpet. "Sorry," he muttered.

Had he really just said that? Was he really bending down now, picking up the buttons, and handing them to her? He was a chump.

Quinn stepped around her and went to the grizzly bear's head. He lifted it off the wall and exposed the safe.

Gwen seemed to forget all about her dress. "I should have known it was behind that thing," she said, hands on her hips. "Please tell me you didn't shoot that. Please tell me you don't literally have a bearskin rug in your house."

"No, it's not mine. It was Shankton's—the former CEO's. I don't like killing animals for sport." His grandpa Jack had loved to ramble around in a drunken stupor, shooting at whatever moved. A damned miracle he hadn't shot off his own nuts.

Quinn input the combination that he'd always used, and tugged at the safe door. No dice. "They've changed the combination. Not surprising." But he banged his forehead on the steel door.

"It's not a problem," she said.

"Of course it's a problem."

"Move, please." Gwen pulled a strange little electronic device from the pocket of her dress and affixed it to the door of the safe. She programmed a series of numbers into it and then waited, stretching her arms behind her back.

This, of course, pushed her breasts forward and up, and Quinn found himself staring at them again like the village idiot. He tore his gaze away. "Sweetheart," he asked as casually as possible, "when did you learn the fine art of safe-cracking? Did you take a class on that, too?"

She nodded. Gave him that sweet, endearing smile of hers. The one that had devastated him the very first time he'd ever seen it—glowing under a silver mask with her hair flying in the breeze.

He'd grinned helplessly back.

She'd extended a delicate hand.

He'd taken it and pulled her to him.

They hadn't exchanged a single word. Their two smiles had met in that moment, shimmered in the night, connected in bliss, and spoken volumes. They'd replayed the whole history of male and female up against that wall . . . and then rejoined the crazy, raucous crowd.

They didn't try to speak at all that night, surrounded as they were by laughter and music and thousands of other voices.

He still didn't know how he'd held on to her for the next few hours, but he had. He'd woken with her in his arms; she lay spooned against him. Her hair smelled of jojoba. The silver mask lay on the floor.

She stirred sleepily, and he'd tightened his arms around her, kissed the back of her neck. She woke with a start, turned slowly, and stared at his face.

A rosy tinge of shame swept up her cheeks and she closed her eyes for a moment. He reached out and touched her nose, and she rewarded him with a curve of those gorgeous, dirty-angel lips. She opened her eyes again and he fell, headlong and helpless, into them. He'd loved her from that moment on. Before he'd even known she could speak English.

A tiny beep alerted him that the little red numbers on Gwen's safecracking gadget had stopped.

"What were you thinking about just now?" she asked.

"Nothing."

She nodded and turned to the safe.

"What is that thing?"

"Nothing." She detached it, dropped it back into the pocket of her ripped maid's uniform, and pulled open the door of the safe.

Inside, the mask smirked up at them, sparkling and gleaming under the concentrated beam of Gwen's flashlight. The peacock eyes spoke of preening vanity, pulsing ego, primal jealousy, and simple revenge. Again, she felt evil emanating from the thing—which was ridiculous, especially since this was only a copy.

Quinn stood silent, gazing at it.

She didn't want to touch it. Silly, but she remembered the horrible images that had come to her the last time she'd picked it up. Copy or not, she couldn't forget the driving force behind the original. Carnevale. Dante's voice, saying *Voilà . . . the husband's rival meat was removed.* Castration. Vengeance. Death.

"That damned thing gives me the creeps," Quinn said.

"Yeah. Me, too."

Gwen inhaled, mentally braced herself, and then stuck her fingers right into the eyes of the mask. She turned it over and examined the back. Real gold—no mistaking the color or the shine. But if she had to make a guess, it was eighteen-karat plate.

Using the safe door to hide the beam of the flashlight, Gwen propped it between her chin and shoulder and scratched at the surface of the mask with a fingernail. That told her nothing, so she reached out and palmed a pen from Quinn's desk.

"What are you doing?" he asked.

"Just bear with me." She made sure the pen's nub was safely inside and scratched at the gold surface with the end of it. Nothing—no sign of a mark. Gwen unpinned the plastic name tag from her uniform and used that to make a deep gouge. She still couldn't be sure. She then poked the point of the pin into a tiny gap in a seam of the mask, a place where it had been soldered.

Quinn just watched.

The pin sank deeply into a material that seemed softer than the surface. She tried to scrape some out. After several tries, she pulled up a soft curl of grayish metal. She didn't know what it was, but she knew what it wasn't: gold.

Carefully, she placed the tiny curl of metal into a tissue and dropped it into her pocket. She noticed a funny smell, sweet and a little like hot asphalt. And also . . . what was it? Maybe turpentine?

This was definitely no solid-gold mask . . . but it had to have been made by someone skilled. A jeweler or goldsmith of some kind. The thing had been dipped into gold, and skillfully. Or the gold had been layered on somehow. Someone had also set the gems into the face of it, which required a good deal of skill and patience. The copy wasn't worth a fraction of what the original was, but it couldn't have come cheap, considering the expertise required to make it.

Knowing a jeweler was involved narrowed the field . . . but which jeweler? One in Miami? South America? Gwen sighed audibly and searched the back of the mask for any identifying marks. She peered closely at an odd cross-hatched area near the upper left corner. She made out what she thought was the letter B.

She took detailed pictures with the camera on her cell phone and then put the mask carefully back into the safe in the exact same position they'd found it.

Quinn shut the door, and Gwen restored the sequence of numbers on the combination to what they'd been before.

He stuffed his hands into his pockets. "I liked your silver mask a lot better."

She smiled wistfully. "Me, too."

Then he added, "I still have it." He reached out and traced

the line of her jaw with his index finger. He brushed her lower lip with the pad of his thumb.

Heat streaked through her body and eviscerated her breath. Knowing that he'd kept her mask all these years both touched her and scared her. "You do?" she whispered.

Quinn nodded. He closed the rest of the distance between them and tilted up her chin. Whisper light, his lips brushed hers, swept across them again, returned a third time. She opened to him and he deepened the kiss, licking inside her mouth, stroking her with his tongue.

Her bones turned to butter and her knees began to quiver. Heat, her own response to him, softened her. He groaned and picked her up. She wrapped her legs around his waist, a pulse throbbing at her core without shame.

He settled his hands under her bottom to support her and kissed her some more. He buried his face in her cleavage.

How good it felt; how right it felt . . . except he was *Quinn*. And they couldn't do this here. They were both guilty of breaking and entering. They could be discovered at any moment.

Gwen pushed at his chest and broke the kiss.

"What?" He leaned his forehead against hers.

"We have to get out of here."

"In a minute . . ." He tried to kiss her again, but she dodged.

"No. Now. Put me down."

He deliberately slid her down the front of him before he set her on her feet. He was more than aroused. "Sure you don't want some of that, honey?"

God, did she want it. Slick and hard between her thighs. Driving inside her until she shattered.

"We have to get out of here," she repeated, double-checking with the flashlight to make sure she still had the tiny, wrapped curl of metal in her pocket. That and all her little B-and-E toys.

She rounded up the discarded body padding and stuffed it into one of the trash bags she'd brought in with her. She added the wig and the old-fashioned feather duster, pulled the plackets of her dress together, and made for the door.

"Coward," he whispered in the dark.

"I'm not a coward. I just think it's a bad idea, that's all."

They left Quinn's old office and headed for the elevators in silence. She tried to step into the main car when it arrived.

"No, we'll take the freight elevator," Quinn directed. "No cameras in that one, and I'll get us out the back way." Once inside, he leaned against the grungy padded wall, folded his arms, and semiglowered at her. "You know you want me, Gwen."

Her gaze flew to his and she got drunk immediately on those tawny-port eyes of his. *Fudge.* He could read her like a book.

"Yes, Quinn," she said slowly. "I do want you."

A look of triumph crossed his face, and he took a step toward her.

Her defenses went into high gear and she stepped back. "I want you in my body, but not in my life."

His pupils widened. Other than a swift intake of breath, though, Quinn didn't comment. The elevator opened and he got out, stone-faced.

He shepherded her through a back passageway and out a door marked LOADING DOCK ACCESS. He reset the alarm code. "Where's your car?"

"I don't need—"

"Where's your damned car?"

He walked her to the Prius, two blocks away, in silence.

"Thank you," she said.

"You're welcome." His tone said she was anything but.

"Quinn, I didn't mean—"

"I know exactly what you meant, Gwen," he said. "And so do you. Good night."

chapter 11

"I'm so terribly sorry," Sir Liam James said to a middle-aged couple from Chicago. "But this room is temporarily closed." To all appearances a gentleman tour guide, he stood in front of the double doors to the grand dining room at Château de Cheverny in France's Loire Valley.

Liam looked pleasantly absentminded and professorial, with the addition of some stodgy spectacles and a tweed jacket with patches on the elbows. He certainly didn't seem the sort of dastardly fellow who'd disarm the château's metal detectors to smuggle something inside.

Cheverny, a stately home of white stone built in the style of Louis XIII, received tens of thousands of visitors a year. It was notable for its clean, classic lines and lack of any defensive structures. There were no battlements or turrets here, just simple elegance, the house a jewel set into the countryside.

The largest room in the château was the *salle d'armes,* which was full of armor and battle paraphernalia, swords that made Liam think fondly of how he'd met and tussled with Avy over the sword of Alexander.

An aristocratic country house, Cheverny also boasted a trophy room hung with two thousand pairs of antlers. In the winter Cheverny's seventy hounds were released twice a week for its famous hunt. Liam had participated in it several years before, but had conveniently fallen and walked back to the house so that he could accomplish other things on his then-nefarious agenda.

The tourist couple from Chicago were not pleased to be barred from the grand dining room. "But we wanted to see the magnificent Don Quixote scenes by Mosnier—"

"And I assure you that you will. However, we're trying to revive a lady who fainted," he confided. "The room will be open again in just a few minutes. I'm sure you understand." He aimed a charming smile at them.

"Why not visit the king's bedroom or the Teniers tapestry room first?" he suggested. "The wall hangings are truly breathtaking—you won't want to miss them. Or you might take a peek at the Mignard portrait of the Countess of Cheverny, which hangs in the large drawing room. Lovely girl, that Marie-Johanne."

The couple nodded and went on their way, while Liam repeated his story to the next tour group. And the next and the next. What was taking Avy so bloody long?

After another couple of minutes, Liam slipped inside the room and simply bolted the doors behind him. Avy stood near one of the magnificent built-in sideboards, part of her skirt bunched up around her waist, and her head down. She was rummaging in the left of a pair of thigh-high black leather boots, and she made quite a stunning picture.

Her light brown hair streamed over her shoulders, catching the sunlight and turning to honey. He glimpsed about two inches of taut, bare thigh emerging from her boots, and this provoked wicked thoughts in him. Who gave a fig for Don Quixote or Pancho Villa when his fiancée was in the room?

"Avy, my love. Whatever is taking you so long?"

She swung around and glared at him. "These damned

fish forks are stuck in the lining of my boot—and I can't get it off!"

His mouth worked. "Those dastardly fish forks. Here, allow me to assist you." He walked toward her and knelt in front of her. "Foot, please, madam."

She extended it to him, scowling. "Only you could talk me into this. Only you, Liam, could convince me to help you put back everything you've stolen over the years. Only you could convince me to load up a pair of thigh-high boots with thousands of dollars of heisted silver! I must be insane."

"Well, I truly don't understand why we have to be in such a tearing hurry. You'll be the death of me if we have to replace everything before our wedding."

"Liam, you don't get it, do you? My dad's a U.S. marshal. As soon as he gets wind of you, he'll use anything he can to take you down. That get-out-of-jail-free card that you have with the FBI *doesn't apply* in Europe! Have you heard of Interpol? Dad's got some good buddies who will be happy to help him out."

"But I'm going to be the man's son-in-law," Liam reasoned. "Surely he'd cut me a break?"

"Not a chance," said Avy. "Don't delude yourself. We have to rid you of anything to do with your past, *now*, or he will use it against you."

She strained to lift her leg, puffing a bit. One couldn't blame her after walking the entire grounds loaded with service for twenty-four. "Only you," she growled again.

Sexy little growl, that.

He caught her foot and caressed it lovingly before pulling on the boot to get it off. This resulted in a faint clanking noise. "And only you, my darling, have the muscle required to gracefully walk that silver all over the grounds of Cheverny and up a flight of stairs."

The boot slid off her leg at last, baring her skin to the

cold winter draft. Goose bumps popped up all over her leg as Liam plunged his arm into the still-warm leather shaft to retrieve the fish forks. "You're done with the coat? You got everything out of it?"

Avy nodded. They'd each worn coats that concealed more of the haul, and her fashionably large leather bag had hidden the rest.

"Voilà!" Liam said, brandishing the forks in their felt wrappers. "Into the sideboard with them. Excellent."

Outside, someone pulled on the door handles. "These should not be locked. Why are they locked?" a man's voice said in French. "Call someone and get them opened immediately."

"Oh, dear, is the room still closed?" This voice was the middle-aged Chicago woman's. "The man outside said that a lady had fainted. . . . I hope she's all right."

Avy grabbed her boot from Liam, and they both looked toward the glass terrace doors. She stuffed her foot inside the shaft, worked it down, and then frantically began helping him unroll the fish forks from the flannel. One of them fell on the floor with a clatter.

"Who is in there?" the male voice asked suspiciously. "Open the doors!"

"Coming!" Liam dashed to the sideboard and loaded his share of the forks. Avy followed. She looked at the terrace doors again and they exchanged a glance. No way—they were probably rigged with an alarm of some kind.

"I demand zat you open these doors!"

Liam seized Avy, smeared her lipstick, and messed up her hair. He pulled half her tailored shirt out of the waistband of her skirt. He adopted a dazed, stupid, sexed-up look and dragged her to the door. She rolled her eyes at him. He grinned.

Then he unlocked the doors, looking sheepish. Avy

smeared her lipstick even more, stuck out her hip, and adopted an annoyed, sluttish expression.

"I beg your pardon," Liam said to the outraged château employee. "We couldn't help ourselves."

The group of tourists took in their disheveled appearances with varying degrees of disapproval.

"Well, I never!" said Mrs. Chicago. "Shame on you for telling fibs."

"Get a room," Mr. Chicago told them.

"A most excellent idea." Liam beamed at him, then turned to Avy. "Come along, my love." He grasped her hand and towed her from the room.

The man who worked for the château glanced quickly around to see if they'd stolen anything, but nothing appeared out of order. Liam waggled his fingers at him and winked.

Avy said, "You have a real nice day, okay?" and gyrated her hips as they walked down the stone hallway, her boot heels clicking seductively.

What a woman. Liam thanked God, not for the first time, that he'd managed to steal her from all other men.

As they strolled out of Cheverny and onto the pebbled path that led to the old stables, Avy's cell phone rang. She dug it out from the depths of her cavernous bag and went a little pale when she glanced at the caller ID.

"Something wrong, my darling?" Liam asked.

"It's my dad again. I don't know what to say to him— and he's going to know something's up, because I've been avoiding his calls."

Papa apparently had very stodgy, inflexible ideas about truth and morality. A pity, that.

"Why are you so afraid to tell him that we're engaged, Ava Brigitte? You're a grown woman leading your own life."

Avy sent him a speaking glance as she pressed the on

button. "Avy Hunt. Oh, hi, Dad. Sorry I haven't called you back—I've been up to my neck in work. Listen, can I give you a jingle in the morning? This is a really bad time—I'm about to go into a meeting."

There was a pause as she listened. Then she swallowed hard. "Um . . . well, yes. I do, uh, have a boyfriend. Dad, I have to go. The meeting starts in two minutes. Yes, he's British. Why?" She sighed. "Liam. Liam James. He lives in London. Mmm-hmm. He's nice."

Ha. An outrageous lie. Liam knew very well that he was many things, but nice wasn't one of them.

"We have a lot in common. He's an art"—she glanced quickly at Liam, panic rising in her eyes—"an art dealer."

Liam grinned. Quite true. He did deal in art. He just didn't necessarily pay for what he acquired. The grin faded. *Right.* But that was all in the past.

"Dad, why the third degree? Of course you'll meet him—if things ever get serious."

Liam narrowed his eyes. *If?* This was veering toward insulting.

"No, no. I told Mama that because she was trying to set me up with an acquaintance's son who lives in Coral Springs."

This was news to him. "Avy, *bellissima,*" Liam said. "We are *quite* serious. Marriage serious. Children serious. White-picket-fence serious."

Be quiet! she mouthed. She hunched her shoulders, and Liam didn't think it was because of the brisk breeze. "Dad," she said, a note of desperation now in her voice, "I will call you in the morning. No, I'm out tonight. Business dinner. Okay? Okay. Love you. Bye."

She turned the phone off and picked up her pace, her shoulders still nearly level with her ears. She dug her hands deep into her coat pockets and refused to meet Liam's gaze.

"Avy," he said, his voice as pleasant as he could make it. "What the devil was that?"

"You don't know my father," she said.

"True. However, since I'm going to be his esteemed son-in-law, I should *like* to know him. Don't worry, my love. We'll get along like the proverbial house on fire." He smiled at her reassuringly.

Avy closed her eyes. When she opened them, she still insisted on gazing straight ahead, looking for anything to distract her from the topic at hand.

Her boots crunched faster on the gravel as she made a beeline for the seething mass of black, brown, and white ears and tails inside a concrete holding pen. The baying of Cheverny's hounds was an aural assault.

Liam frowned. Going straight to the dogs, were they? That didn't suit him at all.

"The poor things!" Avy exclaimed. "They don't have any room in there."

The closer Liam got to the pen, the more he regretted it. Cheverny's hounds were in dire, dire need of baths. He clapped a hand over his mouth and nose.

"I'm sure that they get plenty of exercise when all the tourists have departed," he said. "The grounds of this old pile are enormous."

Avy looked dubious.

"My darling, I do hate to be a spoilsport, but we should be on our way. Who knows when the silver will be redis-covered, and we weren't awfully inconspicuous. May I add that the canine fumes are commencing to asphyxiate me?"

She rolled her eyes at him.

"And I do believe that we have quite a row ahead of us, for which we will need our oxygen." He bared his teeth.

"Liam, I don't want to fight. I just don't know how to tell my father that I'm marrying a *burglar*! Can't you un-derstand that?"

He pursed his lips. "Somewhat. But lying to him is only going to make it worse. And besides, I'm retired now. I'm making restitution. I'm a solid citizen."

Avy started walking toward Cheverny's exit. "No, Liam, you're not. Not until everything's been returned and you've worked a little harder at redeeming yourself with the law."

"It's only a matter of time, Avy. I swear to you."

"He's going to think I've lost my mind. He's going to think I've ignored every value he's tried to instill in me. He's going to be—"

"What?"

She whispered the words. "So disappointed in me."

His chest tightened. "Yes, well." Liam took her elbow solicitously. "My father's been disappointed in me for almost twenty years. One lives, you know."

"That's different."

"How?"

"You know very well how. It isn't as if you and your father were close. My dad and I did everything together."

"It seems to me that your dear old dad engaged in a lot of extracurricular activities without you, Avy."

She cast a furious glance at him. "Stop it, Liam. I mean that he taught me how to ride a bike, how to shoot, how to sail—"

"Yes, yes. And how to parachute, hang glide, dive, and ski double blacks. You've told me all of this. You adore your father. You don't want to upset him or displease him. Perfectly natural. But I was—forgive me—under the impression that you were quite infatuated with me. You did promise to marry me, and you must have known then that Papa Hunt wouldn't like it."

"That's the understatement of the year," Avy said, brushing strands of her hair out of her eyes.

"You're so worried about disappointing him. Have you ever told him how much he disappointed *you*?"

"No. He has no idea that I know about his affairs. I don't plan to enlighten him. That's not a conversation I will ever have with my father. It's not right."

Liam noticed, out of the corner of his eye, someone running from the main entrance of the château. A person who looked like an employee. "My darling, it's time we went on our way," he said, hurrying her across the parking lot to the gray compact they'd rented from Eurocar. He produced the keys, unlocked and opened her door, and stuffed her into the passenger side.

He checked to make sure the piece of cardboard he'd taped over the license plate was still there. And then he dove into the driver's seat and torpedoed the little car out of the lot.

"A change of chariot becomes necessary," he murmured. "What do you say we go for a Jaguar?"

"Fine—if you can get that Bernini bust into the trunk."

"Ah, the Bernini. One does hate to let it go. . . ."

"Yes, but *one* is retired now, remember?"

Liam sighed. "How can I forget?" He pulled over into a copse long enough to remove the cardboard from the license plate. Then he climbed into the backseat and lay on the floor while she tucked her hair up into a dark, bobbed wig. Within five minutes they shot onto the A10, headed northeast toward Orléans.

chapter 12

"Just keep denying everything," the man said to Angeline Le Fevre over a secure line, while he typed one-handed on his computer.

He heard her exhale a lungful of smoke. "I am telling you, she doesn't buy it. She's inexperienced but not stupid. How did I let you talk me into this, you *canard*?"

He snorted. "Talk you into it? As soon as I mentioned the Borgia piece, you salivated like one of Pavlov's dogs. You jumped at the chance."

"The copy was supposed to be foolproof. I can't have this getting out. I will be *ruined*."

"You knew the risks." His tone was callous, but he didn't care.

"I truly did not think they'd test."

"Your problem, not mine."

"Well, you must be feeling very clever yourself," she said waspishly, "since your target and her fiancé are vacationing in Europe while your plans and your money circle the drain."

Rage, not acid reflux, burned a trail from his gut right up to his esophagus. He didn't like being reminded of his failure. He would put an end to Avy's little vacation, but he still had to decide how and when.

"Careful, Angeline. You'd do well to treat me with the utmost respect, or I will send the police to your doorstep. Forget ARTemis."

"I would return the favor."

"You have nothing on me, Angeline, while your own hands are dirty. What did I contribute but an idea?"

"And thousands of dollars! Your half. There's a money trail."

"Ah. That's where you're wrong. Wire transfers of under ten thousand, all made from an anonymous Swiss account. Opened under an alias and now closed."

"The Velasquez brothers—"

"Won't be a problem. And neither will you. Do you understand?"

Silence.

"Do I make my meaning clear, Angeline? Or must I spell it out for you?"

She drew in a sharp breath.

"Smart girl. Now why don't you go find another stud to bend you over your desk, mmmm?"

"*Bastard!*" she hissed.

He laughed. "That skirt of yours rolls up every day, like a window shade."

She slammed down the phone.

chapter 13

Gwen fought consciousness and the alarm. Quinn was inside her and she was close, so close. . . .

Beep-beep-beep! Her eyes flew open, forcing the realization that she was alone, without a big, handsome bed buddy to bring her off. And she remembered what she'd said to Quinn the night before. *I want you in my body, but not in my life.*

Was she a bitch? A liar? She didn't know.

She'd hurt him. She knew that. Why? Because of the past, or because she wanted to ensure they had no future?

If she let Quinn into her life again, he'd smother her. Mess with her freedom. Get in her way. Bring back memories and pain she wanted nothing to do with.

Gwen wished she hadn't woken up. She silenced the alarm clock—it said six thirty a.m.—and rolled out of her four-poster bed, leaving the sheets and blankets askew.

She pulled on some running shorts and a tank, slapped a Marlins cap over her sleep-scary hair, and staggered into the kitchen to make coffee. That done, she jammed her feet into socks and trainers and headed out the door. She locked it with a key that she hung around her neck and then started down the street at what could charitably be called a lope. It didn't even qualify as a jog. But she'd gain speed after her muscles were warmed up.

Gwen hated to run, but she did it anyway two mornings a week. She loathed the humidity of the morning air in Miami, which hadn't abated this winter. Where was the typical four-month break from wet, sticky air? Living in south Florida sometimes felt like being trapped in a fat man's armpit.

After a mile and a half through the funky streets of Coconut Grove, she turned for home, a shower, and freshly made coffee. By eight thirty she was fully dressed and headed downtown to meet Quinn at the office by nine.

She wouldn't tell him that he'd been the starring stud in her dirty dreams. God, what was wrong with her? Maybe she needed to stop by an adult toy store and buy something to take her mind off of him.

Gwen pulled into her space in the parking garage. She'd gotten out and reached back into the Prius for her purse and fruit smoothie when the prickle started at her neck.

She kicked straight back with the silver spike heel of her baby-pink Mary Janes and connected solidly with a padded shin. Cato had struck again.

She whirled to block his next move, her fists up and ready to batter his chin.

But a dark green-and-denim blur toppled him, sat on him, and began to beat the crap out of poor Cato. The blur came into focus as Quinn.

"No!" Gwen yelled. "Quinn, stop it! That's Cato! It's all right!"

But Cato managed to unseat Quinn, and the two rolled around on the filthy concrete, trading blows. Cato's sunburst of hair stood up in angry spikes. Quinn's lips had drawn back in a feral snarl.

"Cato!" Gwen shrieked, as he landed a punch into Quinn's face. Blood spurted from over his left eye, but that didn't stop Quinn from smashing his own fist into Cato's nose. She heard a sickening crunch; then blood gushed from it like a geyser.

She ran forward. "Stop it, you idiots, both of you!"

They paid absolutely no attention. Cato head-butted Quinn, whose skull cracked into the cement. But Cato had made the mistake of straddling him, so Quinn knocked him back, then brought his knee up hard into the other man's crotch.

With a howl, Cato rolled off him and curled up into a ball like a pill bug.

Quinn lay prone in a patch of motor oil, panting.

"Are you deaf?!" Gwen shouted. "Or are you both just morons? What is wrong with you?"

"He attacked you," Quinn finally managed. "I wasn't gonna stand there and watch, for chrissakes."

Cato just moaned and rocked back and forth.

"It's his *job* to attack me," Gwen said, exasperated.

Quinn squinted at her out of his one good eye. "Huh?"

"Cato, meet Quinn, my ex-husband. Quinn, meet Cato, aka Armando Romeu. He works for ARTemis. He's our trainer. He's also paid to surprise us, keep us on our toes. Well, all except Avy. She broke his hand the last time he tried it on her."

"It was an accident," Cato said weakly.

"You sure about that? Anyway, I'd like you two gentlemen to kiss and make up."

Now they both squinted at her. Then at each other. Then back at her. "No kissing."

"Well, at least apologize to each other and shake hands."

Quinn sat up with some help from his elbows. Grease smeared his hair. Half his face and his shirt were covered in blood, which had also run into his mouth so that he looked as if he'd just bitten someone. He looked like a character out of *Shaun of the Dead.*

Cato rolled onto his knees and gingerly straightened. His shirt was torn and he winced as he put a hand to his pulverized nose. The lower half of his face oozed blood, too. His shirt was soaked with it. He had a contusion on his forehead from head-butting Quinn. Dirt and grease blackened his buff, bare legs. He could have stepped off the set of a *Rocky* sequel.

"Well," said Gwen. "What do you have to say to each other?"

"*Mierda,*" said Cato. "You broke my fuckin' nose, you prick."

Quinn grinned at him through the blood. "Yeah. But it's real nice to meet you."

"*Vete a singar por—*" Cato broke off and looked sheepishly at Gwen. "Sorry."

"Yes, best to stop there. Get into the car, both of you," Gwen said severely. "I'm taking you to the emergency room."

"We're fine," Quinn protested.

"Nothing but a flesh wound or two," Cato said.

Gwen took a deep breath and counted to three. "Get in the car before I either Mace or shoot you both!"

"Yes, ma'am," they said glumly. Quinn rode shotgun. Cato rode bitch.

Cato's nose was indeed broken. Quinn had a minor concussion, and the doctor advised that he not be alone that night in case of complications.

Gwen dropped Cato off at the parking garage and then drove the purple-eyed Quinn to her house while he protested. He didn't need to be babysat. The quack was just being paranoid. Really, a shiner was no big deal. He'd had dozens of 'em.

She smiled, nodded, and utterly ignored him until she pulled the Prius into her driveway.

"Nice mailbox," he said, taking in the dolphins and flamingos.

Was he being sarcastic?

"Out," Gwen ordered. She got out of the car herself and went around to his side. She opened his door.

"Honey, you're such a gentleman." Quinn got out and appraised her little house with his good eye. "I like it. Much smaller than I would have thought. But honestly, why are we here? I thought you were mad at me for beating up your buddy."

"I am mad at you. And at him. But how are you feeling?"

"For real? Like I was shot at and missed, then shit at and hit."

Quinn had a way with words. Her lips twitched in spite of herself. "I'm not sure which one of you looks worse. But Cato doesn't have a concussion, and you do. So you get to cozy up to a bag of frozen peas on my couch, at least for tonight."

A gleam appeared in his good eye. "Well, since I'm your hero and all, can I take the bed and cozy up to you? You did admit that you want me—that way."

"You are *not* my hero, you idiot."

"Not even a little bit? I was trying to protect you from that yellow-haired freak. How was I supposed to know he gets paid to harass you?"

"Oh, gee, maybe when I yelled, 'Stop, I know him'?" Gwen threw up her hands. "And while there is some sick, girly part of me that appreciates your caveman response, I am fully capable of protecting myself, Quinn. When will you get that?"

Quinn hunched his shoulders. "Fine," he muttered.

"We'll just call it even, then, since I'm still mad at you for going to Jaworski alone the other night."

Gwen unlocked the door and pushed it open.

He brightened. "Hey, maybe we can have some great angry sex?"

"Unbelievable," Gwen said, shaking her head. She walked straight to the kitchen, opened the freezer, and pulled out a bag of mixed vegetables.

He followed her. "That's the same fridge we had in Brazil."

"Yeah. I liked it. Homey."

"And the same stove, just a nicer color."

She shrugged.

"Where did you find them?"

"Through a junk dealer. I had them fixed up and re-painted." Gwen handed him the frozen veggies.

"Remember how Maria Elena taught you how to make *Camarão na Moranga* in that old earthenware pan?"

Gwen nodded. Maria Elena, a tall, dark-haired girl studying history, had lived in the next apartment.

"Did you keep in touch with her?"

"We exchange Christmas cards. That's about it. Quinn, go make yourself at home on the sofa. Can I bring you anything?"

"A beer, if you have one."

"I don't think beer is great for a concussion." She watched him as he looked around her little house.

Quinn was too big for the space. Too overpowering. Too much. That was Quinn. He towered over her sofa, making it look like a toy.

Most of her furniture dated to the fifties and was made of blond wood with clean lines. The curved dining room chairs would probably splinter if he sat in them.

Her floors were refinished hardwood and creaked as he walked on them. They were warmed by area rugs woven to resemble famous modern paintings—a Kandinsky, a Rothko, a Mondrian.

Black-and-white photographs of Brazil, of Europe, and of friends and family lined the walls, which she'd painted a very pale, buttery yellow.

"I like it," he said simply. "It's you; it's designed deliberately—but it's not 'done up' to within an inch of its life."

He moved to the dining room, admired the big abstract glass piece that held court on the sidebar, and then walked to her china cabinet. "Get out," he said, turning with a grin. "You have Wonder Woman china?"

"I'm not sure it qualifies as china, but yes."

He chuckled. "I remember that you had a pair of Wonder Woman panties."

"They got holes in them," Gwen said, heat creeping up her neck. "I had to throw them out a long time ago."

"So . . . what kind of panties do you wear now?"

"That is so none of your business, Quinn. Now, what would you like to drink?"

"Beer," he said again. "Come on. Just one. This is a minor concussion, remember? My skull is too thick to sustain much damage."

She smiled at that. "Okay, one. But that's it—I don't want you going into a coma on my couch."

"Yeah," he said. "Because then I'd never leave. And since you only want me in your body, and not in your life . . ."

Oklahoma had strolled lazily back into his voice. It wasn't a strong accent, not like a Texas drawl. It was just a little bit country. Gwen had always thought it was sexy—though now was a fine time to be remembering that.

"Quinn, I didn't say that to hurt you. You know that a part of me will always love you. But . . ."

"But what?"

She didn't know how to explain to him. If she let him in, he'd take over her entire world again. He was already distracting her from doing her job. Instead of talking to the Velasquez brothers and consulting with a jeweler, she'd spent her day in an emergency center because he'd misguidedly tried to protect her. He'd harassed her about breaking into the lab. He was getting in her way, and he'd only become worse.

"I don't think we should have this conversation," Gwen said. "We should focus on our search for the mask."

"What conversation? How can I agree not to have a conversation with you when I don't even know the topic?"

Gwen sat down in the armchair opposite the sofa. "Okay. I'm going to say this as simply as I can, and then you're going to rest and I'm going to go back to work."

He waited, peering intently at her with his good eye from around the frozen vegetables.

"Quinn . . . all I know is that fifteen years ago, I went to Brazil to escape, for freedom and adventure. But I met you within weeks, and suddenly I was pregnant. And then married, for God's sake. Whisked off to California—"

"So I'm the bad guy, huh? Because I did the right thing, unlike my own sperm donor? Because I didn't want my kid to be born a bastard like me? Because I wanted you to have decent medical care?"

"I didn't say you were a bad guy. You've never been a bad guy. But you just made all these decisions—"

"You could have said no. I didn't force you to marry me!"

"You didn't hold a gun to my head, Quinn, but you backed me into a corner with your logic and your manic determination that your child would have a legal father. You built a cage around me—"

"A cage? What melodramatic crap is this?"

"You just *took over*. And you're doing it again right now. You won't even—"

"Bullshit."

"—let me finish my sentences!"

"I didn't take over anything. I offered you a ring because it was the right thing to do, and you took it. Plain and simple."

"Plain and simple, huh?" Gwen's eyes filled. "Not so much."

"What are you talking about?"

"You gave me a ring because it was the right thing to do. I took the ring *because I loved you.* Do you see the disconnect there, Quinn? Do you?"

The bag of vegetables fell into his lap, exposing Quinn's battered, bruised eye. The good one stared at her.

"It wasn't convenient for me to love you. It was the wrong time and the wrong place, and you loved me for the wrong reasons, but I couldn't help it, and that's why I walked into the damn cage," she said quietly. Then she picked up her purse and headed for the door.

"What do you mean, I loved you for the wrong reasons?" he demanded.

She didn't answer.

"Gwen," he said. "You've got this all backward. So damned upside down. I loved you, too. I wasn't just stepping to the plate because of the baby. Sure, the baby speeded things up. . . ."

She couldn't bear to think about the baby. "I have to go," she said.

"Where? You don't have to go anywhere. It's almost five o'clock."

"Waiting six hours in the emergency room didn't help me accomplish much today."

Quinn got to his feet and stepped between her and the door, blocking her exit. "Don't go. Please don't run away."

"I'm not running away from anything, and—"

"You *are.*"

"—you are not allowed to interfere with my job. So please move."

He didn't.

So she stepped to the right and squeezed by him. But he turned to face the door, putting his hands flat against it and trapping her between them.

"Quinn," she said despairingly. "You're doing it again. Taking over."

"And you're running away again. Admit it."

She sighed, leaned her forehead against the door. "Okay," she said. "I'm running. I'm sorry—I don't know any other way to deal with you."

"How about by turning around and fighting?"

She did turn. Faced him. "I've tried that, Quinn! You just steamroll me. You don't respect boundaries. You never *stop* fighting."

"Better than never starting. You weren't in a damn cage, Gwen. You were never my prisoner. You were captive to your own passivity."

That hurt. She sucked in a breath. "Fine. You want me to admit it? You're right. It's not something I'm proud of, and I struggle with it."

He nodded, his gaze intent on her face. "You're not used to struggling."

"No," she said quietly. "I've never had to. Everything was given to me on a silver platter, and you resent that. But believe me, it brings its own set of problems. Makes it hard to know what you want . . . when you never want for anything."

He nodded as if he understood. Did he?

"And it makes you feel guilty," she continued. "Determined to give back, be useful, not take everything for granted."

His eyes seemed to go darker as he focused on her face. He smoothed a strand of her hair back and tucked it behind her ear. Just the simple touch of his fingers undid her. Then his hand flattened on the door again, invading her space and curdling the tenderness.

"So, you gonna stop running?" he asked. "It's the ultimate passive-aggressive act."

Gwen stiffened. "Great, Dr. Freud. Thanks for that insight. Tell you what: I'll stop running when you stop *badgering*."

He blinked at that; he didn't seem to have a response.

"*This* is why you're impossible, Quinn. *This* is why it's a bad idea for us to work together."

"Sorry," he muttered. "I didn't mean—"

"I need to go," she said. "I can't get through you. You're in my way. And when you're in my way, you leave me no choice: I get around you."

They stood barely an inch apart from each other. "You get around me, huh?" His deep voice rumbled in his chest, vibrated in her ears. She could smell him again, those unique essences that made him Quinn. His skin underlying the light aftershave, his soap, his detergent, the starch of his shirt. It got to her, the scent of Quinn. It always had.

"Yes," she whispered. "I get around you." She stared at the third button on his shirt, which was at eye level for her. Annoyed and upset as she was, she wished the shirt would disappear.

"Well, that's not going to work again." Quinn the roadblock. He'd blocked her search for freedom fifteen years ago. He'd effectively blocked her from finding anyone else during the past fifteen years, too, just by being an aggressive memory that she couldn't banish, no matter how many dates she went on. And here he was, being a barrier again—to her exit right now and to her career.

"I *have* to get around you, Quinn," she whispered. "Please understand that."

But he didn't move—and neither did she.

chapter 14

With reluctant fingers, Avy dialed her father's number. She sat curled in a ball on a hotel bed in Tours, France, looking into a broad expanse of antique mirror. If she looked into the mirror, she could pretend that her reflection was going to have this conversation with U.S. Marshal Everett Hunt, not her.

Her reflection looked just as uncomfortable as she did, though, and borderline nervous. The woman in the mirror stretched her long legs out into a hurdler position and touched her toes, too.

The muscle burn felt good. Avy switched legs and touched the other toe with her fingertips as her dad answered with a deep, Southern bark. "Avy, that you?"

"Yes, sir. The one and only." She kept her tone light.

"How'd your meetin' go?" he asked.

"Fine."

"Don't lie to me, girl. There was no meeting, was there?"

She sighed. "No, but I was with someone and couldn't talk right then."

"Can you talk now?"

"Sure." Avy glanced uncomfortably at Liam, who was clad in nothing but a white hotel towel, draped none too discreetly. He blew her a kiss from the small table he sat at, enjoying some of his beloved Camembert on a chunk of baguette.

"Look, I have some information on this boyfriend of yours."

Avy took a deep breath. "Dad, about that. He's not just my boyfriend. We're engaged."

A thunderous silence ensued. A bad sign, very bad.

"Engaged," her father repeated. "As in, engaged to be married? No. No, absolutely not. You have no idea—"

"Dad, I know exactly who he is."

"No, Avy, you don't. You *can't*, or you'd never have gotten involved with him. Listen to me—"

"Dad—"

"Avy, the man you're engaged to is a goddamned thief. He's got four different aliases, lives in a residence owned by a shell corporation, and is a suspect in thirty-three different heists. He's wanted in seven different countries!"

Avy Hunt listened to her father rant while Liam continued to lounge half-naked at the little breakfast table. He winked at her, his hair tousled, his face creased by sheet marks, his eyes very green this morning. A small crumb clung to the overnight bristle on his chin. He looked like sizzling original sin, sunny-side up with toast.

No wonder he was wanted in seven different countries. Avy wanted him, too. Again.

"Dad," she said. "Maybe you should meet him before you pass judgment."

"I don't have to meet him! This guy is a world-class con artist and a lousy cat burglar." He'd raised his voice and it was clearly audible, even across the room.

Avy winced.

Liam frowned. "I beg his pardon, but I'm a *top-notch* cat burglar."

Avy shot him a warning glance and laid a finger over her lips, but it was too late.

"Is he there with you, right now?" her father demanded.

"Yes."

"Avy, you're exhibiting spectacularly bad judgment, and I don't know what's gotten into you. I don't know how you got tangled up with this guy, but he's one hundred percent bad news. You *cannot* marry him."

"Dad, I love you. But I'm an adult, and I make my own decisions. You have to trust me on this. He's all right. You'll like him, I promise."

"He's a *criminal*. Please listen to me, sweetheart. He's got you snowed."

"No, he doesn't," she said calmly. "I know about his past. But it's just that: *past*. He's retired. He's going to return—"

Liam shook his head violently and made wild gestures with his hands.

"—everything," she continued. "I told him that I wouldn't have anything to do with him if he didn't."

From Atlanta, U.S. Marshal Everett Hunt made a strangled noise that was unintelligible and yet communicated his feelings quite clearly.

If he hadn't been so upset, Avy would have been tempted to laugh. But he was her father and he was worried sick, and really, who could blame him? On paper, in a black-and-white report, Liam James was a terrible prospect for a husband.

"Avy, how long have you known this guy? A couple of weeks?"

"Three months."

"You can't marry someone you've known only three months."

"We'll have a long engagement," she said reassuringly.

"We will have no such thing," Liam said crossly, in his

most Etonian accent. "We'll have a bloody short engagement and a rollicking long honeymoon."

Avy narrowed her eyes at him and mouthed, *Be quiet!*

"I heard that," her father growled.

"Dad, I really think you should meet him and get to
know him. He's not the man you think he is. He's been
helping the FBI. . . . "

Down the wire came a snort that would have done a
warthog proud. "Avy, only because he was caught and
turned! They arrested this joker in the Getty Museum.
They caught him red-handed and gave him a choice: He
could go to jail and become someone's girlfriend or he
could help out the feds with a case. If they hadn't grabbed
him, he'd have committed burglaries until he died."

"No, Dad. He'd already retired. He was only in the
Getty trying to get something back for a friend—"

"Avy," he groaned. "You can't have fallen for that crap.
You're smarter than that, baby girl. I didn't raise the kind
of fool you're bein'!"

"Let me talk with him," Liam said. "Man-to-man. I'll
get this straightened out, my love."

Avy shook her head at him. "Dad, this is hard for you.
But you have to trust me. You raised me to make my own
informed decisions. I've read Liam's file. I know all of
this. I didn't walk blind into the situation. And I'm telling
you, he's all right."

Liam rubbed at his chin. "It occurs to me why Papa's
nose may be out of joint. I didn't ask him for your hand!"

Avy waved dismissively at him, and his expression became annoyed.

"He's not all right!" her father shouted. She held the
phone away from her ear.

Before Avy figured out his intention, Liam stood up in
one lithe, muscular motion, crossed the room, and neatly
twitched the phone out of her fingers.

"Hey!" She lunged at him, but he sidestepped and pirouetted, playing keep-away with it.

"Mr. Hunt," he said. "Liam James here. How are you, sir?"

"Liam James?" her father barked. "Or Trenton Smathers? Or Clifford Mansfield? Or Dag Friedlander?"

Liam had the grace to blush, but only faintly. "Very good, sir. We are indeed one and the same man, which I daresay is somewhat off-putting. Yet I assure you that we're frightfully good fellows when you get to the bottom of us all. . . . "

Was that an actual snarl coming from the phone?

"At any rate," Liam continued blithely, "we should *all* like to request your permission to marry your daughter. We love her, you see."

"Over my dead body, you scum-sucking bottom-feeder. Get the hell away from her!"

Avy winced.

"I'm afraid I can't do that, Mr. Hunt. I'm going to marry her with or without your permission. But we'd like you to—"

"You're gonna marry the Remington twelve-gauge I shove up your ass, you dirtbag."

"—walk her down the aisle and give her away at the wedding."

"Throw her away, you mean? Uh-uh. You leave her alone. Don't you so much as touch my little girl, do you hear me? Don't even look in her direction, or I will hunt you down like the belly-dragging rodent you are, James."

Liam paused, lifted an eyebrow, opened his mouth to respond, and then decided against it. He pursed his lips. "Right. Well. I don't believe we need any further clarification of your position on this matter, sir. It's been a sheer pleasure to speak with you."

"Put my daughter back on the phone and fuck off."

Liam ruefully handed the phone back to Avy. "That went well, did it not?"

"You had no right to butt in that way," Avy said, as they cased a Renaissance villa in Florence. Brunelleschi's great Duomo was only a hundred yards away, soaring into the evening sky over the red-roofed buildings of the ancient city. She wished she could enjoy the view, but she was too upset.

She had refused to speak to Liam all during the train ride from Tours to Paris and during the drive from there to Firenze. "You knew the situation with my father was already volatile. How could you have done that?"

"Because I'm a bloody idiot?" Liam asked.

"Exactly!"

"Do you have to agree with such alacrity, my love? In truth, I disliked him shouting at you. I disliked you being forced to defend me. It made me feel quite flimsy in the bollocks department. I thought he and I should sort it out ourselves."

"Oh, so you rode to my rescue with apparent schizophrenia? What the hell was that, Liam? 'We should all like to request your permission to marry your daughter.'" She smacked her forehead. "What possible positive outcome could that have had?"

Liam cast her a downtrodden glance. "Had the man possessed a sense of the ridiculous, he might have seen the humor in it."

"Well, he doesn't!"

"That much is evident. 'Belly-dragging rodent,' indeed." Liam ran a hand over his rock-hard, flat abdomen, looking insulted.

Avy sighed. "Look, if it's any consolation, I could probably bring home a marine who's also a doctor and a lawyer and my dad still wouldn't think he was good enough for me."

"Thank you. That's ever so comforting, since I'm none of the above. And as you can tell, my poor ego is positively shattered." He calmly raised his binoculars and squinted into the middle distance.

"Nothing could shatter your ego, Liam. And I'm worried . . . as a U.S. Marshal my father can make things *very* uncomfortable for us. You don't know what he's capable of." Avy had decided not to share Kelso's warning that someone else—someone affiliated with the disgraced Greek ambassador—might be gunning for her. After all, looking over her shoulder was all in a day's work, and Liam lived the same way.

"Excellent," he said, ignoring her words about her father. "That moonfaced, stoop-shouldered fellow in the Gucci shoes is locking up the building. Now he'll toddle off and we'll wait a few hours. Then we'll make our move, and voilà! In the morning, the public will awake to their Bernini again." He chuckled. "I must say, this replacing things is much more fun than stealing them ever was."

"That Bernini bust weighs a ton," Avy said, a little bitterly.

Liam grinned at her. "Yes, and it was the *small* one."

"How did you . . . ?" Avy stopped. "I'm not sure I want to know."

"Of course you do, love. Natural curiosity. I put on a deliveryman's uniform. Then I simply loaded the Bernini into a padded carton, stacked another on top of it, and walked them out with a handtruck." He looked delighted with himself.

"Nothing about it was simple. You had to contend with infrared sensors, alarms, security cameras. . . ."

"Yes, but I have my ways around those things, my darling. You know that."

Avy shook her head and looked at her watch. "Well, what's your ingenious plan for getting the bust back *in*?"

"It's truly brilliant," Liam said immodestly.

"Right. I get that part. Can you fill me in on the rest?"

Liam *tsk*ed. "Cheeky, cheeky."

Avy raised her brows. "The details?"

"We're caterers, my dear. We specialize in Italian wedding cakes, and someone has ordered one of our confections for the Capozzo reception, to be held here at eight p.m."

"You're not telling me—"

"Yes! We're going to waltz right in with the most spectacular cake you've ever seen. Underneath it will be the Bernini."

Avy gaped at him. "Liam, you've got to be kidding me."

"Never, my love."

"This isn't going to work. . . . Is the actual baker in on it?"

"Of course not. Do you think I'm a fool? There's a compartment under the service trolley."

"You did just call yourself a bloody idiot."

"*Very* different context."

"Ah."

"So at any rate, we deliver the cake and fade into the woodwork. Later, during cleanup, the cloth is removed and the bust is found in the service compartment. We're long gone."

"Disguises?"

"Taken care of."

Avy nodded. "Okay. This might work."

"Of course it will work. It's altogether too outrageous not to work." Liam flashed her his sin grin.

"Yeah," Avy said. "I can't wait for you to carry me over the threshold—"

He eyed her fondly. "Neither can I, my love. . . ."

"—of some European jail."

chapter 15

An ocean, a continent, and a culture away from Florence, Quinn felt drunk on the cognac color of Gwen's eyes. Her citrusy perfume had addled his brain and he wanted to taste her again. He wanted to taste her in places that he shouldn't be thinking about: dark, shadowy, and forbidden places. He wanted her stark naked, wearing nothing but a simple silver mask—to hell with this jewel-encrusted gold fake that was causing both of them so much trouble.

Quinn ran his hands down her bare arms. She shivered, and her skin erupted in goose bumps. He took her hands.

"Quinn . . ." But she didn't pull them away.

He kissed her neck, then moved his lips up to her jaw, feathering kisses in a trail to her mouth. She opened to him and he licked inside, whispered across her lips, and moved on to her ear. She gave a deep shudder as he dwelled there for a moment, releasing her hands to caress the nape of her neck.

She wore a camisole of cream lace with beige ribbon woven through the fabric. It barely skimmed the waistband of her low-rise jeans and made that olive skin of hers glow.

The camisole had thin spaghetti straps that left no coverage for a normal bra, and judging by the range of movement he saw, she wasn't wearing a strapless one. Quinn wanted badly to prove this scientific hypothesis. He also wanted to feel the texture of her nipples in his mouth.

He remembered making her come once just by toying with her breasts, suckling them until she was begging for release . . . and then with one single touch of his tongue at her center, she'd been all his.

"Gwen," he said softly. "You can't get around me. I can't get around you."

A sound of distress came from her throat. The protector in him wanted to comfort her, but the wolf in him closed on his wounded prey.

"*We* can't get around this," he said. "This thing between us. You can't dodge it—neither can I. Even though that pisses me off."

She started to say something but he kissed her again, tired of grappling with language that always came up short at expressing what he felt. Whatever was between them had to do with biology, with chemistry. Their formula was correct, plain and simple.

She gave in for a moment, but then her small hands pressed firmly against his chest and pushed. She packed a lot of power for her size. His onetime debutante could damn near bench-press a Volkswagen.

"Quinn, this is not going to happen. Turn off the thrusters, because that rocket is staying in your shorts. We have a job to do, and this . . . this . . . attraction we feel for each other is only getting in the way."

She ducked out of his arms, dropped her purse on a chair, and walked across the room to lean against the doorjamb that led to the kitchen. Shit, his heart moved with her hips. He sat back down on the couch, squinting at her through his one functional eye and feeling like a jackass. A question still burned in his mind: What did she mean, that he'd loved her for the wrong reasons? What the hell was that all about?

She took a deep breath. "Okay. Back to business. You want your name out of the mud. I want to save my reputation—and my firm's. If I don't, ARTemis will be sorry they ever hired me, and I'll make Avy look bad, too, for recommending me. That's not acceptable, so I'm going to focus on solving this mystery and tracking down the original mask—and you are not going to distract me. Got it?"

Quinn just looked at her.

"Are you going to say something?" she asked.

"Yeah. Finding the damned mask shouldn't be difficult. Because you know who's responsible for taking it. They just set you up."

She shook her head.

"You recovered the fake from someone, Gwen. *Who?*"

"That's not important. They're minor players. Someone else is behind the scenes, calling the shots."

"How do you know that?"

"Because this is a sophisticated crime, Quinn. The guys who broke into Jaworski Labs are burglars, smash-and-grab guys. One of the reasons I needed to see the duplicate so badly was to examine how it was constructed."

"And?"

"Most Venetian masks are handmade of paper and painted. This one is different, made of gold, or it wouldn't have survived the centuries. If I'm right, the technique used to make it is ancient and takes a lot of skill and knowledge. I want to take that little curl of metal and the photos to a jeweler I know and see if she can give me any clues as to who might have made the mask."

Quinn nodded. "All right. We'll do it first thing in the morning. But something is bothering me about this whole situation, and that's motive. Why would someone go to all the trouble of doing this when it would be much easier to have grabbed that Matisse? Or the Brancusi sculpture? Those are worth just as much."

Gwen said slowly, "I don't think this is a financially motivated crime."

Quinn frowned. "What other motive could there be?"

She shrugged. "Art collectors get passionate about things. Some of them will stop at nothing to get what they want."

"But . . . they'd never be able to display stolen work."

"Sometimes that doesn't matter. They just want to own it, have an object all to themselves and enjoy it in private."

"But why bother with duplicating it, then?"

"The obvious: They thought we'd recover the fake, put it back in the collection, and not discover the difference for years. By then the trail would be cold and they'd be home free."

Gwen frowned and tapped her fingernails on the windowsill. "But something about this feels personal. . . . The mask is such an unusual object."

Quinn shrugged. "It's gold. Studded with jewels. Worth quite a bit, even melted down. I doubt the motive is personal. I'd say it's financial."

"Unless, as you said before, someone at Jaworski is trying to make you look bad."

"Or someone's trying to make *you* look bad, Gwen. Have you thought about that?"

She walked to the kitchen counter and picked up an open bottle of wine, poured some into a glass, raised it to her lips, and drank. "I suppose there's a possibility that Kelso cooked this up to test me."

"Who's Kelso?"

Gwen grimaced. "Kelso is the ghost who owns fifty-one percent of ARTemis. Nobody's ever met him, but he's known for his practical jokes. If you ask me, he's a human headache."

"What do you mean, no one's met him?"

She sipped some wine and held it on her tongue before

swallowing. "Exactly that. The guy is a faceless presence. He issues orders and dispenses unwelcome advice from the ether."

"C'mon," Quinn said. "You're telling me that ARTemis is a bunch of Charlie's Angels?"

Gwen choked. "Hardly. First of all, we employ men, too. Second, we've never even heard his voice. But he does like to pull strings behind the scenes." She made a sound of mild disgust.

"Meaning what?"

She walked into the living room, sank into the chair opposite the sofa, and crossed her legs. "Do you want to know what Kelso had me do as an initiation rite? To prove my competence and value to ARTemis? You won't believe it."

He waited.

"Kelso had me break into a palazzo in Rome. Sid Thresher's palazzo, to be exact. To steal his dog—and then replace it."

"Sid Thresher of Subversion?"

Gwen nodded.

"You're shitting me."

"Nope."

"That was *you*?" Quinn laughed in disbelief.

"That was me. But if you tell anyone, I'll deny we ever had this conversation."

Quinn shook his head. Then he looked at Gwen. "You're having fun with this job."

Her lips parted and she shot him a wry smile. "Yes. Seventy percent of the time, Quinn, my knees are knocking together. But I feel *alive*. Not suffocated and overprotected and insulated."

He sat back and evaluated her words, turning them over in his mind. "You zigzag," he said finally.

"Pardon?"

"You veer wildly between wanting adventure and wanting

safety. You ran off to Brazil at age nineteen, but then ran into marriage with me—"

Her mouth tightened.

"—then you ran out of the marriage and back into high society. It took you, what, a year to flee again from that environment, and you went careening off to the projects to teach art to at-risk kids. . . ."

"How do you know all that?" she demanded.

Quinn shrugged. "I kept tabs on you for a while."

"Kept tabs," she repeated, not looking as though she liked the sound of that.

"Yeah."

Gwen's eyes glittered with hostility. "You mean you spied on me."

"I didn't spy. I just wanted to know how your life was going. I almost called you, but you got engaged to that putz."

She glowered at him. "Putz?"

"C'mon, Gwen. Mr. Mayonnaise? You can't tell me you loved that guy." She'd been briefly engaged to the heir of a condiment fortune, a rumpled-looking sap with a weak chin who'd mooned at her adoringly in the newspaper photo. Quinn had stuffed the paper into his grill and held a match to it.

She flushed. "He was sweet."

"And you could push him around."

"Shut up, Quinn! I didn't marry him. I made a mistake, okay? Haven't you ever made a mistake?"

He looked her dead in the eyes. "Yeah."

Gwen broke eye contact and got up. She walked to the kitchen and splashed more wine into her glass, her hand shaking almost imperceptibly. She set the bottle down with a thud. Unlike her.

"So what happened next?" he continued. "You got roughed up one day by some delinquents and that was the end of art in the projects. Next thing I hear you're taking self-defense classes and you've gone back to school in interior design. Zig, zag, zig."

Gwen rubbed at her neck and rolled her head back and forth. As she came back to the living room, her expression was ominous.

"Then zag: You've left the fabric swatches behind; you're working for ARTemis and stealing rock stars' dogs. What's the next zig?"

"There is no 'next zig,' Quinn, and I don't like the implication that I'm flighty—it just took me a while to figure out what I wanted to do. I'm happy at ARTemis. Assuming Avy doesn't can me for screwing up this recovery, I'm staying here. What's *your* next 'zig'?"

"Good question. I'll think more about it once we find the mask."

She rubbed at her neck again. Kneaded her shoulders. "Have you been happy as a big-shot CEO?"

Quinn slugged down some beer. "I've achieved all my goals."

"That's not what I asked. Are you happy?"

He shrugged. "I have money. A lot of it. And stock. I had a title. I got to run the show. I had everything I always wanted. You should have stuck with me, honey. Do you want to know how much I'm worth?"

"No."

"More than that stupid mask." He threw the figure out there, and it clattered onto the coffee table like a pair of dice.

"I said I didn't want to know!"

"No shame in that number, huh? Not bad for a little bastard shit-kicker out of small-town Oklahoma. Son of the town whore, grandson of the town drunk . . ."

"You still don't get it, do you?" Gwen looked at him

with something akin to pity. Something that burned his ass, bad.

"Oh, spare me the lecture about how money can't buy happiness, darlin'. Just spare me."

"Fine, I'll spare you. But realize that money doesn't erase shame, either."

"I have *nothing* to be ashamed of!"

"That's right, you don't. It's nice to hear you say it out loud. Now maybe you'll start to believe it one of these days, Quinn."

His jaw dropped open and he just stared at her.

"Your money, your stock, your title—none of that impresses me. You want to know what does impress me, Quinn? The fact that you came out of that horrible childhood a decent person. A guy who didn't turn into a delinquent—"

"I stole cars," he said. "I stabbed the school principal. I smoked pot."

"—and put himself through not only college—"

"I had my way paid by schol—"

"*Let me finish my damn sentences!* Not only college but business school. You turned out to be a guy who does the right things despite being set the wrong examples. That's what impresses me, Quinn. So don't ever talk to me about your money again."

He tossed the bag of vegetables back and forth from one hand to the other. And he let out a short, unamused laugh.

"Funny thing is, Gwen. . . when you left, I figured it was because you came to your senses. Saw me for what I was— somebody who wasn't good enough for you. A guy who couldn't give you the lifestyle you were used to."

"That's so insulting that I can't even think how to respond to it. You projected your own feelings of inadequacy onto me."

"What was I supposed to think when I read your little Dear John note?"

"Anything but that."

"Well, you didn't stick around to explain in person, did you?"

She stood up and clutched at her neck again. "I don't want to rehash the past with you. I'm going to go take a hot bath."

He paused. "I noticed a Jacuzzi out there. And I'd be happy to massage your neck and shoulders for you. I'll even keep my mouth shut, if you want."

She gave him a sharp, mistrustful look.

"Innocent. No funny stuff."

She wavered.

"Oh, c'mon, Gwen. I won't bite."

She wavered some more. Finally she said, "You stay on one side. I stay on the other. Got it?"

That didn't sound like any fun at all, considering she'd be wet and almost naked. But he nodded. "I don't have any swim trunks on me."

"Your boxers will work fine." She moved toward the small dining room and a set of patio doors covered by wood blinds. "Just duct-tape your fly."

"Funny," he said.

"I'm going to turn the spa on, and then I'll get changed and find some towels. The water will take a few minutes to heat up."

He nodded.

She unlocked the doors, went outside for a moment, and then came back in, sparing only a brief glance for him before she disappeared into her bedroom.

He stared at the white-painted door and thought about her peeling off her camisole and shucking off her jeans. Sliding her undoubtedly minuscule panties down her thighs as her full breasts brushed her upper arms.

He was a poor slobbering bastard, and no amount of duct tape was going to help him now. Quinn cracked his neck and avoided his battered reflection in the dark glass of Gwen's television screen. As Grandpa Jack would've said, he looked like he'd been drug through a knothole backward.

Screw it. He set down his beer and stripped stark naked. He tossed his pants and shirt on the arm of Gwen's couch and then arranged his boxers over the lamp shade so she couldn't miss them.

You can duct-tape my ass, Daddy's Girl.

Then, with a swagger and a flourish, he opened the doors to her patio and stepped outside into the breezy evening.

Gwen's neighbors to the left had thoughtfully hung their sheets to dry over a clothesline, blocking their backyard from view. *Excellent.*

To his right on the other side of the hurricane fence stood a parade of plastic trellises attached to plastic flower boxes on plastic wheels. Out of the boxes grew a tangle of mixed magenta and purple bougainvillea.

Beautiful.

The night air was tinged with salt, charcoal smoke, and freshly cut grass. The wind felt odd under his arms as he lifted them to stretch, and it blew cool between his legs, eddying erotically.

What in the hell was he doing here, though? Naked as a jaybird in Gwen Davies's backyard? Quinn rubbed at his chest and wondered briefly if she'd dropped something into his beer to make him stupid.

He heard the door open behind him.

"Quinn?" she said suspiciously.

He figured she'd seen his boxers draped over the lamp and wasn't happy about it.

"Quinn, are you *naked* out there?"

He turned around with a smile. "Why, yes, darlin', I am."

chapter 16

Gwen shut her eyes and pulled her head back inside. Okay, so she clearly shouldn't have made the comment about the duct tape. She shouldn't have agreed to get into the hot tub with Quinn, either, but it had been a long, frustrating day, and her shoulders and back were killing her.

"C'mon, Gwennie. It's not like you haven't seen it before." Quinn's voice held amusement at her expense.

She stuck her head out again. "Yes. But it doesn't hold the magical appeal you seem to think it does."

"Chicken," he said.

She rolled her eyes and stepped out, closing the door behind her. "You're being juvenile. But if you want to wave your johnson around my yard, go right ahead—I'm sure it gives you a thrill."

She actively felt his gaze on her body, roving over the muted silver of her bikini and stopping, riveted on her navel.

"Is there a problem, Quinn?"

"That had better not be what I think it is."

He started toward her, and though she refused to look below his waist, she watched the shadow of his cock bounce with each angry step. She bit her lip, because right now was a very unwise time to laugh.

Quinn stopped a foot short of her and peered at her navel. His mouth worked, but no sound came out.

She took advantage of the moment to wrap a towel around his waist, tucking the edge in as he straightened with a thunderous expression.

"You turned the diamond I gave you into a . . . a . . . *belly ring*? How could you?"

"Zigzag," said Gwen, shrugging. She brushed past him and swung her legs over the side of the spa. It was luke-warm. He was hot.

"You . . . you . . ." Quinn had no words.

She'd never seen him like this, and guilt set in.

"I didn't mean it to be disrespectful," Gwen said.

"*What the fuck*, Gwen!"

"You wouldn't take it back. What was I supposed to do with it, make a necklace out of it? Pawn it?"

He practically growled at her. "You wear that with Mr. Mayonnaise?"

She sank into the water up to her neck and leaned her head back. "We're not going to talk about Curtis," she said firmly. "That chapter is over and done, and there's no sense in revisiting it."

Quinn's mouth twisted. "How about the others, Gwen? How many men have gotten up close and personal with the diamond that I gave you?"

She glared at him. "None of your business. How many *women* have you been with, Quinn? Don't even try to tell me that you've been a monk for fifteen years."

His mouth tightened, he looked away, and she pressed her advantage. "Oh, but that's different, isn't it? Because you're a man."

"That's not the point," he said, finally climbing into the water. We were discussing—"

"We weren't discussing anything! You were interrogating me, and you have no right. We've been divorced for fifteen years, Quinn, and you don't get to be jealous."

"I'm not! It just grates on me, that's all."

Gwen raised an eyebrow and pointed at his biceps. "You wore that with those other women, right?"

"My tattoo? Yeah, but it's not like I can take it off at night and leave it by the door."

She shrugged. "Same difference."

"Not even. You didn't pay thousands of dollars for this, like I did for your ring. And I couldn't afford it, not being a trust-fund baby like some of us."

Gwen froze. She leaned forward, jabbing him in the chest with her index finger. "I never asked for anything but a wedding ring. It was your pride that demanded a diamond."

"How could I marry the daughter of banking's Andrew S. Davies without a big rock? He was already pissed enough that his daughter was getting hitched to some worthless shit-kicker, a guy who'd make change in a church collection plate."

"You have a chip on your shoulder about my family background, and I'm tired of it. My family never had a problem with yours. I never thought I was better because I grew up privileged. That's all in your head."

Quinn closed his eyes and laughed mirthlessly. "No, babe. It wasn't all in my head. Daddy never told you that after you left, I showed up looking for you?"

Gwen stopped breathing. "What?"

"Yeah. Jesus, it was like a scene out of some Victorian novel. He actually offered me money to go away."

Dear God. Horrifying . . . but she could see it. Anything for her father to have his daughter back, not realizing or caring about the scars he'd inflict on someone who didn't deserve any more.

Quinn's expression and body language could have

chipped marble. She reached out a hand to touch his shoulder. He looked at it as if it were a tarantula. She dropped it.

"You should never doubt that you're loved, baby doll. That son of a bitch, he wrote me out a check for a hundred thousand dollars."

Gwen felt ill. "What . . . did you do?"

"Oh, I proved I was a real class act. I took the money. I said thank you, real polite. I pulled the wad of Wrigley's out of my mouth and stuck that check to his hundred-dollar tie. Then I told him to have a nice day and left."

The burble of the water jets and the hum of the spa's motor filled a long silence between them.

"Quinn . . . I'm so sorry. I didn't know. That's unforgivable."

He shrugged. "Your mom came running after me in tears, trying to make it right. I made her swear she'd never tell you."

Gwen stared at him, at the cynicism and moonlight playing across his face. "Why?"

Quinn's mouth twisted. "I didn't want you to be mad at your dad."

Gwen shook her head in disbelief. "You didn't want me to be mad at him?" She reached out and gripped his shoulders, shaking them as best she could. "That makes no sense—and I *should* have been mad at him! How *could* he?"

"He did it because he loved you, Gwen. And I realized that in his shoes, maybe I'd have done the same thing." Quinn caught her wrists, looking down into her eyes with an expression of such sadness and tenderness that it broke her heart. And yet, shards of old anger scraped at the edge of her consciousness. These two high-handed men had both done irrevocable damage with their power plays, their need to control things.

Quinn stroked the insides of her wrists with his thumbs,

and Gwen closed her eyes as sensations streaked along her nerve endings, eddied into shivers, and broke the surface at her erogenous zones. *Kiss me, Quinn. Please* . . .

What was she doing? She'd been in hot water with Quinn years ago, and here she was again.

He tugged her closer, brushed her cheek with his lips, and turned her so that her back was to him. Then—*oh, heaven*—he began to knead her shoulders, using his thumbs to work the knots and the tension out. She moaned and dropped her head forward, unable to resist. The hot water enveloped her, and the massage made being between her ex-husband's naked thighs a little less threatening.

Gwen dropped her elbows and let her arms rest on those powerful, hair-roughened thighs, her hands draping over his knees. She traced her fingers over them, feeling the scar on the left one that he'd had since he was a kid and had fallen off his bike onto some broken glass.

Quinn being Quinn, he'd never gone for stitches, just picked most of it out himself and bandaged it with a paper towel and some Scotch tape. His mother hadn't noticed until it was festering and infected.

Gwen had gotten stories like this out of him in bits and pieces. He didn't talk much about his childhood, but she knew that he had pretty much run wild while his mother worked two jobs—as a waitress in a diner during the day and as a checker at Wal-Mart during evenings and weekends. There'd been a lot of men on her few nights off. Gwen couldn't bring herself to condemn a lonely single mom, though.

Quinn's hands moved up to the base of her skull and into her hair, making her scalp tingle and a deep shiver run down her spine. He dropped a quick kiss at her neck, and then rested his chin on her shoulder, putting his arms around her.

It was odd, it was intimate, and for a moment she

wondered if he was simply staring at her cleavage, but a quick glance reassured her that his eyes were closed.

His arms around her felt dangerously good. She sensed his reluctance to move, and she felt it, too. Then his hands moved lower, to her belly, and smoothed along the skin until they reached her navel. Quinn fingered the diamond there, toying with it, and her breathing quickened.

"I'm glad you didn't pawn it," he said softly.

Her heart turned over. "Me, too."

He didn't say anything else. She could feel his own heart beating against the muscles of her back, and his expelled breaths teased the nape of her neck.

She wanted him to . . . She didn't know what she wanted. Gwen sat there between his legs in a state of heightened awareness, as caught between the possibilities as Quinn was himself. Would he touch her breasts? Slip his hands down her bikini bottom? Do nothing at all?

His stillness made her crazy, and yet she wasn't sure she wanted him to make a move. He was hard against her backside, had been for some time, but she hadn't teased and he hadn't pushed.

Gwen found his hands and laced her fingers between his. Then she brought them up to her breasts. Quinn palmed them, gentle but expert.

"You sure about this?" he whispered.

She bent her head back and kissed him.

He kissed her in response, but a little warily. "What are we doing, honey?"

"I don't know, but it feels good."

He turned her to face him, caught the edge of her bottom lip between his teeth, and stroked it with his tongue as he lifted her breasts with his hands and circled the tips with his thumbs. Heat shot through her, and it had nothing to do with the spa.

Quinn placed her in front of him again. He undid the

bow at her neck with his teeth, and the ties of her swimsuit fell into the water. She felt the bristle of his chin scrape down her spine, and he did the same with the bow at her back.

He let the two silver triangles of her string bikini fall into the water and churn with the bubbles. His hands cupped her naked breasts, and a hard pulse kicked up between her legs, stealing her breath.

He turned her slightly in his arms and took a nipple into his mouth. More heat streaked through her, and she felt as if she were liquefying, becoming one with the water. She was living her recurring dream.

She closed her eyes and then opened them, focused on his hard biceps, the tattoo ringing it and accentuating the muscle.

Quinn changed breasts and slipped his fingers into the front of her swimsuit bottom. She bucked uncontrollably as he touched her there, shocked as orgasm ripped through her without warning.

She automatically went to push his hand away when the intensity undid her, but he ignored that and hit the replay button, forcing her to explode again and tremble with aftershocks.

Quinn made a sound of male satisfaction, a sort of growl with smug overtones, and stripped off her bikini bottom while she lay gasping in his arms. Then he pulled her on top of him so that she straddled him face-to-face and his cock nudged her intimately.

"Do you know how long I've dreamed of doing that again?" he asked. His forehead glistened with water droplets, and his lids were heavy. That touch of smugness on his face was really rather dear—he was happy that he'd made her happy.

"Almost as long as I've dreamed of doing this." He took her almost reverently by the hips and pulled her down onto him, inch by inch, until he was fully sheathed and she could barely breathe. They stayed like that, savoring the joining of their bodies.

Then Quinn made a confession that clearly cost him a fortune in the coin of male ego. "I'm afraid to move," he said. "One stroke and I'm done."

She moved for him, wanting to give him pleasure. Wanting to share the intimacy of seeing him come apart in front of her. She slid her body up his and then took him in again as his hands dug into her hips. His eyes closed. His legs trembled.

"Gwen," he murmured.

She slid up him again and he lost control. He grabbed her and plunged up and into her, convulsing. His breath rasped into her ear; he said her name again hoarsely. His lower body slammed into her almost violently while his arms wrapped around her as if to protect her from himself. He withdrew and then pushed her down onto him again. He bit into her shoulder, hard, as he came.

She felt him everywhere inside her: at her core, in her blood, in her heart and mind. The sheer, primal power of it overwhelmed her, and impossibly, she splintered around him again.

"I'm sorry," he said within moments, taking her face in his hands. "God, I'm sorry—did I hurt you?"

She shook her head.

"You're sure?" His worry was palpable.

She smoothed the wrinkle from his forehead with her thumbs and kissed it. "I'm sure."

After a moment he said gruffly, "I, uh . . . Normally I last longer than that—"

"Shhh. I take it as a compliment." She stroked his jaw, then, gently, the periphery of his swollen eye.

"Well, but that was kind of embarrassing."

A door slammed to the left, and heavy footsteps shuffled along the brick patio behind the sheets on the line. "Not as embarrassing as it's going to be in a second," Gwen said. "Because I have a really bad feeling that my neighbor just came out to take down her laundry."

chapter 17

Gwen woke to the damned dream early the next morning after a mostly sleepless night alone in her bed. Despite his pleas, she'd made Quinn stay on the couch, because clearly she'd lost her mind.

She *hadn't* dreamed making love with Quinn and his shiner in the hot tub. The irony was that they'd remained locked, literally joined at the hip in mortification, as old Mrs. Santos had indeed come out to take down her laundry—bless her heart.

Without her sheets to camouflage them, Gwen and Quinn had had to stay submerged to the neck in the hot tub until they were raisins.

Mrs. S had dropped the sheets into her laundry basket and then plopped herself down in a wrought-iron chair on her patio to have a long conversation with her daughter in New Jersey about whether the daughter should invest in a new kitchen or save the money for her kids' college tuition.

The forty-minute conversation, during which Mrs. S had oh-so-casually looked over into Gwen's yard at least five times, had been an effective mood killer.

Gwen had mentally kicked herself all night for being so stupid. Quinn had been pretty disgusted with himself, too, by the time they emerged. What were they, thirteen? How many times did they have to learn this particular lesson? Last time this had happened, Gwen had started puking up her organs every morning and Quinn had used his savings not on grad school but on a ring.

Now Gwen went straight into the shower, got dressed, slapped on some makeup, and left her hair wet. Carrying her shoes, she tiptoed out to the living room, where Quinn sprawled nude on her couch like a gently snoring Mr. February. The blanket she'd given him had fallen onto the floor.

His face was turned in toward the cushions, hiding his damaged eye, and his breathing was even and deep. He slept peacefully on his side, giving her a spectacular view of his muscular, naked backside. Honestly, it was hard to look away.

She ran her gaze upward, along his spine to the powerful shoulders, honed from a youth working so many summer construction jobs and fixing cars and God knew what else. The back of his neck looked oddly vulnerable compared to the rest of him, the dark blond hair curling slightly where it would meet his collar.

Stupid to bring him back here. Stupid to get into a hot tub with him. Stupid to let him—

A triple flash of heat streaked through her body, ending between her legs.

Well, she'd gone and done it, hadn't she? And someone had needed to babysit him. At least he'd been right—his darn skull was too thick to have sustained much damage. He hadn't had any seizures or gone into a coma during the night.

Gwen resisted the urge to stroke his hair or kiss him. She left Quinn sleeping, tiptoed out, and went to the office.

As she approached the glass doors of ARTemis, she reached out for the brass handle that would open the right one and then stopped dead at the sight of Sheila as the office manager straightened her tight skirt.

It was black with bright red cherries printed on it. Her shoes were black and red and festooned with plump plastic cherries on the toes. Her red top left nothing to the imagination and had two green stems over the bust—very subtle. And naturally, she wore black cat's-eye reading glasses with tiny plastic cherries glued near the hinges.

Gwen recovered and tugged open the door. "Good morning, Sheila."

"It's not a good morning at all."

"I'm sorry to hear that. Why not?"

"We just had a power blink, so I lost a document. And Marty's being cheap again."

Marty was not only Sheila's husband, but the accountant for ARTemis, and his cheapness was legendary. He'd once tried to institute an office policy that limited the amount of toilet paper each employee could use daily. That plan had come to an abrupt end when the entire staff (directed by Sheila) started taking the elevator down to the third floor and using Marty's firm's facilities instead.

"What did he refuse to buy you?"

"A silver fox coat. Full-length. Gorgeous. And on sale, thirty-five percent off, at Bloomie's. I want it to wear to my mother's funeral."

"But . . . your mother is alive and well and living in Brooklyn."

"Yeah, so? You have to seize your opportunities. The coat is on sale *now*. This way I'll have it when the sad day comes."

Gwen wasn't quite sure how to respond to this piece of reasoning, but she nodded noncommittally.

McDougal walked in from the back. He'd obviously heard the exchange. "So, Sheila, have you decided what you're wearing at your own funeral?"

"Couldn't you have stayed in Scotland?" Sheila complained.

McDougal shrugged. "Easy job. Sorry. So, do tell us about your burial outfit."

"A purple St. John suit with a big pink silk rose on the lapel. Pink readers with rhinestones. Still haven't found the right shoes. Why, you planning to off me, McD?"

"I think about it every day, sometimes twice," he said, grinning.

If sarcasm could be bottled and sold like tequila or mescal, McDougal would be the drunken worm at the bottom. Not that Gwen had ever seen McDougal drunk—his hard Scottish head could take on anything. He was the guy whom they sent to the casinos and strip joints to get information out of pickled marks. Dante or Gwen did the upscale events, where McDougal would stick out like Opie at a black Baptist church.

"Any messages, by the way?" he asked Sheila before he left.

"Yeah: You can kiss my left butt cheek, sailor."

"Ooh, don't get me all excited." He turned to Gwen, sweeping his eyes over her apricot linen blouse. "By the way, sweetness, I was about to text you back. No sign of the Borgia mask in Angeline's panty drawer, though she does have a nice collection of paper ones hanging on her bedroom wall."

"Did you look *everywhere*?"

"I did," he said with a lascivious grin. "It wasn't in Angeline, either."

"Ugh! Was that detail really necessary?"

He shrugged. "You're the one who called me McManwhore."

Sheila burst out laughing as he sauntered out.

"And where are you off to today, Miss Thing?" she queried.

"I'm going to track down the Velasquez brothers."

Sheila nodded. "Take your SIG."

"Always."

"And your cell."

"Got it."

"And watch your back."

"Thanks, Mom. I took my vitamins, too."

"I worry about you," Sheila said with a scowl. "You're fragile."

"I'm *what*?"

"Not too much in the brains department, either."

"Sheila!"

"Just saying. Anyone playing with a full deck woulda told Kelso to go to hell on that dog-napping thing. But you . . . you actually flew to Rome and *did* it."

Gwen gaped at her.

"And then," Sheila continued, "you don't take advantage of the fact a famous rock star wants to date you." She shook her head.

Gwen set her jaw and blinked in irritation as she counted to ten. "Sheila, trust me on this: Sid Thresher doesn't look like he used to. He's also borderline insane and heavily medicated."

Sheila spread her hands wide. "So?"

"I have to go," Gwen said, smiling politely. "Please tell me he hasn't called again."

"Four times. He's getting very insistent about prying your cell phone number out of me."

"Sheila, if you give him any of my personal information, I will wring your neck with my oh-so-fragile hands. Are we clear?"

The receptionist pushed her reading glasses up to the bridge of her nose. "It's a crime," she said, shaking her head.

"Why don't *you* date him?" Gwen asked, exasperated.

Sheila drew herself up to her full height. "Oh, I couldn't. Marty would be devastated."

Twenty minutes later, Gwen was playing bumper cars with all the other lunatics on the Miami freeways and headed back to east Hialeah, a part of town that was seedy, to say the least.

The Velasquez brothers lived in a one-story stucco box of a house that was painted an unappetizing flesh color. They had a gravel driveway and a sagging carport held up by metal poles of the same color. The brown plastic garbage cans next to the back door overflowed with debris and fast-food cartons. A mangy cat poked its head out from under a truck and gave her the feline stink-eye.

Gwen parked the Prius at what passed for the curb, which was really just a line of demarcation where grass met tarmac. She made sure that both the SIG Sauer and her compact stun gun were readily available.

She'd worn jeans with the apricot linen top, and a pair of high-heeled sandals with spike heels in case she had to do any instep stomping. They might look delicate, but they were great weapons. Gwen got out of the car and took a deep gulp of air that was unfortunately redolent with the smells of gasoline, spoiled food, and dog poop. She managed not to gag and made her way up the cracked sidewalk to the two cement steps that led to the front door.

Wrought iron reinforced the screen door, which she tugged open in order to knock on the wooden one behind it, which wasn't quite closed. Nobody answered.

"Hello? Anybody home?"

Only silence greeted her. Carlos and Esteban might well still be asleep. Gwen checked her watch. It was almost ten a.m., but they often kept late hours.

She knocked again and the door creaked open a few inches. She peered inside. "Hello? Carlos?"

Then she saw the feet protruding from the hallway. Male feet, bare, dark olive skin tone.

Fear chased adrenaline to her heart, which hurled itself

against her rib cage. Gwen drew the SIG from her bag and used it to push the door open the rest of the way. She listened. What if someone was hiding in the house?

Not too much in the brains department, she heard Sheila say.

Maybe not. But what if the man lying on the floor needed medical attention?

She told herself that it was just as likely that he'd been partying and passed out cold the night before. But . . .

Gwen stepped inside, keeping her gun leveled in front of her and her back to the wall. She walked the short distance to the feet, which she could now see had a bluish tinge. *Dear God.*

One more step and she was looking into the dead eyes of Carlos Velasquez, who still wore the tiny shark earring.

He also wore two neat, clean, horrifying holes in his forehead. Blood had pooled underneath, soaking his shaggy dark hair. His arms lay spread to the sides, palms up. The coppery smell of blood mingled with the undertones of urine and the stale, faintly sweet stench of death.

Shock fluoresced through Gwen's system, and bile shot up her throat. Cold sweat broke out of every pore and she heaved once, then twice. She ran to the door, just making it outside before she threw up ingloriously into the raggedly pruned bushes.

She wiped her mouth on a tissue from her purse, and then fumbled with shaking hands for her cell phone. She'd never had such difficulty dialing three numbers, but finally stabbed them out with her malfunctioning, rubbery index finger.

The emergency dispatcher told her to stay right where she was, so Gwen sat down on the steps and got her breathing under control. She was tempted to call Quinn, God only knew why. But Quinn didn't need to be anywhere near the dead body of Carlos Velasquez.

The cops were already going to interrogate Gwen until her face was blue, and unless she could come up with a heck of a cover story, they were going to wonder why she hadn't shared information about the brothers and the break-in with them.

She dialed the ARTemis office, and as she pressed the last two digits her gaze focused on a tiny shred of khaki cloth that had caught on a finishing nail halfway up the door frame. Someone had attached black rubber weather stripping to keep the heat and humidity out.

"ARTemis, how may I help you?" Sheila's nasal accent made the company name sound like *Ottemis*.

"Sheila, it's Gwen." Feeling as if she were underwater, she reached out and plucked the khaki cloth off the nail, examining the worn cotton.

"What's wrong with you, doll? Your voice sounds funny."

"I just found the body of—"

"Did you say *body*?"

"—Carlos Velasquez."

"As in *dead* body?"

"Yes."

"Oh, my Gawd."

"Exactly. Sheila, is Dante there?"

"Huh-uh. You want McDougal? He's back."

"No—listen, can you page Dante? I need—"

"It's going straight to voice mail. I just tried him for a client. You need someone there with you, doll. I'll send you McDougal."

"I can't deal with McDougal right now!" Gwen said, but Sheila had already hung up.

Gwen threw her phone into her purse and stared a moment longer at the khaki cloth. Something tickled her memory . . . but what? She frowned. She should have left it alone. It could be a clue as to who had done this to Carlos Velasquez. She'd turn it over to the police.

Gwen dropped the fabric into her purse and then put her head into her hands. The cops would be here any minute, and she needed to pull herself together.

Actually, what she needed to do was try to find any link between Carlos, Esteban, and the art world. But if she went inside to search, she'd be further contaminating a crime scene.

What if she went inside and was excruciatingly careful not to touch anything? She got up and stood outside the screen door, gazing at those dead, bluish feet. Gwen shuddered.

There was no dignity in death. The soles of Carlos's feet were dirty, almost black, and stuck to the heel of the left one was a small piece of what looked like tape. Under the middle toes of the right foot was a portion of what might have been a dust bunny. His jeans were frayed at the bottom hem.

Around the corner was the rest of him, soaked in his own body fluids. His belly was visible under his rucked-up T-shirt, and his underwear emerged from the loose, faded jeans. She'd never forget the slack mouth, the dull open eyes. Or the smell.

Gwen's stomach lurched, and she gagged a couple of times outside the screen door. But she had to go in. She had to find a link. She'd steeled herself to do it when a police car came screaming around the corner.

I am such an idiot. Why didn't I look around before I called 911? Now it's too late.

chapter 18

Gwen studiously ignored the repeated ringing of her cell phone, since the caller ID showed Quinn's name and she didn't feel up to explaining her current predicament to him yet. He wasn't likely to be happy.

She waited outside as various investigators and CSI people swarmed in and out of the Velasquez brothers' house and Carlos's body was finally bagged and taken away to the medical examiner for analysis.

The officer in charge was pleasant-looking and harried, with a long, bulbous nose that made him resemble a moose. She privately dubbed him Bullwinkle.

Detective Bullwinkle wanted a statement from her—go figure. He'd already asked where she'd been the evening before, since, judging by preliminary evidence, the crime had been committed then. He'd wanted to know what she was doing there today. He asked to see her gun and the permit she carried for it, but had given it back because it was the wrong caliber to be the murder weapon.

He asked her if she knew where Esteban Velasquez was—there were signs of panicked packing, a suitcase bearing his initials.

Gwen shook her head.

As all this replayed in her mind, the deep rumble of

McDougal's Kawasaki announced his presence before he turned the corner and zoomed up. He brought the bike to a halt across the street, dismounted, and pulled off his helmet, revealing his rumpled ginger hair. He stowed the helmet and crossed the street, his long gait eating up the tarmac.

Gwen was unexpectedly glad to see him, but she resented the fact that Sheila—and all of the ARTemis staff— thought she needed to be babysat. Fragile . . . It pissed her off. "Hi, McD. You didn't have to come over here. Sheila's just being a mother hen."

He raised a pale ginger eyebrow. "The concept of Sheila as a mother is horrifying," he said. Then his blue eyes went dark and serious for once. "Hey. Are you doing okay?"

She gave a wobbly nod.

"Yeah, no." McDougal pulled her onto her feet. Then he gave her a bear hug and patted her back. He smelled of Irish Spring soap and leather and motor oil. "Dead bodies aren't a lot of fun, are they?"

"Not so much," Gwen admitted.

He held her away from him and looked her up and down. "You ever seen one before?"

She shook her head. "Not . . . like that. Only in a funeral home."

McDougal sighed and ran a hand through his hair as his gaze flicked to the house and then back to her. "I'm not sure which is creepier—the satin-lined coffin and the professional makeup job, or the real deal with the unputtied holes still in the forehead. Anyway, let's get you out of here."

Gwen stared at him. "How did you know Velasquez was shot in the forehead?"

McDougal looked into her eyes for a second too long. Then he shrugged. "Friend on the force. He heard it on the police radio."

She nodded slowly, but her legs began to tremble again. How had he *really* known? His explanation seemed a little too glib. She sat back down on the porch steps. "I don't think they'll let me leave yet. They want to talk to me some more."

"You're not a suspect, surely?"

"I don't think so." God, was she? No, it wasn't possible. She had an alibi. She'd been in her house, then in the hot tub with Quinn. Old Mrs. Santos had seen them and would back up her statement.

"Gwen, it's eighty-five degrees in the shade and you're shivering. I think you're in shock."

"I'm fine. Really."

"Hang on a sec." McDougal crossed the street to his Kawasaki and unlocked a small storage compartment at the rear of the bike. He pulled out a rolled-up khaki jacket and stuffed it under his arm while he relocked the compartment.

Khaki jacket. *Oh, God.* Gwen shivered again. She was leaping to ridiculous conclusions. He was probably right and she was in shock.

McDougal couldn't have blown two holes through an unarmed Carlos Velasquez. What motive would he have to do such a thing? It didn't make sense.

McD strode across the street and rounded the back of the cruiser. He shook out the khaki jacket—she saw no visible rips in it—and leaned in to put it around her shoulders.

Gwen gave an inward sigh of relief, only to choke on it when Bullwinkle came out of the house and down the steps again.

"Sir, I'm Eric McDougal with ARTemis. I'd like to take Ms. Davies home now, if you're through questioning her."

Bullwinkle's lips formed a somewhat goofy, disarming smile, but no humor reached his eyes. "We're not quite through with her, Mr. McDougal. And as long as you're here, we may as well ask you some questions, too."

"In regard to what, sir?"

"In regard to that damn peculiar business that employs you two. ARTemis. Hunting down stolen art. You're aware that there's an FBI task force on that, aren't you? And a central database of missing art?"

"Yes, sir." Neither she nor McDougal made any reference to the fact that the Nerd Corps often hacked files they weren't supposed to have access to.

"Then why don't you guys back off and let us and the feds do our jobs?"

McDougal looked him right in the eye. "Because, with all due respect, sir, sometimes the owners and the insurers want things handled quietly. Not to mention that, just like you in the property crimes unit, the FBI task force is overwhelmed with cases."

Bullwinkle's large nose twitched. He drew up his upper lip, exposing his teeth. Then he sneezed forcefully, as if he were allergic to both Gwen and McDougal.

"Bless you," they said in unison.

The detective pulled out a pocket hankie and blew his nose, never taking his eyes off them. "You mind if we search your car, Ms. Davies?"

She blinked at the change in subject. "Go right ahead. I have nothing to hide."

He nodded and signaled to a uniformed officer, who gave the body of the Prius a perfunctory search. He paused longer when he looked at the driver's side floor mat. Frowning, he beckoned to Bullwinkle, who joined him. The uniformed officer spoke into a radio, and a slight man in latex gloves came out with a box.

Gwen and McDougal watched as he took a swab of something.

"What's he got?" Eric asked her.

"I don't know." Still cold, she shoved her arms into the sleeves of his jacket and they waited.

Gwen insisted that she was able to drive. McDougal insisted that she was not. Bullwinkle asked if there was any reason that she'd have blood in her Prius.

Blood? "No," Gwen said blankly.

Then Bullwinkle solved the dispute between her and Eric by giving Gwen a ride down to the Miami-Dade police headquarters to fingerprint her and get a DNA sample.

Eric looked worried as they pulled away in the squad car, but she couldn't ignore her doubt. Had he been at the Velasquez brothers' home before she had? Was he a murderer? Had he set her up?

He had access to her fingerprints—and lip prints, for that matter—just by virtue of being an office mate. He could have taken a discarded coffee cup and pulled prints from that. What if he'd planted them inside the house? What about her DNA?

Gwen's stomach churned acid. Why would McDougal have gone to the house, though? What motive would he have had? Was he trying to horn in on her case?

Five-point-four million dollars, the value of the mask, was a lot of money, and the ten percent commission on it was more than five hundred thousand dollars. McDougal made great money, but he had expensive sporting tastes. He'd been talking a lot about buying a boat. He'd been dating Angeline Le Fevre, who was tops on Gwen's list of suspects.

But he couldn't hate Gwen that much—not enough to let her go to jail for a crime she didn't commit. She couldn't reconcile the idea with what she knew of him. People did do desperate things to save their own skins, though. . . .

"You're awfully quiet back there, Ms. Davies," said Bullwinkle from the front of the Crown Vic.

She met his gaze in the rearview mirror and nodded. "Yes. I'm not in the habit of stumbling over dead bodies."

"I have to wonder, ma'am, if that's Carlos Velasquez's blood in your car. Did you shoot him last night, throw the gun under the floor mat, and go dispose of it, not realizing that it would leave trace evidence?"

"No, Detective. I was in my hot tub last night, as I told you. And if I had done such a thing, why would I come back to the house this morning and pretend to discover the body?"

"Makes you look innocent."

Gwen sighed. "Your theory is wrong. I don't even have a motive."

"I'd say it's enough motive that you recovered a fake mask from the Velasquez brothers. You want the real one. You went to the house to question them, according to your statement this morning. Carlos wouldn't tell you what they did with it, so you lost your temper and shot him."

"No. That's ridiculous. I don't go around shooting people, Detective. You won't find any gunpowder residue on my hands."

"Scrubbed them real good last night, did you?"

"No! Look, if you continue to question me like this, I'll have to request an attorney."

Bullwinkle didn't answer, just sneezed again. She guessed he was allergic to defense attorneys, too.

"Bless you," she said again.

He nodded.

She thought about redirecting him toward McDougal, but frankly she wanted to grill Eric first. Gwen peeled off his jacket even though she was still cold.

Bullwinkle hit the brake at a stoplight, and Gwen absently watched a too-skinny woman in brown spike-heeled boots cross in front of the car. She had a snakeskin-patterned bag slung over her left shoulder and a briefcase in her right hand.

Wait. Snakeskin.

"Detective, I can tell you where the blood came from," Gwen said, almost smacking herself in the forehead. "I shot a very large python a few days ago."

Bullwinkle's head swiveled. He looked her up and down, from the orange streaks in her hair to her rosy apricot-painted toenails in their four-inch, spike-heeled sandals. "You shot a what?"

"A python. I think."

Bullwinkle looked as if he thought that was a good one. "You think you shot it, or you think it was a python?"

"I definitely shot it. I believe it was a python."

Bullwinkle digested this for a moment. "Right. So you shot a snake. And . . . stuffed it into your Prius?"

"No, of course not. But some blood spatter could have been transferred from my shoes to the floor mat."

The light had changed, and a horn blared from the car behind them. Only in Miami would somebody honk at a cop.

Bullwinkle glared into the rearview mirror but stepped on the gas. "Ms. Davies, this story is colorful, to say the least."

"I'm not lying."

"Where is this python now?"

"Probably still in the warehouse where I shot it."

Bullwinkle pulled a hand over his face, lingering at his mouth. Okay, so maybe her story did sound a little far-fetched, but she was tired of people not taking her seriously. Sheila thought she was fragile; McDougal thought she was dumb enough that he could set her up; Quinn still thought of her as a spoiled little princess. . . . Enough already.

"I'll need the address of this warehouse, Ms. Davies," said the detective.

"Fine," she muttered.

The Miami-Dade police station was a massive concrete block. Inside it smelled of commercial-grade cherry disinfectant, stale, burned coffee, and traces of BO. They went upstairs to a bare-bones room with light gray cubicles and walls and industrial metal desks with faux-wood tops.

While the officers did some paperwork, Gwen balled up McDougal's jacket and mashed it into her Jimmy Choo handbag.

Soon one of the officers took each of her fingers and rolled them on a little electronic pad.

She gave Bullwinkle the address of the warehouse.

He wrote it down. "All right, for the moment you're free to go. But don't take any sudden trips abroad, Ms. Davies."

Darn. And here I'd planned to have lunch in Paris on Sunday.

"You have someone who can pick you up? This, ah, Eric McDougal, perhaps?"

Gwen just nodded. "Yes, I'll find a ride. When will I get my car back?" It had been impounded as possible evidence.

"When we're through processing it. That's all I can tell you."

"I see. Thank you." Gwen hitched her bag over her shoulder and headed for the door, cell phone in hand. She dialed Quinn's cell phone number with her thumb and braced herself for an explosion of angry testosterone.

chapter 19

"Why are you at the police station?" Quinn asked. He listened as Gwen calmly explained that she'd discovered Carlos's body. With each word, his blood pressure went up a notch.

"Let me get this straight. You left me sleeping in your home and you went to east Hialeah *alone*? To talk to known burglars and drug dealers?"

"Yes."

Quinn absorbed this while his brain supplied a movie reel of graphic images as a backdrop. Gwen bruised, bleeding, assaulted, raped. Gwen strangled by these creeps. Gwen tossed into the trunk of a car and disposed of in the open ocean.

"Are you crazy?" he shouted, unable to help himself. "They should put you behind bars for your own safety."

"Listen, Quinn. For one thing, I really do know how to kill a man with a pen. Keep insulting me and I'll show you sometime. For another, it's not like I'm some Gothic heroine descending into a crypt at midnight in my skimpy nightie. I went in broad daylight, armed with a gun, a knife, a metal nail file, two spike heels, a cell phone, and a healthy working knowledge of tae kwon do."

"You took an unacceptable risk!"

"Matter of opinion."

"You sneaked out and left me here deliberately."

"Okay, fine. Guilty as charged. But I've found that a little lipstick and a lot of cleavage work wonders in this job, and you would have gotten in the way of—"

He flat-out snarled at that. "Jesus, Gwen, so leave me in the car! What happened to working together? What happened to—"

"Look, can you spare me the lecture?"

"I've never met anyone who needs a lecture more than you."

"No, what I need is a ride," she told him. "Can you just come get me?"

Silence. "Yes. If only to shake you until your teeth rattle. I'll have to get a cab to your office parking garage. But I'll be there as soon as I can."

"Thank you." Her voice sounded calm. Too calm. As if she'd had a few too many Xanax.

"Gwen, are you okay?"

She hesitated. "Something bad happened today."

"Something worse than finding a dead body and being hauled off by the police?"

"Yes. I'll tell you when you get here. I don't want to talk inside the station."

"All right. Gwen, everything's going to be fine. I promise."

She said nothing.

"Gwen?"

"Yes, I heard you. See you in a few."

That eerie calm weirded him out. "I'm on my way."

He vaulted into his clothes and called a Yellow Cab, spurred on by an image of Gwen standing forlorn in the big Miami-Dade police building, whacked out on Xanax or Valium because she'd been traumatized today.

The cab arrived in record time only because he'd promised a double fare. It ferried him to the Brickell parking garage and his Mercedes coupe.

Minutes later he pulled up outside the Miami-Dade police station. Gwen stood in the lobby, staring out at the traffic. She didn't see him at first.

She had a bag bigger than herself on her shoulder and she was slim as a mannequin, looking as if one good blast of air-conditioning could blow her right off those skyscraper heels. Every protective instinct he possessed surged to the surface and pushed his anger out of the way.

He opened his door and got out. He was halfway to the doors when she noticed him and emerged from the building, walking as if she were underwater. Something was very wrong, but she was doing her damnedest not to show it.

"Hey, Quinn." She gave him a lopsided smile. "Thanks for coming to get me."

He wrapped his arms around her, but instead of melding into him, she stood stiffly and patted his back in a weird, mechanized sort of way. Delayed shock? Drugs? He took her shoulders and held her at arm's length.

"How are you doing?" He peered at her pupils, but they weren't dilated.

"I've been better. How's your eye?"

It throbbed. He couldn't see out of it. Strangers stared at him with pursed lips. He waved a hand dismissively and opened the passenger-side door of the coupe, shepherding her in, settling her onto the cushioned leather seat. "What happened?"

"Jeweler first," Gwen said. "Talk later."

"Jeweler? Don't you want to—"

"No, I don't. We lost too much time yesterday."

"All right. Which jeweler? What's the address?"

"Her name is Trudie Hayward. She has a studio inside a gallery in Coral Gables."

"Yeah, I know it. Hayward Gallery, right? Contemporary American art and crafts?"

Gwen nodded.

"I think I got dragged to an opening there once."

Trudie Hayward was a lively blonde with perfect skin and a taste for kimonos and Converse high-tops. Quinn couldn't guess her age. She wore glasses of a subtle design and silver jewelry as far from subtle as possible. Her long necklace started in a spiral, became a square in the next link, only to transform next into an oval, a shield shape, and so on. The necklace was dotted with semiprecious gems and also sported some gold layered over the silver.

Quinn shook Trudie's hand, mesmerized by the necklace and surprised that it didn't look like an opera-length identity crisis. It worked, somehow. He didn't *know* how, but it worked. It was hip; it was cool; he could imagine it on some L.A. starlet.

Trudie exclaimed over Quinn's eye.

"Ran into a door," he said.

Gwen exclaimed over Trudie's earrings, which were asymmetrical and complemented the necklace. One was longer and one had a doodle of some kind on it, a curly silver thing that swung back and forth. He'd never seen jewelry like this. He liked it enormously.

"Trudie went to the same school as my mother," Gwen told him. "She was several years behind her, but Mummy knew of her because she's made quite a reputation for herself."

Trudie grinned and slipped her hands into the pockets of her hot-pink kimono. "What can I say—I'm notorious. Well, come on back and show me what you've got."

They followed her into a suite of rooms at the far end of the gallery. One was clearly a business office and the other was a studio full of strange machinery, long unfinished wood tables, unassembled parts of jewelry, piles of books, trays of stones, a huge safe, and various odds and ends. In short, it was a colorful creative chaos.

Trudie seemed to do most of her work at a scarred drawing table lit by a powerful lamp. Next to it was what looked like an acetylene torch. Neighboring that stood a very large tree stump ringed by various tools.

Quinn eyed the stump and Trudie laughed. "My other desk," she said. "I beat the hell out of metals there." She gestured to a couple of stools and sat down in a rolling chair.

Gwen set her handbag on one of the long tables and rooted around in it. She pulled out a stack of enlarged prints made from the photos taken with her cell phone.

Trudie whistled as she looked through them. "Very nice work."

Gwen dug into a different pocket of her purse and produced a folded Kleenex. "Trudie, I'm positive the mask isn't solid. I pulled this out of one of the seams." She carefully opened the tissue, revealing the tiny gray curl of metal. "It smells kind of like asphalt."

"Looks like lead. You said the original mask is of solid gold? The person who copied it may have layered gold over lead to approximate the weight of the original. Lead tends to smell like asphalt, too—sweeter, though."

Gwen nodded.

Trudie put on a visual device with big lenses and elastic that wrapped around her head. She turned on the lamp at her drawing table and inspected the little metal shaving. "Yes, it's lead."

She picked up the photos again and continued to look at them under the light.

"*Very* good work. Just a little careless at that one seam. Mmmm-hmmm. This looks like thirty-gauge gold, layered over the lead. The stones are probably colored cubic zirconia. More interesting is the fact that this mask has been laser welded. You can tell by the seams."

Quinn looked askance at Gwen, who lifted her shoulders in a shrug.

"And what have we here? Looks like the beginnings of a signature, which has then been scratched out. But the first letter is a B. That I can tell you for sure."

Trudie looked for a few more seconds and then set the photos down. She took off the strange apparatus on her head.

"So my guess is that this was made by a jeweler who not only knows the very difficult repoussé technique used here, but owns a laser welder."

Trudie elaborated after seeing their blank looks. "A laser welder costs about twenty-six thousand dollars. It's not a tool that a lot of jewelers can afford. And it's only been around for the last ten or twelve years, which tells you that the mask has been made fairly recently."

"And . . . repoussé? Is that what you said? What's that, exactly?"

"It's a very difficult process, and a time-consuming one, in which metal is bulged, or hammered from the back. Basically a sheet of metal is annealed, or heated with a torch to soften and compress the molecular structure. The metal is then laid into what's called a pitch bowl and hammered in. It's bulged from the front, and then from the back. It takes a long time and an expert hand to do this." Trudie drummed her fingers thoughtfully on her tilted drawing table.

"The art of repoussé is ancient and dates back to antiquity. Very few people can do it competently, much less beautifully."

Gwen nodded. "Can you give us a ballpark figure of how many?"

"I'd say only three or four hundred people in the world."

"And out of those, how many do you think might have a laser welder?"

"Maybe a hundred. And it's very likely that your mystery jeweler belongs to the Worshipful Company of Goldsmiths."

"The what?"

Trudie laughed. "I know, it sounds like a cult. It's basically the goldsmith's guild in England. I'm a member. Every piece of gold jewelry made in the U.K. has to be tested in one of five assay offices. It's assayed and hallmarked—or crushed in a hydraulic press if it's not as pure as it's purported to be."

Quinn said, "And what does assaying gold involve?"

"A groove is filed on the piece with a triangular file," Trudie explained. "Then acid—nitric acid or aqua regia—is dropped into the groove. The results are compared to a touchstone to see if the color matches. If it doesn't, the jeweler is in big trouble and the piece is destroyed."

"Okay," Gwen said. "So in order to find the artist behind this mask, we look for a member of this international goldsmith's guild who knows the repoussé technique, owns a laser welder, and has a name starting with the letter B."

"Exactly," Trudie said. "I can make some inquiries for you, if you'd like."

Gwen shook her head, thinking of the dead Carlos. "I think you'd better let us make the inquiries. But thank you."

"All righty, then."

"Well. Thank you for your help. You're a talented woman," Quinn told Trudie.

"I like him," Trudie said to Gwen. "Can I have him when you're done?"

Gwen flushed. "He's . . . not mine."

Quinn glared at her.

Trudie snapped her fingers. "Dang. I forgot for a second

that I'm married. Sorry, stud; it won't work out. You don't want to get sued for loss of consortium."

Quinn said to Gwen, "Not yours? What was that in the hot tub?"

Trudie chuckled. "Sounds divine. Well, kids, I have to get back to work. I'm creating a very special necklace—for Gloria Estefan. And unfortunately, her stylist wants it yesterday, so it's back to the tree stump for me. Let me know if there's anything else I can help you with, okay?"

They thanked her again warmly, and Gwen said she'd be back to shop.

"Citrine and smoky topaz," Trudie said.

"Excuse me?"

"You'd look stunning in a combination of citrine and smoky topaz. Go away and call me in a couple of days. I'll have a design."

Gwen smiled. "Okay. It's a deal. Well, as long as whatever it is doesn't cost a million dollars."

"Nah. I never gouge people. I should . . . but I can't." Trudie escorted them to the studio door, analyzing Gwen's long, graceful neck. "Definitely some gold leaf and an ornate clasp in the back. Something dangling from the nape . . . Where's my notebook?" She fumbled in the pockets of her kimono as the door shut behind them.

chapter 20

Gwen walked out of the Hayward Gallery deep in thought, not focusing on where they'd left the car. She turned left. Quinn took her arm and steered her in the opposite direction. Even on this late January day the sun exercised brutality, shooting at them from the windows of buildings and from every other reflective surface.

The air inside the coupe stifled her breath and immediately dampened the fabric of her blouse. Gwen, knowing it was sacrilegious to feel this way in paradise, prayed for just a couple of days in the forties, sheltered by a thick bank of clouds. What she wouldn't give right now to be able to snuggle into a coat, wrap herself in a scarf.

"So what do you want to do next?" Quinn asked, as he started the car's engine. With clean efficiency, he maneuvered them out of their parking spot in two turns of the wheel.

Enlist the Nerd Corps' help in tracking down this jeweler.

But suddenly Gwen couldn't get the image of Carlos Velasquez's dead bluish feet out of her mind, however hard she tried to substitute the awful picture for the beautiful, unusual pieces in Trudie's gallery.

She tried to replace the feet with a colorful, wild,

abstract coil of glass that reminded her of flame dipped in watercolors. She focused on a hammered silver necklace made of different-size triangles . . . an oil painting of a peaceful forest glen, the trees full of woodland creatures that seemed to look right back at the viewer.

And still she saw Velasquez's feet, dirty on the bottom, a jagged edge on one of the big toenails, as if he'd caught it on something. Those vulnerable, naked feet on such a big, strapping, frankly menacing kid.

Gwen gasped for air once, then twice.

Quinn's head turned sharply. "You okay?"

A man, not a kid. One who knew the business end of a gun himself, and had a rap sheet longer than Quinn's belt. A man who had committed armed robbery. Why did his death affect her so much? He was a common criminal— and yet he'd deserved more dignity than that . . . shot and left to lie rotting in his own fluids.

She gasped for air again, and Quinn hit the button that would lower the window. Then he wrenched the car through two lanes of angry traffic to pull it over at the curb and slam it into park.

"Gwen?"

She gasped again and turned her head toward him, mute. To her vague surprise, her eyes were dry, as if tears were too insignificant to express the horror that had taken over her body.

"Gwen, my God. Breathe," he said urgently.

How could he be so close, his hands on her shoulders, and yet seem so far away? She felt completely cut off from what was happening, as if she were an observer hovering over the car. She gasped again.

"Is something lodged in your throat?"

She shook her head.

Quinn reached across her, unbuckled her safety belt,

and hit the button that would move her seat back. "Put your head down, between your knees," he ordered.

She did.

"Let the air out of your lungs. Force it out, Gwen. Then a slow breath in. Slow. *Slow.*"

How could it be so hard to regulate her own respiratory system?

"And out," Quinn said. "In . . . and out. In . . ."

Quinn had always tried to tell her what to do. Now he was telling her how to breathe, as if she were a toddler or a Barbie doll. While she was grateful along with being annoyed, the very idea of it struck her as silly. No, downright funny. A mad, hysterical giggle spiraled within her, circled her stomach, and then shot upward, popping into laughter in her throat.

Gwen felt crazy as she struggled for breath and battled the awful giggles at the same time. And still she thought about Carlos Velasquez's dead blue feet. Not funny. Not funny at all.

"Gwen, Jesus. Gwen!" Quinn didn't sound so calm anymore. "Listen to me. Force that air out of your lungs. Then breathe in through your nose. Close your mouth. Slow down."

She fought to do it.

So this is what people feel like when they go insane.

"And out through your mouth. In through your nose . . ."

She reversed the order, like an idiot.

"Focus. Come on, sweetheart. . . ."

Gradually, she got control over herself, but her embarrassment grew.

"Good." Quinn's voice was still calm, and when she stole a look at him, he didn't appear disgusted or as if he thought she needed to be carted away to a white padded cell.

Finally quiet, she remained slumped over her own knees.

"Hey," he said, stroking her back and rubbing between her shoulder blades. "What was that all about, hmmmm?"

"His feet," she whispered. "I can't get Velasquez's dead feet out of my mind. It's what I saw first. I'll never forget them. Not ever."

"Oh, honey."

"I know it sounds insane. I'm sorry I lost it like that."

He pulled her into his arms. "You don't sound crazy, and there's no need to apologize. Okay? You found a body today. Most people don't react well to things like that."

"I'm supposed to be tougher than this," she said with a shaky laugh.

"You are tough. You called the cops; then you got grilled by them. You went straight to interview a jeweler with no visible sign of what you'd been through. And, hey, you've been under a little stress lately." Quinn kissed her forehead. "Plus you've got your damned ex harassing you. It's enough to make anyone go hysterical."

"I wasn't hysterical," Gwen said.

He lifted an eyebrow. "Okay, babe, whatever you say."

She scooted back over into her seat and ran a hand through her hair while Quinn started the car and began to drive in the opposite direction from her house.

"Where are we going?"

"My place," he said in a tone that would tolerate no argument.

She was too tired to argue anyway.

You could take the boy out of Oklahoma, but you couldn't take Oklahoma out of the boy. Quinn's condo on South Beach was full of tan and tobacco-colored leather, and a big painting of wild mustangs hung on the wall over the couch. It wasn't strictly Gwen's style, but it was a good piece that complemented the rugged Western look of the furniture. On a pedestal between the couch and an oversize leather chair stood a bronze of a bull. It, too, was rough-hewn and yet brilliantly done, with perfect proportions. She guessed that he'd paid a decent sum for both pieces.

An old trunk took the place of a coffee table. The combined effect was that of a comfortable, luxurious lodge—even if its setting in Miami was a little incongruous. She half expected to see a massive stone fireplace somewhere, and snowcapped mountains outside the floor-to-ceiling windows.

But the familiar stretch of sandy beach framed the surging Atlantic, which disappeared into the horizon.

"Nice place," Gwen said.

"Thanks." He was clearly proud of it. "Make yourself at home."

"Can I look around?"

"Sure. I'll be back in a minute," he said, walking toward the kitchen.

Gwen wandered down a tiled hallway, which would have looked better with wide oak plank flooring, but then, this was Miami and not Colorado. Quinn had few family photos, but he'd hung a framed shot of his mother that must have been taken when she was in high school, along with one of a great-uncle wearing overalls in his machine shop. There were none of friends or girlfriends.

His grandfather was conspicuously absent, too, but that didn't surprise her. She'd heard the stories. And Quinn had never known his father. It made her sad, though, that he didn't share his life with more people. What did he do in his spare time? Did he have any?

Gwen came to a room that held bookshelves and a desk—obviously Quinn's office. On the wall over the desk was a painting of a storm raging over a field, trees bending almost double and a tornado threatening in the background.

It was the sheer aggression in the piece that riveted her, a combination of brushstroke and subject matter and color. The rainstorm rushed at her, sucked her in, almost had her believing that she could feel the angry wind in her face.

Quinn had chosen very high-quality artwork for his home, despite his lack of fine-arts education. Gwen kept walking down the hall. On her right was a bathroom done in a lot of blue-gray marble with brushed-nickel accents and walls the palest, softest silver. Very masculine.

And then on the left again, Quinn's bedroom. Gwen laughed in delight as she looked in. There on the wall over the headboard of his bed was mounted the front grille and headlights of a car, and not just any car. She remembered his favorite: the '67 Pontiac GTO. On the adjacent wall the side of the car had been painted, a real driver's-side door mounted in the appropriate place. This was a sign of the old Quinn, the one she used to know.

"You like it?" His voice came from behind her, along with the subtle tinkle of ice in a heavy glass.

She turned with a smile. "I love it. Your designer did a great job."

He handed her a drink. "The designer thanks you," he said, taking a bow.

"You did this?"

Quinn nodded. "Not like I knew anyone when I moved to Miami," he said, shrugging. "I had to occupy my evenings and weekends somehow—when I wasn't working, that is."

"I'm impressed. I really am," Gwen said. But she saw little else of personal significance in the room. Oh, there were three Rolexes, a Cartier tank watch, and a high-end Movado in a silk-lined case, but no photos at all.

"Ms. Interior Designer is impressed? That's something."

"I wouldn't change a thing." Furniture-wise, she wouldn't.

Quinn's eyes seemed to deepen as they considered her. He reached out and brushed his thumbs gently under her eyes, as if to erase the dark shadows she knew were there. "Me, either," he said.

A lump rose in her throat, and the shaky feeling she'd had in the car threatened to return. Gwen moved away and made an innocuous comment about his choice of reading material on the oak nightstand: *Time, Newsweek*, a biography of Warren Buffett, and a Tim Dorsey novel. He still slept on the right side of the bed, and the nightly glass of water and his antacids stood like sentries next to a digital clock.

Quinn's simple platform bed looked all too inviting, made up with soft blue cotton sheets and a navy spread. The pillows looked soft and she wanted nothing more than to sink her head into one and crawl under the covers for about twenty-four hours.

"Go ahead," he said. How did he read her mind?

The bed called to her, and she thought of Quinn sprawling naked on it, Quinn holding her next to his bare skin and making her forget everything she'd seen today and all that she still needed to do.

Such a bad idea.

An image of them locked together in the heat of the hot tub didn't help. The fullness of Quinn buried in her body and the way he took ownership of her senses.

Gwen took three quick steps backward and slipped out of his bedroom. She took a sip of her drink on her way back out to his living room. "Caipiroska," she said, unable to repress a smile. He'd remembered her favorite Brazilian drink. "Quinn, I do not need to be drinking vodka in the middle of the afternoon."

He checked his watch. "Sun's on the run, honey. It's

four fifty-nine p.m., so you're legitimate in one minute, and you need to relax. You've gone from hyperventilating to so tense you're practically in rigor mortis." He winced. "Sorry."

Her mind swept back to Velasquez's body and she shuddered.

"Boy, do I have a talent for saying the wrong thing. Gwen, c'mere." He walked to the leather sofa and sat down, patting the spot next to him.

Gwen took another sip of the drink and just looked at him. The vodka spread warmth inside her belly and made her extremities seem suddenly light. Slowly, she walked to the couch.

"Christ." Quinn looked mildly exasperated. "I'm not going to bite you."

She sat down and he took her drink, setting it on the floor. He moved to the edge of the couch and turned her slightly, beginning his magic on the muscles of her neck and shoulders.

"This is exactly how we got into trouble the other night," she murmured.

"I'm not—"

"I know." The heat, the skill, the tenderness, and the strength of his hands took over, and she let her head fall forward, relaxing in spite of herself.

Outside she could hear the surf on the beach and birds calling. She inhaled the leather of the sofa and the male scent of Quinn. No cologne or aftershave today, just clean skin and a fresh white shirt rolled to the elbows.

She wasn't drunk on two sips of vodka. She wasn't freaking out anymore. But nevertheless her emotions took charge. She'd taken this job to make her feel alive . . . and it had brought her into contact with the dead. Now she'd gone somewhere inside herself emotionally and she desperately needed to break out again.

Without thinking too hard about it, Gwen lifted the hem of her linen shirt. Behind her she heard Quinn suck in a breath and his hands dropped from her shoulders. With very deliberate movements, she pulled the shirt over her head.

chapter 21

Quinn didn't know how to respond as Gwen whipped off her shirt and then unhooked her bra. She clearly wanted more than a back rub from him at this point, but would he be taking advantage of her? She'd discovered a dead body that morning, and she'd had a clear physical and emotional reaction to it just half an hour ago—this didn't seem right.

But in the few seconds it took him to process those thoughts, Gwen had stripped completely naked and she'd now undone his fly. He was pretty familiar with his cock, and he couldn't say it had much of a conscience.

"Gwen—"

She sealed his mouth with hers and straddled his knees, her breasts brushing his shirt as she fumbled in his back pocket.

Dimly he realized that she was pulling out his wallet, but by then he had his hands all over her and the primitive side of him took over. How did he say no when her nipples were hardening against his palms? How did he say no when his fingers traced the satiny skin of her smooth, fine ass?

Hell, who was he kidding—he didn't want to say no at all. He'd never been able to resist Gwen. He'd wanted her from the moment he'd first seen her lush but just-a-little-prissy mouth under that silver mask in Brazil. Maybe it was that touch of prissiness that got to him. He didn't know.

He broke free of her mouth and looked down her cleavage to the shadowy apex of her thighs, which teased him, the flesh softly brushing against him, sliding up and down his cock. Nothing prissy about that.

Those dark, beckoning, forbidden crevices on a woman were the stuff of fantasies. On her specifically, they were crazy-making. All he wanted was to get inside, into the hot, black oblivion where sanity and identity were lost.

Her hands wrapped around him, rolling a condom down his length. And then without warning she sank onto him in a single, almost brutal thrust. Quinn's head fell back with the shock, the intense pleasure of it as she rode him.

Who was this new Gwen who took over, took *him*, without permission, really, without so much as a word?

Was she making love to him, or just releasing tension?

Her head was thrown back, her eyes closed, her face beautiful and yet desperate.

He struggled with what he felt. On the one hand it was erotic as hell, every man's fantasy. No cuddling, no foreplay, no big tease. And on the other he felt used, even though there were no complaints down there from a certain part of him.

He understood that she needed this and that he could give it to her. And yet he felt left out and forgotten. She was somewhere else entirely. And possibly *with* someone else. Who?

Gwen's body tensed and arched as she took him. He could tell it was a matter of seconds before she found her release. Her lovely face was flushed, her nipples ripe, her stomach muscles clenched. Soft moans came from her mouth.

Why wouldn't she open her eyes and see that he was

here? He found himself almost praying for that as he met
her thrust for thrust and his own tension built until it was
unbearable.

Quinn almost picked her up and took over, but he was
half mesmerized by what was happening. She started to
tremble; her breathing came faster and more shallow. Her
mouth opened wider and she bit down on her lip, then released it with a cry. He felt every tremor as she shattered into
orgasm around him. It was beautiful—she was beautiful.

God damn it.

Quinn hated it, but couldn't hate her, even as his body
betrayed him and wrung him dry. Hell, he hadn't taken advantage of her. She'd taken advantage of *him.*

And he still couldn't help but wonder if she'd been
thinking of another man. The thought made him crazy.
Caveman crazy.

Gwen fell forward against Quinn's chest without opening her eyes. She loved the smell of him, the slight muski-
ness, and the tinge of salt on his skin. Still impaled, she
rubbed her cheek against the soft mat of dark blond hair
and listened to his rapid heartbeat and suppressed panting.

His big hands were wrapped around her hips, and she
found herself not wanting to move ever again. It was too
good: the heat, the satiety, the joining.

But Quinn lifted her off of him without a word and got
up to dispose of the condom. She heard water flowing in
the powder room, and when he came back in he was wiping his hands on a fingertip towel. "Feel better?" he asked,
his eyes enigmatically sweeping her from head to toe.

"What? What do you mean by that?" The heat of a mor-
tifying flush started at her chest and seeped upward. With
two words he'd made her feel shameful.

"You used me to get off," Quinn said flatly. "Where
were you?"

She felt as if a fastball had hit her right in the diaphragm. She tried to suck in some air. "I . . ."

He sat down on the couch and folded his arms, his stare unwavering.

"Quinn," she said, closing her eyes again. "Please don't do this."

"Do what?"

She didn't answer for a long moment. Finally she said, "See. Don't . . . please don't . . . see through me right now."

"Where were you?" he asked again. "Who were you with in your mind?"

"Don't." She turned, then picked up her clothes from the floor.

"Who were you with?"

"*You!*" she burst out.

He shook his head, implacable. "No, you weren't."

"You're right," she said. "And you're also wrong." *Oh, God.* He'd been so sweet earlier. She really didn't want to explain. It would only hurt him.

But he wasn't letting her off the hook.

"Fine. You want to know where I was? I was with you *fifteen years ago*. Not you now. Not this corporate guy who tells me how much he's worth financially and owns more luxury watches than he's got arms and drives the same car as my father and . . ." She shook her head, feeling like a complete bitch.

Quinn's mouth had dropped open. He looked as if she'd run him through with a sword.

"I told you not to push it," she said miserably. "Because I didn't think you'd like the answer." She picked up her drink from the floor and took a huge swallow of it. Then she retreated, naked, down the tiled hall to the bathroom.

Gwen threw her clothes down in a heap and turned on the shower. While she waited for the water to get hot, she drained the rest of the Caipiroska and set the glass down with a snap.

She eyed herself in the mirror and didn't know whether to laugh or cry at the wink of her diamond belly ring. But she was finished with tears.

She needed to toughen up or she'd never make it in this job. To be a rookie was one thing; to be a weenie was another. So she'd seen her first dead body. Big deal.

So she'd just slept with her ex-husband. Big deal. Happened all the time to the best women; it didn't need to mean anything. Natural to feel an old attraction . . .

Gwen stepped into the shower and made free with the soap, trying not to get her hair wet. It wasn't working, so she finally just stood under the spray, let it soak her head, and scrubbed all the makeup off her face, too.

She wasn't sure how to react to the knock from outside. "Yes?"

Quinn opened the door and stuck his head in. "May I join you?"

She stared at him through the pane of clear glass that separated them.

He stared back.

"Why?"

"Because we need to get to the bottom of some things."

He opened a cabinet and pulled out two blue towels, which he stacked on the marble vanity. Then he climbed into the shower and they looked at each other a little warily.

"Soap?" Gwen offered.

He took it with a nod and dropped his gaze as he lathered. His mouth twisted. "I feel . . . like an ass. You're telling me that I was out there getting impossibly jealous— crazy, pickle green, ball-racking fuckin' jealous—of *myself*, fifteen years ago?"

"Yes." She could hardly look at him.

"And you're also telling me that..." He swallowed. "You're telling me that you don't like the man I've become." His jaw worked. "Gwen... I don't know why it matters to me what you think, but... what have I done wrong? Everything I set out to do, I've done. I've worked my ass off. I've made good. I've made better than good! How many guys my age become CEOs of multimillion-dollar companies? So why, *why* do you find me so lacking?" He hit the shower wall with his fist, and she jumped. "What do I have to do to be good enough for you?"

Finished with tears? She started to cry. "Quinn, you were always good enough. You were the best." She reached out and cupped his face in her hands.

"Then why the hell did you leave? Huh?" Raw emotion made his voice gravelly.

"My leaving... it had nothing to do with whether you were good enough. It had to do with—among other things—why you were with me."

"Explain, Gwen. Once and for all, tell me what you mean!" Frustration turned his voice rough.

"I was a trophy to you, Quinn."

chapter 22

Anger flashed into Quinn's eyes. "You were never a *trophy*."

"Wasn't I? You claimed me and I was yours. I became another barometer of the bastard kid done good, like one of your scholarships and awards. 'Look, everyone! Quinn Lawson got himself a rich, pretty society girl to show off. . . .'" Her voice broke and she turned away.

"Horseshit." He hit the shower wall again, and she whirled.

"It's not horseshit! You can't just invalidate what I say, run over it with a verbal tractor. I'm telling you how I feel and what I believe, and you don't get to contradict that. You don't get to control my thoughts!"

He stood there shaking his head, his breathing rapid and labored with denial. "So you really think you were my trophy? Well, let me try to change your mind. Let me tell you my version of things, okay?"

She nodded.

"You weren't a trophy, Gwen. You were . . . a goddess. From the moment I saw you, I wanted to touch you, but I was also afraid to touch you. I was desperate to get inside you—in every sense of the word—but scared shitless that I'd never leave again if I did—not voluntarily. You turned me upside down. Wanna know what that does to a control freak, honey? It fucks him up, every which way. And still, all I ever wanted was to deserve you."

Her hands had gone involuntarily to her mouth. "Then why . . ."

"Why didn't you know that? Why didn't I talk to you? Why was I sometimes a real asshole?"

She stayed mute, so he'd fill the distance between them with these crucial words.

"You think I wanted to be that in love with you? You think it was comfortable? Well, it wasn't. It made me mad. It terrified me. It made me feel like a cornered animal sometimes. So I barked. And maybe I bit—when all I ever wanted to do, honey, was guard you. Prove my loyalty. Prove I was good enough for you."

He broke off and leaned his forehead against the tile of the shower wall. He banged it once, and then twice. Then he straightened and shifted his gaze back to her face. "And here we are. With the naked truth. I'm stupid enough that I could love you again, if I let myself. But you don't even like me."

The words tore through her; she could only imagine what they did to him. To his ego, to his heart.

"Quinn, you misunderstand. It's not that I don't like the man you've become. It's that I don't think *you* like him." She searched his eyes.

He averted his gaze.

"He's not a happy man, Quinn, despite a lot of pride in his accomplishments. He's got a Mercedes coupe and a pile of money to prove that he's 'arrived,' but yes, to use that old cliché, he can't buy happiness."

"Yeah, well. Looks like I'll have to fuckin' steal that." His voice was harsh, sardonic.

"You can't steal it, either! It's a blessing and a gift and a state of mind. It's sharing, Quinn. Not *taking* everything that life can offer you and keeping score, but sharing it with people you love. I don't see people in your life, Quinn. Where are they?" Tears ran down her face and body, mingling with the spray of the water, rushing for the drain.

"People?" His mouth twisted. "People let you down, sweetheart. They fuck you over, as soon as what you're doin' or who you are ain't convenient to them."

"Not everyone's like that."

"So I hear. But I've got enough experience at getting bent over that it makes me real careful." He leaned against the wall, arms crossed. "And I don't like being used, either. You know that old saw, honey: It's lonely at the top."

She wasn't getting through to him, and it frustrated her, made her harsher than she meant to be. "Then it's a damn good thing that this missing mask has knocked you to the bottom again."

Quinn could have been a piece of statuary being soaked by a sprinkler. He didn't even blink. The water sluiced smoothly down his shoulders and chest, pooled in his navel, clung to the hairs on his legs. It spattered around his ankles as it hit the marble shower floor.

She opened the glass door and slipped out, leaving him inside. Running again? She didn't want to think about it. She wrapped herself in one of the blue towels, went into his bedroom, and curled up in an armchair.

She heard the shower shut off, the door open and close as Quinn got out. A moment later he appeared, big and half-naked in the doorway, the other blue towel wrapped around his waist. "Maybe you're right," he said. "Maybe this is my reality check."

Quinn walked over to her and brushed his fingers over her cheek. She turned her face into them. He picked her up and cradled her in his arms. He traced her mouth with a finger and then kissed her. "You," he said slowly. "You're my people. You're the person I want to share things with."

Silly to say her heart turned over. Or stopped. Or beat wildly. But his words undid her. Pure emotion, unnamed, swelled in her throat. Was it love? Was it mounting panic?

Clearly he was developing feelings for her all over again. But *could* he share? Was he capable . . . or could he only direct and control?

Quinn kissed her again. He laid her on the bed. Then he knelt in front of her and pushed her thighs apart.

His mouth on her erased all thought. The wet heat, the shocking intimacy, the sensation of his tongue, the hot, thrashing pleasure took her over. She was at the edge, climbing, trembling . . . when he stopped.

"I want to make you come," he said. "I want to make you forget your own name, honey. But I want it to be me. Me here and now. So if you're thinking of me fifteen years ago, babe, then we have an issue."

"Now." Gwen moaned. "Oh, God . . ."

"I want you to sit up. I want you to keep your eyes open and watch me, Daddy's Girl." He took her hands and pulled her to a sitting position.

She was a rag doll, could barely hold herself upright. "Please, Quinn." Funny how she didn't mind him being alpha in the bedroom.

"Watch"—he took a long lick at her center—"me."

"Yes," she managed. And she did. She could see his big shoulders between her knees, his skewed dark blond hair, the shadow of stubble on his cheeks, the way her body masked the lower half of his face.

She could see his eyes, pupils black with passion, and the satisfaction in them when she struggled for control and lost miserably.

She watched him react to her reactions and hold her thighs apart as she bucked against his mouth. She watched

as he stilled for just a moment and then set off the chain reaction again, sending her into multiple orgasms until she
finally begged him to stop.

And this time she didn't close her eyes when he crawled
onto the bed and slid home all the way. As they spiraled up
and fell together, she realized what she'd been missing for
fifteen long years.

Quinn liked seeing Gwen in his big bed. He liked her
hair messed up and her eyes all sleepy. Nobody else got to
see her this way, without the punk Audrey Hepburn thing
going on. She was carefully done for the public, with her
smoky eye makeup and the deliberately spiked, sprayed-
just-so hair. But this mussed Gwen was all natural.

He toyed with his diamond in her belly button, flicking
it gently with his finger. He didn't know what the hell they
were doing, but here they were, naked in bed and pretty
satisfied that way. It was a little unnerving, given their
history.

"I should go," Gwen murmured.

He found himself very much opposed to that idea.
"Why?"

She propped herself up on her elbow and traced his
knuckles with her index finger. "Things to do, people to
see. Esteban Velasquez, for one."

He tensed. "Gwen . . . Carlos was murdered. That puts a
whole different spin on things."

"Yes, it sure does. Why was he killed? Because someone thought he was about to talk? Maybe to me? About
who hired him to steal the mask . . . and who's got the real
one?"

"It could just as easily be a drug deal that went bad."

"I don't think so. I just have a gut feeling about it, and
now I want to find his brother. Personally, I still think that
Angeline Le Fevre is behind this."

"Angeline?" Quinn didn't know her well. He supposed it was possible. She knew the piece; she had the art world connections to unload the thing.

"But I can't prove it. The Nerd Corps checked her bank accounts and there's no irregular activity."

"She could have an offshore account."

"True. Or she could still have the mask. But it's not in her home or office."

"How do you know that? You didn't—"

"No, Quinn, I didn't break in. McDougal is seeing her. I had him check." Not that she trusted McD anymore, but for some reason she held that back.

"So . . . in the absence of the real mask, we need to keep following the leads on the fake one. They will eventually bring us to the person responsible."

Quinn reluctantly nodded.

"And that's why I need to locate Esteban Velasquez."

He reached for her and pulled her on top of him, crushing her breasts against his chest. "I don't want you to get hurt."

"I'll be fine, Quinn." She kissed him. "I told you, I can handle myself. And this is my reputation. It's important."

"There are things more important than your reputation—or mine. Your life, for one."

"You don't think I can take care of myself," she said.

Dangerous ground he was on here. He tried to be tactful. "I would worry about anyone pursuing this case. It has nothing to do with me thinking you're incompetent. Somebody put two bullets through that kid's head. I don't want the same thing to happen to you."

"It won't." She swung her legs over the side of his bed and wrapped her discarded towel around herself. She seemed to think that was the end of the discussion.

He hated to break it to her, but he wasn't going to be put

off that easily. "Gwen, please drop the case. Let the police take it from here."

She spared him barely a glance. "No." She wasn't rude, just dismissive, which was worse.

"Then I'm coming with you," he said, tamping down his anger.

"Coming with me where? I don't even know yet where to find Esteban. And—please excuse me if this sounds obnoxious—but where is it written that because you have a penis, you're more bulletproof than I am?"

"That's really uncalled for. I'm not trying to be Captain Testosterone, here—I'm just worried about you. Why can't you understand that?"

Gwen went into the bathroom for her clothes, came back out, and dumped them on the bed. She stepped into her panties and pulled them up. Then she put on everything else, including McDougal's jacket, since it was surprisingly, blessedly chilly.

"I'm sorry, Quinn. I do understand. And I think you're sweet. But just because we've slept together doesn't mean that you get to control me or dictate to me."

"I'm not!"

"I know you don't mean to." She came over and took his face in her hands. Kissed him. "It's just your nature. Now, will you take me home?"

chapter 23

The car purred through the gaudy, pastel, art deco–flavored streets of South Beach. The interior smelled of leather cleaner and combustible memories. Gwen thought about the two stupid kids they'd been, setting up house without understanding all the ramifications.

She thought about how livid her father had been at the shotgun wedding . . . and how pleased her parents were to have their daughter back afterward, even under the circumstances.

She thought about how utterly infatuated she'd been with Quinn, his hard body and soft words. His raw ambition and take-no-prisoners attitude. His rebel streak and occasionally incorrect grammar. The way he filled out a pair of jeans.

Quinn turned down Ocean Drive and then cut over to Collins. She looked at his hands on the wheel of the Mercedes. He didn't belong in this thing. He belonged in a muscle car or some kind of truck.

He pulled up into her driveway and she got out. "Thanks."

"No problem."

He stared at her.

She stared back.

"Gwen . . . please. I'm not trying to dictate. I'm not

trying to control you. We can be equal partners in this thing. You'll gain an extra pair of eyes and hands, and I'll gain some peace of mind. Okay?"

She took a deep breath. "Okay."

"Thank you."

She knew he wanted to come in. She didn't ask him to. Gwen needed some time alone and told him so.

He watched her from the car until she stepped into the house and raised her hand in a wave good-bye. She turned on a light, let the door close behind her, locked it.

Gwen stood for a long moment listening to the empty, silent little house. She needed to get a pet. Avy had Kong, her cockatiel, to keep her company when Liam wasn't around. All Gwen had were a couple of dust bunnies.

She made her way into the kitchen and looked into the fridge. A half-empty container of orange juice, a lone stale bagel repressed in its bag by a twist tie, and a bunch of celery stared back at her. The celery made her think of crazy rock star Sid Thresher, who was partial to Bloody Marys.

She shook her head, then went to see what she had lurking in the liquor cabinet. Her reward was three-quarters of a bottle of vodka, a plastic squeeze container of lime juice, and the dregs of some triple sec.

She made herself another almost-Caipiroska and went outside to the patio, where she sat on the edge of the closed-up hot tub and sipped at her drink.

Old Mrs. Santos's house was dark, but the smell of meat cooking on the grill wafted over from behind the plastic trellises to the left. Her husband's name was Jerome, and he called to his wife for a platter.

Gwen took another sip of the drink and set it on the lid of the hot tub. She scooted back and sat Indian-style on it, shoving her hands into McDougal's coat pockets. Her thumb caught on something in the left one. Puzzled, she looked down and pulled her hand out. The pocket lining came out with it. Gwen stopped breathing.

Part of the khaki fabric had torn and there was a small triangle missing.

Morning brought a spectacular pink-and-gold sunrise and another unwelcome realization: For the last fifteen years, Gwen had gotten her period like clockwork on the twenty-eighth day of each month . . . until now. It should have come yesterday.

She told herself not to be silly. She'd been under every kind of stress lately, and her system was just out of whack. She'd get it this afternoon. She stocked her purse with supplies, because after all, the only time she'd had unprotected sex with Quinn was that night in the hot tub, and what were the odds? It was the wrong time of the month.

It's still possible. . . .

But not probable.

Really? The man has turbo sperm. They climb vertically, judging by Brazil. The women in her family were all fertile Myrtle's.

But the chlorine in the hot tub . . .

Is not effective birth control, and you know it.

What if she was one of those women who ovulated twice per month?

Ridiculous. She was being paranoid. She had more serious things to think about—like the missing fabric from McDougal's jacket. The hole was a match to the piece of cloth she still had. Had the pocket been turned inside out when it caught on the nail? McDougal . . . She still couldn't wrap her mind around it.

Gwen got ready quickly, drove down to Brickell, and wiped her face clean of all anxiety before she entered the office and took inventory of the ensemble that greeted her.

Sheila had clearly gotten a pedicure recently and had

decided to show it off in lime green wedge sandals. Her toe-nails were orange with little green palm trees painted on the big toes.

She wore a lime green leather jacket over an orange camisole and white pants. Today's reading glasses were of a brown-and-white giraffe pattern.

"Hi, doll face," she said to Gwen. "You didn't sleep, did you?"

"Not much." So much for the two coats of concealer she'd put on under her eyes to camouflage the fact. "Is Dante in this morning?"

"Yes, our Dapper Don is here," said McDougal, apparently on his way out. "He's in his office on the phone with some poor peasant, making him an offer he can't refuse."

Gwen could hardly look at him. "Thanks."

"How you doin'?"

"Fine."

If this hadn't been McDougal, she'd have thought that hurt flitted through his eyes at her tone. But it was. He merely quirked an eyebrow and then turned to scan Sheila in all her glory. He winced, shaded his eyes, and put on his aviator sunglasses. "Damn. And we need electricity, too?"

"Get lost," the receptionist retorted. "You wouldn't know fashion if it bit you in the left nut."

"If that's fashion, babe, then I'm happy to remain unac-quainted with it."

"Out," Sheila said, pointing at the door. "I have better things to do than talk to you."

"Yeah, like strangling yourself with a chain of paper clips." McDougal winked at Gwen as he sashayed out the door. She didn't wink back.

"Where's he going?" she asked, keeping her tone casual.

"Some obscure errand for Kelso. He's headed to the Hard Rock Casino in Hollywood to try to get some info from a regular gambler there. Wonder how many free drinks he'll suck down as just part of the job."

"Couldn't tell you." Gwen also couldn't tell her why part of McDougal's jacket had been stuck in the Velasquez brothers' doorway. It unnerved her.

She took her morning smoothie down the hallway and stuck her head into Dante's office. He was there, impeccably groomed as usual, in a monogrammed custom-made shirt. His clean dark hair was swept back from his forehead in a *GQ* style, and his brow was knit in concentration.

His crutches lay propped against a visitor's chair, and he'd draped his jacket over them. His elegant hands clicked away on the keyboard.

"Hi," she said.

He looked up with an abstract smile, minimized the screen he had up on the monitor of his computer, and pushed back a little from his desk. "*Ciao, bella.* I hear that you made an unfortunate discovery yesterday morning. I am sorry."

Gwen said, "I'm fine. Really. Everyone seems to think that I'm going to come apart at the seams because I saw a dead body."

"You must admit that such a thing is upsetting."

"Sure, I'd rather see a field of flowers or a great painting any day than a corpse. But what can you do?"

"Call the undertaker. *Eccolo*, how may I help you this morning?" He gestured toward the other visitor's chair.

She closed the door and then took a seat. "Dante, there's something I have to talk to you about."

He seemed somewhat amused. "*Si*, evidently. Talk away."

She didn't know how to begin. "How do I say this? I was waiting for the police yesterday morning and Sheila sent McDougal out to babysit me. He let it slip that he knew exactly how Carlos had died—but when I questioned him he had a good cover reason, a buddy on the police force."

Dante nodded.

"But I found a piece of fabric stuck to a finishing nail in the door there. And McDougal . . . he loaned me that old barn jacket of his. I put my hands in the pocket later and discovered a rip that's the same shape. It's also the same fabric. He was there, Dante. Sometime before I ever arrived. And he didn't call the cops."

Dante no longer looked amused. "What time did you get there?"

"Around nine a.m."

"What's the estimate of time of death?"

"Carlos had been dead for hours. Long enough for rigor mortis to set in."

"Where was McDougal the night before?"

She shook her head. "I don't know."

Dante sat for a moment in thought. "Have you told the police any of this?"

"Not yet. I guess I didn't want to believe my suspicions. Like I said, he had an explanation for his knowledge, and I didn't find the rip in the jacket pocket until last night."

His mouth had flattened into a grim line. "You must inform them. I don't like to say this, because he is one of our own, but . . . if he had anything to do with the murder, then he must answer for it."

"Of course, but I wanted to give the office a heads-up."

Dante nodded, his expression inscrutable.

Gwen threw up her hands. "McDougal . . . why? Why would he be involved? I keep asking myself that question and I'm not coming up with any good answers—except that he's sleeping with Angeline Le Fevre, and I'm ninety-nine percent sure she's behind the theft of the mask."

"Angeline?" Dante's brows shot up. "Why?"

"Gut. Art world connection. McDougal connection."

Dante nodded again. He rolled his chair toward her and took her hands. His were steady, warm, comforting. "Gwen, who knows? It's possible that Eric commissioned the theft himself. . . . We all have contacts in this business or we wouldn't be here. Maybe he saw a way to make money. Maybe he has a special buyer. But you must tell the police, and it's good that you gave me a—what did you call it?— heads-up. I won't put him on anything high-profile until we know what's going on."

Gwen crossed her legs and leaned back in the visitor's chair, withdrawing her hands. "God, I'm so stupid! I asked McDougal to check Angeline's house for the mask. Of course he didn't find it."

"You had no way of knowing."

Gwen stood up. "He gets on my nerves just as much as he gets on everyone else's. But I never thought he was a . . . a killer."

"And perhaps he is not. There may be a reasonable explanation, for all we know." Dante rolled backward again, pushing himself with his good leg. When he reached his desk, he propped an elbow on it.

She nodded. "Yes. But I doubt it." She moved toward the door. "Avy is going to come unglued when I tell her this."

"She won't be pleased," Dante said.

"Thank you for listening. I'll keep you up-to-date. Right now I need to find Esteban Velasquez to ask him some questions, and he seems to have disappeared. I'm sure the Nerd Corps can track a credit card of his or something."

"You're doing a good job, Gwen."

She lifted a shoulder to acknowledge the words, but they bothered her, simply because he wouldn't have said them if he didn't think she needed to hear them. Gwen didn't want people to feel that she needed reassurance.

"Ciao, bella."

"Bye." And she went off in search of Miguel, who could almost certainly help her track down the mysterious jeweler, too.

chapter 24

Avy remembered Venice as an antique, cut-glass perfume bottle of a city: delicate and exquisite as long as the sterling stopper remained closed. Once opened, especially in summer, it smelled like a rotting fish head.

She'd never visited Venezia in early February, though, and it retained all of its fluid, romantic charms without the ripeness of June or July.

She and Liam shivered in the crisp air as they sat entwined on a noisy vaporetto, headed down the Grand Canal. Despite the overcast day, she felt that they were motoring straight into a Canaletto painting. The light from the Venetian sky gleamed metallic and silvery on the warm-toned buildings, which were reflected in the moody gray-green water.

Other than the noise of the vaporettos, or water taxis, Venice was a quiet, upscale city that pulsed with both old poetry and crass tourism. It had survived against the odds for centuries. While it reflected a mélange of architectural styles—Byzantine, Gothic, Renaissance, baroque—the actual layout of Venice had changed little over the past five hundred years.

The shabby-chic yet elegant buildings seemed to float on the waterways, impossibly buoyant. They were all built on pilings sunk into the *caranto* below the water, a mixture of sand and clay. Avy found it miraculous that the pine pilings hadn't decayed over the centuries.

Liam, of course, wanted nothing to do with anything shabby, no matter how chic it might be. He insisted upon staying at the Gritti Palace, one of the best-known five-star hotels in Venice.

"Isn't that a bit too high-profile for what we're doing?" Avy cautioned him.

"Not at all. Besides, nobody will even begin to guess what tricks we're up to, my love. Think about it: All of the security measures taken in each villa, palazzo, or museum are geared toward one thing, and one thing only: keeping inventory in. Not a single one will have taken precautions against keeping it *out*."

Avy had to admit that this was true. What they were doing was probably unprecedented in the entire history of art theft.

"Now, things to be aware of tonight, my darling," Liam said into her ear. "Our magistrate snores like a tuba, so his long-suffering wife sleeps in a separate room. Ideally they will both be unconscious when we pay our visit, but *il signore* is known to have various other sleep disturbances, as well."

"He's an insomniac?" asked Avy.

"No. He's actually narcoleptic during the day—falls asleep on the bench quite often—and occasionally sleepwalks at night."

"Then why don't we break in during the day when he's gone?"

"Staff, wife, and children scattered about then, I'm afraid. Also nosy neighbors. We're still better off dropping in on the other side of midnight, my darling."

"I don't like this sleepwalking issue at all," Avy said. "What if he wakes up and sees us and starts hollering?"

"That would be rather tough luck," Liam admitted.

She stared at him. "Tough luck? You have a talent for understatement. I'm not going to jail for you."

"We're not bloody well going to jail," Liam said crossly. "We're returning something, after all."

"Right. Which means first we get slapped for possession of stolen property and then we get charged for B and E. No, thank you."

"Do stop being dramatic, darling. Nothing's going to go amiss. Trust me."

"Dramatic? You want to see dramatic, I'll push you off this farting tub of a taxi. . . ."

Liam seized her and kissed her to shut her up as the vaporetto sputtered under the Scalzi Bridge. He was warm and annoyingly sexy, and his lips distracted her from her doom-and-gloom thoughts.

She barely noticed as they passed the Casa Adoldo and the Palazzo Foscari-Contarini, and then their hotel, the Palazzo Gritti. Liam finally released her as they sped by San Geremia to play tour guide, pointing out the early Renaissance Palazzo Vendramin Calergi.

"Beautiful, isn't it? Venice's casino is there. We could go and play later, if you like."

"I think I'm gambling quite enough on this trip," Avy said, "But thanks."

"Ah. Well, in that case, you will be delighted to know that the cat-strangling German composer Wagner died there."

She laughed. "He's not my favorite."

Liam shuddered. "Nor anyone's, I daresay. No one cheerful or good fun, anyhow."

They were thoroughly chilled by the time they got to the dock at the Ca' d'Oro, where Liam tugged her off. "Lunch, my darling! Then we'll explore what this house of gold has to offer. It was commissioned in the early fourteen hundreds and designed to be the most fabulous palace in the city, but fell upon hard times in later centuries. Then it was torn to pieces by a mad Russian ballerina with atrocious taste and no reverence for history. I wonder if she listened to Wagner? What do you think, my love?"

"It's hard to say, Liam."

"At any rate, an Italian baron, unable to stand the barbarity of it all, rode to the rescue and restored it. It is from him that I acquired—"

"I knew there was a point to all of this."

"—my magnificent Caravaggio Bacchus."

"Which you're going to replace after lunch?"

"You're wonderfully quick-witted, my love."

"I'm actually going to miss that painting," she said. It had hung in the living room of Liam's London home.

He brightened. "Then you'll let me hang on to it?"

"No stolen goods," Avy said in severe tones.

"Such a stickler for law and order, darling. Not that I don't adore you, but your morals get rather onerous at times."

"Yeah?" She shrugged. "Well, it's just the cross you have to bear. You'll get used to it, given twenty or thirty years."

Liam looked perturbed. "Then may I gamble our fortunes away?"

"No."

"Become an arsonist, an alcoholic, or an addict?"

"No."

"You won't let a man have any fun, will you?"

"There's always kinky sex."

"So there is," Liam mused, brightening.

"But it has to be with me."

"How wretched." He cast a furtive look over his shoulder and slipped his hand inside her coat and up her skirt.

"Liam!"

"I'm doomed, am I?" His wayward fingers slid under her thong. "A prisoner to the marital flesh, ending my days in abject misery . . ."

"Stop that!" She squirmed and sidestepped, trying to catch her breath. Her body had gone from freezing to electrified in a matter of seconds.

" . . . just begging for a little slice of . . ." His eyebrows waggled and he whispered a dirty word into her ear. Heat blazed between her legs and she caught at his wrist, trying to pull his hand away.

Liam just chuckled and maneuvered her down a side street and into a dark doorway. He stood in front of her, his coat open, so nobody could see what he was doing.

Avy gasped and clutched at his shoulders, no longer willing or able to stop what he was doing to her.

His diabolical grin widened as her head fell back and a tiny whimper left her lips. She exploded against his hand as he rubbed it between her thighs. Her knees trembled and she fell forward against him.

"I don't suppose you'd let me keep my Bacchus now, would you, darling?" he murmured into her ear.

"You," Avy said raggedly, "are the devil."

He seemed unfazed by this opinion. "Yes, occasionally. I'm a Renaissance man, after all, and temptation is just one of the many services I offer."

Caravaggio's fleshy, sly, exuberant Bacchus did seem more at home here in Italy than he did in the respectable areas of London. He sprawled decadently across a sofa not monitored by the security cameras when Liam and Avy made their exit from the Ca' d'Oro.

It had been frighteningly simple, really. Liam had walked in with the unframed Caravaggio rolled tightly and attached inside his London Fog coat by small loops of black Velcro.

Once inside the building, they played tourists. They duly admired Andrea Mantegna's *St. Sebastian* and Carpaccio's *Annunciation* and *Death of the Virgin* on the first floor. They strolled through the *portego* gallery, which faced the Grand Canal, and admired the sculpture.

On the second floor they wandered through the exhibits of tapestries and ceramics, viewed a couple of paintings by Guardi, and double-checked the positions of all security cameras.

Liam disabled the only relevant camera, pulled the rolled painting out of his coat, and gently spread it out. Avy stood casually in the doorway, making sure they weren't disturbed.

Liam eased the Bacchus onto the sofa with a small sigh of regret. "Cheerio, old boy," he said. "Carry on with the hedonism, eh?" Then he walked away.

That had been hours ago. Now it was time to replace the Tintoretto Venus. They slipped through the shadows in a black sliver of a gondola, not encountering anyone at this hour. Most of Venice was sleeping at four a.m., which was too late for any drunks and too early for even the most industrious workers.

Avy didn't much like trusting a gondolier with their destination, but Liam assured her that this particular one was a jolly fine fellow and accustomed to dark doings. She wasn't to get her knickers into a twist.

The jolly fine fellow knew how to handle a gondola, at least, which was more than they did. He also knew the back waterways of Venice like his own palm.

They pulled up to a dilapidated old lady of a house that had once been quite lovely. But this poor villa was in her dotage. Her facade showed cracks and peeling paint, her arches looked dingy and gray even by moonlight, and some of her architectural details reminded Avy of old gums and false teeth.

She knew it was hideously expensive to live in Venice, and she couldn't imagine what it took financially to keep up these stately old homes. "Liam," she whispered. "You took that Tintoretto from people who couldn't afford to lose it."

"Yes and no," he said. "The old codger certainly enjoyed spending the insurance settlement he got, and as far as I know not a penny of it went into the upkeep of this place."

"Maybe he has an aging parent to take care of, or children to put through college."

"Your faith in humanity is touching, my love. But he spent it on whores and the casino we passed earlier today."

"How do you know?"

"Ah." Liam smiled in the dark. "How do you get your information, Avy? We each have our ways, do we not?"

The jolly good fellow guided their gondola around to the back of the home, and Liam leaped out with a flash of white teeth. Then, ever the gentleman thief, he extended his hand to Avy.

They crept around the side of the house and came to a halt.

Then Liam produced two masks from an inside pocket of his coat. She wasn't surprised that they were genuine Venetian Carnevale masks—this was just up Liam's warped alley. His was the traditional Il Dottore mask, the medieval plague doctor. The mask featured a long beak and painted black round eyeglasses.

Avy quietly snorted with laughter until she saw her own mask, which Liam handed to her with a smirk. It was the Burrattino, or puppet mask. "Oh, I'm your little marionette, am I?" she said wrathfully. "Insignificant until you pull my strings?"

"Avy, love, it's just a joke. Now put it on like a good little cat burglar and let's get on with things."

They each made a bizarre appearance, dressed in form-fitting black with the Carnevale masks over their faces. Liam led the way toward the back entrance of the house and produced a key.

"How in the hell did you get a *key*, for God's sake?" Avy whispered.

He shrugged. "Little boys should be more careful of where they leave their schoolbags."

"That's low," Avy said. "That's really low, Liam."

He rolled his eyes, turned the key, and eased the door open. He listened for a moment and then stepped inside, gesturing her to follow.

She had a funny feeling in the pit of her stomach, and if Avy had a rule it was, *Listen to your gut.* She grabbed his arm and shook her head. "Something's not right."

That put Liam on alert, but he just held up a finger. He cocked his head in the ridiculous mask and listened some more. Then he took two more steps inside.

"Liam, I'm warning you. Get out now. Leave the painting right there if you must, but something's off. I'm not going in."

"You don't make much of a puppet!" he hissed at her, but she was already crouched low, heading back for the gondola.

"We can always try again tomorrow night," she tossed back at him.

He shook his head. "We've a schedule to keep to, darling. And besides, we're going to enjoy the real Carnevale while we're here. Thousands of people will be out over the next few nights—too many eyes for what we have in mind."

"Don't. Go. In," Avy tried one last time, but Liam's body language remained stubbornly committed. "Fine. I'll do my best to bail you out of Italian jail, then." She slipped back into the gondola with their jolly fine fellow, and

Liam, damn him, ignored her advice and crept inside the house. Within three minutes, lights blazed in a room on the middle floor of the palazzo.

Avy's heart leaped into her throat. Liam was in serious trouble, and she might be the only person who could get him out of it. Cursing under her breath, she palmed her SIG and climbed back out of the gondola, stopping only to make a promise in fluent Italian to the man still in it. "If you leave us here, I will hunt you down like a dog and shoot you, *capisce*?"

chapter 25

The bitch was now in Venice. The man didn't know what she and the thief were up to, but he seriously doubted it was a vacation.

He had a way to pay her back for all the headaches she'd caused him. He sent an anonymous tip to someone he felt sure would be interested in the whereabouts of Sir Liam James.

Avy Hunt was about to regret very much that she'd ever messed with the man's family.

Frankly, with all the cleanup he was having to do on the original plot, he would quite enjoy killing her, too. Yes, it would give him great pleasure. But . . . he wanted to come up with a *creative* death, something that would resonate. Bullets were so boring, so uninspired, so common and pedestrian.

As he savored an excellent, full-bodied cabernet at the Delano on South Beach, he turned the issue over in his mind. A couple of drunk models stumbled in, giggling, and made eyes at him to see if he'd buy them drinks. They were beautiful, but a bit too skinny for his taste. Still . . .

They hovered over the cocktail menu, shamelessly flaunting cleavage and bare skin and thick, fake nails painted in eye-popping colors. Finally they turned to him and asked what he recommended, with naughty giggles. He'd bet a hundred dollars that they each knew exactly what they wanted.

But then, so did he. "I think," he said, lighting a cigarette, "that you would simply adore the Ménage à Trois."

They laughed uproariously, the little harlots.

"No, really. It's a California white. The 2007 is quite good." He signaled the bartender to hook them up and smiled ferally. Now all he had to do was score a little blow . . . in more ways than one.

In the small hours of the morning, after a sweaty, raunchy romp, the perfect idea came to him.

The Borgia mask he'd begun with had a bloodthirsty history . . . and had been crafted as a tool of revenge. Why not reenact that history? Why not continue its pattern of revenge? He admired the neatness of the concept and its ties to his original plan. Not all of his efforts would go to waste.

While the secrets of the mysterious Borgia family poison had died along with them, plenty of other toxic substances existed. Angeline had the original mask, which suited him fine—ARTemis or the cops would never look beyond her or, without evidence, believe a word she said— but he could easily get his hands on the copy. In the meantime, he'd do a test run.

He woke up the skanks sprawled naked in his bed and kicked them unceremoniously out. They could find their own way home.

chapter 26

Miguel was brilliant: He hadn't let Gwen down. He'd been swamped with other information requests, but had tracked Esteban Velasquez's location by the next morning, and had promised Gwen the results of the jeweler search soon.

Twenty-four hours later, a simple bribe was all it took for the clerk of the Manatee Motel in south Miami to walk Gwen to Esteban Velasquez's room. The clerk made no secret that he liked her body and the long blond hair of the wig she wore.

Gwen made it clear that she, in turn, liked his complete lack of morals and receptiveness to cash.

The room was simple and frankly scuzzy. It smelled of stale cigarettes and cheap industrial cleaning solution, neither of which quite covered a lurking mildew odor. A queen-size bed was covered in a cheap rainbow-hued spread, and the rest of the furniture was laminated faux–wood grain over particleboard.

Velasquez had tossed a small duffel into the room's only armchair, and it contained inexpensive clothing from Wal-Mart with the tags still attached, as if he'd bought some necessities in a hurry.

"We ain't seen him in a day and a half," said the clerk.

It looked as if Esteban had stepped out for a meal or a vending machine soda and simply not returned.

"Like I said," the clerk continued, shaking his head, "the guy's truck's still there, but when the maids knocked on the door they got no answer. One of 'em said something to me just this mornin' about the TV still bein' on after twenty-four hours. I says, 'Well, then turn the darn thing off! Ain't like anybody's watchin' it.'"

"Do you mind if I take a quick look around?" Gwen asked. "I won't touch anything. I'm just worried about him. He hasn't called me like he said he would."

The clerk shrugged and winked. "I figure I'm not s'posed to let you in at all, but it helps pass the time."

Not to mention that he was a hundred dollars richer. Gwen rounded the bed and checked the drawer in the nightstand, but found nothing but a Bible.

The new clothes were half pulled out of the duffel, and there were no papers or anything of interest under them.

"You didn't see him get into a car with anyone, did you?"

"Nope."

Gwen pulled open the dresser drawers, but they were completely empty. She headed toward the vanity area outside the bathroom. A toothbrush lay to the right side of the sink with a miniature tube of Colgate next to it. An electric razor was plugged in on the left side.

She poked her head into the bathroom. A minibottle of shampoo had been half emptied. Nothing else of interest was in the room.

The closet was completely empty except for a pair of brand-new gym shoes. Gwen turned slowly around, surveying everything a second time. She spotted the wastebasket under the vanity and went over to nudge it out from under there with her toe. There was nothing inside.

As she shoved it back, a flash of white caught her eye.

She discreetly toed forward a small, crumpled scrap of paper from behind the little can, but she didn't dare pick it up in front of the clerk.

"You done?" he asked, pulling a toothpick out of his mouth. "Because if the guy comes back, I don't wanna be in his room."

Gwen nodded. "I'm done. There's nothing here."

He nodded, yawned, and turned toward the door.

In a flash she'd palmed the scrap of paper. Gwen followed him out and said thanks. If he saw Mr. Velasquez, would he tell him to be sure to give his cousin a call?

The clerk smirked at her around the toothpick. "Sure, I'll tell him. But, babe, you ain't no cousin. You got about as much resemblance to that guy as my ass does to a lawn mower."

Gwen dimpled and touched the hair of her blond wig. "What gave it away?" she asked.

"Lemme guess: He owes you money." The clerk was eyeing her tits in a contemplative way.

"Good guess."

"Well, don't spend no more looking for him. You could have traded me something else for the key to his room, cutie pie."

Disgusted, Gwen winked anyway and did a classic hair flip accompanied by a strategic jiggle of assets. "I'll keep that in mind. Thanks."

Once she was back in the Prius, she unfolded the balled-up paper and peered at it. In pencil, someone had scrawled, *Costumeria Barzini. Isola di San Servolo, 30104 Venice.*

Venice? Gwen supposed it made sense. The mask she was tracking was, after all, Venetian. And this was a costume shop. There were probably dozens that catered to locals and tourists alike during Carnevale.

She was headed back to ARTemis when Miguel called. "Hello?"

"Miguel the magician, *mi vida*."

"What have you got for me, oh magician?"

"I think I have your jeweler. Tracked him down through that Worshipful Company of Goldsmiths organization. An old guy. He's got the right kind of welder and he's a repoussé expert. In fact, that's pretty much all he does. He's in Padua, near Venice in Italy." He read her the name and address.

Gwen snatched a pen from her bag and copied the information onto her thigh for lack of a piece of paper. "You're the best, Miguel."

"*Sí*, it's true."

Gwen laughed and recapped the pen, dropping it into her open purse. "I owe you my firstborn." Her stomach dropped as she said it. She didn't have a cramp on the horizon. . . . *Dear God.*

He shuddered audibly. "*Coño.* I'd rather have a BMW."

"Very shallow of you."

"Yes, but smart. I don't have to send a BMW to college."

"Bye, Miguel. Looks like I'll be booking a flight to Venice." Gwen hung up. What a chore . . . having to go to that beautiful city for work. It looked as if she were about to fly back to Italy. But this time, she'd make sure to bypass Rome and crazy Sid Thresher.

"Ice, ice, baby," Sheila said, brandishing a package at Gwen when she walked into the office the next morning. Sheila wore sequins today, and nobody wore sequins like she wore sequins. Cobalt blue ones formed a body of water on her yellow shirt. Coppery brown ones created the hull of a ship. White ones billowed out in sails across a baby blue sky, which in turn bulged over Sheila's ample bosom. Her reading glasses were bright yellow.

Gwen eyed the package with misgiving. "Who's it from?"

"Your lover boy."

Sid. Her heart sank. "What's in it?"

"I haven't opened it yet—the UPS guy just came a second ago—but I have high hopes. Can't wait . . ."

"Yeah, me, either," Gwen said without enthusiasm. "Go ahead."

"You thought I was waiting for permission, doll face? Get real." Sheila cackled and dug into her top drawer for a letter opener. She slit the tape on the package and pulled out a red velvet box along with a note that reeked of men's cologne.

Both she and Gwen gagged.

"Holy Mother of God," Sheila gasped. "What's that, essence of rhino 'nads?"

She flipped open the long velvet box and gasped again. Inside was the gaudiest diamond necklace Gwen had ever seen. It was fit for the empress of all hookers and madams. It looked a lot like a rhinestone dog collar with a bow suspended from a two-inch-long squiggle in the center. The squiggle and the bow were both mounted with diamonds, and gauging by the proportions, the bow was meant to nestle right in the lucky wearer's cleavage.

"Yikes," said Gwen.

Sheila was entranced. She unfurled the note with a flourish and approximated Sid Thresher's accent, which was quite funny, given her own Brooklyn one. " 'My dearest Gwendolyn, you don't call; you don't write. What's a lovesick old sod to do? I dream of you nightly. If I don't hear from you soon, I'll be coming to Miami to find you, my sweet. I know you're shy, but we'll be so good together. All my love, Sid.' "

Sheila looked up with an avid expression. "He's coming

to Miami! To sweep you off your feet and into his rock-'n'-roll life."

"Noooooooo," Gwen moaned.

"I'll bet you could get him to buy you a castle, Gwennie!"

"I don't *want* a castle."

"I've always wanted a castle," Sheila said. "But as cheap as Marty is, he'll never be able to save that much. And he wouldn't want to pay the taxes and upkeep on one of those old places, either."

Gwen tried to imagine Marty and Sheila living in a castle, but it was just too much of a stretch. "I'm sure the heating bills would be atrocious," she said.

"Yeah. And even with a ride-on model, Marty wouldn't want to mow a whole moor, d'you think?"

"Probably not."

"No castle for me," Sheila said sadly. She fingered the diamond necklace. "So. I know you're going to let me wear this to my next bunco night before you make me send it back, right?" Her blue-shadowed eyes became orbs of entreaty.

Gwen sighed. "When is it?"

"Wednesday night."

"Fine. Wear it to bunco, but tell everyone it's made of rhinestones. I don't want you knocked over the head for Sid's stupid bauble. Then you have to send it back, okay? With another computer-generated note that says I can't accept."

Sheila nodded, still gazing at the necklace. "Ooh, I'll feel just like Liz Taylor in this."

"Mmmm-hmmm," said Gwen. "Listen, I need to go to Italy. Can you book me a flight to Venice, leaving tonight if possible?"

"Oh, milady wants to leave tonight, does she? Well, la-di-da. We'll just see if we can find an airline to accommodate Her Highness. . . ." Sheila closed the velvet box and shoved it into her desk drawer. "You know, Avy's in Venice."

"She is?" Gwen gulped. She hadn't talked to Avy in a while—not that her friend would answer her phone. "What's she doing there?"

"Vacationing. So she says. I don't believe it. Something strange is going on with that girl, and I'm gonna get to the bottom of it. I want the dirt."

As Sheila's acrylic nails began clattering over the keyboard, Gwen decided that she was over her fear of flying. Because really, her fear of the reception area at ARTemis was so much greater—and she faced that every day.

Venice. Such a romantic city . . . not a city to enjoy alone. *We can be equal partners in this thing*, Quinn had said. *You'll gain an extra pair of eyes and hands, and I'll gain some peace of mind.*

She'd agreed, hadn't she? Gwen rubbed her suddenly damp palms over her skirt. On the verge of asking Sheila to make the reservation for two, she realized that she couldn't—not until she knew for sure whether she was pregnant or not.

Because if Quinn was overprotective and in the way now, what would he be like if he had any inkling she might be carrying his baby?

chapter 27

Avy pulled down her mask again, clung to the shadows, and moved silently toward the house, her gun drawn. She slipped inside the open door, praying that the owner of the old palazzo wasn't armed.

She took a moment for reconnaissance, listening intently. All she could hear were slightly raised voices coming from the second floor. She crept toward the center staircase, only to see Liam sprinting down toward her, taking the steps two at a time. In his wake was a fat, florid man in a nightshirt, brandishing the rolled painting.

"*Per favore, non lasciare il dipinto qui!*" he beseeched Liam. "*La porti via con Lei, La prego!*"

Avy's mouth dropped open. *Please*, he was saying, *don't leave the painting here! Take it with you, I beg you.*

"Hallo, my love," Liam said, leaping past her and running for the door. "Shall we?"

"*No, no, no! Non riesco a ripagare la compagnia di assicurazione, signore. Per favore!*" The owner of the house barreled past her, too, pale, hairy legs pumping, still chasing after Liam and waving the painting. *No, no, I can't pay back the insurance company. Please . . .*

Liam stopped and turned around, bracing his palms on the man's tubby shoulders. "Look here, old chap. I'm doing a good deed to return it, though *why* I'm damned if I know, since you're too cheap to climate control a national treasure. It's going to rot, do you hear? *Rot. Si decomporra!* For God's sake, sell it on the black market and pocket the cash, you fool."

The man babbled at him in Italian. No, he couldn't do that. The insurance company still had eyes on him. They'd catch him for sure. *Please, Signor Burglar, take it away.* He beseeched him to *spegnersi come una lume*, to just fade away again. Yes, back into the night like a good thief.

Half-hysterical, the man pressed the painting back into Liam's hands.

Liam looked at Avy. His eyes twinkled behind the plague doctor's mask, which had slipped slightly to the side so that the beak tilted askew.

This is the man I'm going to marry, she thought hopelessly. *He's enjoying this.*

"I pity the poor *signore*," he said. "Really, he wants us to keep the painting. Why don't we accept it as a token of his esteem? A small wedding gift?"

"Are you out of your mind?" Avy could barely keep from strangling him.

"But, my darling! You heard the man. He doesn't want it back. I think if he had any money left, he'd pay us to take it away. Be reasonable, hmmm?"

She gritted her teeth. He wasn't the plague doctor; he was the plague itself.

"He'll ruin a masterpiece with his cheeseparing ways," Liam continued. "I told you why I felt compelled to relieve him of the damned thing in the first place."

"No!" said Avy, pointing her gun at him.

Liam clapped a hand over his heart. "My conscience begs me to retain guardianship of this painting. . . ."

"You *have* no conscience."

"Unkindness does not become you, my love."

The homeowner looked from Avy to Liam and back. *"Non la ascolti. Ma Lei é un uomo o un topo?"* Don't listen to her. Are you a man or a mouse?

Avy narrowed her eyes on the good *signore.* He was starting to piss her off.

He puffed out his chest, which made him look like a potato on toothpicks. He said to Liam, *"La mostri chi commanda, no?"* Show her who's boss.

In a voice sweet as sugar, Avy said, *"Chi commanda sono io, pancione cretino."* I'm the boss, you fat fool.

He had the nerve to look insulted.

Liam looked at the floor, his shoulders shaking. "Alas, *signore,* it is true," he said in Italian. "She rules me with an iron fist."

Avy was tempted to shoot them both. What in the hell were they all doing here in the small hours of the morning, having this bizarre argument? Surely they'd gone into some weird Italian twilight zone.

The homeowner made one last valiant attempt, saying that gun or no gun, Liam shouldn't let himself be governed by this skinny bitch. Women were attempting to take over the world now that they'd been let out of the kitchen!

"Va bene!" Avy shouted at him. *"Lei é cosi antipatico che rimarremo noi col dipinto."* Fine. He was so obnoxious that they'd keep his painting. She snatched the rolled canvas out of his arms and marched out of the house with it.

Liam didn't seem at all surprised when Avy smacked him as soon as he stepped out the door. He caught her around the waist and deposited a noisy kiss on her ear. "Crimes of passion, love—they give me a stiffie. Won't you do that again?"

I'm not pregnant. I'm just not. Gwen drove into the parking lot of her local CVS pharmacy and cut the engine of the Prius, wishing she could cut off her worries as easily. But that was why she was here, after all.

Inside, she quickly perused the aisles until she got to one in the back that stocked ovulation tests and pregnancy tests. *EZ!* one promised. *Yeah, EZ. Peace of mind. Right away.*

She told herself that it was virtually impossible for her to have gotten pregnant in the very last days of her cycle.

And yet . . .

Gwen prayed as she made the trip back home. She prayed as she opened the package and read the instructions. She prayed as she followed them.

God laughed.

When two blue lines appeared on the tiny stick, she stared at it until it went out of focus and then came back in again. Then she laughed until her ribs hurt, a miserable release of pent-up emotion. She giggled hopelessly, helplessly. There was nothing else she could do. She wiped her overflowing eyes and headed back to the office.

She was horrified. She was overjoyed. She was nuts.

Gwen was indeed pregnant with Quinn's baby—again.

Quinn was sweating like a linebacker. He took off his baseball cap and wiped his streaming face on his already soaked T-shirt. Nothing like hard labor under a hot sun. He'd single-handedly polished every gleaming inch of his thirty-three-foot Sea Ray, and felt better for the exercise. It gave him something to do.

Silvery canals and high-rises and watercraft stretched as far as he could see. A humid breeze off the water felt like the hot breath of a stripper and provided little relief from the sun. The air was redolent with salt and engine grease and the aroma of grilled fish coming from three vessels down.

Old Rusty Harbough grilled snapper or grouper almost

every evening he was in residence. He periodically got kicked out by his wife for bad behavior and sometimes stayed on his boat for weeks at a time. Quinn figured he offended his wife on purpose just to take a break.

It was peaceful out here. Water lapped at the sides of the boats, which bobbed and rocked gently while rigging clanked against the metal masts of the sailboats. Quinn had come a long way from Oklahoma.

Tomorrow, if he still hadn't heard from Gwen, he'd don scuba gear and scrub every submerged inch of the Sea Ray's belly. What else was an unemployed executive to do? He should get in touch with headhunters and find another job, but until they wrapped up this business with the mask, he couldn't focus.

What exactly did a woman mean when she said she needed time to herself? How much time? And what if that was just an excuse to get him out of her way while she did things that she didn't want him to know about?

Quinn grabbed a cold beer out of the little fridge below-decks, closed up and secured the boat, and then headed down the concrete pier for the marina showers. He didn't want to admit it, but he'd thought of her constantly since driving her home.

She was back under his skin again. He could still smell her perfume in his car. He could still taste her . . . still hear her moan as he bit the cookie-shaped birthmark on the inside of her thigh and savored the flesh, leaving his mark on her.

He was hard as he entered the shower, and turning it on cold, full blast, did no good. "Cold" water in Miami was lukewarm, and it only made him want her more.

He'd take her some flowers. A bottle of wine. She couldn't possibly construe that as controlling, could she? Hell, who knew what women could construe.

But twenty minutes later, he handed a small, wizened

Costa Rican man ridiculously little money for a huge bouquet of tropical flowers. Birds-of-paradise, hibiscus, wild azalea, larkspur, lilies, and protea fought for center stage and put traditional roses to shame.

He picked up a chilled bottle of sauvignon blanc and then drove well out of his way to a favorite little restaurant, Salmon y Salmon, to pick up a batch of *chorros* to go. Nobody, not even a moody ex-wife, could turn down these mussels, which were marinated in fresh lime juice and slathered with onion, tomato, and cilantro.

He drove to Gwen's little house in Coconut Grove, gambling that she'd be home by now. Sure enough, the Prius rested in her driveway under a shade tree, clashing with the pink flamingos on the mailbox.

Quinn climbed the porch steps feeling a little silly with the giant bouquet. He rang the bell and waited expectantly. Her light footsteps sounded on the floorboards as she approached the door. There was a pause as she presumably checked to see who was there. The pause stretched on. Did she regret sleeping with him?

Just as he began to wonder if she'd acknowledge his presence at all, the latch jiggled and she pulled open the door. Her face was carefully neutral, devoid of expression.

"You've reduced me to making silly romantic gestures," Quinn said, holding out the flowers.

"They're beautiful. Thank you." She made no move to invite him in, and he felt about as welcome as a skunk at a garden party.

He held out the wine next, hoping that would sway her. What was wrong? Where was the passionate woman of two nights before? Something awfully like hurt clawed at his gut, so he overcompensated for it by being brash. "You are going to invite me in, aren't you, sweetheart?"

Gwen might know how to shoot, crack a safe, and pick a lock these days, but her innate courtesy remained intact and made her unable to leave him on the doorstep. She knew he was banking on that and taking advantage of it, and he knew she knew. "Of course. Let me put the flowers in some water. Make yourself comfortable."

Nothing would make him comfortable at this point, but he faked it. Proximity to her was better than comfort right now, and he also wanted to know what was going on in that enigmatic little brain of hers.

She moved toward the kitchen, the chambray shift she wore making her smooth, tanned skin look like caramel. She was very much there physically, because the sight of her had made him hard again. But mentally, she was somewhere else. And this time, an edge of wariness guarded that hidden territory like barbed wire. She wasn't letting him in.

What had happened? What was different? He walked into the dining room, still watching her out of the corner of his eye as she stood at the sink, filling a large amber glass vase with water. He set the bag of *chorros* on the table, along with the wine.

Six Wonder Women stared at him from the plates in Gwen's china cabinet. Wonder Woman. Independent, hell-bent on justice, didn't need the help of a man. She'd zip off in her invisible plane and lasso the bad guy on her own.

Was that what this was all about? Again?

Gwen came into the room and set the vase of tropical flowers on the dining room table. She fiddled with them, rearranging them so that they appeared perfectly balanced in spite of all their different shapes and sizes. He didn't know how she accomplished that, but she did.

Once she had disciplined the flowers into symmetry, she went back to the kitchen and returned with a corkscrew and two wineglasses, which she set on the table. "Would you like to open the wine?"

Sure, if you'll open a little welcome. But Quinn nodded and did the honors. "So, how was your day?"

"Good, good. How was yours?"

"Peachy." He handed her a filled glass and clinked his against hers.

As she took a sip, he inclined his head toward her china cabinet. "So, you think Wonder Woman ever had multiple orgasms?"

Gwen choked. Really choked, swallowing wine down the wrong pipe.

"You okay?" He thumped her on the back as she sputtered and coughed.

Finally, after wheezing and coughing some more, she said, "What kind of question is that?"

Quinn shrugged. "I don't know. I just remember, as a kid, wondering what Wonder Woman looked like naked. I always thought she had a hot bod. Think she ever hooked up with anyone? Ever got married, grew a Wonder Bun in her Wonder Oven?"

Gwen started coughing again.

"You want some water?"

She shook her head, reached for her wine, and tipped half of it into her mouth. Then she froze before swallowing, her expression truly strange. Next thing he knew, she was running for the kitchen sink, where she spit out the wine.

Quinn was perplexed, to say the least. "What's the matter with you?"

"Nothing." She gasped. "I just can't—the wine won't agree with me. Stomach issues."

"Then I guess you won't be eating the *chorros* I brought, either."

"Shellfish? No . . . no, I'm sorry but I can't right now." She patted her mouth with a paper towel. "It was really sweet of you to bring this stuff, though. Thanks, Quinn."

She poured herself a glass of water and came back into the dining room, where she sat down and aimed a fixed smile at him.

Quinn decided to cut through the BS. "You regret sleeping with me the other night. You're afraid that it forces us into a relationship again."

Her eyebrows shot up into her hairline.

"You want to be like your Superfriend, there—alone and free to pursue truth, justice, and the American way."

"You're making a lot of assumptions," she said quietly.

"Maybe. Don't take this wrong, Gwen, but when you won't talk to me, I *have* to make assumptions—just like you've made them about me."

She stayed silent.

"When you walked out on me after losing the baby . . ." He swallowed. Pinched the bridge of his nose. "I assumed that you ended things because you no longer needed a father for it. I thought you'd used me, and then you were done."

Her mouth dropped open. "You don't have a clue why I left," she said, shaking her head. "Not a clue."

He felt his jaw tense. "Then would you like to enlighten me now, sweetheart? After fifteen years?"

Gwen stood up abruptly. Turned her back to him. Hugged herself, hard, as if to hold her own body together. "I left," she said slowly, "because there was nothing remaining to discuss with you when I got home from the hospital. I saw the look on your face, and it said it all. You were *relieved*, Quinn!" She turned, her eyes blazing and throwing the shadows underneath them into even deeper contrast. "You were glad I lost that baby."

Shock knocked the breath out of him. "That's not true!"

"Don't bother denying it. I saw your face."

"I was relieved that you were okay, Gwen!"

She shook her head implacably.

"I was out of my mind with worry. . . ."

She just looked at him. "Yeah. That was so clear when you went out to a bar that night and left me alone." She covered her mouth with her hand.

He closed his eyes and leaned against the wall, remembering: Gwen in a hospital bed, pale against the pillow, her eyes huge, her hair a mess. She'd curled into a fetal position under the sheet and blanket.

He'd sat on the bed next to her and taken her hand. Said he was sorry. And he was. Sorry for what she'd gone through. Sorry for what might have been.

Had he felt relief on any level?

Terrible question.

A question nobody had asked him, too awful to verbalize.

Gwen's mother had said it was God's will, that it was probably for the best, that they were too young to be parents. That there was time in the years ahead.

He'd nodded. What else was there to say?

He'd driven her home to their efficiency in the old green Ford truck that smelled of mildew and cat pee. She'd climbed into bed and curled into her fetal position again. Didn't want the TV on.

Was there anything he could bring her?

Doughnuts. Chocolate-covered doughnuts. Entenmann's.

He drove to the store and brought them home. She stared at the box. She stared at him. He didn't know what to do or what to say or how to make it better.

A buddy of his called. Did he want to go get a beer? *Not a good idea, man.*

She continued to stare. Said it was okay; she wanted to be alone. Go. He should have known better, but . . .

All right, man, I'll meet you for an hour.

He came back in three.

Gwen had eaten ten of the doughnuts and drunk a quart

of milk. He didn't know if she'd been sick afterward. She pretended to be asleep, but he didn't think so, judging by her breathing.

He felt like an asshole, but what was he supposed to do—watch her fake being asleep? He couldn't. He got dressed again and slipped out the door. Walked and smoked. Drove and smoked. Bought a six-pack at a convenience store, sat on the stoop, drank two of the beers, and continued to smoke until the sun came up.

Had she thought that because of his behavior, he hadn't cared?

Quinn opened his eyes and she was still looking at him, as if he were a particularly revolting insect, so gross that she couldn't even bring herself to crush him with her shoe.

"You were relieved," she repeated. "No crying, no diapers. You could go ahead and go to grad school. You were free. . . ."

"I wasn't relieved! I was wrong to go out that night, but you told me to. You didn't seem to want me there."

She just shook her head. "You should've known better."

"Well, I didn't. Stupid guy behavior. I'm sorry! I was twenty years old, Gwen. I didn't have a decent job, much less a career. I couldn't afford the diapers or an acceptable place to raise a kid. I didn't have any concept of how to be a parent. Yeah, I'll tell you straight-out: I was petrified. So sue me. But God damn it, that doesn't mean I was glad when we lost the baby."

She didn't say anything.

"Did I run dancing into the street? Set off fireworks? Christ, Gwen! This is so unfair. I thought, at the time, that your mom was right. We had plenty of time ahead of us. It was sad, but we'd try again one day."

He felt his anger rising up again. "So that's why you left. Because you made an *assumption* about my feelings and condemned me for it. That's great, Gwen. That's just fucking great."

"You still can't admit it, can you?"

"Admit *what*? And who are you to sit in judgment of me?" he said. "I stepped up to the plate. I proposed to you! And that's a hell of a lot more than my dad ever did. He knocked up my mom, refused to marry her, and then took off. I did right by you, which is more than you did by me. You're the one who ran away."

"I had good reason! You went to a bar, Quinn. A bar, after we lost the baby." She turned her back to him as if she could no longer look at him.

"Because you wouldn't fucking talk to me!"

"It was at worst cruel and at best immature."

"And writing me a note and taking off was mature?"

She bowed her head, hugged herself. He could see the tips of her fingers digging into her own ribs. The three tender, vulnerable vertebrae at her nape reproached him, accused him. She was obviously upset—why couldn't he be the one to hug her? Why was she having to hug herself? He took half a step forward.

Then she raised her head, and her hair came down like a curtain over those unprotected vertebrae. She turned to face him and slowly unwrapped her hands from around her body. She gave him a tiny nod. "You're right. I'm sorry. I shouldn't have run. And I owed you a face-to-face explanation."

Fifteen years he'd been waiting to hear her say those words . . . and now she'd said them. He forgave her instantly—so easily that it made him furious. Did he have no self-respect?

Was this all it would have taken, a few words, to salvage their marriage?

No. He knew that the problems had been deeper than that; they hadn't learned, back then, how to grow and adapt to the world individually, much less together. They'd been so young and unformed and naive.

They stared at each other across the table, the flowers and the wine he'd brought now seeming borderline obscene.

"I'm sorry," she said again.

He nodded. "Yeah, well, I'm sorry, too. And the bar—it's not what you think. I wasn't licking tequila outta some bimbo's navel."

"I know that." Gwen looked tired. She slipped her arms back around her body, lower this time. Across her belly. It was body language that blocked him out. Told him to go away. Stuffed him back into that dark, suffocating, communication-starved place where misguided beliefs thrived.

"Tell you what, honey," he ground out. "Don't make any more assumptions about me. Try talking to me instead. Even cussin' at me."

She searched his face, a strange expression on hers. What the hell was it? Hope? Fear? Mistrust? Damned if he could tell. The Oklahoma weather was easier to read than Gwen's beautiful, blank, sphinxlike features.

Air. He needed air. He was suffocating on the past. His boots heavy on her floorboards, Quinn brushed past her and headed out the back door, slamming it behind him. Outside, the humidity embraced him cloyingly like a two-bit whore, and the stars in the night sky sparkled like cheap rhinestones.

In the corner of Gwen's yard stood a palm tree, which had dropped a couple of now-moldering coconuts. He drew back his boot and kicked one, sending it in a neat spiral to the right, over the neighbor's fence.

He winced as he heard a crash and craned his neck to see where it'd landed. Touchdown: right in the barbecue grill.

The motor of a car started nearby, just as the neighbor came barreling out the back door. "What the . . . ?"

"Sorry, man."

Fortunately, the guy laughed, and they exchanged a few words. Then Quinn went back inside.

"Gwen?"

No answer.

"Gwen?"

Music continued to play softly on the stereo, and the lights still blazed. Their glasses, the wine bottle, and the food remained on the dining room table—along with a piece of paper and a key.

Oh, no way. Another goddamned note? After the conversation they'd just had? Stunned, he grabbed the scrap of paper.

Lock up when you're done. Leave key under mat or give to Sheila. G.

Quinn strode to the window and looked out. The little red Prius no longer sat in the driveway. His damned good-bye girl had run out on him again.

He clenched his jaw so hard he thought his teeth might shatter. He sat down heavily in one of Gwen's fifties-style chairs, which creaked under his weight. He thought about smashing every one of those stupid Wonder Woman plates.

And then . . . then things started clicking in his mind.

She hadn't been happy to see him. She'd looked tired and pale. She'd been pacing like a cat on a hot griddle. She'd spit out her wine. She couldn't—or wouldn't—eat shellfish. She'd wrapped her arms around her belly. And finally she'd blurted out the truth about why she'd left him. Why *now*?

He was dumber than a bag full of hammers. Quinn got up so fast that he knocked over the chair. He righted it and then headed for the bathroom adjoining Gwen's bedroom. He pushed the door ajar. He briefly took in all the little details that defined the space as Gwen's: the pretty monogrammed hand towels, the small crystal soap dispenser, the beeswax candle. Even the wastebasket to the right of the toilet was tasteful. He looked inside it. Nothing.

Bull in a china shop, he reversed directions and stormed the little powder room, where he found what he was looking for: a package in the trash. EZ Pregnancy Test.

His heart launched toward his esophagus. Without even registering what he was doing, he sank to his knees and pulled the box from the wastebasket. He searched among the folds of the plastic bag that lined it until he found it. Two innocuous blue lines stared up at him from a window in a small white plastic stick.

Innocuous? *Yeah, right.* He felt like a manatee hit by a speeding Cobalt. How in the hell was Gwen pregnant? He did some quick math. It was possible, of course. Just barely, but stranger things had happened. Or was it not his? He sat there on his knees and scrubbed his hands over his face.

It was his. He knew that instinctively. But even if it wasn't, he didn't care.

She hadn't known how to tell him, unconvinced as she was that he'd wanted the first baby. And now everything had gone hell western crooked *again.*

Quinn got up from the floor, went back out to the dining room, and seized the open bottle of wine. He walked with it to the living room sofa and sank down onto the couch. He thought about history repeating itself, and doubted that he was any wiser or more sensitive fifteen years later, or Gwen would've stuck around to tell him.

He told himself that she'd just gone driving around the block to clear her head, that she'd come back soon.

She didn't.

chapter 28

"I waited at her house for hours," Quinn said to Sheila the next morning. "She never did come back."

Sheila's hair looked freshly frosted, her bosom was upholstered in tiger-print spandex, and she'd painted her fingernails a delicious shade of rusty, week-old-murder red.

"Listen, Ken doll," she told him. "Gwennie's hip to all kinds of sophisticated surveillance techniques. You sittin' there with the lights off won't fool her."

"She won't answer her cell phone."

"A smart man might take that to mean she don't want to talk to you."

"What if something's wrong? Something's happened to her? You have to tell me where she is. You have to let me know how to get in touch with her."

"No, lovey, I don't. Like all the agents, our Gwen keeps a 'go bag' in her car. And when she goes, she goes. She's fine. She's just traveling for work."

"Where?" asked Quinn again.

Sheila sighed, opened the top drawer of her desk, and reached for a nail file.

"I'll pay for the information," he said in a low voice.

For a moment her eyes gleamed. Then Sheila jabbed the

nail file into his chest. "You most certainly will *not*. What kind of gal do you think I am?"

Oh, please, lady. Don't make me answer that question. Quinn removed the instrument from his solar plexus and apologized. "Look . . . I'm not stalking her. I'm genuinely concerned. She's out there trying to find a murderer and a mask, and she's, well, she's not herself."

Behind black cat's-eye glasses with little red devils in the corners, Sheila's eyes narrowed. "What d'you mean, she's not herself?"

He shifted from foot to foot. "She's just not, that's all."

"Spill, Ken doll, or lose me forever."

Quinn cursed under his breath, but she'd folded her arms across her desk, and that gimlet-eyed stare told him she wasn't budging unless she got the dirt. So did her rhythmically drumming, rusty acrylic talons. Sheila had him by the short 'n' curlies.

He pulled a Baggie out of his pocket. Inside the Baggie was the pregnancy test. He dropped it in front of her keyboard.

Sheila turned it over and inspected it. The little red devils on her glasses had pointy tails. Her thickly painted mouth formed an O. She raised her head and ran her gaze up and down his body, stopping for a beat too long around his fly.

He could feel his equipment pulling an instant turtle.

"Naughty, naughty!" Sheila crowed, shaking her finger at him. "Yeah, uh-huh, and I *told* that girl you'd do her in a chicken suit, didn't I?"

"Excuse me?" said Quinn, bewildered.

"But honestly." Sheila slapped her own forehead. "Ever heard of a *rubber*, Kenny?"

Christ, he could feel himself blushing. He couldn't remember the last time he'd blushed. "I . . . uh. We—"

"It's a little jock stocking? Known to prevent this sorta thing from happening."

Quinn just stood there, mute.

Finally she took pity on him. "She's preggers, huh? I can see why you're going nuts."

He nodded.

"Assuming it's yours."

Quinn drew a deep breath at the suggestion that it wasn't; but again, he didn't care. "It's mine."

"All right. She's gonna kill me, but . . . our Gwennie's in Venice, chasing some jeweler and rowing your little microtyke around in a gondola. Go take care of her. Make sure she eats. Hold her hair if she pukes. But don't get on the wrong side of those raging hormones, you hear me? Remember, you're hunting an armed pregnant woman. . . . Good luck to you, Kenny. You'll need it."

She'd been clattering away on her keyboard during this speech, and now she hit the print button on her computer. It spit out a piece of paper, which she handed to him. "Flight schedule. Hotel info. Now give me some sugar." She pointed at her cheek.

Quinn hesitated, then bussed its powdery, wrinkled surface. He smelled a bizarre combination of hash browns and White Shoulders.

"Do you love me, Ken doll?" She smirked at him.

Already sidling out the door, he nodded like a bobblehead.

"Good. I wanna be godmother, you hear?"

Gwen didn't consider her hasty exit running away, exactly. It was more of a dodge. She was in no way ready to have the pregnancy conversation with Quinn even if she'd been wrong about him, all those years ago. Had she been? After all, he had been wrong about her. . . .

The insanity of the Miami airport distracted her from

her thoughts. MIA was always a mess: crowded and illogically designed, with little to no signage. She got her boarding pass and made it through security with little incident, though.

Getting her rubbery knees to actually walk her into the belly of the plane was the real trick.

She always hated to fly, since she was all too aware that she had no control over how she got back down to terra firma—but flying while she knew she was pregnant was infinitely worse. Now two lives were at risk.

Baby. *Baby.* She tried to bend her mind around it. Tried to reconcile the whole concept of being a mother with her high-risk career. Tried to imagine telling Quinn. Just the thought had her reaching for the airsick bag tucked in the seat pocket in front of her.

And yet she felt an indescribable joy . . . like champagne running riot through her veins. Like warm sunshine on bare skin.

The flight was long, and though she tried to sleep, the knowledge that a tiny life grew inside her created a riot of different emotions. Could her body hang on to the pregnancy this time? Would the baby be a boy or a girl? Would it be healthy? How would Quinn react? Would he want to be a parent? How much of a role would he want to play in the child's life?

Worry blurred into images from her own childhood: the Cat in the Hat, Tigger and Eeyore, Mickey Mouse–shaped pancakes. Crayons and coloring books and sidewalk chalk. Easter dresses and Barbies, hula hoops and Twister. Blue Birds and Brownies and Girl Scouts. But all the toys and games were different today, weren't they?

She went back to worrying.

Gwen arrived at Venice's Marco Polo airport, staggered off the plane, and passed through customs quickly.

As she walked outside to the vaporetto, she was proud

of herself. She'd white-knuckled it through the flight without a crutch, bypassing the Xanax and the vodka entirely. Booze and drugs weren't the most effective prenatal vitamins.

The vaporetto was crowded and buzzed with dialogue in Italian. A cranky-looking man stepped on her toe while getting on board, and a black-clad woman in a headscarf knocked her in the head with a baguette when she stepped past. The early February wind was chilly, and the spray off the water contributed to its bite.

But none of this bothered Gwen, with the stunning vista of Venice spread out before her. The water shimmered silver under a gray sky, reflecting and alluding to the centuries-old secrets and intrigue hidden behind the windows of every palazzo.

Miami and Venice: Though both cities had been built on the water, the similarities ended there. Miami flaunted sex and skin openly: vast stretches of sand, money, corruption, and flesh. There was nothing mysterious about Miami. If the city had a symbol, Gwen felt it would be a thong.

Venice concealed its sins behind the facades of history and beauty and charm. Aristocratic, jewel-like, sophisticated . . . Gwen loved Venezia but was also conscious that whispers of ancient, veiled decadence traveled along its canals and lurked under its picturesque bridges. Venice hid its venality, its malice, behind costumes: corsets and panniers, wigs and masks.

And still, though Machiavellian in its beauty, the city was seductive, extraordinary.

Because of her fascination with her surroundings, it wasn't until she got off the vaporetto in the San Marco area of Venice, where her hotel was, that Gwen remembered her cell phone was still off. As she made her way to the lovely Europa e Regina, she turned it on and discovered that she had five messages. She hurriedly checked into her room, which had a breathtaking view of the Grand Canal.

The walls were a soft apricot, and the headboard of her bed and both nightstands were varnished robin's-egg blue with hand-painted floral designs and gilt trim.

The windows were done in soft sheers framed by heavy embroidered brocade. A burled walnut writing desk sat awaiting her, its comfortable chair inviting and cozy. Gwen dropped her purse onto the desk and sank down into the middle of the bed with the phone.

A full-size, bow-fronted dresser with polished bronze handles completed the suite, and her reflection stared back at her from an elaborate eighteenth-century mirror as she listened to the first two messages.

"Gwen, it's Dante. The police found Esteban Velasquez dead, wearing a poisoned mask. I need to talk to you."

What?!

"Gwen, it's Dante again. Call me right away. The police are not happy that you've left the country."

Gwen reeled with the implications of a dead Esteban Velasquez . . . in a mask.

She called Dante immediately, relieved when he answered. "It's me. What's going on? How did Esteban die? Who found him?"

"He was found in the hotel room that you tracked him to. Wearing a cheap Mardi Gras mask," Dante said. "They're not certain of the cause of death—it will take a while before the toxicology tests are back—but it's consistent with nicotine poisoning. He wasn't shot or stabbed or injected with anything, as far as they can tell."

"Nicotine poisoning?"

"Yes. Concentrated nicotine is highly toxic and absorbs through the skin. It can kill in as little as five minutes."

"I don't understand what's going on," Gwen said.

"Neither do I—but the cops would like to talk to you."

Gwen tightened her hand around her phone. "Why?"

"The manager of the Manatee Motel ID'd you from a photo, despite the wig, and you are now officially a person of interest."

Gwen's stomach rolled. "Surely they can't take it any farther than that, though. There's no evidence that can link me to Esteban's death."

"You're seeing your ex again. Jaworski Labs has concentrated nicotine on the premises, which he once had access to. The forged mask is missing from the building. And you've both conveniently left the country."

The *forged* mask was now missing? "Both of us? What do you mean? I traveled alone."

"Quinn Lawson," Dante said, "apparently boarded a British Airways flight bound for Venice late this morning."

"Oh, my God." Gwen tried to absorb this. How had he known where she was going? Why had he followed her? And more important, when would he turn up?

"You need to come home, *bella*. Talk to the police. Put an end to their speculations."

"Dante—I can't. I can't do that yet. I have a couple of important leads."

He sighed. "I very much encourage you to come home. You may be, as the Americans say, in over your head."

Gwen's lips tightened. He couldn't have said anything more calculated to make her stay. "Thanks, Dante. I appreciate it. See you soon."

She hung up the phone racked with guilt. Esteban Velasquez was dead . . . poisoned, in a bizarre repetition of history, by a mask. And apparently *she'd* led the murderer to his location.

chapter 29

After sleeping for a few hours to beat the jet lag, Gwen showered and dressed quickly. She took the elevator down to the grand reception area of the Europa e Regina, where the floors were done in a visually arresting black-and-white marble harlequin pattern, the walls were painted a warm yellow ocher, and every elegant architectural detail screamed luxe perfection. Fabulous Venetian glass chandeliers lit every immaculate inch of the place, but they didn't manage to make her mood any sunnier.

Outside, Gwen walked down Calle Larga Marzo in search of coffee, huddling into her chartreuse suede jacket and wishing she'd brought something warmer and more weatherproof. It was drizzling slightly, and the temperature was in the upper forties.

She crossed the bridge over the canal and meandered through the charming, narrow streets until she got to the Piazza San Marco. There she found her coffee at a little sidewalk café and fed the famous hordes of pigeons some of her pastry.

The Basilica di San Marco never failed to awe her, with its five domes and multitude of spires, the four horses of Saint Mark's, and the magnificent carvings of the Labors of the Month inside the central arch. Outside and inside the basilica were countless treasures—mosaics and sculpture and religious relics.

As Gwen sat there drinking it in, she knew it was well past time to come clean with Avy. ARTemis was her company, after all, her exposure more than anyone else's. Gwen had to put her mortification and her ego aside. She needed help, and she needed it before anyone else was murdered.

She dialed Avy's cell phone number and was surprised when she woke her, since it was early afternoon. "Hi, Avy, it's Gwen. Sheila tells me you're in Venice."

"Gwennie! How are you?" Her voice was raspy with sleep.

"Late night?" Gwen asked.

"You could say that." Avy yawned audibly.

"Anything exciting?"

"Mmmmphhh," her friend said. "Just an evening at the home of a friend of Liam's in Venice. Pretty uneventful, but I don't know. . . . I just couldn't drift off last night."

"Well, you're not going to believe this, but I'm here in Venice, too."

"No kidding?" Avy's voice sounded a bit wary.

Gwen couldn't bring herself to tell Avy what was going on over the phone. "Listen, do you want to get together for dinner tonight, the three of us? I'd love to meet Liam."

Slight hesitation. "Sure. We'd really like that. Why don't we meet here at the Gritti Palace dining room? Around sevenish?"

"All right. See you then." Gwen closed her phone and tapped it thoughtfully on the table. Ostensibly, Avy and Liam were here for a romantic holiday . . . and why not, since Venice was one of the most beautiful cities in the world?

They were in love. They were engaged to be married. Yet she'd known Avy for years, ever since they'd been college roommates. And Sheila was right: There was something very odd about this romantic getaway of hers. She'd left so abruptly from that meeting, saying only that she had to go, that it was important. That Gwen should take on her assignment.

Was she helping Liam, a world-renowned thief, to steal something? That didn't fit Avy's moral profile, but then again, marrying a cat burglar didn't, either. Like Sheila, Gwen wanted to know exactly what was going on. She supposed she'd learn more in a couple of hours.

The Gritti Palace was situated fairly near Gwen's hotel in the San Marco *sestiere*, on Santa Maria del Giglio. A fifteenth-century palazzo, it was luxurious in the way that only old Venice can master, radiating history and grandness from every corner.

Far more interesting to Gwen, who had stayed there with her parents, was Sir Liam James, who was a veritable Gritti Palace of men. She eyed him as she gave Avy a bear hug. Liam looked as if he'd jumped off the pediment of a Greek temple and donned a Savile Row suit, stopping only to imbibe a martini and seduce a young Grace Kelly on the way.

Gwen turned to Avy, who seemed a little too interested in Gwen's reaction to her fiancé. And that was very unlike her.

"You look awfully tired for someone on a romantic getaway," Gwen teased her. "This man has clearly been keeping you up at night."

Avy gave a short laugh and cast Liam a pointed glance.

"Not so," Liam protested with a wicked grin. "She has been keeping part of *me* up at night."

Gwen flushed, while his eyes seemed to go greener.

He took both of her hands in his manicured ones and kissed her soundly on both cheeks. "My dear Gwendolyn, what a pleasure it is to meet you! Come, what can we get you to drink?"

"It's nice to meet you, too, Liam," she said, taking a step back. "But it's just Gwen."

"All right, Just Gwen," he said, his eyes twinkling. "What will you have?"

"Pellegrino," she said. "Thank you." She'd kill for a nice, belly-warming glass of Chianti, but that was out of the question, given her condition.

Handsome, charming, affable, and clearly besotted with Avy, Liam cleared up the mystery of why she was with him in one smile.

God had mixed a powerful man cocktail when He'd created Liam James. He'd combined two fingers of eighty-proof George Clooney with a dash of spicy David Beckham and dropped in three cool cubes of Pierce Brosnan. Then he'd garnished the lethal concoction with an amusing wedge of Johnny Depp in *Pirates of the Caribbean.* One whiff was enough to make the average woman drunk. A single sip would have her naked, and two would make her insane.

Liam James was a man who could melt the panties off a nun in seconds flat, and Avy was certainly no nun.

Curiously, Gwen found that he paled in comparison to Quinn. Liam seemed . . . what was the right word? Frivolous. He struck her as a man who filched what he wanted, whereas Quinn got his hands dirty and created it from scratch.

But Liam did seem perfect for Avy, and Gwen had to laugh at her friend's reaction to him: She seemed annoyed and frustrated by her hopeless attraction to the guy. Gwen had never seen Avy so off balance. She'd finally met a man she couldn't handle, and Gwen thought it was good for her.

As they sat in the bar, Gwen drank her Pellegrino, Liam

drank vodka, and Avy, who still seemed a bit wary, had bourbon.

"What brings you to Venezia, Gwen?" Liam asked politely.

She stayed as close to the truth as possible. "I'm here to speak to a jeweler about a collection of Byzantine items that's gone missing."

"Oh?"

"He's done some pieces for a new collection that are remarkably similar, and I want to question him face-to-face—if you know what I mean."

"I do." Liam nodded. "I absolutely do. So you're representing the insurance company?"

"Yes."

"Which one?"

Gwen uncrossed and recrossed her legs. "I can't really disclose details of a case. Sorry."

"Oh, no worries. Discretion is of the utmost importance in these matters, isn't it, Avy, my love? Insurers can be such sticks-in-the-mud."

Avy's hand tightened around her glass and a muscle jumped in her jaw. "You can't blame insurance companies for getting cranky about theft and fraud." Her glance at Liam was carefully neutral, but Gwen would swear that behind that neutrality was anger . . . and uncertainty. As if she didn't know what to do about something.

"How's your father?" Gwen asked, to change the subject.

It didn't seem to be a welcome change. "Fine," said Avy.

"Isn't he delightful?" Liam said. "A veritable pistol of a man."

"True. He'd like to shoot Liam," Avy murmured.

Gwen laughed. "Nobody would be good enough for Everett's little girl," she said. "Don't take it personally."

"Like anyone would get *your* father's approval?" Avy shot back.

Poor Quinn. He hadn't had a chance in hell with her dad. "My father liked the mayonnaise prince."

"Mayonnaise prince?" Liam inquired, looking amused. "Was he a colorless sidekick?"

"That about sums it up," Avy said, nudging Gwen.

"Curtis wasn't that bad. And I really liked his dog."

"Now, there's a reason to marry a chap," Liam remarked.

"Well, Curtis used to pass out early, and Pickles and I would watch Letterman."

"Pickles. You can't be serious? The mayonnaise prince had a dog named Pickles?"

"Swear to God," said Avy.

"Okay, this is war," Gwen declared. "We're going to talk about some of *your* past flames, Ave. How about the circus clown?"

Liam choked on his vodka.

"He was not a circus clown. He had a business that catered to kids' birthday parties."

"Oh, right. I forgot that he was also the Cat in the Hat and the Easter Bunny . . . not to mention Zorba the Magician."

Liam bellowed with laughter. "Avy, my love! You're upset about *my* past?"

"And what about the medical student who took you on a hot date with a cadaver, Ave?"

"Better than that stuffed shirt who came for the weekend with matching Polo luggage, shoe trees in his loafers, and starched, dry-cleaned boxer shorts."

"That was a blind date," Gwen said. "It's not like I chose that guy. . . ."

"Ladies," Liam interjected.

". . . and what about the pilot, Ave? Mile-high Sly?"

"Shut up about the pilot, Gwennie, or I'll have to bring up Dirk the Defiler."

"Ladies! While this is all very amusing, things seem to be getting heated." Liam signaled to the waiter, who promptly popped over.

"Sir?"

"This lovely lady needs another Pellegrino, *per favore*—though if I were her, I'd choose something stronger, since she actually went on a date with a fellow named Dirk."

"Can I hit him?" Gwen asked Avy.

"Be my guest."

"And we'll have another Basil Hayden's on the rocks for the other lady. Grey Goose straight up for me, *signore*."

They chatted for a few more minutes, finished their drinks, and then went to the grand dining room for the evening meal. After Liam had taken the "liberty" of ordering antipasti for them all, Avy excused herself to go to the ladies' room. Gwen was tempted to go after her and have the necessary chat immediately, but couldn't take the risk that there might be other women in there. She'd have to wait.

There was a moment of silence between Liam and Gwen, but he was far too skilled a conversationalist to let it grow. He eased back comfortably in his chair and tilted his head at her.

"So, tell me what Avy was like as a college freshman," he said.

Gwen smiled, thinking back. "She looks just the same; she just dresses differently now. She arrived at Sweet Briar in army surplus pants and a T-shirt, with this industrial-size backpack that used to be her dad's. There I was, with my matching, monogrammed Hartmann luggage, dressed in Calvin Klein. We weren't sure what to think of each other at first. Avy was different from anyone I'd ever met. . . ."

Liam asked more questions, his expression fond, and Gwen did her best to answer them.

"And now you work together," he said. "That's lovely."

Gwen nodded. Lovely . . . as long as she didn't single-handedly ruin Avy's reputation and future. She swallowed hard. When could she get her alone?

"Now, didn't Avy tell me that your last recovery was of an old Venetian mask?"

Gwen snapped to attention, her stomach rocketing to her throat. "Yes. Solid gold and studded with emeralds, sapphires, and diamonds. It was quite a piece."

"I know it," Liam said. "Since we're all discussing past, er, peccadilloes, I will confess that I used to date a strange woman who's descended from the Borgias. She was quite obsessed with that mask."

Gwen sat stunned. "Really?" she managed. "How interesting. Confidentially, Liam, there's been an odd development with that recovery—"

Avy turned the corner from the hallway leading to the ladies' room.

"Please don't say anything to her," Gwen said. "She's got enough to deal with on her own plate."

Liam raised an eyebrow but nodded. "All right."

Avy approached the table, slim and glamorous in a deep green cashmere sweater with cutouts that showed off her athletic shoulders. She'd reapplied her soft claret lipstick and seemed more relaxed after all the teasing and the two bourbons.

"You know," she said, "there's nothing like an old friend with knowledge of your dark past to keep you humble."

"And a fiancé who makes you wear a puppet mask." Liam's lips curved.

"Puppet mask?" Gwen asked.

Avy looked daggers at Liam. "Lover boy here thought that we'd be the plague doctor and the puppet for Carnevale."

"For some reason," Liam said with feigned surprise, "our Avy doesn't wish me to pull her strings and make her dance."

"I can't imagine why," Gwen said.

"Don't worry, darling. We'll outfit you with something much more grand for tomorrow night." He turned to Gwen. "Will you get a costume and enjoy the start of Carnevale with us while you're here?"

There were masks for sale in street stalls everywhere, and balls and fetes advertised. "I don't know," Gwen demurred. "I'm really here on business."

"I can assure you that I've found mixing business with pleasure most rewarding," Liam said, brushing the backs of his fingers over Avy's cheek. She actually blushed.

Gwen was so astonished by the sight of Avy blushing that she didn't respond. Then memories of her Brazilian Carnaval rushed her, and her own cheeks heated.

Quinn in a tight black T-shirt with a quick smile and a slow hand up her skirt.

A shirtless Quinn with rock-hard abs and his mouth on her breasts.

A naked Quinn with his unshaven face between her legs.

Gwen squirmed and wished she were anywhere but in the Gritti's dining room with two lovebirds, on only the second course of five, but she supposed she'd have to sit through it.

And she did . . . all the way to dessert. Liam and Avy continued their edgy flirting, while Gwen agonized over how she'd deliver the news she had, and wondered what exactly their reaction would be if she were to suddenly announce that she was pregnant. She moved her hand to her navel and rubbed her index finger over Quinn's diamond.

Just full of secrets, wasn't she? Gwen had not the slightest idea how she'd tell him or what would happen between them or when he'd show up . . . but as the espresso and the check were delivered to the table, she found herself praying.

Please, God, let this baby stay with me. She wanted to be born fifteen years ago. Now she's back.

Only a child of Quinn's could be so stubborn.

chapter 30

Gwen made the short walk back to the Europa e Regina by herself, even though Liam gallantly offered to escort her. The doorman admitted her without hesitation and she started for the elevators.

A man uncoiled himself from an armchair in a cozy little sitting area to her left, and without warning she looked up into Quinn's cognac-colored eyes. "Hello, darlin'," he said. "Why is it that you never, ever say good-bye?"

Her whole body began to tremble.

This was it. Unconsciously, her hand went to her abdomen, her fourth finger brushing the diamond beneath her sweater. Would he yell at her, make a scene right here in the lobby? Try to muscle her outside, where he could give vent to his feelings freely? There could be no doubt that he knew.

His eyes were unreadable, and she shivered. "How did you find me?"

"How do you think?"

"You bribed Sheila. How much did she soak you for?"

"You might be surprised to hear that she wouldn't take any money. She just wants to be godmother."

She couldn't even laugh at that, couldn't think, didn't

know what to say. Her eyes filled, and she looked at the black-and-white tiled floor.

He took a step forward, and she took two back.

"It's okay," he said.

No, really. It's not okay.

He closed the gap, put a finger under her chin, and tilted it up. "Are you all right? How are you feeling?"

Kindness was the last thing she'd expected, after the way she'd disappeared. She nodded, and her eyes overflowed. *Damn it.*

"C'mere, honey." Quinn took her in his arms and stroked her hair. "Want to take a walk? Better yet, a gondola ride?"

Conscious of all the hotel personnel and guests surrounding them, she nodded again. She dashed the tears away and let him take her hand as they walked outside. Quinn signaled a gondolier, settled on a price for a half-hour tour, and held her steady as she climbed into the small watercraft. He got in behind her and sat next to her as the other man stood in the bow and cast off the line holding them near the dock.

The night air was cold, but she didn't mind. All around them the city prepared for the start of Carnevale, its biggest tourist attraction. The crowds had started pouring in, and during the day merchants catered to them with souvenirs, specialty foods, colorful displays, and signs advertising costume ateliers, the more upscale operating by appointment only.

Tonight the moon had stolen the show, though, bathing the city in sparkling silver. Quinn's fingers laced unexpectedly through hers, and she looked up at the strong column of his throat, the firm jaw, the proud, slightly Roman nose.

"You're not angry with me?" she asked. "Why not?"

He was silent for a moment, letting the gentle lapping of the Grand Canal and the creaking of the gondola speak for him. "Gwen, isn't it time to let the anger go? Yeah, sure, initially I was mad. You didn't even leave me much of a note this time."

She started to speak, but he tenderly put a finger over her lips. It wasn't a controlling gesture, more of a silent request that she let him finish.

"I felt like busting some things at first. But then, I don't know . . . I guess it hit me that it takes two to make somebody run. And I don't want to be the kind of guy you run from. I want to be the kind that you run *to*."

Oh, Quinn.

"I tried to put myself in your shoes, honey. You'd just found out about the baby yourself, right?"

She nodded.

"And there you were, convinced that I hadn't even wanted the first one—*erroneously* convinced, *wrongly* convinced, but still sure of it. How the hell were you gonna tell me about this one? And we'd just had a fight. So you ran."

"I—"

He shook his head, half smiling. "You're somethin' else, Gwennie. You can break into buildings, crack safes, and kick the hell outta that Cato guy, but you run from me. Why is that?"

Maybe because her feelings for Cato weren't nearly as complicated. "He doesn't scare me nearly as much as you do."

"Whatever. I can't say that I was prepared for this, but I want this baby, Gwen. I want it more than anything in the world. I'll marry you tomorrow, if that will make you happy. You gotta appreciate the irony of a *second* shotgun wedding with your pissed-off parents."

She chuckled weakly. Marry Quinn all over again? She tried to bend her mind around the concept.

"But if you don't want that," he continued, "then we'll

come at it some other way. Some way that works for us and the baby, both."

She couldn't think. Could barely breathe.

Living together? Living separately? Sharing custody? Gwen placed her hand, again, over her flat stomach. Still so hard to believe there was a tiny life growing inside her. Such a fragile life . . .

His next words just about killed her. "Be my people," he said, cradling her. "You and the baby. Please. Give me someone to share my life with."

Oh, God. Her eyes overflowed again. He was saying all the right things, touching her the way her body begged to be touched . . . and yet it was the omission of three little words that stopped her cold.

I love you. He hadn't said it to her. She hadn't said it to him. Perhaps the past had swallowed the sentiment whole. Maybe the future loomed too large. Was it too soon? Or too late?

She didn't have the answer, so she pushed the thoughts away and gave in to other, more immediate ones. Ones that were just as hard to verbalize.

"Quinn, I'm so scared. . . . I'm scared that if my body couldn't hang on to a baby at nineteen, how will it hang on when I'm thirty-four?"

He took her face in his big hands and kissed her, a kiss full of the magic and moonlight of Venice after dark. "It's gonna be fine," he said.

"How can you possibly know that?"

"This baby wants us for parents, sweetheart. It's chosen us twice. And I think it's here to stay this time."

His certainty and his heat soothed her as nothing else had. His gentleness caught her off guard. She realized that she'd grown accustomed to the idea of Quinn as a combatant. Letting him onto her "team," so to speak, didn't come naturally. But it did feel good. Still, she had questions.

"Are you ready to be a parent?" Gwen asked bluntly.

"Scared out of my mind," he admitted. "But . . . in a weird way, yeah. You?"

"Petrified. Overjoyed. Ready? No. I have this urge to run out and buy a hundred books on how to do this. But I'll be ready when the time comes."

"Will you feel trapped?" He carefully didn't look at her as he posed the question.

She put her hand over his. "I'm thirty-four now, Quinn. Not nineteen. I've had some years to live my life. So though it may be hard, no—I don't think I'll feel trapped this time. I'll feel blessed."

He nodded, but still wouldn't look at her.

"What is it?"

He sighed. "You said just a few days ago that you didn't want me in your world. I gotta tell you, Gwen, I'd walk through hell in gasoline-soaked underwear for you—but what I won't do is back out of my own child's life. No way, no how. You can't ask that of me."

"I wouldn't." She squeezed his hand.

"So you've changed your mind?"

"Quinn, hasn't everything changed? Hasn't everything turned upside down since the day I walked into your office?"

"Yeah. I guess it has."

They fell silent as the gondolier took them around the darkened, lovely old city. Gwen held Quinn's hand on the water, and when they returned to the hotel's dock, she was surprised to find herself attached to him still. As he helped her out of the gondola, he murmured a few words. "You don't seem to want a proposal, so how 'bout a proposition instead?"

She had to smile at that.

"Let's you and me shack up for the night. It might just

grow on you." He bent down and kissed her, sending familiar heat rushing through her system.

Gwen held his hand all the way through the lobby and up to her room.

Venice by dawn was just as breathtaking as Venice by moonlight. Spectacular striations of pink and gold lit the still-drowsy sky, bathing the old palazzos and villas in warm, honeyed light.

Quinn lay on his side next to Gwen, his big, nude body radiating comforting heat. His breathing was deep, even, content. During the night he'd unconsciously curved an arm around her, and his hand rested protectively on her abdomen. This simple gesture convinced her more than any words that he truly wanted this child.

And so did she. But she knew instinctively that she didn't want to stop working—and what about Quinn himself? He was a high-powered executive who was sure to find another job as soon as they cleared their names. Where did that leave the baby? In day care? With a nanny? Gwen couldn't say she liked either of those options, though they were reality for millions of children all over the world. Children who grew up just fine.

Outside the hotel she heard heels on cobblestones, murmured conversations, and a few businesses opening their doors and hosing off the sidewalks of debris from the night before. The smell of baking wafted up, even through the closed windows of her room. Life went on, ignoring the momentous decisions ahead of her and somehow reminding Gwen that she could hardly make them all this morning.

"Hey, sleepyhead," she said, nudging Quinn. "Since you're here, you may as well help me get on with things."

"Mmmmm." He opened his eyes. "Yeah, where were

we?" He moved his hand south of her stomach with evil intent.

"*No*," she said. "We have to get up."

"I am up." Quinn placed her hand on a part of his anatomy that evidently needed no caffeine. Then he rolled her onto her back and made free with her breasts.

"Really, you cannot distract me this way—"

He spread her thighs. "No?"

"Naaah!"

"Nah? I'm getting mixed signals here," Quinn said, gently easing home as if she were made of glass. Like glass at four thousand degrees Fahrenheit, she melted. "You still want me to stop?"

"Stop and you're a dead man," she promised. He was certainly full of himself . . . but then again, she was full of him, too.

"I can give it to you fast, baby, if you're in a hurry." He teased her with clever fingers, scraping teeth, hot mouth.

"T-take your time."

"Yeah, I can do that," Quinn said, smoothing her hair back from her face as he moved masterfully inside her. "It's been fifteen years, so what's another half hour?"

After breakfast, Gwen and Quinn walked over to Costumeria Barzini. The shop was tucked down a small side street and held an astonishing number of costumes for its size. Ball gowns, breeches, cloaks, petticoats, wigs, and masks of every size, shape, and color confronted them. Sheila would love this place—it was a theatrical gold mine.

Gwen laughed as Quinn tried on a jester's cap in orange and silver, complete with tinkling bells. He struck a pose.

The shop smelled of mothballs, old fabric, and fresh lavender, with an underlying odor of ripe shoe leather. In the far northeast corner, a tired-looking woman in a navy blue dress busied herself with steaming costumes.

In the northwest corner was a cash register, where a man—maybe her husband?—took money from a line of customers and handed them their rentals.

Gwen left Quinn donning another hat—this one something like a musketeer's—and approached the woman, since she was alone. *"Buon giorno, signora, come sta?"*

"Bene, grazie." She barely looked up from her task.

"Signora," Gwen said in passable Italian, "I wonder if I may ask you . . . have you seen this particular mask before?" She reached into her handbag and produced several snapshots of the elaborate jeweled Columbina. She held them out.

The woman hung the end of the steamer on its hook, wiped her hands on a small cloth, and took the photos. Her eyes widened in shock or alarm, and she handed them back immediately, then crossed herself. She shook her head.

"We do not have this mask, *signorina.*"

"But have you seen it?"

"It is cursed. Stay away from it."

"I'm looking for someone who duplicated a mask like this one. It's very important. Please. Can you help?"

To Gwen's surprise, the woman was very close to tears. "No, I cannot help you. Please leave."

"But—"

"Leave now. *Per favore.*" Her aghast expression and tone of voice had attracted her husband's attention. He looked over at them, curious.

"And don't come back here again." Her voice was sharp enough to alert Quinn, and he immediately took off the hat.

"Mi dispiace, signora." Mystified, Gwen took his arm and they left.

"What was that all about?" he asked.

"I don't know, but the sight of the mask clearly upset her. She says it's cursed."

"I'm beginning to agree with her."

Gwen nodded and looked at her watch. It was still early, and Avy might not yet be awake, so she and Quinn took a train to Padua next, the jeweler's address burning a hole in her pocket.

Padua was a bustling little university town, lively with students and two street markets around the Palazzo della Ragione. Gwen checked her map and they made their way on foot to the Piazza dei Signori, where the jeweler's shop was located.

The front room was small and sunny, with scrupulously clean glass cases displaying traditional gold jewelry— necklaces, earrings, rings, bracelets, and watches. On the floor was a large Oriental rug that Gwen pegged as an early-nineteenth-century Chelaberd in the Kazak style, a little worn but in decent condition for its age. Overhead hung a sparkling Murano glass chandelier, which added a touch of modernity to the otherwise classical room.

"*Buon giorno*," she said to a young, chicly dressed salesclerk who had eyes only for Quinn. "May I speak to *Signor* Brancato?"

With difficulty, the girl tore her gaze from Quinn's biceps and responded. "May I tell him what business you have with him?"

"It's a private matter of some urgency."

The girl nodded and disappeared into a back room. She returned almost immediately and gestured to Gwen to follow her.

Quinn raised his brows, asking a silent question. Did she want him to go back with her? He didn't speak a word of Italian, so she shrugged, leaving it up to him. He glanced toward the jewelry cases. "I'll stay out here."

Gwen nodded and followed the girl into the rear of the store.

An aging man with surprisingly broad shoulders and arms ropy with muscle sat at a battered desk. His shirt-sleeves were rolled up and he wore a lamb's-wool sweater-vest to keep him warm. His pale blue eyes were myopic and watery, but shrewd behind thick jeweler's glasses. The glasses were held on his face by an elastic band that went around his head. The band had mussed a few strands of his hair in back so that they stood up like antennae.

The girl went a little too eagerly back out front, no doubt to flirt with Quinn.

"*Signor* Brancato?" Gwen queried.

"*Si?*"

She launched into Italian. "*Mi chiamo* Gwen Davies, and I work for an American company called ARTemis. We're hired by insurance companies to track down and re-cover stolen art objects."

Signor Brancati looked at her for a long moment. Then he took off the jeweler's glasses and set them down. He rubbed wearily at his eyes. "Yes? Continue."

"A couple of months ago, a very valuable gold Venetian mask encrusted with jewels was stolen from a U.S. company."

Signor Brancati dragged his age-spotted, blue-veined hands down his face and clasped them in front of him on his worktable, almost as if he were praying. He nodded.

"A duplicate of this mask was made by a jeweler using a technique called repoussé. You're a well-known master of this technique. You also own a very expensive laser welder, which was used to seal layers of gold over the lead needed to approximate the weight of the real solid-gold mask."

Brancato wouldn't look her in the eye.

"*Signore*, I'm afraid this isn't just a case of simple fraud. Two people have been murdered."

Silence.

"*Dead*, *Signor* Brancato. Please, if you know anything or if you created the copy yourself . . . please help me."

Brancato sighed. At last he spoke. "I expected you," he murmured, "but not so soon."

"You expected me?" Gwen was mystified for the second time that day. "Why?"

"My daughter called me. You went to see her earlier today—Silva Barzini."

"She was very upset when I showed her pictures of the mask."

"And for good reason. The safety of my grandchildren has been threatened." He raised his clasped hands to his mouth, and she noticed a visible tremor.

"*What?* Why?"

"Because initially I refused the job."

"Who—"

"Sit down, *Signorina* Davies," he said, gesturing to a wing chair covered in threadbare tapestry.

Gwen sank into it and waited as he gathered his thoughts.

"I will talk to you, but you must keep in mind that I have done nothing wrong: To make a duplicate of a famous piece is not illegal. It is laborious, it is time-consuming, but in itself the process is not a criminal act."

"I realize that, *Signor* Brancato. Were you paid?"

The edges of his thin mouth turned down, seeming to slice into his jowls. "*Si*, she paid me, but I only kept enough to cover my materials and expenses. The rest of it I gave to the Scrovegni Chapel for the preservation of Giotto's frescoes. The woman who came to see me would do well to spend time kneeling in front of the *Last Judgment* on the west wall."

"What is this woman's name, *signore*?"

He shook his head. "I do not know."

"What did she look like? Was she Italian?"

"She wore a black wig and dark glasses. She spoke in an assumed German accent."

"How do you know it was assumed?"

"It sounded stilted." He rubbed at the back of his neck. "She came only once herself. She asked if I would duplicate the mask. I wished to know her reasons.

"She told me that she wanted to display the copy but keep the real one in the vault. I didn't believe her story. I thought she was up to no good. I turned down the job.

"She offered double the money, which made me even more suspicious. I turned her down again. She told me that I would regret my decision, and left."

Gwen leaned forward as Brancato got lost in his own thoughts for a moment. She waited. "And then . . .?"

"Then a man—if he can call himself that—showed up at my daughter's shop two days later. A man with a Spanish accent, rough-looking. He had video of my grandchildren at school, playing in the yard. He knew where they took piano lessons, dance lessons. He told my daughter that he could find them anywhere, and that he advised me to make the mask. If we told the police, they were dead."

Signor Brancato had tears in his old eyes now. He looked at Gwen and spread his hands wide, palms up. "What was I to do, eh? I told myself that making a copy of a cursed mask was no big deal. And to be frank with you, *signorina*, to keep my grandchildren safe I would do anything. Wouldn't you?"

Gwen's chest tightened and ached with sympathy. She reached into her purse and pulled out a package of tissues. She handed him one. "*Signor* Brancato, I am going to find these people. I promise you."

She didn't want to tell him that they would quite

probably kill again if she didn't figure out the motives behind their sick game.

Gwen took his hands. "I think your grandchildren are safe, *signore*. You did what these people wanted, and they have no reason to harm your family now."

"*Si*, this is what I tell myself every night before I go to sleep. But I pray to my dead wife, God rest her soul, to be their angel, to keep them safe."

A lump rose in Gwen's throat, and she squeezed his hands in hers. "She will do that, *signore*. I'm sure of it." She hesitated. "However, you may want to take a little vacation for a bit, until we solve this mystery. Don't tell anyone where you're going."

chapter 31

Quinn stood with his hands in his pockets, chatting with the salesclerk in her broken English. He looked . . . smug. Like he had a secret. But Gwen didn't pay this much attention, since her head was still spinning with the information she'd gotten from Brancato.

They got on the train back to Venice and she shared the results of the interview with him. Was the mystery woman Angeline? It seemed all too likely.

She and Quinn reviewed everything, trying to connect the dots. The mask: stolen in a smash-and-grab job. ARTemis: given the task of recovering it. Gwen had then found a copy, which damaged her reputation. She'd discovered the body of Carlos Velasquez and called the police. Then the police had found the body of his brother . . . and they now wanted to question both Quinn and Gwen.

What was going on? To all appearances, someone was out to embarrass ARTemis and destroy Gwen. But why? And who? Nothing made sense. All they knew was that a woman was somehow involved.

"Dante thinks we should go back immediately and talk to the police to clear things up," Gwen said to Quinn, as the train rocked rhythmically back and forth and the Italian countryside rolled past.

He frowned. "He's right, of course, but something's bothering me. Didn't you mention that the assignment of recovering the mask originally went to Avy?"

"Yes . . . why?"

"But she had to leave the country suddenly and so she gave it to you."

"Are you saying that maybe there was a plot afoot to discredit Avy—that it never had anything to do with me?"

"You have to admit that it's a possibility."

Gwen nodded, lost in thought. "I have to talk to her. *Immediately.* It was a foregone conclusion that Avy would get the mask as the plum assignment. Nobody could have foretold that she'd squirrel out of it, take off to Europe on a whim, and give it to me. It's very unlike her."

Quinn leaned forward and took her hands. "But now you're in the middle of it, asking dangerous questions, and whoever's behind the original plot is tying up all the loose ends to avoid discovery." His eyes had gone dark and serious. "I don't want the next dead body that turns up to be yours."

They disembarked at the station and took a vaporetto to the Gritti Palace, entering from the rear. Quinn listened to reason and agreed that she was safe there. She offered a suggestion—not an order—that while she talked privately with her boss, he might round up some costumes for them for later, since Carnevale launched that very night.

Gwen saw him off with a kiss and then did her best to calm down before confessing to Avy, who would be well within her rights to fire her. Her only hope was that Avy might be able to put herself in Gwen's shoes . . . and admit that she'd have tried to recoup on her own, too.

But then there were all the secrets that she'd kept from her best friend. How could she possibly explain those?

Again, her only hope was that Avy had a few of her own—
which went without saying.

With shaking hands, Gwen called Avy's room and asked
if she could come up to see her.

She found Avy in a terry hotel robe with wet hair, again
tired and groggy. She yawned. "Hi."

"Hi."

"Hi. Where's Liam?"

"He went out for some pastry that he says I've got to
try." She sent Gwen a wry look. "He gets very passionate
about food. Camembert, for example. Goes into raptures
over stinky cheese."

Quinn loved a good beer. He'd once made it his mission
to visit almost every pub in London.

Gwen tossed her bag into an armchair and, like a true
chicken, headed for the bathroom. "Hope you don't mind,
but I've had to go since I boarded a train back from Padua.
I hate public toilets."

Avy yawned again. "Be my guest. I'll still be here when
you get out." She plopped down on the bed and crawled toward the pillows.

Gwen went into the sumptuous marble bathroom, still
searching for the right words. She was washing her hands
when she heard a heavy knock outside, and Avy muttering
something about Grand Central Station as she got off the
bed to answer it.

Liam, returning with his pastries? Gwen opened the
door as Avy set an ornate, hand-painted box on the bed. It
looked vaguely familiar. Avy opened it and stared.

"My God. Liam had the Borgia mask copied? Just in
time for Carnevale tonight. . . . Does he want me to wear
it?"

All the breath left Gwen's body as Avy reached for a familiar gold, gem-encrusted Columbina mask with green
velvet lining.

Esteban Velasquez, found dead in a poisoned mask. The forged Borgia, now missing from Jaworski Labs. What if . . . ?

As Avy's fingers came within inches of it, Gwen launched herself across the room, unaware that she'd even moved. Pure instinct took over. She knocked the mask out of Avy's hands and sent it flying. It hit the wall with a thud and a soft clatter as the jeweled fringe was knocked askew.

"Don't touch it, Ave! It's *poisoned.* I'm sure of it. Don't go *near* it."

Avy stared at her as if she'd sprouted horns. "That's ridiculous."

"It's not! The real mask is missing—unless that's it. I recovered a fake. Someone is trying to reenact history. The curse of the Borgia cousin, remember? He poisoned the original. Liam didn't send you that. *Who did?*" Gwen heard the hoarse urgency in her own voice as if from far away. "Who delivered it to the room?"

"A porter . . ."

"Call down to the front desk. Ask them who brought it here."

Avy blinked. "You're serious."

"Yes, I'm serious! A man in Miami just died from a poisoned mask, Ave. The second Velasquez brother. The first brother was shot."

"How . . . what do you mean, you recovered a fake? Does the client know? What's going on?"

Gwen took a deep breath. "Wash your hands. Then we need to talk."

"Damn right we do." Grimly, Avy scrubbed her hands, then called the front desk and asked who'd delivered the box. Some kid from a local courier service. She called the courier service. A nameless, nondescript man had paid cash.

Meanwhile, Gwen turned over the mask with her foot

and bent to examine it. Fake. The same fake—she could
see the mark where she'd dug out the curl of lead. No wonder the police wanted to talk to her. She wondered if they
had surveillance tape of two shadowy figures leaving
Jaworski Labs—she and Quinn.

Avy's face looked as stern as she'd ever seen it as she
turned to face Gwen. "You'd better start from the beginning. Now."

"You'll probably fire me," Gwen said, "and I won't
blame you. But here's what happened. . . ." She left nothing out, not even the secrets of her past.

Avy listened in absolute silence, her expression growing
darker by the minute. "Let me get this straight. We have a
week before Jaworski Labs files suit for breach of contract,
destroying ARTemis's reputation?"

"Yes. But at least Quinn doesn't think they'll go to the
press. They have a vested interest in keeping this
under—"

"Great. I'm so glad a man I've never met—even though
my best friend was married to him!—has an opinion on
this."

Gwen didn't feel that right now was the best time to
bring up the fact that Avy was engaged to Liam, but Gwen
had only just met *him.*

"ARTemis is my company, Gwen! When were you
going to tell me?" Her voice was low with suppressed fury.

"I—I—I tried to call you more than once. You wouldn't
answer your damn phone, since you were off on some
honeymoon with Thief Boy. And then you hung up on
me. . . ."

"Oh, so it's my fault. You could have left a message."

"Look, the bottom line was that I wanted to take care of
this myself. I felt responsible. I was mortified—here it was
my first case, and I screwed it up. I just wanted to make it
right."

Avy said nothing.

"Ave, you would have done the same thing."

"No." She shook her head violently.

Gwen met her gaze steadily, without flinching.

"All right, all right," she snarled. "I would have done the same thing. That doesn't excuse your actions."

Avy sat propped against the headboard in her white terry bathrobe and socks, clutching a pillow to her stomach. With her damp hair and freshly scrubbed face, she looked exactly like the girl Gwen had warily introduced herself to freshman year, a lifetime ago. The girl who'd unzipped an army green sleeping bag to use as a comforter, while Gwen had brought matching quilted bedspreads and pillow shams to make the room nicer.

Avy didn't look like anyone's boss. She looked like Gwen's best friend . . . except that Gwen was very afraid that she'd managed to destroy not only their professional relationship, but their personal one as well.

"Ave, I'm so sorry. It was never my intention to damage the company. I'll resign if you don't want to fire me."

Avy fingered the Swiss army knife that hung on a cord around her neck. Her hands shook slightly, but she said nothing.

They both looked at the mask in the corner.

The silence stretched on, and finally Gwen went to pick up her coat and handbag from the chair. Clearly, she was finished. Clearly, Avy couldn't forgive her. She shrugged into the coat, her heart heavy, her blood sluggish with shame. She headed for the door.

"Take that off," Avy snapped. "You're not going anywhere, Gwennie. I can't in good conscience fire someone who just saved my life. And you're not resigning, either: You're going to see this thing through."

Gwen almost collapsed with relief.

"But I'm still really, really, *really* pissed off at you. And if you ever keep information like this from me again—"

"Understood," said Gwen. As she peeled off her coat, she spotted a large, rolled canvas emerging from the window treatment. "Hey, Ave? You been buying art while you're here? What's that?"

"Nothing," Avy said too quickly. "Listen, we have to figure out what's going on. Why would someone send me a poisoned mask?"

Gwen had a flashback to the original assignments meeting: Sheila popping in. Communiqué from Kelso. The Greek ambassador, out for revenge . . . "Could this be related to Kelso's warning?"

Avy sat up straight.

"Worse, could that guy behind the Sword of Alexander plot be gunning for you? Gautreau?"

Her friend lost color and passed a hand over her mouth, her fingers creeping up to finger a tiny scar on her cheek, a nasty souvenir of her experience with Gautreau. "There's no doubt in my mind that he'll rear his ugly head one day. But I didn't expect it to be quite this soon."

Avy hugged her knees again, while Gwen felt a knot of cold, hard fear deep in her gut.

Then they both jumped as a key rattled in the lock and Liam came in with a pastry box, humming. "Hi, honey, I'm home!"

chapter 32

"Oh, hallo, Gwen. Greetings and salutations and all that rot." Liam flashed a grin at her, then came over to peck her on the cheek. He smelled of damp wool, expensive soap, and coffee.

"Hi," Gwen said.

"Liam, you didn't send me that mask in the corner, did you?" asked Avy.

"No, my darling. Why?" He walked over to the mask. "Good God, it's the Borgia."

"*Don't touch it*," Gwen and Avy said at the same time.

His eyebrows shot up toward his hairline. "Why not?"

They explained.

He looked shaken and moved immediately to Avy's side. "We need to take this to the proper authorities—if it's actually poisoned."

"I'll bet you any amount of money that it is," Gwen said. "But I'm not volunteering to be the guinea pig who finds out the hard way."

"No, indeed." Liam seemed lost in thought.

"Do you think this is Gautreau?" Avy asked.

He shook his head slowly. "Not his style. He's not the kind of man who'd operate from a distance. He'd be here firsthand to watch." He swallowed and drew Avy into his arms, holding her tight.

"But isn't he in prison?"

"Yes. He'd still want firsthand details from anyone he sent. Instinct tells me this isn't him."

"Avy?" Gwen asked. "You agree?"

A brief nod.

Gwen cut her gaze back to Liam. "All right. I need to ask you a question. You mentioned a woman from your past whose ancestors were the original owners of that mask. What's the woman's name?"

"Angeline Le Fevre. She works as an art consultant—"

"She's the key to all of this," Gwen said. "I knew it."

"Angeline?" Liam thought about it. "But why? She's a ruthless businesswoman and a first-class bitch, but a murderer?"

Gwen filled them in on the mystery woman at the jeweler's. "You said last night at dinner that Angeline was obsessed with the mask. Clearly she had it stolen and then planned to keep it while a copy went back into the collection."

Avy said, "Why wouldn't she have just given the copy to Jaworski in the first place? No need for the smash-and-grab job, or for outsiders who could talk about her involvement."

"Because Christie's would have caught it. And failing that, if the switch were ever discovered, that copy could be traced right back to her. This must have been her way of covering her tracks."

"Why send a poisoned mask to Avy, whom she's never even met?"

"I do know who she is," Avy said slowly. "And vice versa. From some art world networking event. Long dark hair, too much gold jewelry, fire-engine red lipstick with darker liner? A chain-smoker?"

Liam nodded reluctantly.

"I was on my phone on the terrace and she walked out there. She eyed me, pulled a gold lighter out of her pocket, and lit up. Then she walked past and deliberately blew smoke right into my face. I remember looking at her name tag and thinking, 'What is that woman's problem?' "

Liam hesitated. "We didn't have the friendliest parting, Angeline and I. She made some rather nasty remarks when I ended things."

"Nasty remarks, or death threats?"

He lifted a shoulder. "There may have been a small discussion about feeding parts of me to wild boars."

"Is that all?"

"No."

"Did she threaten to turn you in to the police?"

"No, love. She was under the impression that I was an art dealer, so she simply threatened to ruin my business. I closed it and skipped town before she could do much, but imagine: She began to tell people that I was a con artist and a thief!"

Gwen blinked. The outrage in his voice was real. "But . . . you are."

"I *was*. But she didn't know that. She was simply spreading vicious gossip. She has no integrity at all."

Gwen stared at him. Then she gave Avy an is-he-for-real look.

Avy fiddled with the bedspread and sighed. "What can I say? Liam exercises his own twisted logic. It makes sense in his world."

"Thank you for explaining my peculiarities as if I weren't in the room, my love. Now, back to our little problem . . ."

Gwen rubbed at her eyes and thought about the gaps in their theory. Someone had taken nicotine and the forged mask from the safe at Jaworski Labs. Who else had the capacity and know-how to do a complicated B-and-E job?

She didn't like the best answer: someone at ARTemis.

Like McDougal, who'd been at the scene of Carlos's murder. "I think we need to look at the possibility that Angeline is working with someone else."

"Why?"

"Because I have evidence that puts Eric McDougal at the first Velasquez murder scene."

Avy's head came up. "You *what*?"

Gwen nodded. "He was there, Ave. He knew how Carlos had died and covered it with a lame excuse. And I found a piece of his jacket stuck to a finishing nail in the doorway."

"McDougal?" Avy shook her head. "That's crazy."

Gwen said, "Is it? Let's review everything again. I thought at first that someone was trying to ruin *my* reputation. But the recovery of the mask, Avy, was supposed to be *your* case. Remember? Then you had to leave the country immediately, for whatever reason, and you suggested me."

"Yeah . . ."

"That would have screwed up the plan. McDougal resents you. You get all the best cases. Remember how pissed he was when you got the Sword of Alexander assignment? How he questioned it?"

Avy nodded.

"Well, we all know he's a man-whore. He hooked up with this Angeline woman, and I guess it came out how they both felt about you: Angeline because you're dating her ex, McDougal because you're the queen bee at ARTemis—or maybe for some more sinister reason. Could he be working for the Greek ambassador? Anyway, between them, they hatched a little plan to make you look bad, destroy your reputation. Meanwhile, she gets to keep her family heirloom."

Avy thought for a moment. "McDougal's definitely not fond of me. But then, neither are some of the other team members—Valeria, even Dante."

"Do they have anything against you?"

Avy laughed mirthlessly. "Sure. I didn't want Valeria hired because of certain, ah, irregularities in her past."

"What do you mean?"

"I can't discuss it."

"Okay . . . and Dante?"

"Dante." Avy's mouth twisted. "Dante's macho Italian leg is broken because he disobeyed a direct order on that Berlin job we did together. Did he tell you that?"

Gwen shook her head.

"Yeah, well, his pride wouldn't allow him to. Ostensibly, he's doing office work and handling the assignments research and meetings because of the leg. The truth—and you don't know this, understand?—is that he's on probation for that little German stunt."

That was a piece of news. "But neither of them—not Valeria, not Dante—was at the murder scene," Gwen pointed out.

"That you know of."

"Come on, Avy. They're not sleeping with McD, either. Angeline is. McDougal and Angeline hatched this thing, and they hired the Velasquez brothers to pull off the actual burglary. Then maybe the V brothers tried a spot of blackmail, which backfired."

Avy frowned. "I can see them gunning for my reputation, but my life? McDougal?" She shook her head.

Liam raised his chin. "Are you certain that this mask was meant for you, love? Was there a note? Or could it have been meant for me? Not to be arrogant, but Angeline was rather devastated when I tossed her."

"No note," Avy said.

"But they waited until Liam had left the hotel," Gwen reminded them. "No, the mask was meant for Avy."

Avy and Liam looked at her grimly. "Gwen, be careful. What if they look at taking you out next?"

Gwen's stomach roiled as the coffee she'd had earlier tried to revisit her esophagus. She should give up caffeine, too. "No . . . I doubt it."

"Why?" Avy climbed back onto the bed and sat Indian-style while she used a wireless connection to get onto the Internet with her laptop. "Gwennie, you and what's-his-name are going back stateside immediately."

"Quinn. But the police are looking for us there. How are we going to get anything done? My first priority is to search Angeline's property myself."

"I'll send you with aliases, so your names don't pop on the flight manifests."

"And you're going to get these new IDs how?"

Avy shot a quick glance at Liam, who nodded and said, "Got it covered, love. No worries."

"What about you?" Gwen asked. "What about this mask?"

"Liam and I . . ." Avy glanced at him again, her color rising. "We still have a few things to take care of. But we'll take the mask to the Venetian police."

Gwen looked at Liam. "Is that a good idea, given his, um, colorful past?"

"No." Avy skewered him with a look. "So I'll take it."

Liam blew her a kiss. His gaze drifted casually over the rolled painting Gwen had spotted, and once again she wondered just what these two had up their sleeves.

"Alitalia or British Airways, Gwennie? Preference?"

"Ave, I can book my own flight."

"That's nice," said Avy, her fingers clicking away. "Here's one that leaves in the morning. Perfect."

Gwen nodded. "Okay. But I want you two to meet

Quinn, as soon as he's back with our costumes. We'll all stick together, go to the kickoff of Carnevale this evening. It's a once-in-a-lifetime opportunity."

Avy hesitated.

"It'll be fine. Who's going to pick us out of the crowds in costume? We'll be unrecognizable."

"All right."

Gwen looked at her. "That was easy. And I still can't believe you didn't fire me. Careful, Ave, or your employees will think you're getting soft."

Avy glared at her. "You are on double-secret probation, and I'm so mad that you can get my coffee and pick up my dry cleaning for a month. Two."

Gwen did her very best to look suitably horrified.

"You want to try being the boss? I'm telling you, it's not easy. Either people hate you or they try to take advantage of you."

"Thanks."

"I didn't mean you, Gwennie. You just freakin' lied to me, that's all."

This time she did squirm.

Avy noted it with evident satisfaction. "Okay . . . now we need to work on getting the same flight out of Venice for your ex—or is he really ex at this point?"

Gwen shifted uncomfortably. "Why would you say that? Quinn is most definitely ex."

"Not for long," Avy said cryptically.

Gwen gaped at her.

"Hon, it's written all over your face whenever you mention the man. You're still in love with him."

chapter 33

Gwen went down to the lobby of the Gritti, in denial of Avy's words. She was not in love with Quinn Lawson. She . . . cared for him.

Uh-huh. And you're having his baby, girlfriend.

Oh, that. It hadn't happened on purpose, though.

What about the fact that he asked you to marry him?

But he didn't—he said he'd marry you if that's what you wanted. He never said he *wanted it. He didn't mention love.*

He wants that baby. Badly.

But does he really want me with it?

Oh, please. Can't you tell by his actions?

I need to hear the words. . . .

And why is that?

She tried to push the question away, asking herself yet another. *Do you really want* him *back on a permanent basis? He's not an easy man.*

Quinn walked into the lobby as though, once again, she'd conjured him. His hair was windblown and his eyes danced as he crossed the space, his powerful arms full of zippered garment bags and boxes.

"How'd it go?" he asked.

Gwen pulled herself together. "Better than I expected. I can't believe it, but she didn't fire me."

"Good. Well, I think you'll like what I have to offer," he said, kissing her on the lips as the plastic bags crinkled between them.

Oh, hell. I do. I do. And in that moment, there in the Gritti Palace's lobby, Gwen realized that she was indeed hopelessly in love with her ex-husband . . . but she didn't know quite what to do about it. She was glad that she'd have a mask to hide behind for the rest of the evening.

When they met up with Avy and Liam, Gwen gasped in delight. Liam must have chosen everything the two of them wore. Avy was ridiculously resplendent in an enormous, multicolored headdress rimmed by pearls. It looked a bit like a giant, upside-down heart with her head in the center. She blinked from behind a chalk white mask with cherry red lips.

Her costume matched the colors in the headdress; it looked like a cross between an Elizabethan doublet and a rainbow-hued fairy gown. Four ropes of pearls dangled under Avy's chin.

"I feel like a complete idiot," she growled.

"You look magical!" Gwen clapped her hands and walked around her to get the full effect.

"That's me: a one-woman Magical Mystery Tour." Avy stalked to the window, the strands of pearls under her chin clicking together.

Liam gazed at her through a chalk white mask of his own, looking like a scarlet-and-gold maharaja. His doublet was slashed to reveal crimson lining, and little gold instruments hung from his shoulders, elbows, and colossal turban. Two small, enameled violins dangled like earrings on either side of the thing.

Gwen stared up at the headpiece in awe. The base of it

looked a lot like a small upholstered hassock. Scarlet, white, gold, and black ostrich plumes shot up from it like Seussian flames, and in the middle of those sat a doll dressed exactly like Liam, its tiny feet dangling above his forehead.

In his theatrical element, Liam nodded at Quinn and swept Gwen a bow, not realizing that he'd rake her face with the crazy plumes. "*Buona sera*. The dove is a lovely touch."

"*Grazie*," said Gwen. "Liam James—excuse me, Sir Liam—meet Quinn Lawson. And Quinn, this is Avy Hunt."

The three of them shook hands and took stock of one another while Gwen removed a gold feather from the left eye of her mask. While Quinn had chosen a plain outfit of green and gold with a matching mask, hers was cerulean blue, painted with pink blossoms, silver stars, and ribbons of a deeper blue. A white silk scarf wrapped entirely around her head and crested in folds around her shoulders. Her gown was simple, long, voluminous, made of material the same hue as the mask. She held a bouquet of hot-pink silk roses crowned by a white dove with outstretched wings.

The four of them posed for a photographer in the archway of the Gritti's main entrance before bracing themselves for the crowds outside. They all held hands as they swept along en route to the Piazza San Marco, the core of the festivities.

Opera music and the buzzing of thousands of voices filled the air. The rustling of elaborate costumes, the shuffling of feet, the rhythmic lapping of the water in the canal, shouts and mingled conversations in Italian—all of these sounds blurred together into a sort of loud Venetian poetry.

Gwen could almost smell the tradition and history of Carnevales past, carried by the cold currents of wind. The briny scent of the gray-green canals mingled with the essence of old stone and the aroma of pastries; here she caught a whiff of fresh paint, there a puff of a reveler's winy breath.

This Carnevale was nothing like the Brazilian celebration where she and Quinn had met, with its pulsing sexual undercurrents and wild party atmosphere. Venetian Carnevale was pure pageantry, a colorful vogue that possessed an odd dignity. It was more parade than party, a fusion of theatrical fashion. Venice had become a giant stage, hosting a self-styled production with no clear structure.

In the midst of the Piazza San Marco, backlit by the Basilica, hundreds of revelers danced a minuet. Liam laughed with sheer pleasure and squeezed Avy around the shoulders.

Gwen simply watched Quinn's smile as he took it all in. It was impossible not to be impressed with the great spectacle of Carnevale in Venice, and she took pleasure in his pleasure. His white teeth flashed under his mask, and his hand strayed to her neck, caressing it and making her shiver.

She tried to pretend that everything was normal and that the last thing she wanted was Quinn back in her life, having any kind of power over her or her feelings. But her own masquerade was obvious to her. She no longer wanted to run away. She didn't even want to *walk* away.

Gwen shook off the thoughts, and had to laugh at a woman in a gorgeous jester's costume and mask who carried a little dog dressed exactly like her.

A couple holding hands passed by, dressed severely in ivory and black, the headdresses above their masks easily a foot and a half tall. They looked daunting, melancholy, a bit creepy.

She spied three clowns next, in matching black hats and black gloves worn over funny, baggy costumes in orange, yellow, and red velvet.

But it was the dark demon that unnerved her and shot foreboding to the pit of her stomach. He wore a black helmet, a gigantic collar, and a cape. His giant dark wings rose like vengeance into the night, and Gwen shivered as he turned his head and stared straight at Avy and Liam, who were executing the steps of the minuet.

The demon held his wrist in front of his mask, and with sudden clarity Gwen realized what he was doing: He was speaking into a wrist unit.

"Quinn," she said urgently. "Something's wrong."

His head whipped around, and she pointed as subtly as she could. "Surveillance."

She saw the demon's head turn and followed his gaze to a stocky man who looked uncomfortable in his blue cape and brocade trousers. Gwen checked his feet. The guy wore white tennis shoes. Clearly he was American.

Not Greek. Not Italian.

Another attempt on Avy's life? Or something else entirely?

"That man over there . . . they're tracking Avy and Liam. I can't let this happen. We're not going to let this happen."

Quinn squeezed her hand and she knew he was on board, if out of his element. She squeezed back.

She kept her eyes peeled and saw another guy, this one in a plain black half mask and a deep purple cape over street clothes. Something was definitely going down. But this was an operation, a group effort, not a lone assassin.

In the crowd ahead, Avy slipped her hand into the crook of Liam's elbow and they pirouetted in time to the music, oblivious. They were out in the open because of Gwen. There was only one thing to do.

She said to Quinn, "Block the demon when they start to close in. Use surprise. Go for the knees. I'll take the guy in the brocade pants."

He nodded. *Careful*, he mouthed. But he didn't protest. He didn't get in her way. And that sealed things: Quinn was her next recovery. He'd give her his heart again . . . or she'd steal it.

Gwen worked her way over to Liam and Avy and tapped Avy on the back. "May I cut in?" And then quickly, "You're under surveillance. Liam, too. And they're closing in. Americans. Four."

Avy swallowed. "Oh, Jesus. My dad?"

"Or whoever sent you the mask. Either way, get out of here!"

Avy stepped back, weaving her way over to the arcade of a nearby building.

Liam steered Gwen into the steps of the dance. She leaned her head in toward him. "Don't look now, but there's a man—the demon—at your four o'clock. He has a wrist unit and is communicating with guys at your ten o'clock and six o'clock. They appear to be ready for a takedown. Could be Avy's father. Could be assassins. Disappear."

Liam stood stock-still for a moment, then nodded to let her know he'd understood. Then he swept her a bow.

In a flash she saw that he'd discarded his headpiece and she moved to block his body from view. Out of the corner of her eye, she saw the demon step forward, then topple as Quinn dove for his knees. She almost cheered.

In half a second flat, Liam had his doublet off, too. He vanished into the crowd and the shadows wearing only a black T-shirt and the bottom part of his costume.

Gwen wormed back into the crowd, working her way behind Brocade Pants. She neatly tripped him, fell over him, and then made a big show of apologizing and dusting him off. By the time he got rid of her, he was screwed.

Gwen found herself near the clown trio and took one clown's arm, urging him into the dance. The demon in the black costume was unfortunately back on his feet, pushing his way through the crowd, but his enormous wings made it difficult for him to move.

He spoke into his wrist unit again.

She'd lost sight of Quinn. Oh, God—was he hurt? No—there he was, tackling Purple Cape. He had a flair for this; he really did.

Full of a strange pride, Gwen looked over at the arcade, but Avy was nowhere to be seen. Ave could go back to the Gritti for safety, but Liam could not. If Everett Hunt was behind this and had tracked them to the Piazza San Marco, then he surely knew where they were staying.

What a mess. Liam was going to need a cloak of invisibility. Avy was going to need a friend. Gwen wove her way through the crowd, which had packed even more tightly into the square. She looked up at the winged lion of San Marco, supervising the festivities from his pedestal high in the air.

She hoped Liam would sprout his own set of wings.

An hour later, after ditching their own now-filthy and torn costumes, Gwen and Quinn tapped on Avy's hotel room door at the Gritti.

"Go away," said a ragged voice, barely recognizable as hers.

"Avy, it's me. Let me in. Please." Gwen waited for a couple of long moments, unsure whether Avy would open the door.

"Is anyone with you?"

"No," Gwen said, begging Quinn with her eyes to go back downstairs.

Bar, he mouthed, and she nodded.

Avy opened the door, but wouldn't look at Gwen. Her face was red, swollen, and blotchy. Taken aback, Gwen realized she'd never, not in all the years she'd known Avy, seen her cry.

"Oh, sweetie." She closed the door and pulled Avy close for a hug, but it was like putting her arms around a block of granite. Avy didn't really know what to do with female affection—she was more likely to punch a friend playfully in the arm, like a guy.

"Yeah. This really sucks," Avy managed, pulling away and wiping her eyes on her sleeve.

"What do you think went down? Were those guys out to kill you, or grab Liam?"

"There wouldn't have been four of them if they wanted to kill us. There'd be one guy, with a silencer. No communications equipment. No big white tennis shoes in Venice, at Carnevale. I'll swear on a Bible," Avy said with disgust, "that was Everett Hunt in action."

Gwen nodded.

"I was afraid of this. It's why I didn't want to talk to my dad. Liam has to get back to the States, where he has his get-out-of-jail-free card with the FBI. Problem is, they can pick him up right in the airport if he buys a plane ticket. Same with the train or a rental car. They'll be watching his credit cards and mine, too. They'll be watching the flight manifests for all four of his aliases."

"Sounds like it's time to get him a new one. And pay with cash."

Avy nodded. "Yeah, given another day we can do that, same as we're getting yours. But even after we bring him back to the U.S., it's not like I can invite him home for Memorial Day weekend, Gwen. This is going to boil down to a choice between my dad and Liam. I don't know how to make that choice. How can I have put myself in this position?"

Gwen sank down on the bed and just looked at her. She

shook her head as Avy's cell phone rang. And rang. And rang some more.

"That's Dad," Avy said bitterly. "He keeps calling and I won't answer."

"Has Liam called? Do you know where he went? Is he safe?"

"He's all right. He can't call—they'd pinpoint his location—but he gave a kid some money to bring me a message. He said that"—her voice cracked—"he loves me and he'll be in touch when he can. He said"—she laughed wildly—"to trust him."

Tears streamed down her face and she went to the window, feeling behind the drapes. "I have a stolen painting that he wants to keep, but he says to trust him!" She yanked out the rolled painting Gwen had seen before.

She extended it to Gwen. "You have to take it, Gwennie. It belongs to the insurance company. They paid out for it. It technically belongs to them as soon as they sign the check. Please, will you get it to them?"

"Who?"

"Hiscox."

"Where do I say I got it?"

"You don't. You recovered it; no questions asked."

Gwen nodded. "I'll have to smuggle it in my suitcase, and God help me if I get caught."

"You won't. You look like the type of woman who jets to Venice for a little shopping trip. That's the beauty of your work for ARTemis. Nobody would ever suspect you."

"Because nobody takes me seriously."

Avy looked miserable. "I didn't mean it that way, and you know it."

"Well, take this seriously: I do think you can trust Liam. More than you can trust your father at this point."

"Why?"

"Gut. You're the one who told me never to argue with it."

Avy tried to dash her tears away with her fingers and succeeded only in smearing her mascara under her eyes so that she looked like a woeful raccoon. "He didn't give me any warning," she whispered.

"Avy. In your dad's mind, he's trying to save you from a mistake worse than death. Of course he didn't warn you."

"Doesn't he care if I'm happy?" She grabbed a tissue and blew her nose. "Stupid question."

"He thinks you'll be happier with this threat—Liam—out of the way."

Avy honked again into the tissue, then balled it up in her hand. She closed her eyes for a long moment. "What if he's *right*?"

Gwen stared at her.

"What if Liam really can't go straight? I'm so afraid, Gwen. What kind of man have I fallen in love with?"

"I don't know, Ave. That I don't know."

chapter 34

The man was beside himself. While the trial run on Esteban Velasquez with the Mardi Gras mask had worked like a charm, once again, the bitch had slipped through his fingers, this time courtesy of that cursed Gwen. And now Avy was holed up in the Gritti Palace, not leaving her room.

He hoped she was crying her eyes out over the loss of her limey lover. He thought about showing up as house-keeping and blowing a hole through her, but it was far too risky, for a variety of reasons. Since the incident with the mask, the Gritti had tripled its security.

He'd have to wait until she was back in Miami.

He was developing a tic in his left eye, and his fingers literally itched to strangle her. His uncle was impatient after all this time, and had actually begun to mock him, the old bastard.

The man threw his clothes into his Italian leather car-ryall, checked out of his hotel, and took a train over the border. Then he ditched his alias and flew back to Miami.

God only knew when Avy would see fit to come back herself. In the meantime, he had to pretend that everything was normal. And unfortunately, it was time to dispense with Gwen as well. She was causing too many problems, and she wasn't as dim as she appeared to be, damn her.

chapter 35

Life itself got more complicated than the most intricately plotted thriller. Gwen sat next to Quinn in first class on the flight home and evaluated what lay ahead.

Her heart ached for Avy. How would she make a choice between the two men in her life, between the one who'd raised her and the one she wanted to grow old with?

Though Gwen's father might not be happy if she married Quinn, he'd get over it. She was a grown woman now, not a college kid.

Everett Hunt was a different personality altogether. He'd never quit. And Avy wouldn't, either.

Quinn smoothed a hand over her stomach, distracting her. "Baci for your thoughts." He held out one of the famous Italian chocolates between thumb and forefinger.

She laughed and snagged it. "You knew better than to offer me a penny, didn't you?"

His teeth flashed. "Mmmm. I may not be wiser after all this time, but I'm more cunning."

She tossed the chocolate and caught it. "Okay. I'm worried about Avy. She's so miserable about her personal life right now that I'm afraid her reflexes are slow. That she's off her game. And there's someone out there trying to kill her. I have to find that person, and yet here I am on a plane back to the U.S. while he may be on her heels in Venice."

"You're a good friend," Quinn said.

"I don't know about that. I screwed up royally, I hid everything from her for too long, and the company's still in danger—while she's too upset to care at this point. *I have to fix this*. She's always had my back. I'm going to have hers."

"You certainly had her back at Carnevale." Quinn shook his head. "I gotta tell you, Gwen . . . you were impressive."

"So were you." His words made her feel better. His presence soothed her. She realized that she hadn't thought about Xanax or vodka once during takeoff.

"Here's a thought," Quinn mused. "Avy's probably fine. Her father's going to be watching like a hawk to see if Liam makes contact. And whatever their differences right now, he won't let anything happen to her."

An anvil rolled off Gwen's chest. He was 100 percent correct. "Anyone ever tell you that you're pretty smart, Quinn Lawson?"

He caught his lip between his teeth and eyed her lazily. "Whiz kid, that's me. Check the *Wall Street Journal* for confirmation."

Something about Quinn had changed since she'd first walked into his office. He looked . . . happy?

"Do you miss your job?" she asked, already reading the answer in his eyes.

"Not a bit. I'm thinking of doing something else entirely. My only regret is not seeing Alaban, a drug of ours, all the way to market. I'd love to invest in it, but that'd be insider trading for sure."

Gwen waited but he didn't elaborate. "What *kind* of something else are you thinking of doing?"

Quinn stretched his legs out in front of him and pulled down the window shade. The corner of his mouth turned up. "That's top-secret. If I told you, I'd have to marry you—and that's not a conversation we're ready to have quite yet." He slid down in his seat and closed his eyes.

Wait . . . but they'd talked about it that night on the gondola. "What do you mean? We've discussed it already."

"Ah. But not to my satisfaction."

He didn't say anything else, the tease. Annoyance made her a little petulant. "Isn't my satisfaction important, too?"

He opened his eyes and scanned her body from knees to lips. "Always, honey. Always."

A streak of hot electricity lit all her naughty zones.

Then the damned man closed his eyes again and went to sleep.

His cryptic words made it hard for Gwen to focus, even once they were back in Miami. The heat, the vast expanses of highway and concrete, the urban sprawl—all of it took getting used to after jewel-like little Venice.

But for the moment, she had no time to mull over Quinn and his enigmas. Right now, she had to focus on justice—and, if she were honest, revenge.

Angeline Le Fevre and Eric McDougal had tried to kill her best friend, and that wasn't okay. She was going to make sure they didn't succeed.

Home in Coconut Grove, Gwen booted up her laptop and searched for Angeline's home address, with no luck. This was a job for the Nerd Corps, which was fine, since she needed to talk to Dante anyway.

She threw off the clothes she'd been wearing, quickly showered, and re-dressed and made sure she had her company-issued SIG stowed safely in her bag. Then she headed downtown to the ARTemis office. A long line of cars slowly snaked into the parking garage, meaning that it would take a good fifteen minutes before she found a spot in there.

Gwen sighed and inched forward toward the line just as

a man in a Firebird pulled out of a metered space across the street. *Yes!* She snatched it, fed the metal money-muncher seven quarters, and she was good to go.

"Hi, doll face," Sheila said as she walked in the door. "What'd you bring me back from Italy? Gold, I hope."

Sheila didn't need any more of that. She sparkled in a stretchy, low-cut gold top and so many gold chains that she rivaled Mr. T. She wore three or four rings on each hand, and they clanked against the keyboard as she typed. Or was that sound from the multiple bracelets? Gwen couldn't be sure. Even Sheila's reading glasses were gold.

But today, instead of making her cringe, Sheila's outfit comforted her. "I brought you half an unused airline ticket and some chocolate Baci. How's that?"

"Hmmmph."

"Do I have any messages?"

Sheila handed over a stack of them. "You might be real interested in that top one, there."

Gwen scanned it and felt the blood drain from her face. "What does Sid mean, he's on his way?"

Sheila shrugged and displayed most of her capped teeth. "I guess lover boy got itchy and boarded his jet."

"No. No, no, no . . . he doesn't know where I live. You didn't tell him, did you? You'd better swear to me that you've given him absolutely no personal information about me."

"I haven't. But maybe he figures that since you found his dog for him, he can now hire one of our agents to find you." Sheila cackled. "Wouldn't that just beat all."

Gwen glared at her. "Look. You have to make him go away. This is not a joke. You tell him that if he doesn't scram, I will get a restraining order against him and charge him with stalking."

Sheila assessed her silently. "Something's different about you. Did you get a haircut? Nope. Change your makeup? Nope. What is it? You're harder around the edges."

"Is Dante here?"

"I don't think I can call you fragile anymore. It's like you've lost your innocence. Our Gwennie's been devirginized."

"Sheila, *is Dante here*?"

"All right, already! Yes, he is."

"And have you seen McDougal?"

"He hasn't been around for a couple of days. He took some time off."

Time off to attempt murder?

"Thanks." Relieved to hear she wouldn't have to run into McDougal, Gwen strode past Sheila and down the hall to Dante's door, which was partially open. He lounged in his chair, his bad leg propped on another one, staring out over the bay with a grim expression.

"Hi."

He turned at the sound of her voice. "Hi. Come in. So how did you find Venezia? It's one of my favorite cities."

"Still magical. A little cold."

He nodded. He looked as if he hadn't been sleeping well; the shadows under his eyes made them look darker and more enigmatic.

"Dante, I tracked down the jeweler who made the copy of the mask, and he said that the original was brought to him and then taken away again by a *woman*. I also discovered that Quinn's art consultant, Angeline Le Fevre, has ties to the mask. Her ancestors were the original owners, and she has an obsession with it."

Dante's eyebrows shot up, but other than that he made no comment. He remained almost unnaturally still.

"But here's the kicker: Someone delivered a poisoned mask to Avy's hotel room in Venice! If I hadn't been there, she could be dead right now."

"Da tutti i santi . . ."

"Sheila says that McDougal hasn't been around for a couple of days. That he took time off. I think that he and Angeline are working together. He's always had a grudge against Avy."

Dante rubbed furiously at the edge of his cast.

"Who knows how they met, but I caught him half-naked in her office. I need to get Angeline's Miami address from the Nerd Corps. She's unlisted."

Dante stared at her. "You're not thinking of going over there?"

"I still have a recovery to complete, Dante. I'd swear on a Bible right now that Angeline has the original of that mask, and I'm going to find it. If it's not in her home, then she's got it in a safety-deposit box somewhere."

"She could have taken it out of the country by now."

"Maybe so. But I wouldn't be doing my job if I didn't check."

"Breaking into her house could be dangerous. You need backup. Let me come with you."

She shook her head. "I'm not dumb enough to do it when she's there. I'll be fine. If you want to help, track down McDougal. He killed the Velasquez brothers, and I think he's responsible for the missing nicotine at Jaworski Labs. Someone had a knowledge of B and E and the general skill set that we have here at ARTemis—and no other drugs were missing."

"And the attempt on Avy? Why would he try to kill her?"

Gwen shrugged. "He hates her. I think this whole thing began in an effort just to ruin her reputation. Remember, the recovery of the mask was supposed to be her job, not mine. And everything else just snowballed from there."

Dante was silent. Finally he said, "It's a plausible theory." The shadows under his eyes had deepened.

"Are you all right?"

He nodded. "Just tired. And disappointed, disillusioned—whatever you wish to call it. I don't like discovering nasty surprises about my colleagues."

"Neither do I. McDougal must have something in his past, and you'd think Kelso would have caught it before hiring him."

"It appears," murmured Dante, "that even the great and mysterious Kelso makes mistakes." He swung his leg down from the chair and struggled to his feet. "Well. Let's get hold of Miguel and find the information that you need, shall we?"

Cato loved it when his prospective victims were sprawled comfortably on their sofas, watching television. Through a crack in the blinds, he could see a pair of men's Nikes resting on one arm of the couch, while an elbow hung off the opposite end.

The TV was tuned to ESPN, loud enough that the volume covered the sound Cato made when he popped the lock and slid open the glass patio door. Couch Potato didn't move.

Talk about being caught napping, man! I'm gonna scare you into next year. Cato crept forward in gleeful anticipation. *Dude, you're gonna owe me a case of Negro Modelo.*

He sprang without warning, complete with Comanche yell.

Nothing. No reaction. And when Cato landed, straddling the guy's shins, he understood why.

"Mierda!" He knocked the phone over in his haste to dial 911.

chapter 36

That evening, Gwen stuffed Angeline's address into her purse and headed out the door. A special surveillance team had confirmed that Angeline was at an art opening.

Gwen hesitated briefly before pulling out her phone to call Quinn, but he'd made her promise to keep in close touch. Should she drag him into a breaking-and-entering situation, given the fact that the police wanted to talk to them?

She'd *promised*. She hit his cell number on speed dial. "Quinn? It's me. So, I'm headed to Angeline's. If you want to help, you can be lookout. . . . You'll have to meet me there, though. I'll text you once I'm in." She snapped her phone closed.

Her car was across Brickell, with seven minutes left on the meter. She unlocked the door as a white stretch limo pulled up next to her. One of the tinted windows lowered, and she heard the words she least wanted to hear.

"Gwendolyn, me beauty!"

She whirled and stepped back, slamming her hip into the driver's-side mirror.

Sid Thresher peered out at her from behind his rock-'n'-roll shades, which he'd lowered in an attempt at seductive-ness. His crinkled-leather skin retained a suspiciously orange glow. His sparse corn-husk hair had frizzed in the humidity, and the whites of his eyes gleamed crazily from the gloom of the limo's interior.

He wore a silk Versace shirt that showcased a heavy gold chain and a single tuft of gray-blond hair on his skinny chest. In defiance of any open-container laws, he brandished a Bloody Mary. His ugly shar-pei, Pigamuffin, sat next to him on the limo seat, wearing a black Subversion T-shirt from the popular Big Banger tour of 1983.

"Sid, what are you *doing* here?"

"Oy told you that me and my big banger were eager to see you, luv! 'Ere, hop in and oy'll fix ye a Bloody!"

Gwen forced her face into some semblance of a polite smile. Sid was, after all, a client. And she had (unbeknownst to him) once stolen his dog, for which she still felt guilty. "Sid, it's lovely to see you and I wish I could stay to chat, but I'm on my way to an appointment."

His face fell, but then brightened again. "'Ere—so I'll just come with you."

"No! No, I'm afraid that's not possible."

"Then we'll 'ave us a spot of supper afterward. D'you fancy a stone crab or two? We'll go to . . ." He pulled his head back into the limo and addressed the driver. "What the fuck's the name of that place, eh? Bob's? Ed's?"

"Joe's," said the driver's voice.

"Joe's! Right, then, we'll go to Joe's. Oy'll bet you look right sexy, me Gwendolyn, with your knockers nestling under a plastic bib." He leered at her and bit the end off of the celery stalk in his drink, chewing enthusiastically.

Did they make men more appalling than Sid?

"Come on, then." He lodged the Bloody Mary in his crotch and extended both hands out the window, making pincers with his fingers. "Come get crabby with Sid, ya?

And we'll save us some melted butter for later." He waggled his eyebrows.

"*No*, thank you," Gwen said, her level of aggravation rising fast.

"If ye're a good girl, now, oy'll let ye gum Sid's big banger! 'E's quite a tasty morsel, 'e is."

"Sid, we've had this conversation, remember? On your yacht in the south of France. Now, I have to go. I'm sorry, but I don't have time for this." Gwen turned her back on him and opened the door of her Prius.

"She doesn't 'ave time for us, if you please!" Sid said, apparently to Pigamuffin. "What d'you think about that? Oy think she's right cheeky, is what methinks."

Gwen got into her car. "Good-bye, Sid. Enjoy your stay in Miami. I think you'll find plenty of playmates on South Beach."

"'Ere!" he said, clearly miffed. "Oy came all this way to play with *you*, ye ungrateful bit o' tail."

Gwen straightened her shoulders and put her hands on the wheel. Then she opened the door and got out of the Prius again. She stalked over to Sid's limo, bent over, and poked him in the chest, avoiding his revolting little tuft of hair. "Shame on you, Sid Thresher. I am *not* a bit of tail. It's extremely impolite of you to speculate about *any* part of my anatomy, and I will never, *ever* gum or otherwise touch what you like to call your big banger. You *will respect* me, do you hear?"

Sid blinked his watery blue eyes behind the bug glasses.

"*Do you hear me?*"

"Yes, madam, oy do."

"Good." Gwen removed her finger from his bony chest and resisted the urge to wipe it off on her pants.

"Oy must say, this puts a whole different spin on things, it does. Oy've gotten quite the wrong idea about you."

"Yes, you have," she said sternly.

"Been a bad, bad boy, Siddie has. 'E most humbly begs your pardon, 'e does. Ye're angry. Got your knickers in quite a twist. So . . ." He squinted up at her hopefully.

Why did she have a bad feeling about this apology?

"Yes?"

"Oy don't suppose ye'd care to spank me?"

"No!" yelled Gwen. "Now, *please*, for the love of God, *go away.*"

But Sid was nothing if not persistent. As Gwen drove south down Brickell, took a left on the Rickenbacker Causeway, and crossed the bridge to Key Biscayne, the limo followed at a discreet distance. She could hardly allow him to tail her to Angeline's house.

She couldn't just shoot him, so she would have to lose him, and that was going to be challenging, with the straight, narrow miles of Crandon Boulevard ahead of them. She coasted for long minutes, lulling his driver into boredom, and then seized her opportunity. She wrenched the wheel to the left, diving down a side street and then peeling around the next right. The limo simply couldn't keep up. Gwen pulled a few more evasive maneuvers and finally made her way back to where she needed to be. She parked down the block and around the corner from Angeline's house, just to be safe.

The house crouched by itself in a charming little inlet. It was an older home that Gwen suspected had been recently remodeled and landscaped, judging by the brand-new roof of barrel tiles and the small size of most of the plants.

A fountain played softly under the yellow glow of the porch light. Night creatures scraped, hummed, and warbled. Other than that, there were no signs of life in the dark house. Gwen's dark slacks and blue halter top blended seamlessly into the shadows. She'd taken off all her jewelry so that nothing could catch the light and alert anyone to her presence.

Close neighbors weren't a problem, fortunately, because of the inlet. She was careful not to attract any attention, though, since people took strolls and walked dogs. Gwen cased the whole house and chose a side window, hidden from a frontal view by a lattice of climbing roses, as her entrance.

There was an alarm system, but she disconnected it by clipping a couple of wires. There was a surveillance camera, which she also dismantled. She'd have to get the tape from it when she went inside.

The catch on the window was secure, so she had two alternatives: She could either break the glass or cut a hole in it to reach inside. She pulled a cutting tool from her bag. Avy had taught her how to fix the adhesive to the pane, then cut it in a neat circle and pull the cut glass out without making more than a small scraping noise as it came free.

Gwen detached the circle of glass and hid it behind the lattice. Then she put her gloved hand inside the hole and unfastened the window catch. She raised the window, hoisted herself up to the sill, and climbed through. It was fortunate that Angeline had no dog.

She found herself in a sparsely furnished office. Two very fine paintings hung over a spindly eighteenth-century ladies' writing desk, one a portrait by Vigée le Brun and the other an early Cézanne landscape. An Oriental rug—a Kuba with a Kufic border—covered the cool, beige tiled floor.

The old-school furnishings looked incongruous in the modern Miami home, which still retained some of its original art deco characteristics.

Gwen took a moment to listen to both the house and her gut. Nothing appeared to be amiss, so she texted Quinn.

Then she moved into a narrow hallway, which contained nothing but a hanging floral tapestry and two wrought-iron architectural pieces.

The living room housed an entertainment center, a shelf of books on art, a beige sectional sofa scattered with yellow suede pillows, and a large abstract in greens and yellows by a painter that Gwen had never heard of and didn't care to meet, judging by his work. What caught her eye and froze her in her tracks was a pedestal with a stand on it inside a Lucite case. On the stand was a Venetian mask—though it wasn't *the* mask—yellow with blue and green feathers around the eyes and gold bric-a-brac trim. Though of course it had no mouth, it seemed to leer evilly at her.

Gwen stared right back at it as she walked past.

The kitchen was small, a basic black-granite-and-stainless-steel design. There were no signs that Angeline cooked; just a cup, half-full of black coffee, and a couple of diet breakfast bars lying on the countertop.

Angeline's bedroom was something of a shock. Over an elaborately carved mahogany headboard hung eight Venetian masks of varying designs and colors. Matte gold, glittering silver, flat black, blue brocade, red satin. Some had elaborate, curled ostrich plumes and peacock feathers worked into their designs. Others were studded with jewels or hand-painted motifs.

All of them had hollow, lifeless, unseeing eyes that sent a shiver down Gwen's spine. And none was as magnificent as the mask she'd been sent to recover. She hoped none was as deadly, either.

The presence of the masks reinforced for Gwen that she was on the right trail. But where was the Borgia one? Had Angeline stuffed it into some bank box, or would she have it right here in her home?

Gwen glanced at Angeline's bedside clock and saw that

it was almost eight thirty in the evening. She needed to work fast—the woman could be home at any moment.

Gwen started with the dresser drawers, which yielded nothing but clothing, and then checked under the bed, where she found a flat, wheeled, plastic box of shoes. She moved on to the nightstand drawers, which contained ibuprofen, a broken necklace, condoms, massage oil, and a couple of naughty paperback books.

The closet was stuffed with clothing and boasted a full-length mirror on the back wall. Angeline had very nice taste; Gwen would give her that. She also had a lot of gorgeous Italian shoes.

But the mask did not appear to be in her closet. Gwen searched the rest of the house: the bathroom, with its welter of perfume bottles and cosmetics; and the kitchen, which contained no pots or pans of any sort but a large microwave and a lot of disposable plates and cups.

She searched two bedrooms, the office, the living room, and a linen closet in the hallway opposite the bathroom. Nothing.

The smell of barbecue came wafting in from the water, and from around another bend in the water a party got louder as the guests moved on to what she guessed were their second and third drinks.

Think. Hurry.

Gwen went back to Angeline's bedroom, where she ignored the creepy eyes—or lack thereof—of the masks and opened the closet again. She gauged the distance from the door to the mirror in the back.

She stepped out of the closet and then eyeballed the distance along the drywall that the closet should run. Her interior-design background had trained her well. There was approximately a foot and a half unaccounted for inside the closet.

Gwen walked into it again, to the back wall, and ran her

hands down the left edge of the mirror, where she found what she sought: hinges.

She pulled at the right edge and the mirror opened to reveal a shallow hidden space inside with several shelves. On one of those shelves was a hand-painted wooden box that she'd seen before.

Gwen lifted the lid and the Columbina glittered up at her, a beautiful and menacing piece of family history. An object of intrigue, passion, and murder.

She knew without needing to test it that this mask was the real deal. She'd find no seams from any kind of welder on the back of it, no curls of lead where there should be only solid gold, no cubic zirconia substituted for diamonds, sapphires, and emeralds.

She didn't touch it, even with gloved hands. Angeline could have poisoned this one, too. At any rate, whether it was fresh or hundreds of years old, there was blood on this mask.

Gwen couldn't look away from it, even though she wanted to. The thing mesmerized her, evil and seductive and haughty. It was the craftsmanship and the premeditation that got to her. Angeline's ancestor—and then she herself—had planned murder so meticulously and with obvious pleasure.

As she stood there, a car door slammed outside. Quinn? Then another. *Fudge!*

Gwen quickly snapped a picture of it in Angeline's hiding place with her phone, then closed the box, tucked it under her arm, and scrambled out of the closet. She ran a blue streak back to the office where she'd entered and backed toward the window.

A key clicked into the lock at the front entrance, and the door flew open, followed by two sets of footsteps.

"How dare you follow me home?" Angeline's voice demanded of her companion.

"How dare you commit fraud and murder?" Quinn's voice said.

Quinn? What are you doing? Well, that one was easy: making a frontal assault so that she could exit fast.

"You're crazy," said Angeline contemptuously. Her heels clicked across the tile in the living room. She unlatched the big patio doors and walked outside. Quinn's footsteps followed. Gwen heard the click of a lighter.

"Am I? You set this up from the very beginning, Angeline. You brokered the deal when Jaworski purchased the mask. We have a witness in Padua, Italy, who swears it was a woman who forced him to produce a copy, and I'm sure a good detective can piece together your travels, even if you used a false name.

"I'll bet we'll find the original mask in your possession, possibly here on the premises. Where's Eric McDougal, Angeline?"

"Eric? I have no idea."

"Was it you or him who sent the last mask to Avy Hunt in Venice?"

She laughed. "You could not be more mistaken. I barely know Eric McDougal—I had a brief, very brief fling with him. And I haven't been out of the U.S. for a month."

"It's over, Angeline. McDougal helped you steal the nicotine and the fake mask from the lab, didn't he?"

"No. You're wrong."

"But you only did that to distract the police. You already had it. Let me guess—prescriptions for smoking-cessation patches from ten different doctors and ten different pharmacies?"

"I don't know what you're talking about," Angeline said. "Get out of my house." But her voice shook a little.

"They'll trace those prescriptions back to you. Where'd you purchase them? Did you use a credit card?"

"I said leave!"

"Florida has the death penalty, Angeline. You should cut yourself a deal with the cops right away."

"I didn't kill anyone!" she shouted.

Gwen wondered where the hell McDougal was. Had he been the one to take the whole game to the lethal point? She reached behind her in the dark and felt for the windowsill. She turned, threw a leg over it, and then froze. A glint of moonlight reflected off the muzzle of a Glock that was pointed straight at her. A highly illegal silencer was screwed onto the end of the barrel.

"Oh, Jesus," she said. "McDougal."

chapter 37

Avy walked down the jetway in Venice without really noticing her legs move. She felt numb. She operated on autopilot. She couldn't wait to leave one of the world's most beautiful cities behind.

But she felt as if she were leaving her soul and her happiness in Venice along with Liam. Her BlackBerry buzzed inside her well-worn Dior saddlebag as she filed along the narrow, dingy corridor that led to the gaping rectangular mouth of the plane. It had buzzed two other times as she sat in the waiting area, but it was probably her father, and she couldn't bring herself to look.

Finally a stern voice in her head told her to stop being self-indulgent and immature. She had a business to run, and other people depended upon her. This was no time for her to sink her nose into her navel and give in to depression. She had to at least look at the screen.

There were three e-mails. One was from Gwen, saying that she and Quinn were safely back in Miami. One was from Kelso, simple and to the point: *Plot against you has escalated. Possible rogue agent at ARTemis. Be on your guard.*

She responded, typing with her thumbs. *Aware of McDougal's activities and agenda. Gwen will repossess original Borgia mask and then we will involve cops. On my way home now.*

The third message was from an unknown sender. She almost deleted it, but the subject line stopped her cold: *Plague doc seeks puppet.* Liam. It had to be.

Her hands shook as she opened the message. *Meet me in Moscow, darling. Details to follow.*

Avy stood frozen on the jetway, staring at the words until they blurred and then came into focus again. Moscow? Was he high?

"*Signorina, per favore,*" said a businessman behind her. It took her a moment to register that he was talking to her, and that she was holding everyone up. She stared at the words on her BlackBerry again.

Trust me, he'd said.

Could she?

Gwen's words came back to her. *I do think you can trust Liam. More than you can trust your father at this point.*

"*Signorina!*" said the man behind her, seriously annoyed now.

"*Scusi,*" she said, unable to make up her mind. She held the BlackBerry tightly to her chest as she stumbled forward, torn. She'd made it onto the plane and past the flight attendants to her seat in first class when her body rebelled and turned almost of its own accord.

She stepped back into the aisle and fought her way past the startled, disgruntled boarding passengers. "*Scusi, scusi . . .*"

"*Signorina!*" said the flight attendants.

Avy pointed at the lavatory, and they allowed her past them. Then she bolted out the door of the plane.

"*Signorina!* Stop! *Signorina!*"

She muscled up the jetway, inconveniencing more people along the way, bumping past them.

You're crazy, the sensible part of her said just as she got to the corridor's entrance. *What the hell are you doing?*

I don't know. All she knew was that she had to get to Liam.

"Signorina!" The ticket taker grasped her arm. "You cannot get off the flight now—"

She jerked out of his grasp without thinking and barreled forward.

You're crazy to meet him in Moscow. You'll be an accessory to whatever he might be doing. . . . And what about Gwen? You can't just leave her alone to handle McDougal.

Oh, God. Gwen. Avy stopped. Gwen had saved Avy's life. She'd saved Liam's freedom. And she was potentially walking back into a lion's den there in Miami. Avy owed her backup even if her heart lay with Liam.

Feeling discombobulated and torn on every level, Avy turned around again to head *back* to the Miami flight—only to have two security guards take her roughly by the arms.

Belatedly she realized that she wasn't going anywhere. For all they knew, she'd gotten on that plane to plant a bomb and was now trying to escape.

"No, no!" She tried to explain that she'd left her wallet at security and had panicked. The guards looked unimpressed, and even more so when one of them opened her Dior bag and produced the wallet she'd supposedly been going to find.

"I made a mistake. I want to get back on the flight," she insisted.

They ignored her, and radioed the pilot. "Evacuate the plane," they ordered in Italian. "And then remove every bag for screening." They gazed at Avy sternly. *"Signorina,* you will come with us."

Avy's heart sank. She knew she'd get out of this eventually, but it might take hours. The guards had now confis-

cated her BlackBerry, so she couldn't even e-mail either
Gwen or Liam.

Avy tried to reassure herself. Gwen was a tough cookie.
And once she had the mask, she'd get the cops involved.
She wouldn't be stupid enough to face McDougal alone.
Quinn, too, would be by her side.

And Liam? He'd simply have to wait for her. If he
didn't, then she'd know at last what kind of man he truly
was. . . .

chapter 38

Gwen slowly registered that the man holding the gun was the last person she'd expected. Dante smiled through a sheen of Miami moonlight that refracted from the gun's barrel to his teeth and back again. "I'm afraid McDougal can't help you right now," he said. "He's indisposed."

Gwen gaped at him. "Dante, what are you doing?"

"Get back into the house, *bella*; there's a good girl. Don't run or try to pull anything, because I will not hesitate to shoot."

For a moment she simply could not register what the words meant. Dante couldn't be doing this. . . .

She'd been so sure it was Eric. Oh, God, McDougal— she'd misjudged everything.

"What do you mean, McDougal's indisposed?" she said urgently. "Is he okay?"

Dante shrugged, and she stared at him, horrified.

Think, Gwen, think. She was in such a state of shock that she felt paralyzed. *Note and exploit your opponent's weaknesses.* The words came back to her from Avy's intensive training sessions.

Broken leg. She eyed it. He was going to have a difficult time getting it through the window. She might be able to knock him off balance. . . .

Dante followed her thoughts. "Don't try it." He lifted his good leg to the sill without any hesitation, keeping the gun trained on her the entire time. He slid his leg inside, bent at the waist, and, with supreme muscular grace and discipline, put his weight on the floor while he lifted the bad leg and brought it straight through, too. Then he reached out and pulled in his crutch.

Gwen's SIG was in her shoulder bag, but she didn't dare try for it.

"Throw the bag on the floor," Dante commanded, not bothering to keep his voice down. "Angeline!"

"Dante?" Angeline called from the patio, panic in her voice.

"Stay where you are. My friend and I are coming down the hall."

"What—"

"Just stay there!" he barked. "Now, hands on your head and move," he said to Gwen. He shoved the crutch under his arm.

Her pulse hammering, blood roaring in her ears, she left the office and walked down the hall toward the living room and the patio doors. *Quinn.* She was probably dead, but Quinn could still get away. She couldn't, wouldn't, think about the baby.

"Quinn!" she shrieked. *"Get out!"*

Dante flung the crutch against the wall and grabbed her by the hair. "Shut up!"

"Get out! He's got a gun!"

The Glock dug viciously into her spine. Where were Dante's old-world manners now? "Make another noise, Gwen, and I will kill you. Do you understand?"

She couldn't nod, since he had her head pulled back. "Yes," she said.

Dante let go of her hair and picked up his crutch. He

awkwardly propelled her around the corner, and she saw Quinn's white face, his whole body tense.

"Jesus God," he said. "Gwen." He swallowed.

He was here only because she'd asked him to be. Why, *why* had she called him?

Dante shoved her with the gun and they both stepped over the threshold and outside.

"Gwen." Quinn looked agonized.

"Shhhhhh. Quinn . . ." She might not have another chance to say it. "I love you. Always have."

"How touching," Dante said.

Quinn's jaw worked. His eyes flickered from hers to the gun, which was now shoved hard against her back, to the left of her spine, lined up roughly with where her heart would be. "I love you, too."

"Dios mio, it's a regular romance novel around here," Dante said. "But she won't look as pretty with a few holes in her, will she?"

"Let her go," Quinn said hoarsely.

"What are you doing here, Mr. Lawson?"

"Looking out for Gwen."

Silence reigned. No script seemed adequate. Finally Angeline said, "He thinks *I* killed Esteban Velasquez. With Eric McDougal's help."

Dante ruminated for a moment. "A very plausible theory. Yes, I quite like it."

"I didn't kill anyone! That was your idea."

"McDougal," Dante mused, "will work very well. He resents Avy. And I've conveniently arranged things so that he has no alibi for this evening. That Scots bastard has been spying on me for Kelso."

"All I wanted was the mask," Angeline insisted, to nobody in particular.

"Be quiet, damn it!"

"I didn't kill anyone. . . ."

"But you are going to," Dante said calmly.

She stared at him.

"Get the mask," he said. "And apply the nicotine. I want a little insurance, Angeline, that you won't talk to the police. You've been very vocal just now about your limited role, and I don't like that. You're about to put a little more skin in this game."

"You're crazy."

Dante just raised his brows. "Get the mask, Angeline, or I will shoot these people and arrange for your fingerprints to be all over the gun."

"It's still registered to you."

"Get the fucking mask or I'll shoot you as well. I am losing my patience."

Angeline ran from the room.

Quinn said to Dante, "Don't do this. I will transfer every cent I have into an offshore account for you. Just let Gwen go."

"Believe me, I would like to. I once had hopes of getting to know you better, *bella*. . . ." Dante shrugged. "But it wasn't to be."

Ugh. The thought made her skin crawl. Gwen watched a struggle take place on Quinn's face, and closed her eyes, knowing what he'd say next.

He cast her an agonized glance, as if to apologize. "Then kill me and take her with you."

Her breath caught in her throat. *Oh, Quinn. Oh, my love . . .*

"I'm afraid that I cannot do that. She knows too much."

"She can forget it again. Can't you, honey?"

Gwen hated the pleading look on Quinn's face. He'd never begged for anything in his life.

"Why, Dante?" she asked. "For God's sake, this doesn't make any sense. Why would you want to kill Avy?"

"I've been engineering this for some time now. It's what

you Americans like to call payback. You remember a recovery she made from a certain ambassador's home three years ago?"

"Tzekas," Gwen said slowly. "There was a scandal; he was deported from the U.S. in disgrace."

Dante smiled. "My mother's brother. And that's all you need to know, *bella*."

"I can't believe Kelso missed that when he hired you."

Dante shrugged. "The names are different, and Kelso is not Superman. If it's any consolation, we didn't originally mean to kill Avy . . . only to destroy her reputation and disgrace her. But because of you, *cara*, all that has changed. Things are now too complicated; she must die. And you, too."

Gwen seethed. They were in this mess courtesy of her. She had confided in Dante; relied upon him. She'd gotten them into this, misread the whole situation.

Now it was time for her to somehow get them out. If she could only get to her SIG . . .

Angeline returned with the mask. She held it by the edges with two facecloths.

Dante nodded curtly. "Give it to Gwen."

She held it out, and Gwen eyed it as she had the python in the warehouse on the Miami River. At least she'd had a fair shot at the python.

"Take it," Dante said.

Quinn lunged forward. "She's *pregnant*, you bastard!"

Dante dropped his crutch and grabbed Gwen's hair again with brutality, jabbing the gun into her ear. She saw Quinn's expression and bit down on her scream, which would torture him.

Dante said one word in lethal tones: "*Don't.*"

Quinn stopped, his hands opening and closing helplessly, his eyes never leaving her face. "Pregnant," he whispered again.

Dante had the grace to look regretful. "This I am sorry to hear, but it makes no difference in the end."

"God in heaven, you can't do this!" Quinn shouted.

"Take the mask, Gwen."

Sweat soaked every inch of her body, perversely chilling her in the night breeze off the water. Dante tightened his grip on her hair but used his fist against the back of her skull to shove her forward. Strangely enough, the pain gave her something to focus on besides fear. Gwen stretched out her still-gloved hands and took the mask.

Angeline stared at her through those dark gray, Borgia eyes of hers.

She stared right back, concentrating on the pain at her scalp because it made her angry. Angry in a good way: a calculating kind of angry, not a blind rage.

"Put it on and say good night, *bella*." Dante's café-cubano voice and his hot breath gusted against her bare, vulnerable neck. "It's time to end the charade. You're lovely, but you've been a lousy recovery agent."

Fuck you.

"Put it on!"

She brought the mask up inches from her face.

"Don't, Gwen!" Quinn said. "God, don't do it!"

"Enough!" Dante jerked the gun out of her ear, aimed it at Quinn's thigh, and pulled the trigger.

Quinn went down.

Gwen screamed, and Dante released her hair to clamp a hand over her mouth. He shoved the gun back into her ear. "I'll shoot him again if you don't put on that mask."

Quinn struggled to sit up. "No! Gwen—"

She held it up to her face.

Three inches until death.

Two.

Dear God.

One.

No. She wouldn't let this happen. The bastard wasn't killing her baby. He wasn't killing Quinn. And she wasn't about to let him get Avy in the end, either.

Gwen stomped her heel into Dante's instep and slammed her elbow into his stomach. She sliced the edge of the heavy mask down onto his wrist. The Glock hit the ground, and she kicked it into the pool.

Quinn came flying past her and knocked Dante to the patio. His fists were a blur. Gwen heard sickening sounds of flesh and bone being pulverized.

Angeline whirled and ran.

And then the latch of the garden gate rattled. "*There* you are, my beauty!" Sid Thresher called. "At last, I've found you. Been driving all over this bloody, godforsaken island—" His eyes bugged out as he took in the scene.

"Sid!" Gwen screamed, launching herself at the Borgia bitch and taking her down. "Call an ambulance!"

chapter 39

" 'Ere," said Sid, "I've got a perfectly good limo out front. Why wait for a bloody ambulance?"

So they took Sid up on his offer of a ride to the ER, declining his generous offer of Bloody Marys for all.

Dante lay on the floor, shackled with clothesline and unconscious, while Angeline sat hunched in the corner with a split lip and a filthy face, her hands manacled. Sid had just happened to have a pair of mink-lined handcuffs in the "boot."

There were also fishnet stockings, a black leather shorty catsuit with cutouts in inappropriate places, and spike-heeled, shiny patent thigh-high boots in Gwen's size.

A phone call to Sheila yielded the information that McDougal was bloody and concussed, courtesy of Dante, but alive and cranky as hell, thanks to Cato. He was pissed that he'd "let down" Kelso, who'd smelled a rat and sent McDougal to investigate—though not to sleep with one of the objects of said investigation. McD simply had his own way of doing things.

Gwen stripped off Quinn's shirt and fashioned a tourniquet from it for his leg. He wouldn't let go of her, which made things difficult. She pressed her lips to his. "Quinn, sweetheart, let me do this. It's going to hurt, though."

"I don't care. You're alive. You're *alive.* And the baby . . . " To her shock, he broke down. "My people," he said. "My people."

Tears came to her own eyes. "Stop it. You're getting me all emotional. Now let go, so I can try to stop the bleeding."

"I'm never letting you go again," he said. "I love you. More than anything. Marry me, Gwen. Make me happy."

She nodded, unable to speak.

"This isn't how I'd planned it," he continued. "Brancato hasn't sent the ring yet, but he's working on it."

No wonder Quinn had looked smug that day. She kissed him and he tried to pull her on top of him, then hissed in pain as his leg informed him that was not a good idea.

"I have to warn you," Quinn said when he could speak again, "your dad's gonna be livid."

"We knew that."

"No, I mean about my new job."

"When have you had time to find another job?" She stared at him, incredulous.

"I don't have it yet. Serious inside track, though. I know the director of operations."

"So don't keep me in suspense! What's the position?"

"Mr. Mom."

Gwen's jaw dropped open. He put his finger under her chin and gently closed it again. "Well, for a few years, anyway. I know you don't want to quit *your* job, honey. And I've made enough money. . . . Hey, my mouth is gonna fall off if you keep kissing me that hard."

"'Ere!" Sid said irritably from the front seat. "Gwendolyn, me beauty, may I point out that snogging the shirtless, shot-up bloke with the shiner in the back of *my* limo is in very bad taste?"

Gwen ignored him and took the opportunity to tighten the tourniquet.

Quinn erupted into foul curses.

"That's much better," Sid said in tones of approval. He scowled, though, when Gwen kissed Quinn again to distract him from the pain.

"You'd better not be wearing the bustier I sent for *that* rotter."

"Bustier?" said Quinn against her mouth.

"Nor the diamonds, neither! I should bloody well ask for them back."

Gwen raised her head. "What?! I returned everything to you."

"In a pig's eye, you did," Sid said in tones of indignation.

"He sent you *diamonds*? Gwen, I think you have some 'splainin' to do," growled Quinn.

"*Sheila*," Gwen uttered, her wrath rising. "Sheila kept everything! She was supposed to send it all back. I'm going to kill her."

"Fine," Quinn said, his voice soothing as he placed his hand on Gwen's belly. His fingers crept under her top and played with the diamond at her navel. "You can kill her after we get married again, okay?"

She nodded.

"And from now on, nobody gets to give you another diamond except for me, understood? It may take me two times to make you mine, honey, but after fifteen years I'm a little stubborn."

Read on for a special preview of
Karen Kendall's next novel,

Take Me for a Ride

Coming in November 2009 from Signet Eclipse.

Manhattan, September 2008

Some people stole money. Others stole cars, liquor, or big-ticket items like jewelry. Art recovery agent Eric McDougal stole women.

He did it with wit, style, passion . . . and guile—since they never knew they were missing in action until he returned them to reality.

McDougal took his women for a ride and a good time was had by all. Afterward he set them down gently on their own two feet, gave 'em a sweet smile, a wink from his Newman-blue eyes, and a swat on the backside. How they handled things from there was not his problem. Well, not usually.

This evening as he trained his gaze on the pretty target two blocks ahead, McDougal contemplated the horrifying memory of what a tasty, busty little psychopath had done to his Kawasaki Ninja ZX-14. He'd almost bitten through his own tongue when he saw it. Even now, three days later and a thousand miles from Miami, he winced.

Pink. She'd painted the Ninja *pink*. His jaw worked.

Why? He'd taken her to nice places. He'd never made any promises. He'd given her—if he did say so himself—

the mother of all orgasms. And just because he hadn't called afterward . . .

Okay, so maybe he wasn't much of a gentleman. He'd never advertised himself as one. But . . .

Pink.

It was cold. Beyond cold. Vicious, conscienceless brutality was what it was. Carnage.

He was tempted to press charges. But then he pictured the cop's face as he filled out the report, and he deep-sixed that bright idea.

Focus, you bonehead.

Natalie Rosen, his mark, had nothing to do with the destruction. An art restorer and probable thief, she lurched left on the crowded Manhattan sidewalk between Ninety-second and First. The door of Reif's opened and swallowed her.

Reif's? She didn't look the type for a seedy old neighborhood bar run by three generations of Irish. Reif's was a blue-collar place in a now-affluent neighborhood. North of Ninety-sixth got dicey as it eased into Spanish Harlem, but south of Ninety-sixth had become gentrified. Still, there were a few old holdouts like Reif's, where electricians and plumbers mingled with white-collar yuppies and argued politics over cheap beer. The Yankees, the Mets, the mayor, the weather—those were typical topics.

Reif's was situated on the ground floor of a six-story apartment building. It smelled like beer and dust, but it was also homey and offered a sort of tobacco-stained comfort that suited McDougal . . . but not a girl like Natalie Rosen.

Natalie had dark, glossy, straight hair and dark, serious eyes that looked a little at odds with her snub, lightly freckled nose. She was cute in a repressed, academic sort of way. Not tweedy or preppy—more earnest and artsy. The chick wore a lot of black, but there was a difference between severe New York black and sultry Miami black.

New York black covered while Miami black revealed. New York black involved tights, turtlenecks, scarves, and coats. Miami black involved thongs, skirt lengths just shy of illegal, spike heels, and fishnets—particularly on some of those little Brazilian hotties, with their bras clearly showing under skimpy tops . . . oh, yeah. McDougal was a big fan of Miami black.

Focus. He frowned. What the hell was a girl with an art degree from Carnegie Mellon doing in a beer-sodden joint like Reif's? Surely not unloading a $2 million necklace.

It was his job to find out, but he needed to hang back for a few. Let her get settled. Have a drink or two. He pegged her for the type who would walk into a pub like Reif's and order, say, white wine. A little naive. A little out of touch with reality.

Twenty minutes later, McDougal shoved his hands into his pockets, crossed the street, and entered Reif's. He sighted his quarry immediately: She was perched on one of the old, wooden, backless barstools, staring sightlessly into the dregs of a short glass of whiskey, rocks.

His opinion of her went up a notch—at least she hadn't ordered a white Zinfandel. Of course, his opinion of her didn't matter much—he'd get what he came for, regardless. He always did.

In all that black, Natalie looked as if she'd smell of sulfur or mothballs, but as she dug into her nylon messenger bag for a tissue, he caught a waft of fresh laundry detergent and a tinge of 4711, a cologne his sisters used to wear.

Over the bar hung a four-by-eight-foot mirror, which reflected among other things Natalie's drawn, downcast face. Something was on the lady's mind.

McDougal nodded at the bartender and mounted the stool next to hers. It was covered in cheap green vinyl and had seen better days, but the upside of worn was comfortable. It announced his presence by creaking under his solid 180 pounds, but Natalie didn't look at him.

Didn't matter. She would. Women always did, eventually—not that they always liked what they saw. Some of them summed him up as a player in one glance and dismissed him. Others focused on the bare fourth finger of his left hand. The fun ones started shoveling verbal shit at him immediately. Which type was she?

As Eric casually ordered a Guinness, he watched her in the mirror. Watched as her pointed little chin came up, as she pushed some hair out of her face and cut her eyes toward him, her lashes at half-mast.

Then came her first impression, the undercover evaluation of his six-foot-two frame, muscular forearms sprinkled with freckles and golden hair, his denim-clad legs. She took in the brown leather jacket and the reddish brown stubble on his chin; then the grin that widened as he watched her.

That was when she realized that he'd seen her inspecting him in the mirror. Her gaze flew to his in the reflected surface and froze. A slow blush crept up her neck—a blush so fierce, he could see it even in the dim light of Reif's.

"Hi," McDougal said, turning to face her with the full wattage of his grin.

She blinked, stared, then looked away as the blush intensified. She put a hand up to her neck as if to cool the skin off. "H-Hi."

She was a babe in the woods—without mosquito repellent. He prepared to feast on her tender young naïveté.

"I didn't mean to embarrass you," McDougal said, taking his grin down a few notches, from wolfish to disarming.

She seemed to have no adequate response to that.

"It's very normal to check out the guy sitting next to you. He could be a vagrant, a pervert, or a serial killer."

She laughed reluctantly at that, and it transformed her

face from mildly pretty to dazzling. She'd gone from librarian to . . . to . . . *Carla Bruni* in half a second flat. It was McDougal's turn to stare.

"So, which one are you?" she asked, evidently emboldened.

"Me? I'm just a tourist, sweetheart. The only cereal killing I do involves a bowl of raisin bran or cornflakes."

That got a smile. "Where are you from?"

"Miami."

"Florida," she said, sounding wistful. "I'd love to be on a beach right now, not in the city."

"You work here?"

Natalie nodded. "I'm a restoration artist."

"A restoration artist," McDougal repeated. "As in, they call you to touch up the Sistine Chapel?" He nodded at the bartender and pointed at her glass.

"Something like that. But I specialize in rugs and tapestries, not painting." A wary expression crossed her face as the drink was set in front of her. "Um, I didn't order—"

"It's on me," McDougal said.

"Oh, but—"

"What's your name?"

She hesitated. "Natalie."

"Natalie, it's just a drink. Not a big deal. 'Kay?"

"Thank you," she said after a long pause. She curled her small but competent hand around the glass. "Actually, you have no idea how much I need this."

Yes, I do. First heist, honey? It always shreds your nerves. But all McDougal said was, "You're welcome. I'm Eric." And he proceeded to chat her up while she got lusciously tipsy on her second whiskey.

Really, he should be ashamed of himself.

Natalie Rosen's eyes had gone just a little fuzzy, her gestures loose and her posture relaxed. She'd also gotten wittier. "So, you said you're a tourist. Are you an accidental one?"

He smiled. "Nope. I do have a purpose. Are you an accidental barfly?"

"No." She averted her gaze, then looked down into her whiskey and murmured, "I'm an accidental thief."

"Do tell," McDougal said, showing his teeth and signaling the bartender again. If he had his wicked way, she would soon to be a naked one.

•

About the Author

Karen Kendall is an award-winning author of contemporary romance who started writing at the age of four. An art history major with a concentration in twentieth-century art, Karen worked in museums and galleries before she was a published author. She lives with her husband in Florida. Please visit her Web site at www.karenkendall.com.